TOUGH ALLIANCE

First Published in Great Britain in 2023 by
LOVE AFRICA PRESS
103 Reaver House, 12 East Street, Epsom KT17 1HX
www.loveafricapress.com

Available as eBook and paperback

YADILI SERIES

<u>Prince of Hearts</u>
<u>Killer of Kings</u>
<u>Bad Santa</u>
<u>Rough Diamond</u>
<u>Tough Alliance</u>

DEDICATION

To Oluwakemi, Queenie, and Ngozi, thank you for riding this creative roller-coaster with me. Ladies, you rock!

BLURB

It started with a blind date…

Zoe Himba is working to succeed her father and steer the family empire into the next generation. She has the brains, the beauty and sheer boldness to make it happen.

Nothing will stop her ambition. Not her father's ridiculous idea to use her as a bargaining chip in a marriage with another powerful family so he can bolster his stronghold. Nor the unfortunate consequence of an anonymous one-night stand.

Certainly not the recent knowledge that the man she spent one glorious sensual night with is Maddox, the Odili enforcer—a family her father despises.

So when he shows up at her home, serious and sincere about marrying her, she rejects his proposal in the most brutal way possible. It's **tough luck** if he thinks he can ever be her husband.

It will end in a vendetta…

Maddox Ejiofor does not bear his name lightly. For centuries, his ancestors have been the embodiment of justice in the Yadili secret organisation, and he is proud to be one of the best enforcers of his generation. Family and fairness are two crucial tenets of his existence. He'll die to uphold them.

So when the Himba's arrogant contempt threatens his family and blood, he vows to end their iron-fist reign in the central region. But then Zoe shows up, needing his protection. He must apply **tough love b**ecause he can't afford to make the mistake of falling for his wife.

PLAYLIST

Right to be Wrong ~ Joss Stone
Lie to Me ~ Bryan Adams
Suspicious Minds ~ Elvis Prestley
Unavailable ~ Davido
Wanna get to know You ~ G-Unit, Joe
Last Last ~ Burna Boy
Cherish ~ Madonna
No One ~ Alicia Keys
We Can ~ LeAnn Rimes
Water no get Enemy ~ Fela Kuti
My Power ~ Nija, Beyonce, Busiswa, Yemi Alade
Unstoppable ~ Sia
Who runs the world (Girls) ~ Beyonce

ONE

Not even if you were the last man alive.

The phrase blazed through Zoe's mind while she typed a brusque, insulting note and sent it to the conceited man who'd dared to ask her on a date. He would not like her barbed words or her rejection.

But to Hell with Abdul Sani. He was widely reputed to be hunting for a wife since his marriage arrangement with Carla Owo fell through after she married Duke Odili.

Zoe didn't need a husband. Certainly not the insufferable, misogynistic buffoon who acted like he was better than everybody else, all because of his father's status in the country's north-western region.

With a huff, she tossed the phone on the charcoal-grey modular desk and shut her laptop. The AC hummed quietly, keeping the air in her office close to freezing.

The white walls, tall, dark wooden shelves stacked with Law tomes, and grey metal file drawers created a severe atmosphere. However, the strategically located plants in terracotta pots added colour and warmth.

Her mother's handiwork. Mrs Iyua Himba was a keen gardener. Everywhere she went, she left a little flora and Feng Shui.

After she'd graduated from Law School, Zoe worked at a firm in the Federal Capital Territory for a year before coming home to Lokogi to set up her own operations. Focusing on commercial and property law, her father was her first and most prominent client, although she'd gradually grown her reputation as a fierce professional. In turn, her client list had increased over the years. She now employed fifteen people and was seriously considering leaving suburban Lokogi to set up shop in the metropolitan FCT.

With a distracted smile, Zoe raised her left arm and glanced at the gold wristwatch. Half past six. Damn. She swivelled and looked out of the window. The sky was a purple-orange hue due to the sun setting over the low brick houses in the old city built on the confluence of two major silver rivers.

Where did the time go? She had fifteen minutes to get to her next appointment.

Reaching into the bottom drawer, she grabbed the black leather tote and placed it on the desktop. Then she inserted her laptop into the empty compartment, pushed back her armchair, and straightened.

Phone pocketed, tote in one hand, keys in the other, she headed out.

"Shugaba." Her personal bodyguard stood outside the door and extended his hand as she exited. A tall, dark-skinned, good-looking man, he wore a black suit over a matching T-shirt, which clung to bulging muscles underneath. Sturdy dark boots completed the monochromatic ensemble.

Despite his hulking size, they stood almost at the same eye level. She wore these impossibly high heels so no man around here would look down at her—physically and figuratively.

"Noah, we're going to the restaurant," she said, handing him the bag before locking the door.

This was their routine. Not the restaurant bit. The carrying-her-items thing.

"Yes, Shugaba," he replied, tailing her down the corridor.

And the following-her-around bit. He'd been her shadow for almost a decade.

She didn't mind it. Actually, it was a requirement, considering her family's status.

Plus, they had a good relationship. He was one of the only few people she trusted.

Her stilettos tapped on the smooth, glossy, polished flooring. The other offices were empty. The staff had left. It was Friday night, and most people started their weekends early.

Not her. Not usually. She was first in and last out, even as the employer.

There was a lift, but she took the stairs because she always did. Plus, it was only four floors. Their footsteps echoed in the concrete stairwell--tapping and thudding. She liked the sound they made--of familiarity and vitality, of movement and progress.

At the bottom, they exited the stairs and entered the main lobby, where an unfamiliar security man sat behind the large counter. Although the building was owned by Himba Holdings, it housed two other businesses besides Himba Law Associates.

"Good night, Ma," the man behind the counter said, wearing a blue, short-sleeved shirt, black trousers and polished shoes, the standard uniform for their site security team.

Grimacing, she halted halfway through the lobby, swivelling in his direction. "I haven't seen you before. What's your name?"

Standing, he mentioned his name and bowed. "I started yesterday, Madam, on the night shift."

"I can see that." Because every time he referred to her, he used terms she abhorred. Titles she'd banned everyone from using to address her. "My name is Zoe Himba. You can address me as Ms Himba or Ms Zoe. Ma or Madam are for my mother. And I'm definitely not your Auntie."

She added the last comment because 'Auntie' seemed to be the default title for addressing a woman when Ma and Madam were removed from the equation. The informal term implied familiarity, which ultimately bred disrespect.

"Yes, M--Ms Himba," he stammered.

She smiled when he corrected himself. He would learn like everyone else, eventually. "Welcome to Himba House, and have a good night."

"Thank you," he replied as she sashayed out while Noah held the swinging glass door.

Outside, the warm night air embraced her in the concrete forecourt. Her driver hurried over to the SUV, the lights flashing as he unlocked the vehicle. The bodyguard held the back door as she climbed into the seat. He deposited her tote beside her before settling the front passenger position. The chauffeur drove out of the premises, turning right onto the main road as they began the journey from Himba House in the GRA to the riverside where the restaurant was located.

"Noah, why didn't you tell the new security guard the correct way to address me," she commented.

Noah was her security chief and, therefore, responsible for anyone involved in her protection, including the chauffeur.

He turned his head to glance at her. "You're such a great teacher. I didn't want to deprive him of his first encounter with you. This way, he'll never forget it."

Although he kept his tone neutral, she didn't miss the twinkle in his eyes. She had a reputation as a no-nonsense person, and he was teasing her but didn't want to be obvious to the driver.

"He better not." She groused, looking out the window and stifling the smile tugging the corner of her lips.

But instead of admiring the old city's significant landmarks, including the country's first colonial settlement and the governor's residence, she checked her emails on her phone. Most of the messages were work-related. But one stood out and made her heart skip a beat.

Sender: Star Arufin
Subject: You made a match!

Excited and with a trembling finger, she clicked the subject line to read the email.

Dear Mimi,

Congratulations! You passed the screening process, and your application to participate in our Blind Date programme has been approved. Your profile has been successfully matched to another profile that meets all your requirements. He wishes for you to address him as Nnanna.

"Nnanna," she whispered the name, savouring it with delight as her pulse skyrocketed.

Looking for a secure and discreet dating app, she'd downloaded the Star-Arufin software and registered for their Blind Date programme because it promised anonymity for the users. She could use an avatar instead of her photo, and nothing in her profile could identify her publicly. Hence, she used an abbreviated form of her middle name, Mimidoo, known by her immediate family only.

She didn't know anyone named Nnanna, but it was an Igbo name. So, was the bearer an Igbo man? It was easy to make the inference, although it could also be a pseudonym. She doubted the person would use his real name or first name.

The driver beeped the car horn, making her look up. They'd arrived at their destination, and the vehicle stopped in the reserved parking spot outside the restaurant named after her.

Quickly, she closed the email app and stowed her phone in her pocket. She couldn't let anyone glimpse the message or who had sent it. Her father forbade any members of the Himba clan from visiting the Arufin nightclub and its VIP annexe, the Star Club in Lori Osa.

The last time someone—Xandra, their former assassin—had defied the order, she'd been disciplined severely.

Zoe hadn't approved the punishment meted out to Xan because of her sexual proclivities. The woman was an adult, and whatever she'd done had been between consenting adults.

Yet, her father had ordered their enforcer, Norbert, to punish Xandra and commanded Zoe to ensure the assassin showed up for her penalty. She'd had to obey the order because no one defied the Don.

Afterwards, Zoe regretted her involvement in Xandra's capture. She'd seen the woman's life-changing injuries following Norbert's handiwork and wished she'd warned Xan about what had been in store.

After the incident, Zoe started pushing back on her father's orders when necessary. She'd convinced Don

Himba not to punish the assassin again after Norbert was killed.

Norbert had abducted Xan a second time, and an Odili crew had rescued the assassin, killing the enforcer during the shootout. Afterwards, Zoe persuaded her father to accept Duke Odili's truce to avoid a war between the families.

However, none of her previous defiance would be seen as terrible compared to visiting a sex club. Her father would punish her if he found out, although she doubted it would be as life-altering as what happened to Xandra.

Still, better to be safe and keep it a secret.

Leaving her tote in the back seat, she exited the vehicle. Everything she needed was on her person—phone, weapon, even a stick of lipstick. Nevertheless, she didn't expect this meeting to take long as she strode along the harbour into the restaurant premises.

The building was part of a row of old structures renovated when the area was gentrified about ten years earlier. The restaurant was built on stilts along the shore to give the illusion of floating. It also came in handy when the river overflowed because they stayed above the embankment.

Outside, her mother's decorations were evident in the brown wooden boxes of orange tulips and green leaves designed to blend with the wooden facade and terrace.

Her father's henchmen sat at a table and nodded at her in greeting as she entered. Baba's offices occupied the top floor, while the restaurant was on the first level.

The brown, orange and green theme continued inside with the velour cushioned chairs, wooden tables and plants. Even the bar area held similar earthy tones.

Talking about the bar, was that her half-brother? She paused instead of heading upstairs.

Vershima sat on a counter stool, sipping an amber liquid from a crystal glass while watching the sizeable flatscreen telly on the far corner.

"Vershy, what are you doing here?" she asked, narrowing her eyes.

He swivelled and straightened. "I don't know, sis. Baba said I should come and see him. When I showed up, I was told to wait down here until you arrived before going upstairs."

He sounded grumpy, like he didn't want to be there. Vershima was ten years younger than Zoe and the first son of her father's second wife. He had recently graduated from university and seemed to spend his time partying and chasing women instead of finding a job.

"Then why are you drinking if you're here to see Baba?"

"What else is there to do? I was bored."

"You were bored!" Instinctively, she shoved her hand inside her jacket.

Her fingers curled around the contours of the handgun hidden in the pocket. But she didn't pull it out. Anyone else, and she wouldn't hesitate to whip them into shape with her weapon.

Still, this was her brother.

Instead, she got into his face. Although he was slightly taller than her, her heels put them at the same eye level. "Do you think you're a baby? You're going to see The Don, and you're stinking of alcohol?"

At his age, she'd been working. She would not have gotten away with half the things he did, even as the sole daughter of the Himba patriarch.

He wasn't bothered about taking up responsibilities, although he spent the money happily. And there appeared to be different rules of engagement for him, as a male child, which rankled.

"Dide, get him some mouthwash!" she snapped at the bartender.

"Yes, boss," the man replied before disappearing through the staff-only door at the back of the counter.

"Go with him and freshen up. You have five minutes," she ordered Vershy.

"Why are you always giving me a hard time?" he grumbled, following Dide.

Zoe suppressed the eye-roll. She had a good mind to ban her brother from drinking at the restaurant. But she knew it would be unenforceable because the staff would give him drinks unless the order came directly from their father.

Unfair and annoying.

TWO

As the first child and only daughter of Don Himba, head of the cartel controlling most things from local politics to organised crime in the country's central region, Zoe knew all about the imbalance and unfairness of family life and marriage.

Her parents—Tiye and Iyua—wedded thirty-seven years ago, supposedly in happy matrimony. A look at old photo albums and family videos from when she was a child would tag them as ideally in love with each other.

Iyua Himba was a devoted wife and mother, the consummate homemaker if such a thing existed.

Baba was always focused on his business ventures. As head of the family, his role was authoritarian and as a provider.

Zoe had the perfect childhood. Pampered and given whatever a young person would need—a father's seemingly endless wealth and a mother's overwhelming adulation.

However, the idyllic life didn't last forever.

She initially noticed the crack in her parents' relationship when her father introduced another woman—a pregnant one—as his second wife. Subsequently, Zoe, a once lone child, acquired siblings. Male ones, at that. Future heirs to Baba's wealth.

And Zoe's perspective on marriage changed forever.

Apparently, her mother hadn't known about the other woman until she had become pregnant, and Baba had installed her in his home as wife number two. He justified his actions by blaming Mum for not giving him male children after ten years of marriage.

"Zoe is going to get married and move in with her husband when she grows up," her father yelled in an accusatory tone at Mum. "Do you think I'm building an empire just to hand it over to another man's son? Is that what you think? I want my own sons. Otherwise, who else will carry on my lineage and legacy?"

"Me! I will, Baba," Zoe wanted to scream as she'd hidden at the top of the stairs and listened to her parents' first significant argument. She'd known better than to interrupt their quarrel.

Still, she'd learned a valuable lesson.

Regardless of the privileges she enjoyed as the daughter of a wealthy man, she was still viewed as less than a male child, incapable of progressing her family legacy because of marriage.

Marriage diminished a woman. It had done so to her mother.

Not to be misunderstood, her mother wasn't miserable. At least there were no outward signs of unhappiness. If anything, after the second-wife argument, Tiye Himba overindulged his first wife. It seemed they had arrived at an agreement, which worked for Mum.

Iyua Himba lived the charmed life of a well-kept spouse. She travelled the world in luxury, shopped in the best stylish places and holidayed at least twice a year. She was the named proprietor of a restaurant chain in their city and nearby towns. But she barely made appearances in those locations. There were branch managers in charge of daily operations.

***

After graduating high school, Iyua took Zoe to Europe— London, Paris, Milan. During the trip, they had a long conversation. Zoe asked her mother why she didn't leave Baba because of his infidelity.

"Why should I?" Mum said. "I was with your father when he had little to nothing. I suffered with him. I invested my time, sweat and money on him. The initial money he started his business with was mine. Now that it's time to reap the rewards of my labour, you think I'm going to walk away? No. I worked for this money, and I will damn well enjoy it."

"But what about Baba having a second wife? Are you happy with it?"

"No. I'm not happy with it. But considering the options, I can live with it. I prefer that she is where I can see her and control her. Rather than out there where it would be more difficult to influence her and your father." She shifted forward and met Zoe's gaze. "Listen to me, Zoe. In this life, you must learn to make the best out of any situation. Things will not always go to plan, so be adaptable and keep your end goal in mind."

"So this is part of the plan?"

"Not the original plan. But as I said, plans have to be adaptable to changing situations. Men have fragile egos. Your father thinks he controls everything. My dear, it's an illusion I make him believe. The reality is that I pick my battles. I allow your father some latitude. He doesn't feel stifled. He feels in control. Meanwhile, I know his weaknesses. Hell, I know where the bodies are buried. He needs me as much as I need him."

"Hang on, Mum. When you say bodies, you mean metaphorically, right?"

Mum's tinkling laughter indicated Zoe had much to learn. "Yes, metaphorically and literally. I'm not blind to your father's business activities. I never was. Sure, I never got my hands dirty. But I was able to boost your father's profile. I humanised him, taught him how to be respectable, and made him more acceptable in polite society. Otherwise, he would have been seen as just another thug with money. And I will tell you now, you should know any man you're involved with. Understand him, his strengths and weaknesses. Most especially the man you're going to marry."

"I get it, Mum. But I'm not going to get married," she replied.

Her mother frowned. "I can understand why you feel that way now. But when the time comes, you will get married. Your father will insist."

"I won't," Zoe refuted. "I want to run Baba's business when he retires. I can do it better than Vershima or Dooshima ever could. If I get married, I won't be able to because Baba doesn't want the business to go to whoever I marry."

She remembered her father's angry words from long ago.

"I see what you mean. It's true. Your father will not hand his empire over to someone who isn't his blood." Her mother stayed silent for a while. When she spoke again, her tone was quiet and serious. "Do you really think you can handle the intricacies of the cartel business? Do you have the boldness and bravery for it?"

"Of course I can," Zoe replied without hesitation.

"Good. Because I don't want your brothers getting their hands on the business if possible. The majority of it should rightfully be yours as the first child. They can have whatever crumbs you decide to throw at them."

***

From then on, Zoe held a newfound respect for her mother. Through the years, her mother had been her sounding board as she went to university to study and then to law school afterwards. When she'd returned home and bid to become part of his legal team, her father hadn't resisted her offer. Her mother had convinced him Zoe was best placed to support and protect the Don's interests as a lawyer.

She stayed away from relationships and focused on work, on the Himba business interests. She dealt with all the commercial contracts, property and land acquisitions. She'd excelled too, earning her promotion to legal adviser to Don Himba, which meant she was no longer reporting to one of his deputies and was directly working for him.

But it seemed things were about to change again.

***

The squeaking door made her look up. Vershima had returned.

"Come on," she said and started up the stairs.

She walked past the bodyguards standing in the corridor and entered the large office, followed by her brother. Through the window, river boats bobbed in the glistening water, and there was a dark outline of warehouses in the distance. Her father loved this view. Hence, he preferred working from here rather than the more centrally-located Himba House or any other buildings he owned.

"Good evening, Baba," Vershy said quickly.

"Good evening, Boss," she greeted, using the honorific their old man preferred outside the home. If her brother worked, he would know this already.

Since he invited them here, this was about business and not personal.

The Don sat behind a massive desk, wearing a three-piece tailored charcoal suit. He waved at the two bodyguards who stood inside, and they exited, shutting the door.

"Sit down, both of you," Baba said, leaning back in his leather chair.

Zoe settled in one of the armchairs across the wooden desk. Vershima sat in the other one beside her.

"Edosa's shipment was hit last night," Don Himba said without preamble.

"Another one?" Zoe asked, sitting upright with a frown.

Baba may have worked on the docks only metres from here when he was young. However, as godfather to the Himba clan, he'd ascended to a level far above the working class. He didn't get his hands dirty or labour in the usual sense. Instead, he oversaw multiple business operations led by his shugabas. Plus, anybody who was anyone paid him a fee to conduct business in the region.

Edosa was the shugaba handling merchandise logistics, otherwise known as human trafficking. A couple of weeks ago, a truck used to smuggle people through a route across several countries heading to the northern African shores was ambushed. The runners were killed, the merchandise stolen.

By itself, this would barely impact Edosa. The people on the train had paid upfront to be transported across the borders, and the fees were non-refundable. The traffickers knew these were high-risk ventures before they signed up.

However, if such incidents occurred too often, Edosa's outfit would be considered unreliable, and the recruiters would take their business elsewhere. Competitors always waited to steal the market if one wasn't careful.

"Yes!" her father's tense, loud voice cut into her thoughts. "Once is a coincidence. Twice is intentional. We are being targeted purposefully. Being eliminated. This is because Norbert is dead. No one would dare do this to us if he was still alive because he would fish them out and make them suffer. Now, I'm losing business and money. And it's all the goddamned Odili family's fault. I want to burn them all to ashes."

"Baba, I understand your frustration. But you made a deal with the Odilis. They paid blood money for Norbert's death."

They couldn't renege on a deal without bringing the wrath of the powerful Odili family on all of them. Plus, they'd paid a very generous amount, considering Norbert's unpleasant actions against Xandra.

Still, Zoe wouldn't say it because her father had trusted the man and had treated him like a son.

"I know how much they paid. But it doesn't make up for Norbert's absence now." Her father bashed his hand on the table, making the items jump. "Anyway, there's no point crying over spilt milk. We must look at quick alternatives to plug the gap in our crews." He spread his arms out before bringing his hands together to steeple his fingers.

She glanced at her brother, who wore a disinterested expression, and her neck stiffened. He hadn't said anything after the initial greeting. If he wasn't contributing, he could leave.

"Baba, this is a business matter. Vershima doesn't need to be here for it," she said, fighting another bout of annoyance.

"What have I done now," Vershy grumbled.

"Shut up and listen, both of you," Don Himba said before directing his gaze at Zoe, his hand folded on the desk.

"We need a show of force, which means we need more men. So all hands need to be on deck."

"Fine, I'll take on more responsibilities," she said simply. It was second nature for her to step up and fix her father's problems.

"No, you won't."

"I won't?"

"I need you for something else. As I said, we need more men, and the quickest way to get them is through an alliance with another outfit."

Dread curled in Zoe's stomach. Before her father said it, she knew what he would order her to do. She clenched her lips to stop herself from yelling with a tactical refusal.

"You want to use me as a bargaining chip to expand the business. To offer me in marriage to the highest bidder. But instead of a dowry, you'll get a larger crew," she said coldly without inflexion.

She could be as cold-blooded and unfeeling as the men. As her father. She wouldn't let him see how much this new development rattled her. In fact, she'd been preparing for such an occasion for years.

"Yes," her father said as if they were discussing selling one of their properties rather than his only daughter. "Any man marrying you knows he is getting the best—educated in the best schools in the world, a first-class lawyer and an astute businesswoman. They will pay whatever I demand for your dowry."

"I can see the merits of that process, and I hope to negotiate the best deal for the Himba family," she said in a reasonable voice so it would not seem as if she was trying to defy her father with her next words. "However, considering the current situation, this is not the time for me to be distracted with screening suitors or planning a wedding. I have plenty to do here. Like fixing the problem with our security. I'm sure I can—"

"No," her father bit out. "Are you trying to refuse my order?"

"No, Baba." Her cheeks flamed because it was precisely what she'd been trying to do. Beneath the surface, her rage simmered. Jumping through hoops to appease anyone was ridiculous. But this was her father, and as her mother once told her, men had fragile egos.

So, instead of calling bullshit, she swallowed her temper and softened her voice. "I was just concerned about who would do my job while I work on this new assignment."

"This is where your brother comes in. Vershima will take over from you."

"What?" Vershy sat upright, suddenly looking interested as a smile spread on his face. "Are you serious, Baba?"

"Of course, I'm serious," their father replied.

"No way. He knows nothing about the business or the job," Zoe finally snapped, unable to contain her shock and annoyance any longer.

She'd worked for a decade to get where she was. Ten goddamned years. She'd put up with having to prove herself in a male-dominated environment. Having to work twice as hard to be accepted as an equal.

Yet her lazy, inexperienced kid brother could just waltz in the door and take it away from her at her father's command? Not happening.

"I can learn," Vershima gave her a gotcha smile as if he'd been waiting for an opportunity like this.

Wanting to wipe the smirk off his face, she shoved her hand into her pocket, wrapping it around the weapon. But her father's voice made her pause.

"There you have it. He's keen to learn, and you, Zoe, are the best teacher he can have. So you will train him to do your job and hand it over to him so you can concentrate on finding a husband."

The marriage proposal she'd received earlier made her spine prickle.

"Hang on, have you already sent invitations?"

"Of course. I sent a message to all The Board members this morning."

Damn it! No wonder Abdul Sani sent a random electronic message offering marriage to her.

The Board consisted of the heads of the five prominent cartels in the country. Each cabal operated within a region.

Abdul's father ran the northwest.

The Garba family controlled the northeast.

Don Himba owned the central region.

Chief Odili dominated the southeast.

The southwest used to be controlled by The Baron, John Bull Owo. But after the war with the Odili family, resulting in his and his son's death, Carla Owo, now Carla Odili, was the sole heir to the Owo empire. Since she was married to Duke, and Duke was an Odili, Chief Odili was the de facto head of the southwest region.

It could all change, as the region was rife with tribalism. The locals grumbled that Duke wasn't a local because his late father was from another tribe. And they conveniently discounted his late mother, a Yoruba daughter-of-the-soil.

Another woman dismissed as irrelevant. Typical!

Zoe's hands balled into fists.

Still, it wasn't her beef to resolve. She had more pressing matters.

"You sent out invitations before informing me. I'm an adult." Never mind the disrespect.

"You're my daughter. You will do as you're told," he bellowed.

"The hell I am." She'd heard enough. Threatening her brother wouldn't help because the problem was Baba. The old man was being unreasonable.

But she could be stubborn, too. She shoved up from the chair and stomped towards the exit.

"Zoe, don't you dare leave," her father gritted out.

She ignored him. She'd worked herself to the bones to grow the business alongside her father. She'd earned her place in the Himba empire and would not hand it to anyone else.

Then, she stopped in the middle of the room, swivelled and faced them.

"Here is my counteroffer. I will accept the marriage auction because we need the cash injection. However, I will not give up my position as your heir-in-waiting. So, if Vershima or anyone else wants my position, they will have to go through me first."

Her brother's mouth dropped open in shock, his gaze darting to their father. He probably had never seen anyone challenge the old man before.

Truthfully, she was probably the first to do it.

The Don didn't receive it well, either. His expression was thunderous and puffed up like he would explode with rage any second.

To be fair, she was surprised he had no response. No decree to punish her immediately for her insubordination.

Perhaps he realised her proposal had merit.

She was offering him something he couldn't resist. After years of working for Don Himba, she knew what motivated him.

Money. That simple.

She earned a lot of money, and the marriage auction had the potential to be lucrative. Nothing said she had to stay married long, even if she accepted a proposal. She could be divorced within months, and they'd still keep the money.

An ingenious racket. He understood this because he was the king of racketeering.

But she couldn't forget his ego. His reputation.

She was still defying him, and he couldn't be seen to cave in readily. Not in front of Vershima.

She puffed out a breath and added a sweetener.

"Baba, I will make you a lot of money from the auction. I promise," she said in a calm voice, a skill she learned from watching her mother. *How To Tame Male Egos 101.* She only applied it to her father, though. She had no patience to put up with other men like this. "I'm going away for the weekend. When I return, Mum and I will start making arrangements for the suitors."

Bile filled her mouth at the thought of actually screening suitors. She would rather shoot them than entertain them. Still, she swallowed the bitter taste. The alternative was just as repulsive. This was the lesser of the two evils.

Her father's expression eased, and he nodded once.

It was the best she would get from him for now.

She swallowed again. "Goodnight, Boss."

She swivelled and hurried out of the door.

THREE

The blacked-out SUV stopped in a dark alley, and the giant doorman in all-black opened the back door. Zoe stepped onto the dimly lit passage. To her right, the queued partygoers meandering around the block and glittering lights of the city-that-never-sleeps, also known as Lori Osa, beckoned.

Instead, she shoved hands into the pockets of her flowing, hooded cowl-neck gown and headed to the open door of the grey five-storey building. Her high heels tapped against the concrete as she stepped across the threshold of the side entrance into a small foyer with sleek black granite surfaces.

A woman in a black uniform and blonde braids sat behind a glass screen. "Welcome to the Star Club, Madam. Please present your card."

Zoe grimaced at the 'Madam' and pulled out a black Perspex card embossed with gold lettering and a chip from the dress pocket. She tapped it against the digital card reader on the counter, and it beeped.

The receptionist glanced at her computer screen. "You are in the Black Room on Level Three. Your session tonight will be in total darkness."

"Total darkness? There is no such thing. Surely, the window will let in some light," she huffed.

"The Black Room has no windows. All the surfaces are matt black, so nothing reflects light," the woman commented.

Zoe gasped, surprised at the design detail. However, while it solved the problem of anonymity, it raised another. "How do I navigate the room without bumping into furniture?"

"You have the option of wearing the VR goggles, which pick out the shapes of objects and show you a virtual reality of the room so you can avoid bumping into things. Or you can choose to go in blind, and your date will guide you through any obstacles. Which would you prefer?"

"I'll go with the goggles," she replied immediately. Going in blind meant giving up control to her date, a man she didn't know. The info pack provided details about the VR specs. She hoped the device would reveal the shape and stature of the man before they made physical contact, even if it would be an artificial impression rather than reality.

"Of course." The receptionist pulled an oblong box from a drawer and placed it on the desk. Opening the case, she took out the white visor, which appeared slightly wider and thicker than Zoe's favourite pair of sunshades. "You should put it on now, but it won't activate until you get to your room."

"Now? How will I get upstairs if I can't see?"

"My colleague will take you up and ensure your safety." The woman nodded at the giant, bald-headed man with a white beard who stood next to the open doors of the lift. He'd picked her up from the hotel, introduced himself as Idehen, and had driven her here. "Once you're in the room, the sensor will trigger the VR mode on the goggles."

Zoe leaned back, her stomach rolling. It seemed she would have to remove the Venetian mask, which meant showing her face to the receptionist. A hazard, considering she wished to minimise the number of people who saw her in this location. She opened her mouth to request a restroom, but Idehen's baritone voice cut through her thoughts.

"You can wear them in the lift."

Zoe turned in his direction, her muscles relaxing. The lift would provide some privacy and not reveal her identity to the woman behind the counter.

"Okay. Thank you." She took the visor as she headed towards Idehen.

He followed her into the boxcar and pressed the button for the third floor before the doors closed.

Then, pushing down the hood, she removed the mask and replaced it with the visor. It covered half of her face above her nose to the top of her forehead.

Making her totally blind, surrounded by darkness.

An unexpected, insidious wave of unease flooded her. It crawled under her skin, raising her pulse and quickening her breath. The total absence of light made her dizzy. She wasn't used to relying on others and expected Idehen to manhandle her.

Muscles stiffening, she shoved her hand into the pocket of her gown, seeking the reassurance of the small handgun. She rarely went anywhere without a weapon. Some people tried to take advantage of the vulnerable, and she learned early in life never to put herself in a susceptible situation. Yet, here she was without sight, all because she wanted an anonymous sexual encounter. Why, again, had she thought this was a good idea?

"You're safe," Idehen's deep, soothing voice encompassed her. "I'm going to take your hand. Is that okay?"

He was asking for permission to touch her. A welcomed rarity.

She drew in a long breath and exhaled. Her back muscles relaxed, the apprehension dissipating.

He was truly here to keep her safe. Just like Xandra had promised when Zoe had called her friend to enquire about Arufin and the Star Club.

"Yes, you can hold onto me," she replied, loosening her grip on the gun.

A warm palm settled on her upper arm for a few seconds as if waiting for her to get used to his touch before he wrapped the hand around her elbow. "Are you okay?"

"Yes." After a few seconds of him holding her arm, she finally relaxed. "Is my date here?"

"Yes. I believe he is awaiting your arrival."

"Good." Warmth spread through Zoe, her pulse accelerating as the lift pinged.

Nnanna was punctual and keen to meet her, to have the encounter. He would be reliable and responsible. The kind of man she liked.

She had zero tolerance for reckless, immature men.

Then again, this encounter was supposed to be temporary, for one night only. She wasn't here to find a husband and wanted nothing beyond sex.

Spine tingling with excitement, she allowed Idehen to guide her out of the lift and down a corridor, their footsteps muffled by the thick woven flooring, which surprised her. It must be expensive to maintain carpets in busy hallways. Yet it heightened the sensual experience and her anticipation because they'd paid attention to details.

"We're here," Idehen said when he halted, making her stop, too. "I'm going to open the door. But remember, you can stop the session at any time. Simply use your safe-word. There are night-vision cameras in there, as well as sound monitors. Any sign of distress and the session will be ended. So don't feel pressured into doing anything."

She huffed. "Do I look like the kind of person to be pressured into anything?"

"No." he sounded amused. "But these encounters can be overwhelming, especially under certain sensory deprivation."

He had a point. The lack of vision unsettled her. If she wasn't strong, she would feel helpless.

"I'm ready," she said.

"Good." The sound of creaking wood alerted her to a door opening. "Take three steps forward."

She did, and his body heat receded. The air shifted with the door closing behind her, surrounding her with darkness *and* silence. The feeling of being unanchored and falling into a bottomless pit returned. She fought the vertigo and swept her head from left to right, trying to make out something. Anything.

Suddenly, something clicked, and the visor lit up, showing an illustrated suite.

Zoe lifted her hand in front of her, and it appeared like an animated artwork in the visor. *Interesting.*

She glanced around the room. There was a settee with soft furnishings, a large bed, a chest of drawers, a closet and a bathroom. Movement in the corner of her eyes drew her attention.

A man rose from an armchair and swivelled in her direction. Like the rest of the room, he was illustrated in the visor. Interestingly, he didn't seem to be wearing VR goggles.

Hot damn, he was broad and tall and muscular. Well-honed muscles. Not purely sculpted in a gym. But by life and hard work. Perhaps the virtual reality equipment made him attractive, but he was undoubtedly her cup of tea physically.

And he was naked.

Well-hung, even without an erection. How large would he get when fully erect?

Her mouth dried. Her body flushed with heat as she imagined his girth splitting her open.

Damn. She bit her bottom lip, trying to quell her racing pulse.

"Hi, I'm Nnanna," his voice was a rasping, guttural tone, so deep and hot, making her melt inside.

"I'm Mimi," she kept her voice low and seductive. "It's nice to meet you. But you're not wearing any goggles. How will you find your way around the room?"

"I removed the visor after I arrived and acquainted myself with the room's layout. So I know where every piece of furniture is located," he replied in the gravelly voice which should come with a—may induce orgasm—warning!

She swallowed, trying to remember what he said rather than focusing on his sensual cadence. "Really? You can see in the dark?"

"Yes. Don't sound so surprised. It's a skill I learned from my job." He chuckled, the sound warm and melting her core.

"And what job is that?"

Yes, keep asking questions, Zoe. So he won't notice he had you at 'Hi, I'm Nnanna.'

She must be sex-starved. Because what was this? Why was she turning into putty barely ten minutes into the encounter? When was the last time she'd had sex? Okay, it had been a while. But did it warrant this whole swooning act her body was undergoing? She'd never been the woman who fell at men's feet.

"We're not supposed to know anything about each other beyond our sexual requirements. Remember, you were specific about it."

The censure in his voice pulled her out of her reverie, making her cheeks heat.

"Of course." She'd been the one to insist on making the encounter as impersonal as possible.

"Anyway, I didn't want the goggles distorting your image. I would rather allow my imagination to create a picture based on your voice and feel."

"That's fair enough. But we're both here for sex. And the goggles could enhance it."

"Maybe, but I'm not interested in virtual sex. Not tonight anyway."

"Are you saying that if I request virtual sex with you, you will decline it?"

"Yes."

"Hmmm," Zoe muttered to hide her consternation.

She'd tried to change the rules of engagement, a power play. But Nnanna remained adamant about what he wanted and hadn't taken the bait. He would not be easily controlled.

"Take your dress off. It might help you relax if you're naked. There's a coat stand two steps to your left," he said in a husky rumble.

Her clit throbbed, and her panties moistened. Yet, she ignored his instruction. She didn't take orders well and certainly wouldn't jump to please a stranger so readily.

Still, she wondered how he knew her location in the pitch-black space. He hadn't moved and was still across the room from her, close to the bed. Perhaps he'd lied about not using goggles or some other night-vision tool.

"Come here," she commanded and swallowed to clear her croaky voice. "I need to touch your face and ensure you're not lying to me."

He moved without hesitation as if he'd been waiting for the prompt. For her permission. His silhouette in the visor approached until it filled her vision completely.

The air around her shifted, his body heat radiating to her in the air-conditioned room. His proximity made her mouth dry out.

She licked her lips, raising her hands until they grazed the expanse of his chest. His breath hitched. The visor didn't do him justice. Warm skin and solid muscles rippled under her palms.

He was older than her, probably middle-aged, and he wore his maturity like a badge. In the calm, martial stance he adopted, confident yet constrained. He didn't live a typical nine-to-five life. No, he'd indulged in adventures, perhaps even dangerous pursuits evident in the ridges on his skin.

A coldness embraced her, and her heart skipped a beat. Were these scars accidental, or did someone hurt him on purpose? She traced them tentatively, tenderly.

"How did you get the injuries?" she asked without thinking, concern for him overriding everything else, surprisingly.

"You know better than to ask me that. Move your hands to my face unless you've decided you want to have sex after all." He sounded aroused and irritated. Yet there was a trace of something dark and dangerous which appealed to her. Which made her want to find out everything about him.

"Of course," she huffed, her cheeks burning.

Why was she even worried about his scars, about a stranger? She wasn't in the market for a relationship. Her father's marriage auction dictated she couldn't get involved with anyone outside the exclusive list of suitors.

Nevertheless, she'd set the rules about keeping this encounter impersonal. So he was right to be annoyed at her question. Also, exploring his body intimately could be interpreted as an invitation to have sex, considering her suspicions about his sincerity.

So she focused on the objective—discovering if he was using night-vision tools.

Her fingers grazed his collar on the way up. A thick layer of neatly trimmed hair covered his narrow, chiselled jawline, extending around his lush, full lips.

Unbidden images bombarded her. The sensuous scrape of his whiskered jaw over her nether region and inner thighs. The stab of his probing tongue as her core clenched and throbbed. The thrust of his rigidity as he impaled and claimed her.

Heat skittered over her skin. The urge to delve in and feel the flick of his wet tongue on her skin nearly consumed her. She bit her bottom lip to control the moan bubbling inside her as she tried to keep to the task. This man was a whole lotta distraction. And he hadn't even touched her.

Who was he? His presence fascinated her. His quiet confidence and patience. Unlike most men she'd encountered.

Even without illumination, his inquisitive gaze seemed to burn her skin.

She swallowed thickly, wishing she could see him. "What colour are your eyes?"

Nnanna exhaled heavily as if tired of batting back her queries. "You ask a lot of questions."

"Yes, and I'm used to being answered promptly," she retorted, a little irritated by his reticent.

"And you're bossy." His chuckle was warm and easy, softening his chiding words, and making her stomach flip-flop.

Conflicted, her muscles stiffened defensively. Her attraction to him aside, she didn't tolerate anyone attempting to ridicule her.

"Yes, I am. There's nothing wrong with being bossy."

"I didn't say there was."

He sighed.

She stood still, expecting him to say something snide about bossy women.

He didn't. Neither did he move.

The only sound was the whooshing blood in her ears and her thumping heartbeats.

After a few seconds, she raised her hands again, tracing his broad Nubian nose and sharp cheekbones before roaming around the slash of his eyebrows. His lashes fluttered against her palms, sending tingles down her spine. She widened her reach over his earlobes to the nape. The hair on his scalp was shaped into a fade, the skin smooth around the edges and stubbly at the top to indicate he'd had a recent haircut.

"Now you know I wasn't lying to you. I won't lie to you," he sounded sincere.

She dropped her hands. He wasn't wearing anything to aid his vision. But she didn't believe him about never lying to her. People were deceptive, especially men.

"Take the visor off," he ordered.

"You should know I don't take orders from men," she retorted.

"Only men?" he sounded amused, which annoyed her.

"You still haven't told me the colour of your eyes."

"I'll tell you if you take the visor off."

"Fine," she conceded. The image on the visor wasn't nearly as great as the sensation of his skin. From his features, he was a handsome man with an incredible body, and she yearned to touch him again.

She tugged the goggles off and suddenly descended into darkness again as she blinked several times.

"My eyes are black. Obsidian," he said, his warm hand covering hers, taking the gadget.

"That's beautiful," she said and meant it.

"Thank you. Some people think they are too piercing. It makes them uncomfortable when I stare."

"Yes, I can imagine your gaze to be penetrating." She heard a scuffing sound. "What are you doing?"

"I'm putting the visor into a drawer so it doesn't get damaged accidentally. Those things cost thousands of dollars."

He really could see in the dark.

"How do you know how much they cost?"

"We use similar ones in my business, so I know."

Her pulse increased, and she itched to know more about his profession, about him. Yet she didn't ask. Rules were rules.

"So, what do you wish to do now? We can sit and talk if you prefer," he said.

"Hell, no. I came here to have sex. I'll call my friends and hang out if I need to talk."

Hell, last night's conversation with Baba and Vershima had been aggravating, among other things. The marriage bullshit was terrible enough. But trying to install her brother into her position was the last straw. She'd nearly pulled her weapon on them.

So yes, she needed to decompress before she did something crazy, like shooting her brother. She'd travelled to Lori Osa under the guise of meeting up with an old friend, which would happen tomorrow. So not a total lie.

But tonight was for the stranger. For the anonymous, no-strings-attached sex. For Nnanna.

Because for the next few hours, she craved him over her, under her, around her. For him to lay her on her back, bent over, on her knees. For him to caress and cajole, to manoeuvre and master her body.

"Are you sure you want sex?" Nnanna asked in an unhurried tone, sounding concerned.

The cage around her heart rattled, warring with her trust issues. Was he genuinely concerned or playing games?

"For fuck sake, are you going to spend all night talking, or are you going to fuck me?" she snapped.

Without warning, strong hands wrapped around her waist, lifting her and placing her on what seemed like a table or chest of drawers. Her sandals slipped off her feet.

"I told you to strip," he said, his minty breath feathering her face.

"No," she replied. It was bad enough being in the darkness. But taking her clothes off would strip the last of her control. She wouldn't give it up.

His hand searched and found her breast through the fabric. He pinched the nipple, making her gasp and squirm.

"Fine. I'll fuck you with your clothes on," he said in a firm tone, unaffected by her disobedience.

His demeanour proved he held authority and was used to commanding people. Yet he always found a way around her defiance and didn't demand compliance. Was he for real?

Adrenaline spiked her with suspicion. She reached into her pocket, pulled out the weapon and shoved the muzzle to his abs. "Nnanna, I'm warning you. I will use this gun if you try any nonsense."

He froze, one hand on her back, the other cupping her breast.

"Mimi," his deep voice held censure. "I've tried showing you're safe with me tonight. There is no reason to threaten me. But now I'm curious. Why do you need to carry a gun? Who are you?"

Shit. She realised her mistake and shoved the weapon back into her pocket. It was apparent he wasn't intimidated by the gun or by her. "It's none of your business."

He seemed able to defuse volatile situations. Or was a dangerous man.

Yet she wasn't afraid of dangerous men. They were a part of her existence.

However, his calm attitude was new and unnerving. She didn't know any man who would remain restrained after having a weapon aimed at him.

As a distraction, she reached down his body and gripped his naked semi-erect dick. He hissed a breath and swelled in her hand as she stroked him. Her mouth watered, her panties getting wet with her juices.

His hand returned to her breast, kneading and rolling. Anticipation raced through her as she pictured having his erection inside her.

Her other hand caressed his muscular thigh, and his primed dick jutted out from his body, precum beading the tip as she smeared it around him.

Her heart raced. She couldn't wait any longer. Only a few minutes with him and she was going crazy.

"I have a condom." She reached into the other pocket and pulled out the condom foil. He took it, leaning back to open it.

She heard him roll it on, and then he gripped her face and sealed their lips in a searing kiss. It tingled all the way to her toes, making them curl. His firm dick pressed against her belly through her dress. Then his hands were back on her waist, lifting and depositing her on soft sheets.

He followed her, angling his head and kissing her deeply. He knew how to kiss passionately, without concern. This stranger of hers. This Nnanna. He devoured her mouth in a punishing kiss, making her core clench and her clit ache.

She writhed, rubbing herself all over him.

He broke the kiss, nipping her chin and collar. "Turn over. Kneel on the bed."

Potent need flowed through her, and she didn't hesitate to obey this time.

He yanked her dress up, making it pool around her waist. Then hard smacks descended on her bum in quick succession, sending pain, heat and more liquid to her core.

"Ow," she gasped with each thud, more out of shock than discomfort.

"That's for pointing a gun at me," he growled in a deep voice, melting her insides.

Before she could protest verbally, she felt the warmth of his breath on her thigh. Then his wet tongue flicked against her clit, and his mouth went to work, eating her pussy.

"Oh … oh … oh," she moaned aloud, barely able to brace herself on the mattress as sensation after sensation flooded her, her orgasm becoming imminent.

"You're soaking wet." His fingers invaded her insides, curving and stroking her G-spot, making her moan louder with pleasure.

He shoved his face against her pussy from behind as ripples of ecstasy radiated through her. He licked her slit and plunged his tongue inside her. "Your pussy is delicious. I could eat this for hours."

At his dirty words, the orgasm crashed through her, taking her breath with it, and she screamed into the comforter.

Before she would catch her breath, he gripped her hips, tilted her bum up and slammed his dick into her to the hilt.

"Nna…!" Another scream ripped through her as he gripped the back of her neck, holding her down and fucking her into oblivion. She'd never shouted so much as he took her with savage need, his hips snapping against her bum. Each thrust of his dick reignited her pleasure. The way he held her down, he commanded her body like no other man had ever done. She was arched in submission to him, taking him deep with each powerful slam.

Without even knowing it, she had relinquished control to him totally. Worse, she didn't care. She was lost in him, consumed by the vibrations he evoked. She pushed her bum against him, seeking more of him as his dick hit her sweet spot and her inner walls clenched around his length.

Skin flushed with heat, her body quivered, limbs turning to jelly. It was like he couldn't get enough of her, couldn't get enough of the pleasure. He was fucking her hard and raw. Sparks flew all over her nerve endings.

"Mimi … I'm in love with your pussy. Is that possible?" he growled between panting, reaching around, fingering her clit, still thrusting his dick into her.

"Yes! Nna…" she couldn't complete his name as the sensation overload made her shatter in an explosive orgasm. Fireworks burst behind her closed eyelids as ecstasy rocked her body.

The rush of blood in her ears mixed with the roar of his orgasm as he pumped his release into the condom.

The weight of his body pressed onto her back, cocooning her in safety, and she floated in bliss. Their heavy breathing mixed as the sweat cooled on their entwined bodies.

For the first time in a long while, she didn't shove her partner's body aside so she could escape. Instead, she allowed the darkness, his warmth and weight to lull her into sleep.

Her life could wait.

FOUR

Maddox slipped out of the woman's warm pussy and sat on the edge of the bed for a second to get his bearing. When he figured out the direction he needed, he took fifteen steps into the ensuite bathroom, hands outstretched in front of him in case he walked into the wall or furniture.

As soon as he stepped on the metal runner indicating the threshold of the attached washroom, the motion sensor detected his presence, and a dull green light glowed inside the bathroom. He could see the fixtures to use them, but it wasn't bright enough to illuminate beyond the obscured glass door. So, if Mimi wanted to see his face, she would have to enter the bathroom and reveal her face in the process, too.

He disposed the used condom in the small plastic bin, used the WC and washed his hands in the sink. A glance in the mirror above the counter showed the distorted face of a Black man. His features were not distinct.

This whole suite was designed to obscure the guests' identities, even from the ID owners.

Maddox chuckled, shaking his head as he headed back to the bedroom. The light went off when he left the bathroom, and he was back in darkness. He walked in a straight line until his feet hit the edge of the divan. Then he climbed in and lay next to the woman. She was asleep, the soft sighing of her exhales and inhales creating a resonance he was happy to hear.

He wished to explore her body more. To initiate another round of sex. She'd booked the Black Room for the night. So he'd assumed they would be sexually active for most of it. But she was sleeping now. This meant the consent she'd given previously no longer applied. And they didn't know each other well enough for him to arouse her. He would have to wait for her to wake and consent to more sexual contact.

He couldn't wake her by spreading her thighs, dipping into her honeyed sweetness with his tongue.

He licked his lips, savouring her lingering tang. He hadn't been joking when he said he was getting addicted to her pussy. He wished to drag his aching shaft over her dripping channel once more.

Damn. His balls throbbed, his groin straining to feel her again.

Instead, he pulled down her dress to cover her bum and legs. Then he spooned her, pulling her back to his chest. She came to him, snuggling closer and exhaling a soft sigh. But she didn't awaken. She slept as if this was the first time in days she'd been able to fall asleep quickly. She really must have needed the sex to unwind.

A light, floaty sensation fluttered in his chest because he'd helped her rest. Even if she slept for the night, he had no regrets. He'd been of service to her.

Considering her trust issues when she arrived, her reluctance to relax initially escalated to her pointing a weapon at him. He was surprised she felt safe enough to sleep in his arms.

It had been fantastic sex, enhanced and more intense because of the lack of sight.

But he didn't think it was the only reason for the vigour and passion of their encounter.

A big part of it was the woman—Mimi.

Sure, he didn't know her appearance and couldn't identify her in a crowd by sight alone.

Her trust issue was the size of a boulder she bore like a chip on her shoulder. Never mind her prickly and dictatorial personality or that she'd threatened to shoot him.

Yet, she intrigued him. Hooked him with this one encounter.

He craved her. To know her. Her loves. Her hates. Her passion. Her challenges. Her life.

Crazy, considering he signed up for the Blind Date programme for one reason only. The no-strings-attached sex.

So, how could he possibly want more of her? He didn't even know her real name. Mimi could be an alias. Didn't know her ID.

Although he could investigate while she slept.

A quick tumble out of bed to grab his mobile phone from his trouser pocket, and he could use the torchlight to illuminate her face and body to see her appearance.

Instead, his arms tightened around her and his chest constricted with a determination to protect her. An unexpected, intense need to shelter her overrode his curiosity.

He couldn't violate the trust she'd shown him. Nor the safety and comfort she found in his arms as they'd had sex.

She had requested to remain anonymous for this encounter. He would respect it even if he never got what he wanted—her.

He could only hope to convince her to meet him again, even if it would be anonymous and in the Black Room again.

For now, he held her, revelled in her warmth and fragrance—strawberries and sunshine. Desire throbbed within him. He stifled a groan, tightening his grip on her.

She stirred, moaned softly and returned to sleep.

He closed his eyes, sighing softly.

His life was hectic. Trouble was always around the corner.

As a member of the Yadili network and the Odili clan enforcer, his life was hectic. Trouble seemed around every corner. He'd spent twenty years in military service and the last ten running a private security firm. His life wasn't conducive to full-time relationships. He'd learned it the hard way. Even now, he had no time for round-the-clock romantic relationships. But he was a full-blooded human and still needed an outlet for his sexual energy.

His life changed when he signed up and joined the Star Club. Instead of him seeking out partners for sexual affairs, the Arufin team screened and matched women to him based on his requirements. All with no strings attached. And for the price of the membership fee.

He loved the set-up because it was safe, sane, and consensual. Best of all, it was discrete. He'd been using the service for almost a year and couldn't fault it.

His smartwatch vibrated, and he lifted his arm, glancing at the digital display. He read the message notification:

Code yellow.

The hair on his nape stiffened. Trouble had found him.

Needing to make a phone call, he withdrew his arms from Mimi.

She muttered something unintelligible as if in protest.

"Mimi, sleep," he whispered against her cheek as he brushed his lips to her soft skin.

Then he rolled out of bed and padded to the armchair where he'd left his clothes. He scooped them, went to the bathroom, and pulled his phone from the trouser pocket. He dialled his business partner and younger brother, and the line connected after one ring.

"O mu kwube?" *Should I speak?* Jaxon said without preamble on the other end. They used the simple Igbo phrase to clear the air in case it wasn't a good time to talk.

"Kwube. Ana m ege nti," *Continue. I'm listening.* Maddox replied, wanting to get to the root of the matter. They had three alert statuses.

Code Green meant business as usual.

Codes Yellow and Red meant they had a situation which depended on the critical nature. Code Yellow could escalate to Code Red, so it was best to deal with them immediately.

"One of our boys was ambushed in Isale. He's critical, in hospital. I'm on my way there," Jaxon said.

"Send me the address. I'll meet you there," Maddox replied, shoving his feet into his briefs and trousers. "And send out an alert to all our personnel in Lori Osa. No one is allowed to move without cover. They should pair up wherever they're going. I don't care if they're going to their Mama's house. No one moves alone."

Although a trade hazard, Maddox hated when rivals injured any of his crew. Protecting the Odili clan was his responsibility, and he didn't shirk his duties.

When they'd first started the Lori Osa operations about a year ago, he'd initiated a Code Yellow alert and instructed them to move in groups because they'd been the new crew in town. The locals didn't want them here. There had been several skirmishes. However, things had mellowed over the months, and they'd moved to Code Green. But he'd known it was only a matter of time before problems escalated again.

He couldn't risk anyone else being ambushed and injured. Or worse.

"Sure, I'll do that straight away," Jaxon said. As the digital security expert, he handled all their communications. "I'll see you at the hospital."

Maddox disconnected the call and dressed quickly. Then he returned to the bedroom, searched for his blazer and shoes and slipped them on.

With the phone in hand, he was tempted to turn on the torch light and shine it on the sleeping woman so he could see her face. But he shook his head, dispelling the urge.

He was a principled man. It was in his surname— Ejiofor. He wouldn't sully his name and honour, things he'd sworn to uphold.

Regardless, the people in charge of the premises wouldn't allow him to get away with it. It was their job to protect the participants, and they took it seriously. There were cameras and microphones in the suite. They would see and apprehend him if he turned on the phone in the room. He would lose his membership and be banned because he'd violated the terms and conditions he'd signed. So, definitely not worth the hassle.

Still, it was a shame to end the brief evening with Mimi.

If she wanted to see him again, she could always request another meeting via the Star app. He hoped she would.

He withdrew the visor from the drawer and placed it on the mattress under her hand so she would feel it when she woke. It would help her see in the dark without him to guide her.

Then he leaned over her, brushed the hair from her face and pressed his lips to her cheek again. "Bye, Mimi."

He left the suite, took the lift up another floor, and exited into a corridor. Before he could reach the door to the security suite, a big man stepped out and crossed his arms over his chest.

Maddox knew what was behind the door. Banks of monitors showing the different suites in the building. His firm had won the contract to upgrade the Arufin security system. Jaxon had been the project lead.

"Maddox, if you're trying to get out, you're going the wrong way," Idehen said.

"I know. I just wanted to see you about the lady in the Black Room. Mimi. Don't wake her."

"Why?" the other man raised his brows.

"I just want her to sleep. So don't disturb her."

"Okay." Idehen nodded.

"Good. Have a good night." He turned to leave.

"You like her," Idehen stated.

"Yes. So?" Maddox glanced back.

"So, why didn't you look at her face? You could have. You had your phone in your hand."

Maddox growled in anger, swivelling to face him. "Because she didn't consent to it. Because I cannot abuse her trust. Because if you thought I was that kind of man, you wouldn't let me anywhere near her. At least, you shouldn't."

"That's true." Idehen nodded. "I'm glad you're not that kind of man. Have a good night."

Maddox stood there for a beat, tempted to ask Idehen for the woman's real identity. But he didn't because even if he asked, Idehen wouldn't tell him. The other man wouldn't breach her trust any more than Maddox would.

Satisfied that Mimi was safe, he swivelled and returned to the lift. "See you around, Idehen."

The man grunted in response and disappeared into the security suite.

FIVE

This wasn't happening.

Zoe stared again at the white plastic stick on the bathroom sink counter. The pink double lines flashed, confirming the first and second results.

As the sceptic, she conducted the test thrice with different product brands.

The result remained the same.

She was pregnant.

Her legs gave way, and she sank onto the toilet seat cover and braced her head in her hands. She wasn't prone to hysterics. However, this was a disaster. Pregnancy was the worst thing to happen to her right now.

She lived in a high-pressure situation under constant scrutiny.

First was the threat to her position as heir-apparent being usurped. Hence, she must persistently and consistently prove she could handle the Himba operations as the future kingpin.

She'd convinced her father that Vershy wasn't ready for management-level responsibilities. He had to prove himself and work his way up from the bottom like she'd done when she'd started. Baba had eventually agreed when she'd offered to employ her brother. Now, Vershy was an intern in her law firm, working on the Himba portfolio. She would train him as long as he showed initiative.

The matter would resurface again, so she remained vigilant and suspicious of everything.

Then, there was the matter of the marriage auction. Or marriage alliance, as her mother preferred to call it.

Regardless of the phrase—auction, alliance, arrangement—it was still an obligation she must fulfil for her family, for her father, regardless of her feelings about marriage.

It was a project, something on her to-do list. Once completed, she would move on to the next project, getting a divorce. She would not tolerate a husband for longer than necessary.

In the meantime, she was planning a deal to strengthen the Himba clan and provide them with an organised network of business partners beyond their current boundaries.

However, everything could disintegrate with the pregnancy.

It would devalue her worth at the marriage negotiations if the suitors discovered she was carrying someone else's baby.

Her father would lose money, and his fury would be catastrophic. He would oust her as heir-apparent as punishment. Or worse, disown her.

She would lose everything she'd worked her entire adult life to attain—status and family.

No! She couldn't let it happen.

"Grrrr." She growled in frustration and stood from the toilet seat.

How did she end up in this situation? She was usually cautious with her sexual activities. She always insisted on protection. And even when there was a chance of an accident, she used the morning-after pill.

So how was she careless this time?

She'd only had one sexual encounter in the last six months. With Nnanna in the Black Room of the Star Club.

Remembering the explosive encounter made her core clench, and her ovaries dance. His passionate kiss, the feel of his hands on her skin, his throbbing dick deep inside her. She'd pleasured herself most nights over the past six weeks from the memories alone.

However, she was a practical person. She'd given him a condom and heard him roll it on. So how was she now pregnant?

Sure, accidents happen. But it wasn't so easy.

They'd only fucked once, and she'd fallen asleep. She'd been awakened by a knock on the door, but Nnanna was gone. Idehen had driven her back to the hotel.

Nnanna had used the condom, hadn't he?

Her belly knotted as her breath quickened.

What if he hadn't used it? What if he had pretended to roll it on but had thrown it away. The pitch darkness would have given him the perfect cover because she couldn't see.

Hang on. What if he'd removed her VR goggles so she wouldn't see what he was doing to her? That he didn't use a condom.

Okay. It sounded outlandish.

Yet, she'd read an article recently about a man who had impregnated over twenty women because he poked holes in the condom pack without the women's knowledge. He'd met most of the women via a dating app.

What if Nnanna was doing the same thing? What if he was fucking women in the Black Room and purposefully impregnating them.

She knew people who'd done worse to manipulate others.

A pounding started between her ears, and her pulse elevated along with her rage.

If Nnanna was targeting women maliciously, he'd picked on the wrong one. She would find him and make him pay for his actions.

Yet she didn't know his identity. She'd signed an agreement, meaning his profile was sealed.

Surely, there was a way to unseal the profile and find out.

She could employ one of their contract hackers to infiltrate the app and find the data. But it would mean that her profile might be breached, too. She couldn't afford for the information to fall into the wrong hands.

There had to be an alternative solution.

Grabbing the phone from the counter, she walked into her bedroom, scrolling through the contacts until she found the needed number. The phone rang on the other end for a minute before it was picked up.

"Hi, Zoe," Xandra's breathy soft voice came through. "Is everything okay?"

"Of course, everything is okay. Why do you ask, Xan?" she used the abbreviated version of the woman's name.

"Ha, it's the second time you've called me in about two months. You don't usually call me this frequently."

True. They hadn't spoken for several months since Xandra moved away from Lokogi. Then, two months ago, Zoe called her adoptive sister to enquire about the Star Club.

When they'd been children, Zoe and Xandra had been close. Tiye Himba had found Xan at an orphanage and brought her home. Zoe had been excited to acquire a sister. But instead of attending Zoe's private school, Xandra had been sent to another academy where she'd been trained as a soldier. When Xandra returned, she became her father's assassin for hire, utilised for contract kills.

Zoe and Xandra had maintained a semblance of friendship. They'd hung out sometimes and trained together at the gym. Xandra had taught her how to handle weapons, handguns and rifles, even knives. But Zoe's preference was the handgun.

Everything had been good until Don Himba found out Xandra visited Star Club and ordered Norbert to punish the woman.

Now Zoe was a member of the same club.

"I know, and I'm sorry if I called you at a bad time," she said as regret made her body heavy.

"It's fine. I was cleaning the feeding troughs, so your call gives me a break. So how are you? Did you visit Arufin yet?"

Xandra lived with her partner Ebuka, who owned a cattle ranch, and it seemed the woman loved her new life as a farmer.

"That's what I called you about. I was there about six weeks ago."

"Oh, really. How was it? Did you have a great time?"

"I did. Everything went as you said. They took care of me."

"That's wonderful. Osagie and Co are pretty on the ball. He's all about safe and consensual."

"Yes, it was an amazing experience…" she trailed off.

"I can detect a but. Did something happen?" Her friend was very intuitive and the closest person to a sister.

Zoe couldn't tell her secret to anyone else. However, Xandra was removed from her immediate family and would keep it confidential.

She lowered her body into the settee and spoke in a whisper. "No. As I said, the night was wonderful, and the encounter was amazing. But I missed my period, and I did a test … actually several tests this afternoon. And I'm pregnant."

"Oh… I take it that is not good news," Xandra said quietly.

"No. It's the worst possible news. There's just so much going on right now."

"I understand. I'm sorry. What are you going to do?"

"First of all, I need to understand how it happened. I'm usually so careful and always use a condom. I gave him a condom that night, but…"

"You don't think he used it?"

"It was the Black Room. I couldn't see him put it on, and I didn't touch his erection afterwards, so I have no proof that he used it."

"I see."

"I need to know what happened. Otherwise, my brain won't rest. You know how I overanalyse everything."

"I know. You need to find him."

"Yes, but how. His profile is sealed."

"You can unseal it. Just complete an information request form."

"I can do that?"

"Yes. It rarely gets used because it means your profile will also be unsealed. So your date will know who you are."

"It's not ideal. But I don't have any other choice. I want to know who it is. I want to find out if he did this on purpose. My brain is conjuring all kinds of scenarios."

"Okay. Go to the app, and in the support tab, you should find the button for the form you need."

"Great. Thank you. I'll do it," Zoe said, relieved there was a path to her goal. She could get to the pleasantries with the critical matter out of the way. "How about you? How is life on the farm?"

"It's hectic. Some days, I'm so exhausted. But I love every minute of it."

"You sound delighted. I'm jealous that you managed to escape the craziness of this life."

"I wouldn't say I escaped it totally. Ebuka is Yadili and part of the Odili crew. But his involvement is peripheral. Personally, I'm glad I'm not on contract hire any more. If I ever carry out a hit again, it will be because the person deserved it, not because I'm obliged to unalive them."

"I'm happy for you. Happy you found a new purpose and a new family. I'm sorry my family didn't care for you like we should have."

"It's okay. I don't hold what happened against you. It all died with Norbert."

Zoe squeezed her eyes shut and exhaled heavily. "I'm glad. Now tell me more."

They talked for a few more minutes before they ended the call.

Afterwards, Zoe logged into the Star app and completed the Information Request form.

***

"What the fuck!" Zoe cursed as she stared at her phone screen and the profile details on the Star app a week later.

Username: Nnanna
Full name: Maddox Ejiofor
Gender: Male
Age: 48
Race: Black African
Nationality: Nigerian
Tribe: Igbo
Telephone number: xxxxxxxxxxx [click to reveal]
Address: xxxxxxxxxxxx [click to reveal]
And so forth…

She stared at the name on the screen, thinking it must be an error. But the photo in the avatar proved differently. She recognised the man. She'd met him over a year ago when the Odilis hosted the heads of the five prominent cartel families.

Maddox Ejiofor, the Odili enforcer, was Nnanna, the man she'd spent the night with. Her one-night stand. Her blind date.

The man who impregnated her.

A tremble shimmied through her body as emotions swirled and jumbled inside her—shock, anger, confusion, desire.

How did she not recognise him or his voice that night?

Well, she'd never spoken directly to him before. She'd just known about him.

Still, she clutched her head.

What was she going to do now?

She'd planned to instruct her men to abduct her date and torture the truth out of him. Then, after he'd confessed to breaking her trust and violating her with his sperm, she would execute him and dispose of his body.

A reasonable plan until ten minutes ago when she'd opened the email from Star Arufin with the link to her blind date's profile. She'd clicked on it, and a massive rock of dread had dropped in her belly as soon as she'd seen the name.

Of course, she'd read it twice, three times, before it had sunk in.

Nnanna was Maddox Ejiofor.

There was no way she could stick with her original plan.

Even if she succeeded in abducting him, she doubted her torture technique would yield the result she required or make him reveal anything.

Maddox had served in the armed forces for years, a decorated special ops team member before retiring and entering the private sector. He came from a family of military personnel. His father and one of his brothers were still in the service.

She'd learned of his impressive background when she'd commissioned a dossier on the Fierce Four, the name given to Chief Odili's four chosen apprentices and capos—Duke, Mason, Rocha and Maddox.

At the time, she hadn't paid much attention to Maddox's dossier. She'd dismissed him as just another enforcer. Cartel enforcers earned their reputations from their brute force, just like Norbert. They were necessities to keep the crew in line and settle scores with rivals.

Zoe had barely tolerated Norbert. He'd been a loutish, manipulative Neanderthal. The expensive designer clothes didn't change him. He'd been a thug in a suit. Don Himba's attack dog.

She'd assumed the same thing about Maddox as the Odili's attack dog. His nickname was Mad Dog to his enemies.

Still, the man who'd spent the night with her weeks ago—Nnanna—wasn't a brute. He hadn't been aggressive or abusive. He'd stood patiently while she'd explored his chest and face. Hadn't touched her until she'd given permission.

A-ha! Now, those scars on his chest made sense. Even his night vision skills.

He'd been a soldier on the frontlines, fighting militants and terrorists. It tracked he would have those scars, those skills.

Her fingers tingled with the need to retrace his scars. To explore his skin again. Her mouth watered from remembering his taste. The feel of his lips on her sensitive skin. The pleasure he evoked.

Her core clenched, her body wound tight at the memories.

Zoe, what are you thinking?

Her eyes flew open. She hadn't realised she'd closed them while thinking about Maddox.

Have you forgotten he got you pregnant? This could ruin your life. He could have done it on purpose. Maybe he saw your face since his eyesight was so good. Perhaps he knew who you were and decided to fuck you bare without the condom so you could get pregnant?

Her stomach heaved, and she staggered into the bathroom, making it in time to puke in the toilet bowl.

Afterwards, she sat on the floor covered in cold sweat. Her mind whirled with irrational ideas. Most of all, she felt like her life would implode.

***

Maddox stared at his computer screen, hardly believing what he was reading.

A few days ago, he received an information application from Star-Arufin because Mimi had requested his profile details.

Maddox had jumped at the serendipitous opportunity because he hadn't gotten the woman out of his head since their one-night stand. He hoped her enquiry meant she wanted to see him again.

So he'd clicked 'yes' to the request, and this afternoon, he'd received a link to her personal info.

And to his shock, Mimi was Zoe Himba.

At thirty-four, she was fourteen years younger than him. A babe. Yet again, the assertive woman who'd questioned and challenged and threatened him during their one-night stand hadn't been innocent. She'd been his match. He'd craved her. Still did, if he was honest.

He scrubbed a hand over his face.

He'd fucked Zoe Himba. A mafia don's daughter.

What the hell!

The last time an Odili had gotten involved with a mafia princess, it had resulted in a war between the Odili family and the Owo clan. In the end, Duke Odili married Carla Owo.

Damn. Would his one-night stand with Zoe spark another war?

About six weeks ago, Maddox and his F4 brothers—Duke, Mason and Rocha—met with their godfather in Umudike, their hometown. Chief Odili had mentioned wanting their operation to expand into the northern territories. He indicated that Don Himba was looking for a husband for his daughter, Zoe. At the meeting, Chief instructed Mason to bid for Zoe's hand in marriage.

However, as of last week, Mason had withdrawn his bid to marry Zoe and had married someone else, an associate of theirs, Sophie.

This meant no one from the Odili family was bidding for Zoe's hand. Duke and Mason were taken. When Chief brought it up, Rocha had his eyes set elsewhere and hadn't shown any interest in marrying Zoe.

Maddox was the last man standing.

The woman who'd invaded his mind in the past month was available for a marriage proposal. Was it a sign that he was meant to be with her as her husband?

Did his ancestors approve of their union?

He stared at her name on the screen again, and his grin spread.

He'd wanted her contact details, and now he had it. There was only one thing to do with it.

He grabbed his phone and dialled the number listed on her profile. The phone rang several times before it was answered.

"What!"

He recognised the snappy, surly voice immediately.

"Zoe?" he said. She gasped in recognition. But he still added, "It's Maddox, Nnanna."

"I know who you are, you asshole!"

Huh? Stunned by her response, he didn't speak for a few seconds. Perhaps he'd caught her at the wrong time. "Mimi, what's the matter?"

"Don't you dare speak that name again after what you've done?" She sounded agitated like she was pacing. "I knew I shouldn't have trusted you. I should have shot you that night."

Ice filled his veins, and his voice hardened. "You know better than to threaten me."

"I don't care. You've ruined my life!"

"Zoe, calm the fuck down and tell me what's happened."

"I'm pregnant. I'm carrying your baby. That's what's happened. Don't you ever call my number again. Or I swear I will put a contract hit on your head. Do you hear me? I never want to see you again."

The line went dead.

Maddox sat still for several minutes, trying to process the words in shock, staring at the phone in his hand blankly.

Zoe was pregnant with his baby? How did that happen?

He'd used a condom. Sure, accidents happened. But still, they'd been careful.

"Maddox!"

He came out of his haze to find Jaxon standing next to him with concern on his face.

"What?" he asked.

"I've been calling your name with no response. Are you okay?" his brother frowned.

"No. I'm not," Maddox replied. "Zoe Himba is pregnant with my baby."

Jaxon jerked back. "Zoe Himba? Thee Zoe Himba? How? I didn't even know you were dating her."

She was the daughter of a prominent cartel boss. She was an underworld royalty.

"I wasn't. But I had an anonymous one-night stand weeks ago." He swivelled to show his brother the laptop screen. "I was sent the profile of my date because she requested mine. Look at the name."

His brother stared and gasped. "Wow. It's her. And she's pregnant?"

"Yes, I just called her, and she was furious with me on the phone. She is not happy about the pregnancy. I don't blame her. I used a condom."

"Are you sure it's yours?"

"I don't believe she would lie about it."

"Well, you don't really know her."

"Maybe not. But she sounded too furious to fake it."

"So what are you going to do?"

"She told me not to contact her again. If I did, she would put a hit on my head."

"Wow. The babe is serious."

"I don't care how serious she is. If she won't talk to me rationally, I have to find another way because there's no way I will not ignore my child."

Jaxon scratched his hairy chin. "I agree. But what can you do? She has the aces."

"Maybe. But her father opened an auction for suitors to bid for her hand in marriage. I will ask Chief to put me forward as the Odili candidate. I'm going to outbid all the others. She's going to be my wife."

SIX

Footsteps announced the new arrival before Chief Odili appeared at the top of the landing overlooking the spacious foyer, dressed in his trademark two-piece tunic suit, this time in navy blue.

Maddox straightened from the stiff-back chair he'd been in since his arrival at the mansion in the leafy suburbs of Iguocha City.

"Onye Isi, good morning. Thank you for seeing me at such short notice," he greeted, hands clasped in front of him, legs apart.

"Good morning, Maddox," the old man said as he descended the stairs. "It's good to see you. I hope everyone is okay?"

Chief stopped at the bottom of the stairs, scrutinising him with piercing dark eyes. He must be wondering why Maddox requested this impromptu meeting. He operated an open-door policy with his proteges, meaning they could turn up and get granted access to him at short notice.

However, Maddox had called him yesterday, requesting this meeting, and he'd flown from Lori Osa last night so he could see the godfather first thing this morning.

"Yes, sir," Maddox replied. "Everyone is fine. I just had an urgent matter I wished to discuss with you face to face."

"Okay." Chief nodded. "We can talk briefly in the sitting room before I head to the office this morning."

Maddox nodded and followed the old man, past a bodyguard, into the spacious living decorated in cream and gold. He waited for Chief to sit in his favourite armchair. Then, the old man waved him to the adjacent sofa.

"So what's on your mind that we couldn't discuss on the phone?" Chief said.

"The matter is delicate and time-sensitive. I don't want to miss the window of opportunity."

"Okay. Tell me about it."

"It's about the Himba marriage auction," Maddox said, watching Chief's reaction. "I would like you to put me forward as your candidate."

The old man had previously picked a candidate—Mason—to represent him, although it had fallen through. Zoe had rejected Mason, although Mason had planned to withdraw anyway.

"No," Chief replied, a frown on his face. "We already put in a bid with Mason, which was rejected. The Himbas are not interested in working with us. I'm not going to give them another opportunity to decline our offer. We will find other avenues to enter the central and northern territories."

Maddox's heart dropped at Chief's outright refusal to put him forward. He could understand the old man's reticence. It was his reputation on the line each time he presented a candidate.

It had been bad enough when Zoe declined the offer outright. But Mason's withdrawal had been a direct disobedience of Chief orders. The old man obviously didn't need the reminder.

Still, Maddox couldn't let it go. "Onye Isi, there is a lot at stake this time. It's not just about taking territory. It's about my blood."

Chief's eyes narrowed. "How?"

Maddox cleared his throat. "Zoe Himba is carrying my baby. I'm here to seek your permission to propose to her."

Chief's eyes widened. "She's pregnant for you? How is that possible? Is she your girlfriend?"

The old man stared at him as if seeing him for the first time. The Odili enforcer impregnating the Himba heiress seemed dubious. The two were strange bedfellows because of previous bad blood.

"No. She's not my girlfriend." It was difficult to explain his encounter with Zoe to the old man. He chose to simplify it. "We had a brief affair. She later learned she was pregnant and told me it's mine."

"Wait. When did you have this affair? You were here a few weeks ago when we met with your fellow brothers, and I instructed Mason to propose to Zoe. Was your affair before or after that meeting?"

Oh no. Chief eyed him as if he'd gone after his Yadili brother's intended on purpose. Such things were forbidden and certainly not permissible for an enforcer. If an enforcer was corrupt, how could they enforce the brotherhood laws?

"The affair was only one night before you instructed Mason to propose to her. I only learned about her pregnancy yesterday, so I came to see you urgently."

Chief kept quiet for a few seconds before nodding. "It's good that you came to see me. But why didn't you mention that you knew Don Himba's daughter at the meeting weeks ago? I wouldn't have assigned Mason to her if I'd known you'd made a claim on her."

"No, sir. As I said, it was a very brief affair. Just one night. I didn't know her well and didn't claim her then." He didn't want to spill the beans about the sex club and the anonymous encounter, particularly for Zoe's sake. He wished to protect her privacy as much as he could. It was unpleasant enough discussing their date like this.

"But you want to claim her now," Chief said.

"Yes, I do. I want to marry her," Maddox replied.

Chief nodded. "Good. Do her parents know that she is pregnant for you?"

"I don't think so. She didn't tell them about our affair." Well, he hoped they didn't know. Otherwise, it would be awful since they put Zoe in the marriage auction.

"Okay. I'll do my best for you on this. I'll contact the intermediary to place a bid on your behalf," Chief said. "We have an advantage now because of the pregnancy. Zoe can't take your child into another man's home."

Maddox wished he had as much confidence as the old man. Zoe had been adamant about having no contact with Maddox. So convincing her to marry him would be an uphill struggle, which was partly why he was bypassing her and going through Chief and her father.

"Thank you, sir," he said, feeling apprehensive. He really wanted to get this marriage thing right.

Ordinarily, conversations about his intention to marry someone pregnant for him should be with his father because his father was still alive. But this wasn't a conventional marriage. It would be an arrangement, a convenient alliance where each party and clan would put stipulations in the contract. He needed to seek his clan leader's permission before explaining his intentions to his biological father. Respect where it was due.

"Don't look so worried," Chief said, smiling. "Ihe ọma ga-abịara gị." *Good things will come your way.*

"Ise!" Maddox affirmed the prayer.

***

"There is a new bid for Zoe's hand in marriage." Don Himba said as he ate his meal.

Not again. Zoe's stomach dropped along with her head. The damned marriage auction seemed to be the only topic of discussion around her home.

Even at the dinner table, with her father at the head, her mother at his right-hand side, and Zoe sitting,

At least once a week, Zoe shared a meal with Mum and Baba without the half-siblings or stepmother. Her biological mother instigated it when Zoe was younger to ensure her father found time in his busy schedule to pay attention to his only daughter and oldest offspring. Back then, her parents doting on her had been fantastic.

Right this moment? Not so much. She would rather avoid the attention.

She'd wished to opt out of dinner. However, finding an excuse proved tricky, considering she was already keeping secrets from her parents.

She harboured the constant anxiety of her father discovering her illicit affair with Maddox and the baby. Worse, she feared he would uncover her visit to a sex club.

She'd gone to extraordinary lengths to dispose of the pregnancy test kits because she couldn't leave them in the waste bin for the cleaners to discover. They would provide potent ammunition in the wrong hands. Her stepmother was always looking for opportunities to knock Zoe off her perch at the top of her father's favourite person list.

She hadn't even told her mother, the most trusted person in this house. Her mother would be disappointed. That's how much of a disaster the pregnancy was.

Her insomnia had worsened. Every time she closed her eyes, she woke in cold sweat from a nightmare about her life disintegrating.

"Oh, really? I knew my daughter would be very popular," her mother's proud voice drew Zoe's attention back to the dining room.

Shit. She cringed, unable to meet her parent's gaze. She picked at the food, not eating much to avoid getting queasy afterwards.

All that pride would disappear once her mother found out she'd ruined her chances of securing an excellent marriage deal for her father because she'd been impregnated by the Odili enforcer.

"Who is the offer from?" her mother continued in an excited tone.

"I can tell you I was surprised that Chief Odili—"

"Who?" Zoe gasped, her head jerking up. Surely, Baba wasn't about to say there was another bid from the Odili family. She'd rejected Mason's proposal. Now he was married, and so was Duke, which left Rocha and … *Maddox.*

Nnanna.

Her body quickened instantly, awash with heat and memories of his seductive kisses and caresses and thrusts. His ass-warming spanks and comforting embrace.

Her nipples puckered, and she stifled a moan.

"Chief Odili put in another bid. He presented someone else. His enforcer." Baba's words were a douse of cold water on her hot skin.

"No way!" Zoe exclaimed as her heart kicked in her chest.

"Zoe, do you know the young man?" her mother asked.

Zoe wouldn't call Maddox young. He was forty-eight, thirteen years older than her and only twelve years younger than her mother. So no, not that young.

"Zoe?"

Her cheeks heated as she realised her parents were staring at her. Her mother asked a question which she still hadn't answered. How would she answer without dropping herself in it?

"I know Maddox Ejiofor is the Odili enforcer. I had a dossier prepared for Baba about the Odili capos. Remember?" Her response was vague, and her mother picked up on it with the curious gaze she threw at her. She would bring it up later when they were in private.

"Sure. I remember. He has an impressive resume with his military background. We could use someone with his experience in our crew."

Blood drained from Zoe's head. "Baba, you're not really thinking of entertaining his bid. He is an Odili, and you don't want to work with them."

While her father had invited the other potential suitors to their home for preliminary talks, he had vehemently refused to entertain Mason Maduka when he'd put in his bid. Hence, Zoe met Mason at a restaurant instead of her home because of her father's snub and partly why she'd declined Mason's proposal even though he'd been her favourite from the initial list of suitors. Of course, receiving photos of Mason with Sophie had made her decision easier.

"Well, I still don't want to entertain them. But his bid has my attention because he's offered twice as much as the others. I'm curious to meet the arrogant boy who thinks he can throw money and get my daughter," her father said with contempt. "It will make it more interesting when his bid is rejected."

"Don, I hear the Odili boys are doing very well for themselves," her mother said. "Maybe you should take the young man seriously. He could bring more to the table. With his money and allegiance—"

Her mother was interrupted as the dining room door opened, and Don Himba's second wife entered, drawing everyone's attention.

"Brenda, what are you doing here?" Zoe's mother asked.

"I have an urgent message for our husband," Brenda replied, her hands behind her as she stood just inside the door, waiting for permission to move into the room. The woman definitely knew how to play family politics.

"What is it?" Don Himba said, sounding irritated. He didn't like these sessions interrupted. He probably yearned for the quieter days when it was only the three of them, and he didn't have the hassle of the second family and extra baggage.

"Can I come closer? It's a delicate matter. I don't want to shout," the woman looked around as if she was about to share a secret.

"Brenda, spit it out or get out," her mother said calmly. She'd been handling the woman's antics for years.

"Okay." Her stepmother settled in the chair at the bottom of the table opposite her father. She placed a small white plastic object on the table.

No! Blood drained from Zoe's head as she recognised the item—one of the pregnancy sticks. How did the woman get a hold of it? Zoe had taken all the test kits to the large bin outside in a sealed plastic bag. Someone would have to dig through the week-old pile of household rubbish to discover them.

"My husband, one of the maids brought this—"

"Shut up!" Zoe ordered, cutting her stepmother off. The situation had already gotten out of hand. She wouldn't let the woman spill her secrets. This was her life, and she would take charge of it.

"Don't you dare talk—" her stepmother started.

"I said shut up, Brenda!" Zoe pushed the chair back and pulled her gun out of her pocket in one fluid motion, pointing it at the woman.

She'd had enough of other people trying to control her. It was bad enough that her father put her on a marriage auction against her wishes. Then, Maddox impregnated her without her consent. Now, her stepmother was trying to use it against her.

The woman jerked back, raising her hands in surrender.

"Zoe, what do you think you're doing?" her father bellowed.

"Baba, I will explain everything to you shortly. But first, Brenda needs to get out." She turned to the woman, gun levelled at her head. "Let this be the last time you try to snitch on me and come between me and my father. Try it again, and I will kill you."

"Zoe, you can't threaten my wife."

"She is your concubine! At best, the mother of your sons. But she is not your wife. Your wife is seated right next to you." She pointed at her mother. "And this *Amebo* decided to disrespect her. To disrespect me. I am your daughter. Your deputy. I have served you diligently. My loyalty to you cannot be questioned, Baba."

She slashed her hand through the air.

Her father sighed. "I know. But what is this about?"

"Tell her to leave, and I will explain." Zoe glared at Brenda.

"Go," her father ordered.

"Don?" Brenda looked surprised at being sent away.

"I said go!" her father yelled.

The woman scrambled out of the dining room, taking the stick.

When the door shut, Zoe looked at her parents. They were both staring at her as she sat down and pocketed her weapon.

"Zoe, are you pregnant?" her mother asked quietly.

"Pregnant?" Her father looked confused.

"Yes, I'm pregnant." They both gasped. "Before you ask, it was an accident. I didn't plan it. And no, the person doesn't matter. It's not going to affect anything. The marriage auction can continue as planned. Nothing changes because I'm not going to keep it. I'm scheduled for an abortion."

"Zoe—"

"No," she cut her mother off. "I won't entertain an argument. I know you're not happy with me. I made a mistake. But I will fix it. I promise. Just trust me. I've never let you guys down before. I won't again."

Her father said nothing for several seconds, which surprised and worried her. He was looking at her as if he didn't recognise her.

"I'll leave you two to talk." She stood up to leave.

"Sit down," her father ordered.

She lowered her body slowly.

"Are you sure you've scheduled an abortion?" Don Himba asked.

"Yes, Baba. It's next week," she replied.

"Good. Make sure it happens, and we will not talk about this incident again."

"Thank you, Baba."

"You will have to handle Brenda so that she doesn't gossip to everyone," her mother said. "That woman is a liability. I've warned you she will get this family into trouble."

"I will handle Brenda," her father said as he pushed his chair back and stood. "I need to make some phone calls."

Zoe breathed a sigh of relief, feeling a huge load off her chest.

Her father left the room, and her mother went and shut the door. Then she came around and sat next to Zoe, looking her over with inquisitive eyes.

"Why didn't you tell me?" she asked gently.

"I'm sorry, Mum. I was overwhelmed and stressed out. It came as a shock. I knew you'd be disappointed after everything we planned. I wanted to handle it myself."

"I understand. Come here." She opened her arms and gave Zoe a tight hug. When she pulled back, she asked. "Are you sure you don't want to keep the baby?"

"You heard Baba. If I keep the baby, I know he'll disown me. I can't lose everything I've worked for. Anyway, I've never thought about being a mother. I mean, I admire you. But I don't have maternal cravings. I just don't."

Her mother exhaled heavily. "I respect your decision, whatever it is. But does Maddox know about the baby?"

Zoe's breath hitched.

"Yes. How do you know he's the father?" she whispered, afraid someone else would overhear.

"I saw your reaction when your father mentioned him. Mother's intuition," her mother said. "Now he's bidding for your hand in marriage. Perhaps your father will let you marry him."

"You know Baba will not agree to that."

"I know. It's all so complicated." Her mother leaned forward again, and Zoe welcomed her comforting embrace.

For the first time, she really wished she could uncomplicate her life.

SEVEN

An Igbo man wouldn't go to a marriage discussion with his potential in-laws by himself. Although this was still a preliminary meeting to negotiate a possible wedding, Maddox travelled to Lokogi with an entourage.

He'd arrived at his family home in the Federal Capital Territory two days ago to prepare for the visit.

"I have a bad feeling about this meeting," his mother said this morning before they departed for the two-hour drive. She was intuitive, and her statement unsettled him.

"What is it?" he asked, unable to shift the knot in his stomach.

"I feel like something is not quite right. But it's probably nothing. I just want everything to work out for you with this marriage," she said.

He understood her concern, considering he'd been married previously and was divorced. He'd married young while he'd still been active in the military. His deployments had meant that he hadn't been home often enough, and his relationship with his wife soured, only lasting two years. The back of his throat hurt in remembered anguish, and he shoved the thought aside.

"I know, Mama. But don't worry about it," he said, focusing on the positive signs.

He'd been invited to the Himba family home. Mason hadn't received an invitation or gotten this far with his bid. So Maddox took it as a great indication. Maybe Zoe's anger had thawed. Or her father wasn't so anti-Odili.

Or it could simply be that Maddox's bid impressed Don Himba.

Whatever the reason, he was glad he would get to see Zoe again, and hopefully, it would be the first step towards their future together.

It had been two months since their 'blind date' encounter at Arufin, yet it seemed like a lifetime ago. Then again, he hadn't actually 'seen' her then. The last time they'd seen each other was about a year ago.

He could picture her appearance. However, the sensation of her body against his plagued his dreams most nights.

He imagined her with his child growing inside her. Imagined how her body would change with the pregnancy. He couldn't wait to feel the baby moving against her belly, rippling on his hand.

When his ex-wife had been pregnant, he'd missed most of it because of the military assignments. Even his son's delivery.

However, this time, he intended to be fully present from start to finish. He would be at every prenatal appointment and at the birth. He would be a hands-on father. Just like he was for his son, Abuchi.

But that was still in the future.

He had to concentrate on the present. On getting Zoe to accept his marriage proposal because, despite the discussion being between the Odili and Himba clans, there was a personal element.

He and Zoe had met before. Had made a baby together.

And he wanted to retain the personal element. He wished to know Zoe and understand what motivated her, her passions, and her plans.

He wanted them to build a future together. A future centred around family and love.

Yes, love. Because he thought he could love her.

Despite their brief encounter, he liked her.

And he understood her anger about the unplanned pregnancy.

But it could be a blessing. What else could it be?

Now, he sat in the front of the car beside the driver while his father and sister, Amaoge, sat at the back.

Usually, these types of negotiations would involve only men. However, Maddox invited his sister to show Zoe he genuinely wished to marry her, not just because of her father's auction. He wanted a proper marriage, not just an alliance. Amaoge would be his proxy in case he didn't get to speak to Zoe privately today.

They arrived at the Himba residence, which occupied several plots on a cul-de-sac. It was built like a palace on spacious grounds. Armed men milled around, waving their convoy of cars to the parking bays demarcated from the green lawn by the hibiscus hedges.

"Make sure the boys stay alert," Maddox instructed his lead bodyguard, Otito, who'd been the driver.

"Yes, boss," the man replied. Although this was a friendly visit, they were in the heart of Himba's homeland, and the Himba crew were not always honourable.

Maddox decanted with his father and sister and was directed towards the house. The bodyguards from the other vehicles brought out the hampers.

An Igbo man wouldn't attempt conjugal discussions without bringing gifts.

A servant met them at the front door and ushered them across the marbled foyer into a room decorated in cream, gold and black marble with two demarcated sitting areas. They settled into a cluster of sofas on the raised end, gift boxes beside them. They were offered drinks and informed that Don and his wife were on their way.

A few minutes later, Zoe's parents arrived. Maddox and his family stood as they entered the reception room.

Her father was dark-skinned with a trimmed white beard, wearing a dress shirt, three-piece grey suit, pink tie and a fedora. Her mother was dressed in a pink gown and gold mid-heeled sandals. She sparkled with jewellery and elegant makeup, long hair coiffed in a chignon. The couple oozed style and sophistication.

"Good afternoon, Don Himba, Mrs Himba." Maddox bowed in respect.

The man stepped forward and extended his hand. "You must be Maddox."

"Yes, sir." Maddox took his hand in a firm handshake. "This is my father, Ndubuisi Ejiofor."

His father had asked him to keep things informal and not use his military title. In a country where everyone wanted to be a big man, his father stayed humbled despite his illustrious career in the military.

"Admiral, I'm pleased to have one of our top military officers in my house. A former Chief of Naval Staff no less," Don Himba said, extending his hand for a shake. Then he glanced at his wife. "This is my wife."

"It's good to meet you, Don, Mrs Himba." The admiral shook the man's hand. "But I'm retired from active service. Today, I'm here as a father to support my son." He patted Maddox's shoulder.

"Welcome to our home," Mrs Himba said with a lovely smile." It's nice to meet you."

"Thank you," his father said. "As this is just a first meeting, we didn't want to bring the whole family. My wife and two other sons send their regards. This is my only daughter and youngest child, Amaoge."

"Good afternoon," Amaoge said with a curtsey, then she lifted the hamper with potted yellow roses and held it towards the older woman. "My mother asked me to give you this."

Maddox had found out Mrs Himba was a horticulturist and picked out a significant gift with his mother's assistance. Zoe was close to her mother. If anyone could convince her to marry Maddox, it would be her mother. His mother said the yellow flowers represented friendship and new beginnings.

"Oh wow." Mrs Himba's eyes lit up with genuine pleasure. "Yellow rose plant. It's beautiful. Thank you so much. Please extend my gratitude to your mother."

"And I brought a gift for you too, Don," The admiral said, lifting the bottle of rare, expensive, vintage Highland single malt scotch whisky from the hamper, which had been specially sourced.

The man glanced at his wife with a surprised expression. Then he leaned forward and accepted the gift, clearing his throat. "Thank you. This is unexpected. I'm impressed. Sit down. You are all welcome."

Maddox settled in the armchair while his father sat beside his sister on the sofa.

Now that he'd met Zoe's parents, he itched to see her. His heart raced in anticipation. He patted his pocket, which hid the small box enclosing the black diamond and platinum engagement ring he hoped to present to her today. Why didn't she arrive with her parents? He supposed she would wait to be called in when the initial introductions were out of the way.

"Don, Mrs Himba," his father said. "Thank you for welcoming us to your home. We're here today because my son, Maddox, wants to marry your daughter, Zoe."

"You're welcome, once again," Mrs Himba replied. "I'm going to take Amaoge and check on Zoe." She smiled at his sister. "Come on, my dear."

Amaoge glanced at Maddox, who nodded, and she followed Mrs Himba out.

"Now that the women are out, we can speak frankly," Don Himba said, leaning forward. "What exactly do you think your son or your family can offer me to claim my only daughter as his bride?"

His father cleared his throat. "Our family has a history of proud military officers. Maddox had an illustrious military career—"

"Which is over, right?" Don Himba said as if that was a bad thing.

"Yes. But he entered the private sector and established a successful security services firm."

"I still don't see how any of that will add value to my operations or take care of my daughter."

"Don Himba," Maddox spoke before his father could reply. He knew this was his opportunity to pitch to Zoe's father. "I am a security expert. The best of the best. I can tell you about the security gaps in your business model within forty-eight to seventy-two hours of analysis. I can fix those problems and reduce your risk to minimal levels. In addition, I can train your crew and equip them to counter any attacks so you don't lose merchandise as frequently as you're currently doing, which can't be good for your bottom line."

He paused, gauging the man's keen eyes and stiff lips. He was interested, but he didn't want to give anything away.

"That's impressive, I must say." Don relaxed in his seat. "But as you are aware, there are other suitors interested in my daughter and developing a working relationship with my family."

"I understand. You are also aware that Chief Odili, my godfather, is keen to develop a business alliance with you. For example, we wish to expand our chain of hotels and casinos into the region and would like to partner with you on a fifty-fifty basis."

"Fifty-fifty?" The man sat upright.

"Yes. For example, we bring the capital, you provide the land. Of course, we can work out the details to suit all parties."

"Hmmm." Don Himba scratched his hairy chin.

"But aside from business, on a personal level, I care about your daughter and want to make her happy as her husband."

"Care for my daughter?" Don's eyes narrowed. "How can you care about her? You don't know her, do you?"

Shit. Maddox realised his mistake. Zoe hadn't told her father about him. Did that mean she hadn't told her parents about the pregnancy? What game was she playing?

While he didn't want to put her in trouble, he couldn't lie about knowing her. Not when he was trying to engender a cordial bond between their families.

"Don Himba, I've met Zoe before, briefly, and I like her. I believe I could love her. We could love each other if we get to know one another better."

EIGHT

"Shugaba."

Zoe looked up from the sheaf of papers in her hand at the deep voice of her lead bodyguard. "Yes?"

Noah stood at the entrance to her private suite, his broad shoulders stretching the white shirt and the suit jacket which hid the holster and weapons. He held a phone in his hands and stared at the screen. "The guests have arrived."

Unexpectedly, her stomach flipped over and churned at those words.

Maddox was here. At her family home in Lokogi.

After he outbid everyone else at the marriage auction, her father invited Maddox to visit their home, and he accepted the invitation.

So she'd known he would show up, and she shouldn't care. He was just another man vying for her hand in marriage. He would be rejected anyway, and she didn't want to see him.

Is that why your stomach is quivering, and you're clutching the documents in your clammy hands to your chest? You don't want to see him because you don't want him to know what you've done.

No! Maddox meant nothing to her. There was nothing linking them.

She dumped the papers on the desk, grabbed her phone and stood. It had been a waste of time trying to read the documents. She couldn't concentrate. Although, she'd had a few days off work recently and was trying to catch up on the contracts she should have reviewed.

"Are you okay?" Noah asked, his expression pensive. He'd been hovering more than usual the past week because he could sense something was off with her.

She couldn't blame him. Something was wrong with her.

"I'm okay," she lied and hurried to the door.

His pursed lips and raised eyebrows showed he didn't believe her.

"You can take the rest of the day off." She sashayed past him into the spacious hallway.

He wasn't supposed to be here anyway, as he was off-duty.

"I know. But I want to stay. We have strangers visiting your family home." He shut her door.

"Maddox is not exactly a stranger," she said without thinking and had to continue to cover up. "He's the Odili enforcer."

"Exactly. I can't forget what they did to our enforcer, Norbert. I don't even understand why the Don is allowing him to come here. I don't trust any Odili. So I'm staying because my job is to protect you."

She opened her mouth to tell him it wasn't necessary but shook her head and continued walking.

He was her bodyguard and second-in-command—the job her father wanted her to give Vershima. Her brother couldn't command anything to save his life.

Noah was her head of security and was responsible for protecting her. However, her family home was overrun by bodyguards. Maddox couldn't arrive with more people. Even if he managed to somehow defeat the team here in a battle, he was in *the* Himba stronghold. Every thug and police officer in this city was loyal to her father.

Zoe hurried down the hall and entered her mother's private reception room overlooking the front lawn. Unable to resist, she peeked out the window, and her breath hitched.

Two men and a woman in their middle strode towards the front door from the parking bay, followed by three other men carrying hampers.

Her gaze zeroed in on the man at the right end of the front row. Maddox.

Her pulse quickened, her insides vibrating.

Grey clouds obscured the sun, and she couldn't see his features from this distance. Yet it didn't diminish the man's aura. He exuded such dominant energy, from the long stride to the relaxed gait. Still, he slowed his pace in consideration of the woman in stilettos walking beside him.

Who was she? Too young to be his mother, although the grey-haired man beside her had to be his father.

Zoe lifted her phone and checked social media. Sure enough, the woman matched the photos on Maddox's sister's SM page.

Their understated and stylish attires made it easy to tell they were a cohesive family. The men in black linen tunic and trouser sets. Yet the gold embroidery on the hem of their outfits was picked up in the gold-black print Ankara maxi dress the woman wore.

Hang on. How strange?

The other suitors had attended the preliminary meeting with her father accompanied by their crew. Even Mason had met her at the restaurant with his team only.

Instead, Maddox brought his family—his father and sister.

Why would he do this?

None of the others had brought a female in their entourage. They'd sat with her father, trying to negotiate a deal. They hadn't cared about her, only inspected her briefly as if she were a rare, priceless, fragile piece of art on display in a gallery, not a living, breathing human.

Her palm tightened around the phone, her anger reigniting at the ridiculous spectacle her father was orchestrating.

A flash of yellow flowers in one of the baskets made her breath catch.

Maddox brought flowering plants. It had to be a present for her mother, who was a keen gardener. He must have gone to great lengths to discover what her mother would enjoy as a gift.

Warmth suffused her chest.

So considerate of him to think of her mother. None of the other suitors brought a present for Mum, nothing worth remembering. They'd been so focused on Don Himba as the decision-maker, they'd ignored his wife and their potential bride. One bought cigars for her father. But considering she was trying to improve her father's health, the cigars didn't curry favours with her or her mother.

But if Maddox brought gifts for her mother, he probably also brought gifts for her father. Did he buy a present for her?

She wouldn't be surprised if he didn't. All the suitors seemed more interested in pleasing her parents than her.

However, Maddox behaved as if he wanted her, not her father's territory or business deal. He brought thoughtful presents and his family.

Was she wrong about him?

Did he want her?

Oh, Zoe, get a grip. He's only here because of your father and because you told him about the pregnancy. He thinks you're having his baby.

She paced the reception room as the guests entered the house. Noah stood by the door, watching her, but she ignored him.

Her chest constricted, and her stomach cramped. She needed to get out of here.

Before she could move, footsteps announced a new arrival.

"Is Zoe in here?" she heard her mother's voice.

"Yes, Madam," Noah replied.

Her mother entered the reception room, carrying a potted rose plant in a hamper tied with yellow ribbons. "There you are. I want you to meet Amaoge. She is Maddox's sister."

The new arrival sauntered into the lounge, beaming a smile, arms wide. "I'm so excited to meet you. Can I hug you?"

"No!" Zoe said sharply, raising her palm. "I don't hug strangers."

"That's fair enough. I ask permission because I know not everyone likes them." Amaoge halted, hands raised in conciliation, still smiling as if Zoe hadn't been rude to her.

Her chest tightened with guilt at the woman's understanding.

Hang on… What was she feeling guilty about? The woman was Maddox's sister and a stranger nonetheless. More to the point, why did her mother bring her to the private lounge? They didn't entertain visitors here.

"Mum, I need to talk to you now." She walked out.

"Amaoge, make yourself comfortable. I'll be back." Her mother placed the basket on a table and exited the room, shutting the door.

"Why did you bring her here?" Zoe swivelled, unable to contain her annoyance.

"I couldn't leave her downstairs with the men talking business. I thought it was a good idea for you to meet her."

"What's the point of meeting her? I'm not going to marry Maddox. Baba is just stringing them along."

"Did you see the gift basket? The potted plant? That's from his mother. His father gave your dad rare and expensive whisky. No one else has brought gifts except for those stupid cigars I've binned anyway. These people are intentional about their visit. They are attentive and caring. They came here for you, Zoe. For you."

She could see it for herself. Maddox didn't abide by the unwritten rules of engagement for the marriage auction. He wasn't playing fair. It was apparent he came to obliterate the competition. To win and claim the prize.

Her.

The thought quickened her pulse, making her light-headed.

Why didn't he just do what everyone else did? He was making today difficult for her. Making her flustered about what she'd already done and what she would do to him.

She swallowed repeatedly. "But mum—"

Her mother held up her hands. "I know. I'm just saying they would have been great in-laws. Just go in there and be nice to his sister. I've told you to always be nice to people when you can. You never know when you're going to need them."

Zoe puffed out air. Her mother was right. Her anxiety was making her jittery and irritable. She needed to conquer her apprehension and face whatever challenges the day brought. "Okay."

She opened the door and re-entered the lounge.

Amaoge stood, her hands twisting, and she spoke in a strained voice. "I didn't mean to upset you. Maddox will kill me if he knows I upset you."

Seeing the woman's distress melted Zoe's heart.

"No, you didn't upset me. Sit down, please," she replied in a soothing voice as she sat on an adjacent sofa.

The woman sank tentatively into the armchair. "Thanks."

"Can I offer you a drink? A glass of wine, maybe?"

"No, I can't drink alcohol when you can't drink it with me." Amaoge smiled. "Just a glass of juice will be fine."

Shit. Zoe was really off her game today. She glanced at her mother, who shrugged and settled beside her.

Zoe turned to Noah standing by the door. "Get some drinks."

He raised his brow and moved to obey her order. He wasn't a servant, but since he chose to stick around, he had to comply with her demands.

"So why did you come here with Maddox?" she asked, curious about the Ejiofor family's motivations. "You know today's meeting was really for the men."

"I know," Amaoge answered. "But I wanted to meet you. You've been the topic of discussion in my family."

"Excuse me?" Zoe's spine stiffened, her chin tilting upwards.

"No. It's nothing bad. We're all excited about Maddox settling down and the woman who captures him. I knew the men would spend all day talking. And I thought it would be unfair for you. So I decided to come along when Maddox asked me."

"Unfair? Wait, Maddox asked you to come with him? He knew this meeting was for the men." Zoe was even more confused. It didn't make sense.

"Indeed. I always feel it's unfair that men get to discuss our futures and exclude us from the discussions."

Wow. "Exactly. I feel the same way."

"But Maddox didn't want it to be just about the men. He wanted it to be about you. He knows he might not get to talk to you directly today. He wants to understand you better. He wants a relationship with you. The best for you. I'm here to facilitate that."

Zoe's body flushed hot and cold. Something squeezed her chest tight, and she clutched it, struggling for breathe.

"Zoe?" Her mum reached for her.

But she stood abruptly. "I need to speak to Maddox."

She needed to end the charade.

NINE

"Zoe, wait," her mother called out as Zoe stomped towards the door.

She struggled to accept Amaoge's words, to be pulled into whatever scam Maddox and his family were orchestrating to win her hand in marriage. For a moment, she'd almost gotten carried away by the gifts and presence of his family. Almost allowed herself to be seduced by Amaoge's charm. To be fair, the woman was charming.

Nonetheless, she was here as Maddox's spy to disarm Zoe.

But she didn't trust anyone.

Not Maddox. Not his sister.

So, best to end this encounter so they could all stop pretending and she could move on.

She reached the closed door but couldn't escape because Noah stood like a brick wall blocking her path.

She glared at him but said nothing as her mother approached.

"You can't go barging in there. There's a protocol to these things," her mother said.

"Then come with me and introduce me because I'm going down there," she countered and turned to Noah. "Move out of the way."

He shifted and opened the door.

She drew a long breath and blew it out before exiting the room and heading downstairs, followed by Mum, Amaoge and Noah. When she reached the foyer at the bottom of the grand staircase, she paused, allowing her mother to come around and lead the way. The older woman walked to the entrance, tapped the wooden slab and opened it.

"Gentlemen, forgive me for intruding on your discussion. I would like to present my daughter, Zoe," her mother announced and stepped aside.

Zoe sashayed into the luxurious sitting room. Her gaze collided with Maddox's, and all the air was punched out of her lungs. She craned her neck, following his movement as he rose from the sofa, looking fine as hell in the gold-embroidered black tunic set. At over six feet, he dominated the room, and no one else existed. Her mouth dried out.

Although she'd seen him through the window in the distance as he arrived, nothing prepared her for being in the same room with him again.

The memories she had of him didn't do him justice. Not at all.

He was hot in the flesh, more alluring than in her dreams. Than in the VR goggles.

His low-cut, thick dark hair had shots of grey at the temples. His confident maturity oozed off him.

For a few seconds, she forgot the location and everyone else in it until someone nudged her—her mother—and she blinked and curtseyed, hiding her flaming cheeks in her bowed head.

"Welcome," she said, barely recognising her soft voice or hyper-focus on her former lover.

What was going on with her? How did she get so distracted by Maddox in front of her father?

"It's lovely to meet the beautiful woman my son has chosen for a wife," the older man spoke.

"Thank you." She straightened, smiling as warmth flooded her chest at the idea of Maddox choosing her.

He had a skin tone and stature similar to his father, although Maddox was taller and broader. Harder.

"Zoe, take the young man over to the other side so you can chat," her mother said.

A glance at her father showed he was frowning, but he didn't object, even though this was markedly different from her interactions with previous suitors in their house.

"Okay, Mum," she said, walking down the steps into the recessed section. It proved far enough from her father's seat to provide some seclusion but still within reach in a few steps.

Maddox followed, a step behind her. Close enough to make her skin tingle. Yet not near enough to be inappropriate in front of the elders. He hadn't spoken since her arrival in the sitting room. But he watched her every move with those sharp, obsidian eyes—his description from their night together at Arufin. An accurate depiction. Now she understood why people thought his gaze was piercing.

Her heart thudded as she chose the sofa against the dividing wall and lowered her body. The only way anyone could see her here was to stand directly beside her.

As soon as Zoe sat down, Maddox settled next to her as if he couldn't keep away any longer. His body heat and cologne—bergamot and something else—radiated towards her.

"How are you?" he whispered in a gravelly voice. His concern sounded genuine, knocking down her defences again.

A lump formed in her throat, and she swallowed to speak.

"I'm well, thank you. And you?" she kept her voice low.

The elders were talking and sounded distant, making her feel like she was in a bubble with Maddox.

This close, his features were stark and rugged—sculpted cheekbones, wide nose and trimmed beard around fleshy lips. The cut of the tunic and the way it stretched across the width of his massive shoulders.

"It's so good to see you. I didn't think I'd be this close to you today. May I touch you?" He leaned towards her, and her heart raced.

He was doing it again, disarming her by seeking consent to make physical contact. She shouldn't be near him, let alone allow his touch. But his scent filled her nostrils, taking her back to the night with him—the intense kiss and vigorous sex.

Desire throbbed through her, making her lashes flutter shut as she whispered, "Yes."

His callused palm covered her hand, and his thumb grazed her skin, sending heat through her veins. Then his lips brushed her cheek and trailed to her earlobe, tingling her skin.

She yearned to turn, to fuse their mouths and taste his hidden desires. To feel the sensuous scrape of his stubbled jaw over her inner thighs, making her throb and clench. The stab of his tongue on her sensitive flesh, the thrust of his stiffness impaling her and taking her.

Goosebumps popped on her skin, her mouth moistening.

"I didn't realise I would miss you so much." His breath feathered her nape, making her nipples tighten. "Did you miss me?"

"I …" she started and trailed off.

How could she tell him how much she ached for him? How could she wish to relive their time together? Had she forgotten how stressful the past few weeks had been? That one encounter with him had turned her life upside down?

Nothing good could come from succumbing to the feelings he roused.

She stiffened and shifted away. "Maddox, you shouldn't have come here."

He leaned back and looked her over, frowning. "How can you say that? What kind of man would I be if I abandoned you? Seriously, how are you? You look fragile and tired. Are you having nausea or been sick?"

Something fluttered in her belly at his surprising, astute analysis. She felt fragile and exhausted. The past month had taken its toll on her. He didn't know her well enough. Yet he'd picked up the signs. How?

"How do you know about that?" she asked, studying him in a daze.

He was an observant man, judging from their night together. Still, it didn't explain how he knew about pregnancy symptoms.

"I know some women have a hard time in the early months. My ex-wife hated strong smells when she was pregnant with my son."

"Excuse me," she stiffened, coldness hitting her core. She pulled away, speaking in a loud whisper. "You were married? You have a son?"

"Yes, he's twenty and enrolled in the Nigerian Defence Academy." He sounded proud to have a son following in his footsteps and in the family tradition of military service.

Still, it didn't eradicate the jealous knot twisting in her gut at his revelation.

He'd been married before. Another woman had borne a child for him.

"You didn't tell me you were married before. That you had a son," she gritted out.

"How could I tell you? You refused to take my calls. Anyway, I'm telling you now. Let me show you a photo of him." He reached into his pocket and pulled out his phone. He would show off his pleasant little family as if this was a meet-cute. As if they were getting acquainted. He had no bloody clue.

She would shatter the ridiculous romantic illusion.

"Don't!" She shouted, unable to contain the murderous rage bubbling inside her. If she saw the picture, the boy or his mother would not be safe. "You need to get out."

"What?" He shook his head. "You can't be angry because I was married before. It ended eighteen years ago."

"Makes no difference. I told you not to contact me."

"Zoe, be reasonable—"

"Don't you get it? I'm not going to marry you!" she shouted, and silence descended on the sitting room because the elders had stopped talking. They must have heard the raised voices.

"You can't be serious. You're carrying my baby." His gaze flicked upwards, his posture rigid.

"What?" her father bellowed. "He's the one?"

Zoe stood, distancing herself from Maddox now the cat was out of the bag. She knew he father would flip once he found out Maddox was responsible for her pregnancy. So she had to minimise the damage.

She climbed onto the platformed sitting area. "Yes, Baba. He's the one."

Maddox followed her out. "Don Himba, I—"

"Shut up!" Her father's nose flared as his hands clenched. "Now it makes sense. The Odili family is determined to take territory by any means. I saw what you did to The Baron in Lori Osa. Now you want to do the same thing to me?"

"What do you mean?" The admiral asked, blinking slowly, looking flabbergasted.

"No, Don—" Maddox started but was interrupted by her father.

"You think you can impregnate my daughter and use her to get into my family and my territory. You can go back and tell Chief Odili you failed your mission. Zoe, tell him."

"Baba?" Zoe's stomach dropped, the coldness spreading to her extremities, making her shiver.

She knew what her father wanted, yet the confusion and conflict on Maddox's face gave her pause.

"Tell him what he needs to know. End his misery," her father said sharply.

"What is going on?" Maddox scrutinised her with a concerned expression concerned.

She realised what she was about to do wouldn't end his misery. It would be the start of it. Yet, she couldn't stop. She'd started this journey from the day she told her mother she would become the Himba heir.

"Maddox, I reject your marriage proposal," she forced the words out of her mouth in as calm a voice as she could muster as her insides churned and pain hit her midriff.

"Zoe?" He shook his head, staring at her until he realised she was serious, and then his face hardened. "I won't let you take my baby to another man's house."

"You don't have a choice," she bit out, angry that he would dare to threaten her.

"The hell I don't!" he snapped.

"Well, you don't because there is no baby!" She straightened her spine.

He froze, and his eyes narrowed. "What do you mean there is no baby? You told me you were pregnant three weeks ago."

"I was pregnant. Now, I'm not."

Someone gasped. Amaoge?

Maddox stumbled like blood drained from his head. "Zoe, what have you done? Did you abort my baby?"

"Yes," she said through the lump in her throat.

Uncomfortable silence descended again for a few seconds. Her father wore a smirk. He'd gotten what he'd wanted.

Eyebrows folding inwards, nose crinkled, Maddox stared at her in horror. "You had no right to do this without my permission."

"Your permission? Ha!" she huffed. "It's my body. I don't need your permission."

"Yes, it's your body. But it became mine too when I put my baby inside you. It was your responsibility to protect our baby. And you executed him for what? So your father can sell you to the highest bidder like cattle?"

Zoe recoiled as if he'd slapped her. He might as well. Pain bloomed in her gut, making her want to double over. She fought to stay upright. She wouldn't crumble in front of their guests.

"Watch your mouth, boy," Don Himba shouted.

Instead of cowering, Maddox whirled on him. "I will not watch my mouth. Did you know your daughter had a termination?"

"How dare you question me?" her father said in a snide tone.

"Answer the damned question!" her former lover growled, hands balled into fists by his sides.

"Yes, he knew," Zoe answered for her father because she knew pride would stop him from responding and the situation would escalate. She would rather avoid a battle in her home.

"Tufiakwa," The admiral exclaimed as he stood. "There is no honour in this house. Amaoge, come, let's go."

The other woman rose from the sofa and followed her father towards the door without looking at Zoe or her parents.

She scrubbed a hand over her face with regret because she liked the woman.

Maddox shook his head, grabbing her attention once more. "So you never intended to consider my proposal. Yet you invited us here so you could embarrass us."

He gave a short nod and glared at her. "And you, Zoe, I thought you were smart. You want to be the Himba boss one day, yet you didn't seem to do your research before you chose to make an enemy of me. Do you not know that I am the masquerade? You do not spill my blood in vain. I almost pity you because you have no clue what is coming for you, for all of you."

Blood dripped from his bleeding nose onto the marble floor as he swivelled, and he followed his family out.

Exhaustion slammed into Zoe, and her legs gave way before she slumped onto the floor.

TEN

Maddox's head throbbed with a migraine as he exited the sitting room. He reached into his pocket and withdrew a handkerchief, dabbing his nose. This was his affliction. The blinding headaches caused his nose to bleed, triggered by high-stress situations. The headache had been looming for a while. His fury didn't help it.

"Code Red," he said to Otito, who stood just outside the living room door. The situation had changed drastically. When they'd arrived, they'd been in Code Yellow because they were in a not-so-neutral territory. But the Himba heartland was now enemy turf, so he had to upgrade the alert level.

"Code Red," Tito repeated into his earpiece, keeping pace. "Hostiles in the vicinity. Principals Alpha and Omega are headed towards you. Keep secure. Principal Beta is with me. Leaving now."

His father was Alpha, Amoge was Omega, and Maddox was Beta.

One of the advantages of working with former military personnel was that he'd incorporated martial terminology into their standard operating procedures. He'd been Tito's commanding officer. When the man retired from active duty because of an injury, Maddox hired him.

As they stepped outside the mansion, Tito swivelled to cover his flank. Considering what happened in the sitting room moments ago, he wouldn't put an ambush past the Himba crew.

His hyperalert men hustled his father and sister into two separate vehicles, which was the protocol in a Code Red situation. Although the SUVs were reinforced, splitting the Ejiofor family members was best so attackers wouldn't concentrate their efforts on just one vehicle.

Tito entered the car with the Admiral while Maddox climbed into the backseat with Amaoge. As soon as the door slammed and the security guard got into the front passenger seat, Maddox ordered, "Go!"

The driver accelerated across the driveway and out of the gates, the other vehicle coming behind them.

"Vehicle 1 clear," the guard in the front passenger seat said into his headset as they left the street and headed onto the main road leading out of the city.

Maddox pulled on his earpiece to hear the security team's communications. He'd arrived as a potential groom, but now he was back in protection mode. He needed to get his father and sister back to safety.

"Vehicle 2 clear," Tito spoke from the second car, meaning they were behind them.

"Vehicle 3 clear," another of the guards announced in the earbud.

The third vehicle hadn't been in the Himba compound. They had arrived before Maddox's entourage and had been positioned near the Tiye Himba Crescent entrance. Thankfully, the hotel they'd stayed in overnight had views overlooking the Himba residence. So, their sniper had been positioned to provide cover in case the situation escalated.

The backup crew consisted of currently serving military personnel in plain clothes, hence why they kept their distance. They were Yadili men loyal to his father. Although his father wasn't as prominent as Chief Odili in the political or business world, being a respected retired admiral and former Chief of Naval Staff carried weight.

Maddox remained tense until they left the old city limits before he settled into his seat. A sniffing sound made him turn towards his sister. She had a tissue in her hand and was wiping her face.

"Ammy? Ọ bu gini?" He asked, using her nickname and shifting closer to her. He'd been so concentrated on getting out of the Himba stronghold in one piece he hadn't noticed she was upset.

"I'm sorry you had to go through that." she pointed towards the back window, indicating where they'd come from.

Her words reminded him of the shitshow they'd walked away from, and his gut twisted.

"No, I'm sorry you witnessed the spectacle. I wish I hadn't taken you and Dad there. That you weren't caught in the crossfire." He wished he'd foreseen the Himbas' malicious intentions. Instead, he'd taken his father and sister along on a foolish romantic notion that he could have a future, a new family and correct some of his mistakes from the old one. His anger flared, elevating his body temperature.

"And leave you to experience it alone? Mba nu. Ọ kaara mma na anyị nọ nge ahụ. Jiri anya anyị hụ ihe merenụ," she replied in Igbo. *It was better that we were there. That we witnessed what happened.* "You went to their home with an open heart, with good intentions. Your hands are clean. I can attest to it. So can Dad."

Maddox nodded, swallowing his rage because there was no point venting in front of his sister. She was right. He'd needed witnesses because what happened would be complicated to explain and almost impossible to comprehend for someone who wasn't there.

Because many things remained unexplained to him. Why hadn't Zoe told him her intentions to abort the baby? He'd done nothing to her to warrant the contempt she'd thrown at him.

And why had her father invited him to their house if not to humiliate him?

He'd gone there intending to broker a deal allowing him to marry the man's daughter. In return, Don Himba would have a business arrangement with Chief Odili.

Damn. His muscles cramped. He had to call his godfather and update him on the situation. Chief had been reluctant to present him as a suitor for Zoe and had suspected the Himba kingpin's true intentions. Maddox had been too blinded by his fantasy of a future to foresee the potential malevolence.

He scrolled through his recent calls and redialed Chief's number, which connected almost immediately.

"Maddox, how did it go?" The old man asked without preamble. It proved the importance of the situation.

"Onye Isi," he spoke in a grave voice. "I have bad news. You were correct about the Himbas. I'm sorry I didn't see it myself."

"Hmmm." The old man's deep voice rumbled. "They rejected your proposal? What about the pregnancy?"

"She had—" he swallowed with difficulty before completing the sentence. "—a … termination."

Chief sucked in a sharp breath. "What?"

Maddox didn't respond as emotions clogged his throat. The back of his throat hurt.

"Maddox, please accept my deepest condolences," his godfather continued.

The words brought everything into stark focus. He had lost a part of himself and deserved to mourn in a dignified manner, not the spectacle the Himbas orchestrated.

"Thank you," he muttered. "I need your permission to go scorched earth with this one."

"I understand you're grieving, but isn't scorched earth an extreme response?"

"I consider a cold-hearted termination without being given the appropriate courtesy extreme. I consider the humiliation directed at my father and sister extreme. I consider the whole Himba clan conspiring to terminate my child extreme!"

"Her parents knew?" Chief's voice rang with disbelief.

"Yes, they knew." He bit out. This was the most ire-inducing fact. "I believe she acted on her father's orders."

"Then, scorched earth it is. You have my blessings."

"Thank you. I'll keep you updated," he said before ending the connection.

He leaned his head onto the headrest and closed his eyes. A warm palm covered his hand, and he relaxed a little from his sister's comforting touch.

His hand brushed his pocket, reminding him of the package in there. The present he'd bought for Zoe. He pulled out the box without looking at it and placed it in his sister's palm. "Take this. Sell it."

"Are you sure?" she said in a worried tone.

He opened his eyes and glanced at her. "Of course, I'm sure. I don't need it anymore."

Like all the other gifts, he'd specially sourced this one. Natural black diamonds were a rarity, and this one cost him a small fortune.

"It seems such a shame." She opened the box, and the precious gem and metal glittered. "This was the perfect gift for her. Its dark beauty reflects her impure ice-cold heart."

"It's as well that she's out of my life."

"Maybe … I saw how she looked at you when she entered the living room. Saw the conflict on her face when she revealed the termination. She feels something for you."

"Hatred." Although he couldn't fathom the reason.

"No. She's attracted to you."

"As if that makes a difference!"

"Maybe not—"

The ringing phone interrupted her, and he was glad to move on from the topic.

He answered the call from Jaxon. Tito had called to update him. He ordered surveillance of the Himba family, including the stepmother and half-siblings—comms, locations, everything. They'd developed contacts in the area following the incident between Xandra and Norbert, which they could tap into readily.

Then, he spoke briefly to his mother, who was understandably upset. He tried to reassure her that he was holding it together. What other choice did he have?

"Nwa m, ị bụ mmonwu. You're the masquerade. You will prevail. I'll see you when you get home," she prayed before hanging up.

His F4 brothers called with condolences and offered support. Duke showed the most empathy because he'd experienced the wrath of his late father-in-law and had even gone to war against the man. He'd fought for his wife against her family and had conquered.

However, Maddox accepted there would be no such romantic happy ending for him because Zoe had colluded with her parents against him. She'd purposefully humiliated his father and sister.

In turn, he would destroy the thing she wanted most, the target of her ambition and her reason for terminating his baby. The Himba Empire.

Next, Mason contacted him and surprisingly spoke with emotions. He wasn't usually talkative or touchy-feely anyway. However, he was expecting his first child with his wife, Sophie. Perhaps it brought the whole thing home and helped him connect with Maddox's grief.

Rocha didn't call, but Maddox hadn't expected his call anyway.

When they arrived at his father's house, Maddox didn't stay as long as initially planned. He'd intended to spend the night with his family celebrating his engagement to Zoe. Not happening now. Instead, he needed to return to Lori Osa and get to work. If he stayed here, he would only overthink the situation.

On the drive south, they took a longer route, avoiding the more direct expressway through Lokogi because he wanted to put as much distance between him and Zoe as possible. Ten hours later, they were in Lori Osa. They made quick time because they alternated drivers in the two SUVs.

Because of the early hours, he sent the men to bed. They would meet after daybreak. Tito dropped him off in the small, walled estate with three detached properties. He and Duke had bought the land, and the houses had been built to their specifications by Amaoge's husband, Emeka, who owned a construction company. When Duke decided to move to Lori Osa two years ago, Maddox saw it as an opportunity to expand his security business within the megacity.

The lights were on when he entered the house. Jaxon was probably awake and at his computer. They had an equipped home office they shared. He strode towards the kitchen for a glass of water.

A door creaked behind him before he heard his brother's quiet voice, "Welcome. How are you feeling?"

He shrugged, taking the bottle of water from the fridge before pouring the drink. His brother didn't always need words to understand how he felt.

"We need the war room in place for a briefing at noon. Duke will be present for it," he said instead, focusing on what he needed to do rather than what happened hours ago.

"I've got the ball rolling on the surveillance," Jax said. "We'll have a team out there in a few hours. I'm currently working on hacking their digital communications. Tito planted a disruptor transmitter while he was there, so that should help."

"That's it," Maddox said as an idea hit him. "That's our code for this mission. Disrupt and conquer."

"I like the sound of it," his brother said, leaning against a counter. "But what does it entail?"

"There will be a two-pronged approach to annihilating the Himba's operations. First is to cut off Don Himba's source of support by disrupting the marriage auction."

Many families bidding for Zoe's hand in marriage were very traditional. The thought of Zoe being pregnant by another man would mark her as tainted. Even worse was the concept of her terminating the baby. Not only would she be seen as tarnished, but many of those men would not be happy for their sons to marry a promiscuous woman who could not be controlled and who could potentially kill them or their children. The auction would tank, and Don Himba would scrap the bottom of the barrel to find a suitor who would marry Zoe and finance him.

"And what is the second part of the plan?" Jaxon asked.

"Disrupting his operations. It appears he is already having problems. But I want you to post a message on the dark web that we'll pay any outfits targeting his operations, warehouses and logistics. We don't need to get our hands dirty. Others will do the work for us."

Then, when Don Himba was sufficiently weakened financially, Maddox would deliver the ultimate blow to destroy the Himba family.

ELEVEN

Zoe fell into darkness. Not the pitch blackness of her floating in an abyss. But the night where shadows loomed. She didn't know where she was. Nothing felt familiar.

Her racing heartbeat caused pain in her chest, and she swivelled, trying to find a way out of the darkness. Disjointed voices spoke to her, but she couldn't make out the words. Faceless ghouls in the dark, reaching for her with clammy palms.

She walked deeper into the gloom. "I am not afraid of the dark."

The air became overbearingly hot, sweat pouring from her, and she felt as if she was suffocating.

"You should be afraid of the masquerade," an ethereal voice echoed.

She heard the swish of dry raffia and swivelled towards the sound but saw nothing. Then, the tinkle of bells made her twist the other way, limbs shaking.

She reached into her pocket and pulled out her gun. "Who's there? Show yourself."

"I have come for you." The shadows receded, revealing a tall, faceless masquerade covered head-to-toes in knitted raffia and strings of small metal jingle bells around its ankles, wrists and waist. It held a cane in its hand and stepped towards her.

"Go away!" She raised the weapon in her hand and fired at it.

But it didn't stop and kept coming until it stood over her, and the whip ripped into her skin, setting her aflame with unbearable pain.

She screamed, jerking and spasming. Then, ice filled her veins, wiping away the pain, and the masquerade disappeared.

***

Zoe woke to beeping sounds, eyelids heavy, mouth dry. She blinked several times at the white ceiling and glanced around the small room until her gaze fell on her mother sleeping in a plastic chair beside her.

"Mum?" She tried to sit up, but her body wouldn't respond.

"Zoe." Her mother shot upwards and leaned over her, smiling. "Thank Goodness you're awake."

"What's going on? Where am I?" The last thing she remembered was her father arguing with Maddox.

"You're in hospital. You became unconscious because you were haemorrhaging and had a fever. The doctor said there were complications, and you had to go into surgery. Something about Uterine Atony."

"Oh." Zoe gasped. She'd been feeling tired and achy after the procedure she'd had, but she'd thought it was just her body readjusting postpartum. She hadn't known it was something more serious. But did it mean... She clutched her stomach. "Did they do a hysterectomy?"

"No. Your womb is still intact. I'm glad I didn't have to make the decision." Her mother squeezed her hand.

Yet doubt and regret made Zoe's stomach quiver. "Perhaps it would have been better if they'd removed it."

After what she did, she couldn't shake the horror on Maddox's face when she'd told him. And his accusation, *"…It was your responsibility to protect our baby. And you executed him for what? So your father can sell you to the highest bidder like cattle?"*

Maybe she wasn't fit to be a parent. Wasn't it best to remove the womb totally and not risk ever having to choose between a baby and her life?

"No. Don't say that." Mum looked appalled. "I know you don't want a child now. But don't take such a drastic decision. You don't know how you will feel in future."

She sighed and closed her eyes briefly. "How long have I been here?"

"In this hospital, over twenty-four hours. The doctor said you have to stay for another two days at least so they can ensure you're healing."

Zoe wanted to protest about being in hospital, but she was too exhausted to bother. This was probably her body's way of telling her to slow down. She'd been busy almost nonstop for a month. Perhaps this complication was inevitable.

"You said in this hospital. Where was I before?" Her eyes fluttered open.

"We brought you to the Cedar Hospital in the FCT for the surgery because they couldn't do it in Lokogi."

"Oh. Okay." She knew about The Cedar, a private general hospital with state-of-the-art equipment and excellent services. Lokogi didn't have the options and variety of the FCT.

"So, where are you staying? Don't tell me you've been sleeping in the chair."

"Noah booked a hotel room for me, but I didn't want to leave the hospital until you woke up."

"Noah is here?"

"Yes, he drove us here. He hasn't left except to run errands. Bought me some toiletries, the hotel, food … He is very devoted to you."

"He is." Zoe shifted, her cheeks heating.

"Is there something between you two?" her mother probed.

"Of course not. He's married," she replied.

"Probably because you rebuffed him." Her mother chuckled.

She knew her too well. She'd had an affair with Noah a long time ago when she'd first started working for her father way before he'd met his wife. He was attractive, her kind of man physically. It had been two people scratching an itch, nothing more. Although when he'd met his wife, Mary, he'd come to Zoe seeking her permission to marry Mary. She'd known then he might be a little infatuated with her. She'd given her blessing, hoping he would turn his attention to Mary, which he did. When she became Shugaba, she chose him as her second because he'd proven himself the most loyal to her among all the other men working for her.

"One day, you're going to have to let a man into your heart," her mother said in a sombre tone.

"Really, Mum? You want to have this conversation now while I'm in a hospital bed?" She shook her head.

"Yes, because I have you captive. Whenever I start discussing matters of the heart, you always have something else to do. Now, it's just the two of us in a hospital room, and you have nowhere to run." Her mother smiled.

Zoe chuckled and started coughing. Her mother passed her a glass of water, and she took a sip, quenching her dry throat.

"Are you okay?" her mother asked when she returned the cup to the bedside cabinet.

"Yes, I'm fine." She replied. "Have you heard anything about Maddox since…"

"Interesting." Mum stared at her with curiosity.

"What is?"

"You didn't ask about your father. Instead, you asked about the man whose proposal you rejected."

Zoe's cheeks heated. "Well, I assume Baba is well since you haven't mentioned him. But Maddox … I can't wipe his horror and anger from my mind. I don't know what happened after he left."

"They left okay, and your father hasn't mentioned him."

"Mum, do you think I did the right thing with Maddox? Would you have done the same thing?" She bit her lip, her mind jumbled up. She'd thought she'd done the right thing, but she couldn't shake that disappointment from Maddox.

"I would not have done it exactly like you did. But you did the right thing for yourself. You couldn't go against your father and potentially lose everything else. But Maddox is strong and will get over it eventually. But I'm not happy that his family had to witness it, too. It was unfair on them."

Zoe sighed. "Yes, you're right. I actually like his sister."

"She was friendly, and their father was dignified. They seemed like good people."

Good people that she'd offended, albeit unintentionally.

***

A week later, Zoe walked through a shopping mall, her trusted bodyguard beside her. She'd been discharged from hospital two days earlier. Nonetheless, she'd stayed in the FCT for a few more days to relax and recuperate before travelling home.

She also used the opportunity to search for new business premises in the area. Recent events made her accelerate her relocation plans. Perhaps the sooner she moved away from home, the better for her.

Her mother had returned to Lokogi after Zoe was released from hospital. The knowledge that her daughter was on the mend had freed her to go home. She couldn't leave the house for too long, not when another woman was ready to step into her shoes and rule the household and husband in her absence.

Another reason Zoe couldn't trust a man. Sex was fine. But she couldn't deal with the drama of having cheating spouses and men who couldn't keep their dicks in their pants.

As much as she loved her father, this was one flaw she had low tolerance for. There was no reason for a married man to stray.

Her mind wandered to Maddox. He'd been married and had gotten a divorce. Had he been unfaithful to his wife? It was highly likely. Infidelity was a major cause of divorce in the country. She knew this as a lawyer.

Nah. No point in getting married because any man who was unfaithful to her wouldn't walk away from their marriage. He would be carried out in a wooden box and buried six feet under.

"What does Mary think about you spending the week up here with me?" she asked Noah, handing him a shopping tote as she exited another store.

He'd stayed with her since she was hospitalised and had only gone home once to get some personal effects.

"What's there to think?" He shrugged. "She knows I'm working."

"If I get married, I won't let my husband spend this much time with a woman who isn't his blood relative," she said, smiling.

"Yes, I know. You're too damned possessive." He chuckled.

"You're damned right." She laughed and paused to check her phone notifications. When she looked up, a woman came out of a shop on the other side of the mall. Her heart slammed in her chest. "Do you recognise the woman over there in the yellow dress? Is that Amaoge?"

TWELVE

"It looks like the woman that came to the house with the Odili enforcer," Noah said, his forehead furrowing in a frown.

Zoe shook her head. "His name is Maddox. You can say his name, you know. It won't make him appear suddenly, in case you're afraid."

He jerked back and turned his affronted gaze on her. "I'm not afraid of that man."

She curled her lips into a sly smile. "Then you won't have a problem with me talking to his sister."

She started walking towards the woman. She knew he would try to stop her from speaking to Amaoge, so she tricked him.

"Wait," Noah called out, but she ignored him.

He hurried to her side and growled in frustration. "If you weren't the boss, I would flip you over my shoulder and bundle you into the car."

"And if we weren't friends, I would shoot you for saying that to your boss." She smiled up at him to take the heat out of her words.

He was only trying to take care of her, and she was being a handful. She'd always been a handful. She did what she wanted to do, regardless. Although he tolerated her excesses, he wasn't afraid to object and call her out. Part of the reason they worked well as colleagues. Outside of her parents, he was the only person she trusted.

They didn't always get to banter. Perhaps years ago, when they'd dated—more like friends with benefits—they'd shared easy moments of fun and laughter. But since she became Shugaba, their interactions had been primarily professional.

He shook his head as if he was fighting his amusement. Then, he sighed and grinned. "You seem more carefree. You're never like this at home."

She tilted her head, thinking. "You're right. I feel more carefree. Maybe it's all the drugs they pumped into me at the hospital and the painkillers I'm taking. Make the most of it because this carefree mood won't last long."

She giggled. Perhaps being away from home was helping her relax, just like her trip to Lori Osa and Arufin two months ago. She could never chill out in Lokogi, where she was Don Himba's daughter and Shugaba. Right now, she could just be a woman shopping in a mall with her trusted bodyguard. People here didn't know her.

He grinned. "If you're thinking of talking to her, it looks like she's heading towards the exit."

"Oh." Zoe swivelled and moved to run, but Noah placed a hand on her shoulder.

"Don't you dare run," he ordered. "You had surgery a few days ago. If you end up in hospital again, your mother will kill me. Just walk. I'll run and catch up with her so she can wait for you."

Usually, she would ignore his orders. He knew better than to order her to do anything. However, Zoe didn't argue as he carried her shopping bags and jogged towards Amaoge, who had almost reached the exit. She took her time, ambling towards them as Noah spoke to Maddox's sister, and the woman turned towards Zoe.

Amaoge wore a yellow print maxi dress with elbow-length sleeves and a V-neck crossover bodice. Her natural hair was loose and finger-curled into a gorgeous afro. She wore gold loop earrings and a necklace. Her digital wristwatch had a black strap. Her makeup was natural, and as Zoe approached, her face held no amusement. The woman was not pleased to see her. Understandably.

"Amaoge, hi," she said in a cheerful voice. "It's good to see you again."

"I can't say the same, Zoe," the woman replied. "What do you want?"

The woman was honest and direct, making Zoe like her even more. She wished they were friends. Other people would probably smile at her and grumble later when she was gone. Except Noah. He would complain to her face if he wasn't pleased.

"I wanted to say hello and apologise for what happened the other day," she said.

"Okay, go ahead. Apologise." Amaoge stood, hands akimbo.

"Not here. Let me buy you lunch, and we can talk."

"No. I don't eat lunch with strangers."

"I see what you did there." Zoe smiled. "And I deserved it. But seriously, please let me buy you lunch. I promise I will let you abuse me if you want. I will grovel. Well, maybe not grovel. I don't grovel. But—"

"You know you're not helping your case, right?" Amaoge interjected.

"I know. I'm messing it up. I shouldn't have stopped you. I don't know what came over me." She suddenly felt tired and swayed.

"Are you okay?" the woman asked in a concerned voice.

Noah placed his arm around her shoulders, steadying her. "Let me get you out of here."

"No, wait," Zoe said, turning to Maddox's sister. "Amaoge, have lunch with me, and I'll explain."

"No," Noah said. "You should be resting."

"I'll be resting while I'm sitting down and eating," Zoe retorted and swivelled towards the exit. "Amaoge, are you coming? There's a nice restaurant a few doors down."

"Yes, okay," the woman replied.

"Great," Zoe cheered and started walking.

Noah shook his head in seeming exasperation.

They walked to the Afro-fusion restaurant together, and Zoe requested a private booth at the back. Amaoge settled opposite her, and Noah sat at a separate table. Zoe placed her phone and purse on the table as the waiter approached to take the orders for drinks while they perused the menus.

Zoe ordered wine for the first time in weeks because of you-know-what.

"Let's share a bottle," she said to Amaoge. "You're not driving yourself, are you?"

"No, I'm not. Sure, we can share the wine," the other woman replied. She lowered the menu, concern etched on her face when the waiter walked away to handle their drinks order. "So, what's wrong with you? Are you unwell?"

Zoe couldn't help the grin on her face. She'd met an unadulterated person for the first time in her life.

Amaoge was one hundred per-cent legit and pure-hearted. A person like her would not survive in the Himba household. Too many people would take advantage of her kind nature.

Instinctively, the urge to protect Amaoge sank into Zoe.

"I tell you, I'm buying you lunch so I can apologise for being a bitch to you, and the first thing you ask me is about *my* welfare? You know this is your chance to lay into me. To call me names for what I did to you and your brother—"

"Well, what you and your family did to my brother was brutal and nasty. I know you don't have to accept his marriage proposal, but you didn't have to do it that way."

Even with her disapproval of Zoe's actions, the woman showed understanding. Yes, she was reproachful, but she wasn't condemning Zoe.

The waiter brought their drinks and took their food order.

Zoe paused for him to leave before she spoke.

"You're right. I'm sorry. Not about rejecting the marriage proposal because I don't want to marry your brother. I don't want to marry any of the men in my father's marriage auction, but that's another story." Zoe waved her hand, dismissing it. "However, I'm sorry that I had to reject him so publicly and that you and your father witnessed it. I'm sorry if you felt humiliated by my actions. It was not my intention."

"You don't want to marry any suitors coming for you?" Amaoge sounded flabbergasted.

"No, I don't," Zoe said vehemently. "You said it yourself on the day. Men should not decide how we live out the rest of our lives. Although I have to obey my father's orders. I don't want to marry someone just because he offered my father a great business deal or money—"

"But you know that's not what Maddox was there for—"

"Neither do I want to marry someone because I accidentally got pregnant for him from a one-night stand."

Amaoge flinched, and she shifted uncomfortably.

Zoe realised she must have offended her again. "I'm sorry. I said the wrong thing."

"No. You didn't. You spoke the truth. I admire that."

"You do?"

"You're a woman of conviction. You know what you want, and you go for it. I wish I was as brave and bold as you."

"Are you kidding me? The woman who walked into a strange house and offered a stranger a hug is bold and brave. I wouldn't do it."

Amaoge laughed. "Actually, I didn't see you as a stranger. I saw you as family, as my future sister-in-law. That's what made me bold. Foolishly."

"Nah. It's not foolish. You have a warm heart, which I don't have, as you're aware. I'm a cold-hearted bitch." Zoe chuckled.

The waiter brought their meals. Amaoge had the egusi soup with fufu, while Zoe had the spicy grilled fish platter with plantain. They concentrated on eating for a while.

Amaoge's phone rang. She reached for it and glanced up. "It's Maddox."

Zoe's heart thudded hard, but she feigned nonchalance. "You can answer it. I don't mind."

Amaoge lifted the phone to her ear. "Broda, kedu?"
***

Maddox was finishing a call on his phone when his brother strode into his office.

"We have a situation," Jaxon said.

"A situation." Maddox looked up.

"The team monitoring Zoe Himba just messaged in. She's in a restaurant in the FCT having lunch with Amaoge."

"Which Amaoge?"

"Our baby sister!"

Maddox's spine stiffened. "What?"

After his disastrous visit to the Himba house last week, he'd ordered surveillance on the family. However, they hadn't known Zoe's whereabouts or her mother's for a few days as she hadn't been in Lokogi. It seemed she left their home on the same day after they left. Only yesterday they tracked her second-in-command, Noah, from Lokogi to the FCT and discovered her in a hotel there.

Now she was in a restaurant with his sister. What was going on?

"Are you sure it's Amaoge?" Maddox grabbed the phone he'd placed on the desk. The best thing was to ring his sister and find out.

"It's her." Jaxon raised his phone, showing a video of their sister with Zoe.

The livestream was from across the restaurant. Other people were in the frame but not at the same table. He recognised the bodyguard, Noah, sitting away from them.

"From the shot, Zoe's phone is on the table. This will be a great opportunity to clone it."

"Do we have to, right now? Amaoge is in the vicinity."

"I know, but it's our best chance. We haven't been able to clone her father's phone. Hers is the next best thing. Amaoge doesn't have to know what's going on."

Maddox didn't like having his sister caught up in their surveillance web. Why was she having lunch with the enemy anyway? She'd been there a week ago and witnessed the shitshow. Seen the Himba family's contempt. So how could she do this? There was a sharp pain in his chest that his sister could betray him like this.

Unless she had been forced to sit with Zoe. He remembered when he met Zoe in Arufin. She had a gun. Could she have forced her sister to lunch by holding her at gunpoint?

His pulse sped up, and his body tensed.

"Let me call Amaoge." He pressed his sister's contact number, and the phone rang.

"Broda, kedu," Amaoge said in a cheerful voice. She didn't sound like she was under duress. And she wasn't good at pretending. Still…

"Adi m mma. Ginwa kwanu?" He prodded, speaking in Igbo so Zoe and whoever else was listening wouldn't understand.

"I'm okay—"

"Suo Igbo," he cut her off, telling her to speak in Igbo. "Achoghi m ka onye gi na ya no mara ihe anyi na-ekwu." *I don't want the person you're with to know what we're saying.*

"M na enyi gi nwanyi no." *I'm with your girlfriend.*

"Onye gburu nwa m bu onye i na-akpo enyi m nwanyi. Amaoge, akpasula m iwe." *The person who killed my child is who you're calling my girlfriend. Amaoge, don't make me angry.*

He growled in frustration and shot off the chair. He turned to Jaxon and stuck his thumb up, indicating for him to send in the surveillance person. Then, he spoke to his sister, "M ga-ezitere gi onye ga-echebe gi." *I will send you someone to keep you safe.*

"Maddox, I'm sorry, but I'm safe," his sister sounded contrite.

"You're not safe as long as you're with that woman!" he bit out. "I'm not going to argue with you. Pass the phone to Zoe."

"Okay," she said, seemingly happy not to continue the conversation. "Zoe, Maddox wants to talk to you."

"If he wants to talk to me, he can reach me on my number," Zoe sounded unconcerned.

Maddox fought his rising anger, his free hand balled into a fist.

"Please talk to him. He's angry at me because I'm having lunch with you," his sister sounded subdued.

His gut twisted because he'd taken his anger out on her.

"He's angry at you? How dare he? Give me the phone," Zoe bit out and a second later, her voice filled his ear. "What the hell is wrong with you? Why are you upsetting Amaoge? She did nothing wrong."

Maddox's mouth dropped open. *She* was berating him for upsetting his sister? What the hell, indeed?

"Is that what you do?" she continued, sounding like she was walking. A door slammed, and there was quiet. Maybe the ladies. "Bully your sister when you should be taking care of her?"

Hell, no! She didn't just accuse him of bullying his sister.

"How dare you? I don't have to explain my relationship with my sister to you. But one thing you should know is that we're not as fucked up as your family," he retorted.

"Well, whoopie for you that you have a perfect family," she said in an accusatory tone, which held a hint of hurt.

His chest tightened because he'd used her dysfunctional family as a weapon. Yet, he gritted his teeth. How could she be so annoying, yet he felt guilty for retaliating?

She wasn't even apologetic for what she'd done to him, to his family. And she had the gall…

"What the fuck are you doing with my sister?" he said in a sharp tone.

"It's none of your business," she retorted.

"It's my business. She's my sister. If you harm one hair on her head—"

"You'll do what! Maddox, what will you do? You seem to forget who I am."

"I know exactly who you are, and that's why I want you to keep away from my sister!"

"What exactly are you afraid of? Are you worried that Amaoge likes me? Are you jealous that I'm giving her the attention you'll never get?"

Her words punched him in the gut. Could there be an element of truth? Was he jealous?

No way! She was just trying to screw with his head. Had he forgotten what kind of person she was? What she could do? He didn't want anything to do with her.

"No. I'm concerned for my sister. Because no matter how nice you are to her right now. When it becomes a choice between your ambitions and my sister, you will sacrifice my sister for them. You've done it before, and we both know you'll do it again."

Silence filled the line for several seconds. Maybe he'd hit a sore spot. His chest tightened again, and he rubbed it absently.

"Zoe?" he said in a calmer tone.

"I'm going to give the phone back to your sister," she said coldly.

"Zoe, wait."

She ignored him. He glanced at Jaxon, who gave him a thumbs up. The phone cloning was completed.

Relieved, he watched the livestream as Zoe walked back into the restaurant with the background music and conversation. "Amaoge, here is your phone. Thanks for letting me use it. And thanks for keeping me company at lunch. But I have to go now.”

“What? You’re going? But you haven’t finished your food,” Amaoge’s voice came through.

“It’s okay. I don’t usually eat this much anyway. Noah, please settle the bill for me. Amaoge, can I have my hug now?”

Huh? Zoe was asking for a hug? What was going on?

“Of course,” Amaoge replied as wood scuffed concrete and fabric rustled. “It was nice meeting you again.”

On the livestream, Noah walked towards the counter while Zoe hugged his sister.

“Same here. If you ever need anything, you have my details. Call me, okay?” Zoe said.

“Okay. Bye, Zoe.”

“Bye. Enjoy the rest of your lunch.” Zoe waved at her and exited the restaurant.

Fabric rustled as Amaoge sat on the chair and picked up the phone she’d abandoned.

“What did you do to her?” she accused.

“I didn’t do anything,” he replied, taken aback.

What was it with these women? First, it was Zoe having a go at him. Now, it was Amaoge’s turn. They were defending each other, and he seemed to be the one out in the cold.

“You said something to her for her to abandon her food. We were having a good time before you called.”

That made him feel shitty. But this was Zoe Himba his sister had been hanging with.

“You were having a good time with her? Have you forgotten what she did? You’re my sister.”

“I know what she did, and I’m not condoning it. She apologised.”

“Not to me!”

His sister sighed. "Look, I understand her."

"You understand her? Are you saying you would do what she did?"

He was extremely appalled his sister would contemplate doing the same thing.

"Of course not. I'm not as brave as her. That's the point I'm trying to make. She is brave enough to do what she wants even when others condemn her."

It was Maddox's turn to sigh. He could read between the lines. Something was troubling his sister.

"Are you saying that there's something you want to do, but you're worried about being condemned?"

"Maybe…"

"Amaoge, you know you can talk to me. Is Olamma okay? Did Emeka do something to you?"

Olamma was her two-year-old daughter, and Emeka was her husband.

"No. They're both okay. It's nothing. I have to go. Say hi to Jaxon." She cut off the call.

The speed with which she disconnected showed him something was wrong. But he couldn't put his finger on it.

His frown deepened. "Jax, did Amaoge tell you anything?"

"Like what?" his brother replied.

"I don't know. I get this feeling there's something she's not saying."

"I can call her—"

"No. Not right now. Just give her a day or two. I'll call Mum later. Maybe she knows something. Anyway, did the phone clone work?"

"Yes, it did. We're in. We can view Zoe's digital communications and hear phone oral conversations. We can also use the camera if we need it."

Good. He would soon have the entire Himba family exactly where he wanted them.

THIRTEEN

"Something is wrong," Zoe's mother said as they sat together in her mother's reception room.

Zoe returned to Lokogi earlier today. The house had been in its usual bustle, but she noted a tension in the air. When she asked her mother what was happening, the older woman told her to rest, and they would talk later.

Now they were relaxing after having dinner. Her father hadn't been present. He'd been returning late to the house over the past week.

For the first time in her adult life, Zoe was reluctant to get back into the swing of business. However, her family life was intertwined with her father's business, and she couldn't escape it.

"What's the matter?" Zoe asked, turning the volume down on the wall-mounted TV. The yellow rose plant from Maddox's mother adorned one corner.

"Did you notice anything different in your bedroom when you arrived?" Mum asked.

"No, I didn't notice anything different. Should I be looking for something?"

"Someone tried to access my room while you were in hospital. I believe they tried to access yours, too."

"Really?" Her spine stiffened. If someone attempted to enter her bedroom, there would be one culprit. "Brenda must be responsible."

"She is," her mother said. "She's had your father's ear in our absence and must have been digging for something to use against you. Tell me there's nothing in your room she could use against you like the pregnancy kit?"

Zoe frowned, thinking. "The secure box wasn't tampered. It had my weapons, cash and documents. That's where I keep anything I want to keep safe."

"Good. But I'm concerned Brenda has something up her sleeve. Especially now that there are problems with the cartel. The other shugabas are not giving your father good news. There seems to be one problem after another. The latest is that one of the warehouses was burnt down."

"Which one?"

"The one in Lori Osa."

"Goodness. That's a major setback."

"Exactly. So your father is depending on you for some good news."

"Me? How?"

"Through the marriage auction. He seriously needs the cash injection."

"Shit," she muttered under her breath. This wasn't what she wanted to hear.

"I heard that," her mother chided.

"Sorry, Mum."

"Anyway, it means he will pick a husband for you earlier than expected. He can't afford more delays."

Zoe swore again, silently. She'd thought she could stretch the process for a year or at least six months to give her enough time to broker a deal, giving her leverage to escape her father's marriage auction.

"Is there any way you can stall Baba with the marriage auction?"

"Honey, didn't you understand me? Your father won't allow any delays, not since the pregnancy. He's not happy it was Maddox's baby. If anything, he's going to use it to punish you. So I'm telling you to prepare yourself mentally."

"Punish me?" Her heart nearly stopped. "I'm his daughter."

"You're also his deputy, a part of his organisation. He doesn't tolerate disobedience or disloyalty. Sleeping with Maddox was disloyal to the Don. He will punish you. Same as he would punish all the other shugabas. He knows you dislike the marriage auction, and it's more reason he will bring it forward. He wants to prove a point that he can control you."

Shit. Her mother was correct. Her father would not take her disloyalty lightly, although she'd technically paid for it by having an abortion. It wouldn't be enough for him.

"I could decline whoever he chooses," she bit out, feeling like her life was running away from her again.

Her mother sighed. "You could decline. But you won't like your father's response."

***

Those words came back to haunt Zoe the next day as she headed to her father's den after work. She'd spent the day trying to catch up on the caseload she'd neglected for two weeks.

When she reached the door, she said to Noah, "Wait for me out here."

She didn't usually take him to see her father unless he was summoned, too. But her hospitalisation and her mother's warning put her on edge. She'd seen how her father's punishments could turn disastrous, and she wanted to know there was someone she could trust here as backup.

"Yes, Shugaba," he said, standing at attention as she knocked.

"Come," her father's voice penetrated the wood.

She twisted the handle, pushed the slab open, and her spine prickled with unease.

Baba sat behind his large wooden desk as usual. His first wife sat on a sofa. But the woman sitting opposite her pulled Zoe's attention. Brenda. What was she doing here? She never sat in on her meetings with her father. Neither did her mother most of the time.

All the calm and zen Zoe had gained from a week away from this house drained from her, leaving her agitated.

"Good evening, Baba, Mum, Brenda," she greeted. "Baba, you wanted to see me."

"Yes, come in." the old man didn't sound happy as he waved her in.

She shut the door and walked towards his desk, avoiding the women's gazes. She didn't understand why they were here unless Baba wanted to discuss family matters.

"Sit down," he waved at the chair across the desk from him.

"Thank you." She did as he commanded, hands clasped on her lap.

"Are you well?" he asked.

"Yes, Baba." This was the first time she had seen him since her hospitalisation.

Her mother hadn't mentioned him visiting the hospital, so she assumed this was his first time seeing her in over a week. Her father was old-fashioned. Trips to hospitals and caring for the sick were the women's jobs. His job was to pay the hospital bill.

"And the thing with the hospital is over now?" he asked.

The thing with the hospital? "I don't understand."

"He means do you need another … surgery?" her stepmother replied confidently as if she was now her father's spokesperson.

Zoe swivelled in her chair and surveyed the woman before meeting her mother's collected gaze. She knew the expression. It was telling her to keep calm and keep it moving.

She faced her father, biting back the retort she wanted to throw at Brenda.

"Baba, I'm well and got the all-clear from the doctor," she addressed her old man directly.

"Good, because you have work to do," he said.

"Of course, I'm ready to get back to work." She rotated her shoulders, loosening the stiff muscles.

"Then, I'm bringing forward your marriage arrangement."

Her mother had warned her this would happen. Still, she recoiled in the chair. "Bringing it forward. I thought we still had months and more candidates to sift through."

"There are no more candidates!" he shouted.

"What do you mean there are no more candidates? Two weeks ago, you spoke about raising the bid level to narrow and screen out some people."

"This week, there are no more candidates. They all pulled out."

A chill spread in her veins, her muscles weakening. "They all pulled out? I still don't get it. Was the bid level too high?"

"No. They pulled out because nobody wants to marry a promiscuous woman who aborts her babies," Brenda said in a snide tone.

Zoe shot out of her chair. She'd had enough of the woman already. "What did you say to me?"

"It's true, isn't it?" the woman adjusted her blouse as she tutted.

"Zoe, sit down!" her father ordered.

She growled, still standing. "Baba, what is Brenda doing here? My personal life is none of her business."

"It's my business when your personal life affects this family. We're losing money because of your pregnancies and abortions." The way the woman said it was as if Zoe regularly got pregnant and aborted them.

Zoe's vision tunnelled as adrenaline surged through her. She pulled her weapon out, aimed and fired into the cushion beside Brenda as she stalked towards her.

"Ye!" the woman exclaimed and slipped onto the floor.

"Zoe!" her father shouted, but she ignored him.

Noah shoved the door open, rushed in, and stopped when he saw her. There would be a price to pay afterwards. Nevertheless, she needed to wrest back control of the situation.

"I warned you never to disrespect me in this house." She stood over Brenda, pointing the gun at her head.

"Zoe, stop this at once," her father ordered.

She glanced at her mother, who met her gaze without blinking. She wouldn't intervene because Zoe needed to re-establish her authority over the woman.

"Baba, she needs to be taught a lesson," she gritted out, swivelling to face her father, gun lowered.

"What lesson should I teach you for firing a weapon in my presence without my order," he bellowed.

The woman scrambled across the floor on her hands and knees and rushed to Don Himba's side. She straightened and stood behind him, knowing it was the only safe place. Zoe would not fire her weapon in her father's direction.

She clenched her jaw. "I'm sorry for being disrespectful, but she accused me falsely. I work hard. I earn you the most money in this house. What has she ever done except open her legs for you?"

"Yes, I opened my legs, but I gave him sons, unlike some people," Brenda retorted in a noticeable snipe at Iyua.

"Excuse me," her mother spoke for the first time since she walked in.

Her father stood from his chair, swivelled and slapped Brenda across the face. The smack resounded across the room, making Zoe flinch. The woman collapsed on the floor, holding her face.

"Brenda, you must be stupid. You were busy bartering words with Zoe in my presence as if you were in the market, and I ignored you. But I've warned you never to disrespect Iyua. Don't you know that the day she gives the order for you to be buried is the day you will be buried? It is by her grace that you're here. Now, crawl over there and beg for her forgiveness."

Her father must be in a foul mood. She'd never seen him this enraged before. Noah was still in the office to witness it. She was glad he was here. If her father could do this to his so-called second wife, what would he do to his daughter?

Her rage fizzled into shock, and she couldn't speak as the woman crawled back to the edge of the sofa where her mother sat.

"Senior wife, I'm sorry. I didn't mean to offend you. Please forgive me," Brenda snivelled.

Iyua sighed and waved her hand. "Yes, I forgive you. Sit down and shut up."

Zoe lowered her body back into the chair as Brenda sat on a sofa. Her father would turn his rage on her next.

He took his time settling back into his armchair, making her heart race. This was not good.

"As for you, Zoe," he started. "I always thought that aside from your mother, you would be the most loyal person to me. But you have proven me wrong."

"How, Baba? I've never been disloyal to you."

Don bashed his hand on the desktop, making a loud thump, and she jerked.

"You were disloyal to me when you allowed that Odili boy to touch you and put his baby in your belly."

She recoiled at his venomous words. It was as if he'd slapped her.

But she couldn't tell him she hadn't known her lover from two months ago had been an Odili because she would have to explain where it had happened. She couldn't mention Arufin because it would be much worse for her.

"I'm sorry, Baba. I already terminated the pregnancy on your order." She bowed her head as her guilt resurrected.

"But it is not nearly enough. Brenda is right. You have cost me a lot of money due to the auction failure. But you're going to make up for it."

She lifted her head, searching his angry face. She'd already aborted her baby and humiliated Maddox by rejecting his marriage proposal. What more did her father want from her?

"That Odili boy offered me the most money, so you are going to marry him," her father continued.

Everyone in the room gasped.

"Baba, that's impossible. I already rejected his proposal." Very publicly, she omitted to add.

"You are going to make it possible. He liked you. I could see it when he visited. You seduced him before. You can seduce him again. Beg him, grovel, I don't care. Convince him to pay me the dowry he originally offered. Then, once it is paid, you are going to kill him."

"Baba, no!"

"I warn you. If you disobey me, I will disown you!"

FOURTEEN

She is here.

Maddox read the message from Tito. But instead of anger, anticipation left a fluttery sensation in his gut, and he wet his lips with his tongue.

He'd predicted this would happen. That Zoe Himba would eventually show up at his door.

Yet, a part of him had hoped it wouldn't happen. Hoped she wasn't a cold, calculating killer.

Because there was only one reason she'd come here.

To take his money and murder him.

Actually, two reasons, but who was counting.

Regardless, the intent was devious and malicious.

It only proved him right. And his muscles tightened with determination. He would destroy the Himba cartel and empire.

Proceed as planned.

He sent the reply to his security chief and stared at the large flatscreen mounted on the wall, live-streaming from discrete cameras around his home. The wiring and the closed-circuit surveillance were part of the blueprint of the building. He hadn't needed to use them before. However, he'd had new visual and audio gadgets installed and connected as part of planning for today's arrival.

The screen displayed twelve different cameras in and around his home. He clicked the mouse to take one of the displays to full view—the one showing the main gates for the estate as the security men waved in a black SUV. The car drove past the first two houses and stopped in front of his property. He clicked the mouse again and again to change the camera views. The short crescent was unidirectional, which meant his house was on the exit end rather than the entrance. Duke's house was in the middle. The first house was currently used by the security team or visiting Odili capos.

On the screen, the driver hopped out and opened the back door as Tito stepped out of the front door. Spotlights illuminated the paved-landscaped front patio.

The fluttery sensation returned to Maddox's gut, and he swivelled away from the screen, getting up in a smooth movement. He didn't want to stare at her on the monitor like some love-crazed fool. He wanted to gaze into her devious brown eyes when he saw her for the first time after the disastrous proposal meeting.

He stared out the window overlooking the paved side of the house. A hedge separated his property from his neighbour's garden lit by spotlights. Duke and his Carla were home.

Maddox started counting.

One Mississippi. Two Mississippi, Three Mississippi...

His phone beeped before he got to one-ten Mississippi. He swivelled and headed out of the office, across the white-walled corridor into the open-plan living area. He stopped short just inside the threshold as adrenaline flushed through him.

The woman sitting on the sofa was not the one he expected.

"Mrs Himba," the pitch of his voice indicated his surprise. "Good evening."

"Good evening, Maddox," she said calmly, rising from the leather settee. She was dressed in a black and red print maxi dress. "Is it okay to call you Maddox?"

She was being very diplomatic, considering they'd already been introduced. But the subsequent events had turned them into less than strangers. So they had to get reacquainted.

"Yes, Maddox is fine." He glanced at the window overlooking the paved front patio where the car she'd arrived in was parked. "Are you alone?"

"Yes. I wanted to speak to you first before my daughter comes here," she replied.

Wise move.

To them, he was an unpredictable entity. Although he'd accepted the request from his mother to give Zoe Himba an audience, they were on his turf now and couldn't predict how he might retaliate for their malicious actions about a fortnight ago. Hence their need to tread carefully.

"Take a seat." He waved at the sofa she'd been sitting on.

"Thank you." Smiling, she lowered her body again.

He was under no illusion that the smile hid her sly intentions. She might behave as if she came in peace, but the recording he heard from their family meeting days ago proved otherwise.

"What do you want to speak about?" he asked as he settled on the armchair opposite her. A low coffee table separated them. They might as well get on with it. The sooner she said her piece, the sooner he would see her daughter.

She didn't say anything for a few seconds. Instead, she studied him with assessing brown eyes similar to her daughter's. Was she trying to figure him out? It would track with the intel he gathered about her.

Although she had no direct dealings in the Himba cartel, his assessment of her actions over the past few weeks showed her to be an intelligent woman. She had been the one who had initiated contact with his parents, requesting to see them. When they'd agreed, she'd visited their home and convinced them, especially his mother, who he knew would have flat-out refused any reunions. Still, his mother had subsequently called him, asking him to give Zoe an audience and a chance to explain herself. He'd agreed because he'd wanted the opportunity to enact his revenge.

But instead of Zoe, her mother was sitting on his sofa.

"First of all," she eventually spoke. "I want to apologise to you for what happened in my house when you visited. We treated you, your father and your sister appallingly. On behalf of—"

"No, Mrs Himba," he cut her off, his hands clenching into fists on the arm of the chair. "I will only accept your apology. You cannot speak for any other member of your family. Your husband and daughter were quite vocal two weeks ago. If they want to apologise, they can do it directly to me."

Her mouth gaped briefly before she caught herself and leaned into the sofa, puffing out a breath. "Okay. That is fair. I will let them know."

"So, what was the other thing you wanted to say?" He wanted to move this charade along and get to the nitty-gritty.

"The other thing is about my daughter. Zoe is a lot like her father, as you may have noticed. She has a single-minded focus. When she wants something, she will move the world to make it happen. She adores her father and will do just about anything for him. She is loyal to him to a fault. I say to a fault because her devotion to him blinds her to his flaws."

He angled his body away, eyes narrowing. "Why are you telling me this?"

The information she gave him was privileged inside information he could use against her daughter.

"I'm telling you this because my daughter needs a wider worldview. She needs to experience something different. She needs a healthier outlook."

"Then send her to a shrink." He shrugged nonchalantly.

"Zoe would sooner shoot the shrink than talk to one." The woman chuckled, shaking her head. "I think she is better off with you."

"She made it quite clear she didn't want to talk to me. She'd rather shoot me, too." He watched her expression to gauge how she would react to the concept of her daughter shooting him.

Surprisingly, she nodded. "That's true. She would shoot you."

"And you still want to send her to me?" He held her gaze.

She didn't look away. "Only because I think you can handle my daughter. You're the first man I've met who I think is truly her match."

His heart thudded at the concept Zoe could be his match. He'd thought it was a possibility after their night in Arufin. Even allowed the fantasy to take hold briefly until she'd extinguished it brutally.

But it was interesting someone else thought the same thing.

"Why do you think so?" he asked.

"My daughter is very domineering," she said.

Unexpectedly, he barked in laughter. "You can say that again."

She smiled. "As a result, her encounters with men leave them with bruised egos. Those seeking a submissive wife end up with their tails between their legs. Others don't know what to do with her."

He pursed his lips, nodding.

"But the day you came to our house, I saw a man who was prepared for anything."

He reared back. "I wasn't prepared for the shitshow your family displayed."

Her face paled. "I don't think anyone could have been prepared for what happened."

He nodded, appreciating her honesty. "So you are saying that I'm prepared for your daughter. Does it mean you're offering your daughter to me?"

His heart was racing now.

"Yes. I believe you can be the husband my daughter deserves." She said firmly.

"Me? Two weeks ago, you were all adamant that I was wrong for her. What's changed your mind?" he prodded, wondering if the woman would cave and tell him the true reason for their change of heart.

"Two weeks ago, Zoe and her father were adamant. If you remember clearly, I barely spoke that afternoon. It was really my husband's day, and he had the final say."

"You might not have had a say. But your daughter spoke her mind. She aborted my baby, for goodness' sake!" he bit out, getting angry because she was trying to wash it over with her smooth talk.

She puffed out a sigh. "Yes, Zoe spoke her mind. But as I said earlier, Zoe will do anything for her father. I'm afraid of how far her father will push her and what else he'll make her do while she chases the goal of inheriting his empire. I worry that she will end up disillusioned and heartbroken by her father beyond redemption."

"But what's all that got to do with me?" he asked, feeling like he was falling down a rabbit hole he shouldn't. This wasn't what he'd expected when he'd agreed to this meeting. A lot of grovelling, perhaps. But not this seemingly heartfelt confession.

"Zoe needs a man strong enough to direct her attention away from her father. A man strong enough to love her. She showed an interest in you more than she'd shown anyone else. I believe you are the man who will break Don Himba's hold on my daughter. Zoe needs you to save her from her father. From herself."

Maddox started laughing as he stood up, shaking his head. The woman was crazy. He paced a few times before facing her.

"You do realise that what I feel for your daughter right now is not love. You must realise that." He met her unflinching gaze.

"I know that you're angry with her, understandably. But I believe that you come from a place of love. I've met your parents and your sister. You're surrounded by love. You're capable of love. I want that love for my daughter."

He shook his head, turning away.

"I understand if you don't want to do this. I will head back now." She was baiting him to make him cave in. It only angered him because she was trying to play him.

He swivelled, facing her as she stood, unable to hide his anger.

"Mrs Himba, the only thing on my mind right now is revenge. Is your daughter brave enough to face me? To face my wrath?" he snapped at her.

A small smile tugged the corner of her lips. "Shall I send her in so you can find out for yourself?"

That caught him off-guard, and he jerked back. Didn't she say she was alone when she first arrived?

"She's here?" he asked before he could stop himself.

"In the car." She watched him with clever eyes. She was a strategist, and she'd outmanoeuvred him.

He met her gaze and allowed himself a small smile. "Smart move, Mrs Himba. But I won't let you outwit me again."

"Fair enough." She smiled fully. "So, are you willing to save Zoe from herself?"

"We'll see about that," he replied noncommittally.

She nodded. "It was nice seeing you again. I'll send Zoe in."

She walked towards the door leading into the hallway. Then she paused and swivelled to face him.

"I like you, Maddox. So, stay alive—" he opened his mouth to speak, but she raised her hand "—and keep my daughter alive. You can do it."

Then her footsteps clicked on the hard flooring in the foyer as she left the house.

FIFTEEN

Sitting still and waiting had never been Zoe's strength.

The need to move increased as the seconds ticked into minutes, and the minutes stretched towards an hour since her mother went into Maddox's house.

Her muscles became quivery and twitchy, her mouth drying out. She reached for the cool box, pulled out a cold water bottle, twisted the cap, and took a sip. And another one.

"Everything okay, Boss?" Noah twisted in the front passenger seat to look her over. He knew her purpose for being here and had travelled with her and her mother from Lokogi. He'd been there when her father had her given the order to seduce Maddox, secure the dowry payment and kill him.

No matter her misgivings about the Don's edict, she'd never disobeyed his direct command and wasn't about to start now. So here she was, about to face

Maddox for the second time since their encounter in Arufin. Their last meeting hadn't gone so well for him. This one looked like it wouldn't be much better.

"Of course," she said, replacing the bottle cap. "Just wondering what's taking Mum so long."

She glanced out of the car's back window towards the modern house in the gated estate. Not quite what she'd envisaged as Maddox's home. She'd imagined he would live in an apartment rather than a detached house with a partly paved front yard and landscaped garden. There were only three houses in the private cul-de-sac. They looked similar in design, yet there were recognizable differences in style. Trimmed hedges separated each house.

"Here she comes now," Noah said, and two seconds later, the driver decanted and opened the back door. The woman climbed into the vehicle beside her. The driver stood outside with the shut doors so he couldn't hear their conversation.

The smile on her mother's face unsettled her. "How did it go?"

"You will be in good hands." Mum reached for her and patted her arm, her smile widening. "Just remember what I told you. Take the time to understand the man you're marrying."

Zoe took a calming breath to stop from shrieking in agitated laughter. "I don't have the time for that. You know this is a mission, not a marriage."

Her mother shook her head. "Maddox doesn't know it. As far as he knows, you've changed your mind about marrying him and have come to spend time with him so you two can get to know each other. You must play the part. Otherwise, you won't last, and he will send you home with nothing. Your father won't be pleased if you return with nothing."

She swallowed hard because this was the only reason she was here. She couldn't displease her father again and must accomplish her mission.

She sucked in another deep breath. "So, I need to understand Maddox. I can do it."

After all, he was a man, and she'd been handling men all her life.

"It's not just that," her mother said. "Once you cross the threshold, you are no longer your father's shugaba—" Zoe opened her mouth to dispute, but her mother raised her hand. "—only temporarily. In there, you become the woman who wants to be Maddox's wife. Maddox is angry and won't make life easy for you, not at first. But you are fearless and resolute. So you will endure whatever he throws at you. You will submit to him."

She burst into high-pitched laughter. "Me? Submit to him. What a ridiculous concept. You know that's not going to happen."

"Then, there's no need for you to get out of this car. Noah, call the driver. Let's go home," Mum sounded angry.

Shocked, Zoe glanced at Noah, who looked nonplussed. He reached to lower the window, but she spoke up. "Noah, wait."

Then she turned to her mother. "What's wrong?"

"Do you think you're the only one with pride? Do you think I have no dignity? I've just gone in there and pleaded your case with Maddox. Hell, I went to his parents' house to plead, Zoe, plead. I know you don't understand the concept of pleading. But I swallowed my pride and dignity to beg these people so that Maddox could invite you to his house. Now that you're here, you won't swallow your pride for a goddamned minute!"

The censure was a splash of cold water on Zoe's skin. Mum was always so calm. The only other time she'd heard her raised voice was when she'd been a child, and Baba's mistress got pregnant, making her parents argue.

Her mother had raised her voice again, and Zoe was the culprit. Remorse scorched her cheeks.

"I know you're ready to sacrifice anyone to achieve your aims. To please your father. But does that include sacrificing me?"

"No!" Zoe reared back. "Never."

She gripped her mother's hand tight. As much as she adored her father, she couldn't imagine a life without her mother.

"Then don't unravel everything I've done on your behalf with Maddox. Promise me, Zoe."

She swallowed hard but said. "Mum, I promise. I will swallow my pride." At least for a little while, she omitted to add. "And I will submit to him. Not that I know how."

"He will show you how." Her mother smiled.

"I bet he will," she grumbled.

Mum laughed. "One last thing. Open your mind."

She raised her hand, but instead of tapping Zoe's head, she placed it on her chest above her heart.

Zoe narrowed her eyes. "What does that mean?"

"Allow yourself to experience things you've never done before. Allow yourself to express emotions even if they are new to you. Immerse yourself. You might like what you see and feel."

"That sounds easy enough."

The grin on her mother's face said it would not be easy. "Go on, then. Maddox is waiting."

She nodded, and without thinking, she reached across the seat and hugged her mother. She didn't realise what she was doing or that she even needed the embrace until she was surrounded by her mother's softness and perfume.

"Thank you," she said, her voice clogged with emotions.

"You're welcome, honey." Her mother's voice sounded husky, too. "I don't know when I'm going to see you again. But try to check in at least once a week."

It sounded as if Zoe would be here permanently. However, she'd packed for a month. So, weekly check-ins were reasonable.

"Okay. I'll see you later, mum." She reached for the door, and the driver opened it fully.

Noah was already offloading her luggage from the boot as she stepped out. A man stood by the front door. She recognised him as Otito or Tito as he was known. He was Maddox's lead bodyguard.

She stepped up to Noah. "Make sure mum returns home safely."

"Sure, boss. I'll handle it," he replied.

"Let me know when you sort out the other thing we discussed."

"I'm on it."

She nodded and headed towards the front door. Noah and the driver dragged her luggage behind her.

"Zoe," Tito said and moved aside.

"Tito," She stepped into the foyer.

"Leave the bags here." Tito pointed at a spot against the wall.

Noah and the driver dropped the bags. Noah nodded at her, and they left.

Tito shut the door. "This way."

She followed him into a living room space, and her heart slammed against her ribcage.

Seated in an armchair was Maddox, looking stunning and regal in a black dress shirt, black tie and charcoal trousers. Her breath hitched. Behind him were two burly men in dark clothing and visible holstered weapons. He looked like a dark angel, a dark avenger.

What did her mother say about this being a meeting with her future husband?

This was not a man seeking marriage with her. This man had vengeance written all over him.

This was the Yadili enforcer.

Yet, her mother expected her to submit to him? No way.

She was a Himba shugaba and submitted to no one except Don Himba.

Her spine stiffened as she straightened, chin tilted up.

"Maddox," she said, acknowledging his presence.

"Zoe," his voice was cold, making her spine tingle with unease. "Before we start, you must read and sign the contract."

He pointed at the sheaf of papers on the coffee table.

"Contract?" She hadn't expected one. "Why do I need to sign a contract with you?"

"You're a lawyer," he said in a derisive tone. "You understand the importance of signed agreements to protect all parties involved."

She bristled but didn't reply as she picked up the papers. After a quick glance, she lifted her head and glared at him. "I'm not signing this."

"Then, there is no need to waste each other's time. Tito, inform the gates to hold the vehicle. Zoe will be returning with her mother."

"No!" she ordered without thinking. "I'm not going home."

Tito ignored her and raised a walky-talky, stepping into the foyer.

Maddox flashed his pearly white teeth like a shark. "You see. This is why you need to sign the contract.

You're not in control here. You cannot order anyone around. You can try, but no one will obey you without my permission."

"The car is on the way back," Tito spoke behind her.

"Damn it!" Zoe growled in anger. She wasn't even five minutes in Maddox's house and was already failing in her mission. "This contract is ridiculous."

Well, on the face of it, it appeared like any other contract. It started out looking like something she could have drawn up herself.

This contract is entered on (date) ______________________, between MADDOX NNANNA EJIOFOR (hereinafter 'Husband'), located at 3 Odili Close, Braeburn Island, Lori Osa, Nigeria, and ZOE MIMIDOO HIMBA (hereinafter 'Wife') of (address): 10 Himba Crescent, Lokogi, Nigeria.

This contract is entered into in good faith, and signatures from all parties named herein indicate acceptance of the Contract and the terms described herein.

This contract is valid upon signing and shall remain valid for a minimum initial period of three (3) months from the signing date, with automatic monthly renewal thereafter.

The Husband reserves the same Rights and Obligations in subsequent contracts as enshrined in this initial contract.

"What is wrong with the contract?" Maddox asked impatiently.

"For starters, it says the contract is for three months. I'm only staying here for a month," she bit out.

"This is not a negotiation. Sign the contract or get out," he snapped.

She growled, and her fingers itched to pull out her gun. But the sound of a car pulling into the house stopped her. Oh no! That was her mother's car. She couldn't shoot Maddox, and she couldn't go home.

"Fine. I'll read it, and I'll sign it." She lowered her body onto the sofa and began reading.

Kiru Taye

SIXTEEN

T he doorbell chimed.

"Tell my mother she can go home," Zoe said as Tito walked away from the living room threshold to answer it.

She turned and glared at Maddox. She would keep giving orders whether he liked it or not.

He didn't reply, his gaze unflinching as it bore into her from across the room.

She rolled her eyes. If he was trying to intimidate her, he would have to try harder. Sure, the marriage contract shocked her, unsettled her even. But she would pore through every detail and find any loopholes. For one thing, if the signatures weren't independently witnessed, it wouldn't be legal and wouldn't hold up in civil court.

She lowered her gaze and continued reading.

*

WIFE agrees to grant to HUSBAND exclusive and unique rights to provide for, protect, pleasure, and punish WIFE.

WIFE also warrants that WIFE is owned or controlled by HUSBAND without encumbrance and that HUSBAND holds the full power and authority over WIFE.

*

Owned? Controlled? What the hell?

Zoe's head snapped up. Yet before she could open her mouth to tell Maddox to go to Hell and take his marriage contract with him, footsteps announced a new arrival.

A man dressed in a white shirt, grey trousers, and black shoes entered the living room. Carrying a briefcase, he had a blue lanyard around his neck with his ID tucked into the shirt pocket.

Relief washed over Zoe because it wasn't her mother. She didn't think she could handle the disapproval of not getting past the first hour in Maddox's house without intervention.

Maddox stood and approached, extending his hand. "Welcome, I'm Maddox Ejiofor. You must be Mr Oluwole from the Braeburn Island Magistrate Court."

"Yes," the man smiled as they shook hands. "I'm here with your special license and to check your documentation to ensure you're both legally free to marry."

He turned in Zoe's direction. "This must be your bride. Good evening, ma."

Zoe's heart jolted. There went her loophole about the contract being unwitnessed.

Maddox must have pulled many strings to make this happen at short notice because her visit to his house was only confirmed a few days ago.

She forced a smile. "Good evening."

"You can set up at the table." Maddox led the man towards the dining area at the other end of the room.

The clip-clop of shoes indicated someone else had arrived. How many more people did Maddox invite to witness the contract signing?

She turned, and her mouth dropped at the sight of the woman standing at the threshold. "Mum, what are you doing here?"

"I heard there was a problem." She breezed into the living room. "Tell me what's wrong."

Zoe's cheeks heated. She flipped the papers close and placed them face down on the coffee table. "Nothing is wrong, Mum. You don't need to be here."

She would not tell her mother about the contract and the things written therein. The addendum included the Schedule of Dowry Payment and a Rules of Engagement for Sex!

"Mrs Himba, thank you for coming back. We need you as a witness for the marriage certificate," Maddox said, ignoring Zoe's outburst. "Let me introduce you to Mr Oluwole from the magistrate court."

"Welcome, Mr Oluwole. I'm the mother of the bride," Mum chirped as if this was a joyful occasion and she was bragging about her daughter's wedding.

"Good evening, ma," the registrar said, removing a laptop and a binder from the briefcase.

Her mother came around to where she sat on the sofa.

"I heard there was a problem with the contract. Do you want me to take a look?" She said in a low voice and reached for the paperwork.

"No." Zoe snatched the documents from the table, annoyance spiking through her. "I told you there's no problem."

Mum met her gaze with narrowed eyes. "So, you're going to sign it?"

"Yes." Why did she feel like her mother knew about the contract beforehand? She wasn't perturbed about it or the presence of the registrar here to officially register this farce of a wedding.

"Good. Then, let's get on with it. I have an early start tomorrow, so I need to get to bed." She stood. "Registrar, are you ready?"

"Yes, ma." The man straightened. "If the couple can come here and present their photo IDs, please. Also, I need an official document with evidence of date of birth."

Zoe had packed her passport because she would be away from home and would travel internationally. She hadn't known she would require it so soon. She reached into her silver diamante purse, withdrew the document and walked to the dining area where Maddox stood next to Mr Oluwole.

Her strappy black silk cocktail dress swirled around her legs, and her silver diamante heels tapped the marble floor. She usually wore trouser suits. But Mum advised her to pick a dress for her visit to Maddox as part of the seduction ploy. She hadn't realised it would become her wedding dress.

When she reached the dining table, Mum stood beside her.

Standing next to the registrar, Maddox shrugged on a blazer, completing the two-piece charcoal suit custom-fitted to his tall, broad and muscular form. The silver cufflinks glittered, and the matching folded monogrammed silver handkerchief offset it beautifully. His hair was newly cut, and his designer beard was freshly trimmed.

His outfit matched hers like they had coordinated or had the same stylist. She fought the smile threatening to curl her lips.

Despite her beef with the man, he was drop-dead gorgeous. She would happily wed him in an alternate universe where she truly wanted a husband.

The registrar took their documents and scrutinised them. Then, he typed out their names on the laptop. He took the names of their parents, places of birth, ethnic origins, and hometowns and entered them into the computer.

Then he spoke, "Now, for the oaths. Do you, Maddox Nnanna Ejiofor, swear that you are of sound mind and enter this marriage of your own free will?"

"Yes, I do." He held her gaze with an intense stare. His obsidian eyes swept over her with naked appreciation, making a tingle run through her body. He stared at her as if he took his vow seriously and would uphold it until death.

Her clit throbbed at the idea of having his single-minded attention. Perhaps marriage to him wouldn't be so bad. At least it was only for a few months.

"And do you, Zoe Mimidoo Himba, swear that you are of sound mind and enter this marriage of your own free will?"

The question cleared the haze of lust from her mind, and her jaw tightened. Although she disliked the contract terms, the concept of her entering this by coercion annoyed her. She was here on a mission. At the end of the three months, she would walk away.

And Maddox would be dead.

Something constricted her throat, and she struggled to breathe, her chest tightening.

"Ms Himba?" The registrar caught her attention again. "Do you need me to repeat it?"

"No need to repeat it." She swallowed, pulling in a deep breath. "Yes, I am of sound mind and here of my own free will."

"Just say 'Yes, I do'."

"Yes, I do."

"If anyone knows of any reason that these two should not be joined in matrimony, speak now."

A coughing sound made her turn.

"I have an objection." Noah stepped into the living room, Tito behind him. He must have entered the house with his mother and waited in the foyer.

Maddox growled, and from the corner of her eyes, she saw his hands ball into fists.

Zoe smiled, loving that he was getting riled, too. Guess the night wasn't going as he planned.

Welcome to the club, pal.

"State your objection," the registrar said, glancing at the newcomer.

"Let me talk to Zoe," Noah said, feet planted apart, hands by his sides like he was ready for a fight.

"No!" Maddox growled.

She rolled her eyes again and turned to the officiator. "Registrar, part of the reason for the objection clause in a marriage ritual is to allow the participants breathing space to rethink their actions before the marriage is finalised. Am I wrong?"

The man nodded. "You're correct."

"So I'd like to take a moment to talk to my friend," she said.

The man glanced at Maddox. "She's legally entitled to take a break if she needs it. Otherwise, it looks like coercion."

"Fine," he bit out.

Smirking, Zoe walked past Noah into the foyer. The man followed her.

"What are you doing?" she asked him in a whisper so the others couldn't hear her.

"I should ask you the same. Why are you marrying him? That's not the plan," he replied in an equally low voice.

"Plans change," she said, remembering her mother's words. "And we have to adapt."

"You don't have to do it. You've just walked into his house, and you're getting married? What kind of nonsense is this?"

Zoe could detect some jealousy in Noah's sullen expression, and unease rolled through her. She'd hoped the man had gotten over his infatuation with her when he'd married his wife. She hated any form of extramarital liaisons, considering what happened with her family. So, she wouldn't tolerate it in this case. She could never be the other woman. And any respect she had for Noah would tank if this was true. She hoped it was just her imagination.

"Maddox is playing games. But it's nothing I can't handle. Remember the objective. Baba's order. I have to accomplish it by any means. If Maddox wants to play games, it's his funeral," she said flippantly, although her chest tightened again and her discomfort returned.

"You are more than my boss. You are my friend. My family." He took her hand, frowning as if he detected her unease. "If he hurts you, call me. I swear, I will end him."

"He wouldn't dare," she said, equally pleased and annoyed by his protectiveness.

Maddox could get away with pulling this marriage contract crap only because she'd come in the guise of wanting to marry him anyway. But he wouldn't dare try to harm her.

"Still, you can't let your guard down," he insisted.

"I never let my guard down," she retorted, the annoyance winning this time. She stared at the living room door to ensure no one was lurking there, eavesdropping. "You forget that I can take care of myself. If he tries anything, he's dead anyway. Now, don't interrupt again. Or they could suspect something."

"Okay." He stepped back, although he still looked worried.

Noah had been by her side in one form since she started working for her father about ten years ago. First as her bodyguard, then as her lover and finally as her second-in-command. So, she could understand how her sudden change in status could unsettle him since it wasn't part of their original arrangement. But he had to get with the program.

She ignored him and headed into the living room. He would have to get over whatever was eating him. She intended to fulfil her mission regardless of the roadblocks Maddox and anyone else threw at her.

Everyone stared at her as she entered the room and approached the table. Her mother sat in one of the dining chairs. The two security men were now by the door while Maddox stood beside his brother.

Maddox's gaze burned into her flesh, but she refused to look at him. She stepped up to the registrar. "I'm ready to proceed."

"Good." The man straightened. "I've been informed that instead of exchanging rings, you have opted to sign a special marriage agreement. So let's proceed with that."

Two copies of the contract were on the table. Maddox signed the contract first under the HUSBAND section, initialling each page. Zoe added her signature to the WIFE line on the other, including her initials on the pages to indicate she read them. Her mother signed as the first witness, and Jaxon scribbled his as the second witness. The registrar stamped the signature page. Then they swapped and did it all again on the second copy. One copy was given to Zoe, and Maddox kept the other.

"Now that is done, I can finalise the vows," the registrar said. "Would you like to hold each other's hands?"

Maddox didn't hesitate. He stepped into her personal space and took her hand. His callused hands were surprisingly gentle even as his grip tightened briefly. His eyes flared with fiery possession. Butterflies took flight in her belly, and emotions she didn't recognise whirled inside her.

"By the powers vested in me, I pronounce you husband and wife. You may kiss the bride," Mr Oluwole spoke.

"Hello, Mrs Maddox Ejiofor," Maddox growled and sent her mind reeling as he pulled her into his arms and kissed her passionately and thoroughly in front of everyone.

SEVENTEEN

"Relax, it's your wedding day. The photos will be all over the internet and social media," Maddox whispered into Zoe's ear as he wrapped his arm around her slender waist.

Her scent filled his lungs—strawberries and sunshine. Need punched his gut, like it always did when he scented her. Despite his burning need for vengeance, his body still ignited with lust in her presence.

They were in the living room, posing while Tito took the photographs on his camera. He was a photography enthusiast. They'd taken the group photos first because Mrs Himba wanted to head off early. She'd left already, same as the registrar. Jaxon had popped over to Duke's house for a meeting. So it was just Zoe and Maddox in these shots.

She clenched her hands on his arms, digging her manicured nails into his skin. Still, she forced a smile onto her face as her eyes flared with annoyance.

"What do you think you're doing kissing me like that in front of everyone?" she hissed at him. Despite her anger, she was stunning in the black dress, showing off her toned body and flaring at the waist. Her hair was sleek, straight to her waist and parted in the middle.

"I was kissing my wife. Oh, I love the sound of calling you Mrs Maddox Ejiofor." He grinned, seemingly pissing her off even more, and he chuckled.

He was experiencing euphoria, temporarily, no doubt.

Because she was here with the objective to end his life. And he was on an arduous mission to tame his treacherous wife. A goal he hoped to complete within three months. If he didn't accomplish it, the marriage would be over, and he could be dead.

Still, for the moment, he was alive, and she was his wife. He could bask in the knowledge. Therefore, life was great.

"You can gloat all you like. But if you think I'm going to play little wife to you, you have another think coming," she whispered harshly into his ear. Her high-heeled stilettos brought her close to his height.

"Oh, Mimi. You're so tense," he whispered, brushing his lips against her earlobe. "Would you like Nnanna's tongue on your pussy. It worked wonders the last time."

Her breath hitched, and her body froze. He would bet her pulse was pounding against her skin.

"You wish," she said in a husky whisper. She was affected. "You were not that good."

"Liar." He pulled her toned back flush against his chest as Tito rearranged them. His dick hardened as his hips brushed her fleshy bum, and he remembered taking her from behind. Her slickness. Her heat.

Their night together seemed like such a long time ago. Yet it was getting on three months. Had she had other lovers since then? Any of the so-called suitors her father had been negotiating with could have been her lover.

A burning sensation ripped across his chest at the idea that someone else had touched her since their one-night stand. He tightened his grip around her.

He had three reasons for the shotgun wedding. Three signals he wished to send.

To Zoe: ***Fuck, yes! I own you.***

To Don Himba: ***Fuck you! I married your daughter.***

To the men bidding for her hand: ***Fuck off. She's taken.***

He had three months to enact his revenge. Three months where he would use her any way he wanted. And her father would live with the knowledge that the one man he didn't wish for Zoe was the one who owned his precious only daughter.

Oh, he knew she would fight him all the way. But he was prepared for her rebellion. In fact, he looked forward to it. Because he intended to ruin her, thoroughly spoil her for anyone else. None of her suitors would want her afterwards. Even her father would not want her back.

After all, the man had been malicious to send Zoe to take Maddox's money and execute him. And she was devious to show up here in the guise of wanting to marry him so she could rip him off and kill him. All after what they had already done to his family. They deserved everything coming their way from him.

Zoe's only saving grace was her mother. Mrs Himba. The woman seemed genuinely remorseful about what her husband and daughter had done to Maddox. She was the only reason he adopted a carrot-and-stick approach to handling Zoe. Otherwise, it would have been the stick all the way.

Wouldn't it be the ultimate revenge if she fell in love with him?

The thought had blood surging to his dick, making his erection swell as he nudged it against her bum.

Zoe shoved him, turning to glare at him as she stepped away. "That's enough!"

"Okay. We might as well end the celebrations and get down to reality," he replied, unbuttoning his jacket and shrugging it off his shoulders.

Zoe backed away towards the sofa. "What do you mean?"

He ignored her, undoing his cufflinks and rolling up his sleeves. "Boys, bring her bags in here.

Josiah and Joshua, fraternal twins and two of his team handpicked for their loyalty, picked up her suitcases as if they weighed nothing, carried them into the living room and placed them flat on the floor.

"What's going on?" she asked, gaze bouncing around the living room at all the men.

She didn't even look intimidated, surrounded by men who could squash her.

His heart swelled with pride. He'd married an intelligent, sexy woman who challenged him with every breath. She would shoot him if given half the chance. Yet, he wasn't deterred.

"I want you to remove any weapons in your person and luggage and hand them over to me for safe-keeping," he said.

"Why should I give you my weapons?" she bit out, eyeing him balefully.

"Because you signed a contract which states that you will obey me."

"And if I don't?"

"Then the boys will rummage through your belongings and remove any prohibited items."

As distrustful as she was, he would bet the thought of strangers ransacking her personal items would infuriate her. And he was right.

"Prohibited items!" she screeched, bending forward and reaching under her dress. "Who the fuck do you think you are?"

"Bear hug!" he ordered, anticipating her next move. She was probably reaching for a weapon.

Joshua, who was closest to her, wrapped his arms around her from behind as she pulled out a handgun from an inner thigh holster concealed in a pair of Lycra carry shorts visible under her dress. He lifted her as she aimed the weapon in Maddox's direction.

"Gun!" Maddox shouted, ducking as she fired, and a loud bang reverberated, followed by smashing glass.

Adrenaline kicked in, and he ran full pelt. Just as Joshua twisted her wrist, she cried out, dropping the gun. He grabbed it before it hit the floor so it wouldn't discharge accidentally and hit someone. With quick movements, he disengaged the magazine and released the one in the chamber into his palm. Once the weapon was safe, he handed it along with the ammunition to Tito, who placed them on the dining table.

Maddox visually checked the room. Everyone else was uninjured. The bullet had been aimed at him. But the only damage was the framed painting on the wall with a hole through it and shards of broken glass sticking out of the frame.

Tito's walkie-talkie crackled. "This is Amadi from the gatehouse. Is everyone okay in there?"

Maddox glanced out of the front window. Sure enough, some of the security men were approaching, weapons drawn.

"Tell them to stand down," Maddox said.

"Stand down," Tito spoke into the comms gadget. "Everyone is fine."

"Roger that," came the response and the crackling went silent.

Maddox sucked in a deep breath and faced Zoe, who was still in Joshua's grip, panting.

***

"Get your hands off me," Zoe yelled, struggling and failing to kick the enormous man restraining her.

She never liked people touching her anyhow on a good day. Let alone when violent anger coursed through her veins. Right now, she wanted to kill this man. But he didn't release her, keeping her high enough, making her kicks ineffective.

Realising that fighting the bear of a man was useless, she turned her glare on Maddox, who seemed to be taking a visual assessment of the scene. The gunshot hadn't even touched him, infuriating her because the weapon was out of reach.

"This is you, isn't it? Getting other people to do your dirty work?" she taunted. "You're not man enough to handle me yourself."

"Release her," he ordered immediately.

The bear holding her dropped her gently. She twisted out of his grasp and charged towards Maddox in a haze of anger. She threw a jab, and he evaded it, swivelled and shoved her face onto the sofa arm. Leaning his weight onto her back, he held her down. She yelled and kicked out. However, he grabbed her foot, yanking her stiletto off. Then he did the same with the other one.

Before she could do anything else, a hard smack landed on her bum.

"Shit!" she yelled, more outraged than in pain. "What are you doing? Aww!"

He didn't stop raining his rigid palm across her ass cheeks. "These men have done you no wrong. Yet you nearly injured them."

"I wasn't aiming at them!" She twisted, trying to get away from the nonstop motion of his hand against her heated backside. Anyway, the men were here as his bodyguards. If they caught a bullet, it was part of their jobs.

"I'm your husband. What did I do to you to deserve getting shot?" He paused, waiting for her answer.

"You are infuriating," she wanted to yell but bit her tongue. She doubted it was a good enough reason to shoot anyone, let alone her husband, of less than six hours, although she wouldn't admit it.

When she didn't respond, he continued the spanking. "You don't even have an ounce of remorse.

Another retort sprouted. She bit it back, too. Perhaps if she didn't complain, he would give up on the paddling, which set her body alight and an ache in her core.

"Stand up," he ordered when he stopped eventually.

She moved slowly, feeling lightheaded and wincing as she straightened. Heat bloomed around her bum and groin. Her clit throbbed, and her nipples ached. Her bones felt like noodles. She'd never felt anything like it. It was almost like being drunk.

"If you think losing your weapons was bad, wait to see what's coming next," he said, stepping into her space and holding her chin up.

"Well, you've spanked me. Now, are you going to fuck me?" she jeered, glaring at him. She couldn't help herself. Defying him seemed to be part of her DNA.

Someone chuckled. She turned her head and found Tito shaking his head as he smiled. She'd forgotten the other men were still there. They'd watched Maddox spank her. Her cheeks heated, but she refused to be cowered. Instead, a fierce, sensual energy swept through her, and she winked at Tito.

Maddox grabbed her chin tightly, turning her to face him. "Follow me."

Then he walked towards the door.

But she didn't move, ignoring him. She wasn't a dog to obey his orders.

He came back and grabbed the back of her neck, shoving her forward. She lashed out, hitting his chest. He bent his knees, hauling her over his shoulder.

She punched his back, but he didn't budge, "Let me go!"

Ignoring her, he carried her out of the living room into the corridor while she hung upside down. Tito opened a door for him, flicking a light switch.

Maddox stomped down a set of steps. Her position made it difficult to observe the new room. Not while she got eye-fulls of her new husband's tight butt encased in fabric. Still, it seemed they were entering a light-grey concrete basement. The space was clear except for a narrow bed pushed against the far wall.

"Get the cuffs," he said to Tito, who followed them down.

She heard metal clanking and something clamped around her ankles. "What the hell?"

Maddox lowered her, and she stared at the stainless-steel shackles around her ankles linked by a foot-long chain, hooked to another chain disappearing under the bed.

Mouth agape and speechless, she slumped on the mattress covered in a white sheet. Her bum hurt from the spanking. She ignored it and grabbed the chain instead, yanking it. It didn't dislodge or break.

"What is this?" she looked up, still unable to comprehend her situation.

Maddox stood within reach, watching her. Tito had left already.

"What does it look like?" he replied, arms folded across his chest.

"It looks like you've chained me to a basement." She glanced around. "Are you out of your mind?"

"Were you out of your mind when you shot at me tonight?"

"No. And given what you've just done, when I get my hands on that gun, on any gun, I will shoot you again."

"There you have it. You don't think I'm going to give you freedom of my house when you're threatening to kill me. You could injure one of my team. Hell, Duke and Carla live next door. My job is to protect people. I can't protect my people with a killer in their midst. So, enjoy your new home down here." He swivelled and walked towards the stairs.

She glanced around. There was nothing apart from the bed and chain. Not even a window. A door led to the right.

He couldn't leave her here. Outraged, she jumped off the bed.

"You have no right to do this to me. My father will kill you if he finds out what you're doing to me."

He whirled around. "Do you think you're the only one with a father? What do you think mine will do if you kill me? Hell, I have brothers who will avenge me. Did you consider that? Or what the impact will be on Amaoge?"

She recoiled, feeling like he'd slapped her by mentioning his sister. She hadn't thought about the woman she considered a friend. In her haze of fury, she'd forgotten everyone else. The tunnel vision she experienced whenever she was angry made her focus on the source of her anger rather than the whole picture. She had no valid excuse for firing the weapon at Maddox. Worse, if she'd killed him, her mission would have been a bust, and she would've incurred more of her father's fury.

"Look, I didn't mean to shoot at you—" she started.

"Oh, you meant it, alright," he interrupted her. "You have no regard for human life. You think you can shoot people at your whim. I know you assign the contract kills for your father, so you're apathetic to death. But I'm not some faceless target. I'm your husband. Yet, you have no regard for my life. For the life of my men. Damn it, you had no regard for our baby's life."

"Don't you dare mention that!" She jerked back, slumping on the bed, wincing, and feeling under siege. She struggled to breathe as her chest tightened.

"Get out!" she yelled. Regardless of what he said, she would not feel guilty. She'd done the best thing for herself. For her life. She had an objective. A goal which didn't involve babies or husbands, for that matter. Nothing would change it.

Maddox stood there, staring at her silently with an inscrutable expression. Finally, he swivelled and stomped up the stairs.

Yet, instead of relief, Zoe felt the first strands of her purposeful life unravelling, and she didn't know how she would knit it back together.

EIGHTEEN

The squeak of a metal lock woke Zoe. She groaned as she shifted, blinking up at the white ceiling, a little disorientated. Footsteps against concrete made her turn her head towards the sound, and last night's events rushed back at her.

She married Maddox in a legit albeit fast and unadorned ceremony witnessed by her mother and his brother. Then she'd shot at him because he'd dared to take her weapons away. And finally, he'd chained her down in his basement.

All in all, not exactly how she'd imagined spending her wedding night. Not that she'd dreamt of weddings anyway.

"Good morning, Mrs Maddox Ejiofor." Her new husband stood at the landing splitting the stairs at ninety degrees. He swaggered down, carrying a flowery plastic tray.

He wore a grey shirt, charcoal trousers, and matching leather trainers—his signature style. She loved it because it matched her style. He could have been her fashion twin.

Still, she would not admit to him. And why was she even thinking about his dress code? What was wrong with her? He'd locked her up all night long!

"I have a name, you know," she grumbled. They might be married, but she wasn't changing her name. "My name is Zoe Himba. Use it. I don't need your misogynistic, patriarchal bullshit this morning." Sleeping on the bed put her in a bad enough mood already.

"Really?" He stopped at the foot of the stairs and fixed his dark, challenging gaze on her. "You want to accuse me? Do you want to discuss gender equality? Women's rights? Have you considered that the most sexist person in your life is your father? If you want to show off your independence and freedom, why not change your name altogether? Pick one totally unique and not tainted by your father's legacy."

She jerked upright and groaned as her body ached, laying back slowly. She opened her mouth to challenge him but closed it. He was true about her father. A lot of the things she couldn't tolerate in men were displayed by her father. Yet, she accepted it from Baba. Why? Did it make her a hypocrite?

"Go away." She rolled onto her side, away from him, the chain clanking and the bed creaking. Since last night, she'd started questioning some of her actions and behaviour. He had no right to make her feel uneasy about her life. She was Zoe Himba. She was who she was. Take her or leave her.

"How are you today?" He ignored her order, sounding so damned cheerful she wanted to gouge his eyes out.

"How do you think I am?" She sat up stiffly, using her elbows as support as she swung her shackled feet over the side. "This is the worst, most uncomfortable bed I've ever slept in. The room was hot and stifling. And every time I use the toilet, I hobble around like a prisoner on death row." She'd had a restless night, waking almost every hour from the heat or wanting to pee.

"Hmmm." He looked her over as her bare feet hit the cold concrete floor, his eyes sparkling with amusement. "Maybe I should order an orange overall for you."

His face lit up in a gorgeous smile.

"You think this is funny?" She glared at him.

"No. But I think orange will complement your beautiful skin tone."

Her heart stuttered at his compliment. "You think my skin tone is beautiful."

"Of course. You're a beautiful woman." His heated gaze warmed her skin.

Yet she shook her head in disbelief. Sure, she knew she was beautiful but didn't feel it at this very moment.

Last night, she'd had to wash her face in the washroom sink with cold water and cheap hand soap. She had no toiletries and slept in yesterday's clothes. Her hair was dishevelled. Her skin was sweaty. So she wasn't beautiful right now. He was up to something, and she must keep her guard up. Not to forget, he'd chained her to his basement, no matter how pleasant he seemed this morning.

"I don't believe you. Anyway, I don't wear bright colours," she reverted to the original safer topic.

"Why is that?" He took a step forward, his head tilted to the side.

"I just don't." She shrugged. "I prefer fabrics on the greyscale or shades of silver."

He nodded. "Now, I understand why they call you Ice Queen."

"I think they call me that for a different reason." She shifted uncomfortably, remembering what he'd said last night about her being apathetic to death.

"Tell me." His eyebrows rose, and his body posture perked up in apparent curiosity.

"Are you sure?" She narrowed her eyes, suspicious of his motives. Why was he behaving as if she hadn't shot at him? As if she wasn't locked in chains? "Don't get angry if you don't like the implications."

"Okay. Tell me," he repeated. He came forward and sat on the mattress next to her, placing the tray on his lap. It had two parcels wrapped in paper and an aluminium flask.

She shuffled to the farthest end, not wanting contact. For one, she felt filthy.

"They call me Ice Queen because I'm the queen of ice, as in queen of the kill contracts, because of my designation in my father's organisation."

"Ice Queen," he said as if testing the phrase on his lips. Then he stretched his hand and traced her cheek before brushing the unruly strand of her hair with his fingers. "My Ice Queen. It makes perfect sense."

"Are you mocking me?" She moved out of his reach, standing, rattling the chain. "Last night, you were accusing me of being apathetic to death. Now you want to call me your Ice Queen?"

"I'm not mocking you." He lowered the tray onto the bed and stood, facing her. He cupped her cheeks, and her skin tingled. She wanted to break away but felt frozen by his penetrating gaze.

"I'm just reclaiming the phrase and repurposing it," he continued in a husky voice, setting winged creatures aflutter in her belly. "You are my wife. My queen. The ice is for the iceberg you have in the place of a heart, which I intend to melt. So help me, Chukwuokike."

She ignored his comment about her iceberg heart. It wasn't the first time someone had implied she was cold-hearted. Something she wore as a badge of honour and a requirement in the cartel business. To prove she could take over from her father and run the Himba clan eventually.

However, she was his queen? She felt lightheaded as her hands trembled and became clammy.

"You just have to let me in," he continued huskily. "Let me warm you up from the inside out." His breath feathered her face as he lowered his lips onto hers.

Her brain scrambled. There was something she should be doing. Stopping him? But she didn't, couldn't. Instead, she welcomed his tongue as it invaded her mouth, flicking, tugging, tasting her, claiming her.

She moaned, her hands going around his shoulders without much thought, clinging on, digging into his taut skin. She kissed him back, although his kiss was brutal and punishing. But she didn't back down from challenges. She lived for them.

Kissing, sex, she could handle. It was all the other emotional mumbo-jumbo that freaked her out.

He plundered her mouth, a hand grabbing her bum and pressing his solid body against hers, his erection pushing against her belly.

Lust sizzled in her veins, her nipples hardening. She rubbed her chest against his, needing some friction against the hard points.

She moved her leg, trying to get closer, to climb him. The rattling chain was a wake-up call, cold water on her hot skin. What was she doing? She was his prisoner, and he was taking advantage of her.

She sank her teeth into the flesh of his lower lip, drawing blood.

"Oww." He broke the kiss, eyes blazing as he lifted his head and touched his mouth with his hand. Crimson coated his finger. "Why?"

Her chest squeezed tight, and she swallowed, feeling conflicted.

He genuinely looked confused, as if he couldn't fathom why she would end the kiss so violently.

"You have no right to touch me while I'm down here in chains," she shouted, backing away, chest heaving as she tried to get her breathing under control. How could he think it was okay to touch her when she was defenceless and tied up? "If you want conjugal rights, release me immediately. I won't be your sex slave."

With an inscrutable expression, he stared at her for several seconds as he pulled a handkerchief from his pocket and dabbed his swelling lip.

Eventually, he shook his head and turned away. He walked up the stairs before pausing on the landing. "I brought you some breakfast. I asked your mother what you like, and she said you like Akara, so I ordered some for you. There's tea in the flask."

Her heart thudded. "You spoke to my mother. Today?"

"Yes. She was on the way to the airport for her flight this morning. She sends her love." He continued up the stairs. "I'll send someone down with some clothes and toiletries for you."

Then he was gone, the door slamming and the lock engaging.

He'd spoken to her mother, and she hadn't. She had no phone. No means to contact the outside world. Not even a television to see what was happening in the world.

She stood there for a moment, feeling lost. All she had were the diamond necklace, rings and bracelets and an old-style analogue gold and diamond encrusted wristwatch. She'd taken it off last night. She walked over to the bed and grabbed it, checking the time—a quarter to eleven.

If only she'd worn her smartwatch last night, she would have been able to read messages. But it was in her luggage in the living room the last time she'd seen it. She doubted the bags were still there. They were probably in a cupboard or bedroom somewhere in this house.

Her stomach grumbled, and she hobbled to the washroom. It had a white WC and sink with a wet room style space but a faucet instead of a showerhead. And no bathtub. There was no window in here. Just a layer of thick decorative cloudy glass blocks letting in sunlight. An extractor fan sucked out the humid air when the light switch was turned on.

How was she expected to wash? Not that she could remove her Lycra shorts or panties anyway because of the stainless-steel shackles on her feet.

She used the WC, then washed her face, hands and cleaned her teeth as best she could at the sink, which only had cold water. There wasn't even a towel to dry her hands. She wet her hair and tidied it up as much as she could with her fingers.

Heaven knew she'd never been as dishevelled as this in her adult life. Her appearance always spoke volumes, even before she opened her mouth. When she showed up, people showed respect.

But look at her now. Less than one day married, and it was like she'd been dragged through a bush. She'd always thought marriage was terrible for her, and she had the proof. She had to find a way to escape this dungeon and return to her life.

She had to find a way to convince Maddox to set her free from this basement. From this marriage. She couldn't go through another nine days, let alone ninety days of playing wife to anyone.

Even if it was someone she was attracted to.

That kiss had been awakening. Perhaps...

She gripped the sink tight, rocking back and forth.

Perhaps it was her ticket out of the basement. What if she'd allowed Maddox to continue kissing her? What if they'd had sex? He would have to release her, right? He wouldn't really keep her locked up afterwards, would he?

Well, she had to give it a chance. Next time he came down, she would try to relax, try to let him seduce her again. It would work. It had to work.

Determined, she returned to the bed and sat on it. Then she placed the tray on her lap, unwrapping the parcel. The smell of fried bean balls rushed at her, making her stomach rumble. She bit into the first one, mewling with pleasure. Before long, she was chomping through the pack. Then she opened the flask and poured the steaming black tea into the cap.

She took a sip and moaned. It was sweetened with honey, just the way she liked it.

Hang on. How did Maddox know she liked black tea sweetened with honey? He must have asked her mother. Didn't he also say he asked Mum what she wanted for breakfast and had ordered the akara for her especially?

He'd gone out of his way to find out what would please her, even when he'd locked her up.

The clause from the contract flashed in her mind.

*

WIFE agrees to grant to HUSBAND exclusive and unique rights to provide for, protect, pleasure, and punish WIFE.

*

In less than twenty-four hours, Maddox proved he could fulfil all the clause elements. He was a man of his word, a principled man.

She shouldn't have accused him of trying to take advantage of her. Just like she shouldn't have shot at him last night. She couldn't help herself and didn't know how to be anything different.

A good thing she was already sitting because her knees weakened as she became overwhelmed by feelings she couldn't control. She got light-headed, and her stomach cramped, her appetite receding. She drank the tea to force the food down her throat.

Then, she placed the tray on the floor and bent over, covering her face with her hands.

For the first time in her adult life, she didn't know what to do. Didn't know how to handle Maddox. How to get out of the situation she found herself.

Mum, what do I do?

Her mother was good at providing solutions to matters like this, relationship stuff. This was one aspect of her life that she failed woefully.

Her conversation with her mother from yesterday replayed.

"Don't unravel everything I've done on your behalf with Maddox. Promise me, Zoe."

"Mum, I promise. I will swallow my pride ... And I will submit to him. Not that I know how."

"He will show you how."

That's it. She would have to ask Maddox, as humiliating as that would be. What other choice did she have?

NINETEEN

"So you have a woman locked up in the basement," Abuchi said and chuckled.

"It's like an episode from a true crime podcast," Jaxon commented.

Maddox lifted his gaze from the laptop he was working on at the dining table and glanced at his brother and son, who sat on a leather sofa playing a game on the large TV screen in the living room. It was one of their rituals when his son was on school breaks. The three men sitting in the living room bantering while Jax and Abuchi played video games. Maddox sometimes joined in the video games, but it was mainly Jaxon's and Abuchi's thing.

"Jax, you're talking about my wife. Your stepmother, AB," Maddox replied, using his son's nickname. His words held no heat. Just part of their family chat. It was fair for them to laugh about his situation, even though it was severe.

"That makes it so much worse." Jaxon teased, dropping the controller. He stood, walking to the dining area.

Abuchi stood, too and headed out to the kitchen. He returned a minute later with a giant bag of plantain crisps. That was the thing about having a young adult son around. He never seemed to stop eating. "Dad, I've heard about midlife crisis, but this is mad. I go away for a semester, and you get married and lock your wife in the cellar."

"Oh, you missed out the fun part where she tried to shoot him." Jaxon pulled out the chair beside Maddox at the dining table. "Seriously, bro. You can't keep her locked up for the next three months. What are you going to do?"

A good question. Maddox leaned back into his seat, scrubbing his hand over his face. "I really don't know. She's not making this easy at all."

Zoe had been in the basement for five days.

The room had been set up as a guard room in case he ever needed to secure one of the crew members. However, it had served as storage, and he'd cleared it before her arrival. He'd suspected he would need to use it when he'd listened to the audio recording of Don Himba ordering his daughter to kill Maddox.

However, he hadn't expected her to stay there for this long. Three days, maybe. But not five.

Still, it showed how resilient she was. How irrepressible.

After the first night of sleeping in an uncomfortable bed, he'd thought she would have been ready to do anything to get out of there.

But she hadn't been prepared to give in or leave the place when he'd taken breakfast down to her the following day. Sure, she'd been in a foul mood, but he'd expected it. And she'd gotten defensive when he'd mentioned her father. Same as she'd been cagey the previous evening when he'd talked about her abortion.

However, when he'd referred to her as his Ice Queen, he'd noticed a softening, perhaps from surprise that he would dub her his queen. Seeing the glimpse of vulnerability in her had made him forget every horrible thing she'd done to him. He'd ached to wrap her in his arms, to savour her.

And he'd done so, kissing her.

She'd tasted like he'd remembered. And his craving for her had returned. He shouldn't want her, not after what she'd done. Yet, he couldn't resist her.

She'd kissed him back initially. Then she'd suddenly sunken her teeth into his lower lip, drawing blood.

He'd been swamped by emotions—shock, hurt, confusion. He couldn't understand why.

Then she'd accused him of taking advantage of her, and anger had surged through him.

How could she accuse him falsely? He hadn't forced her to open her mouth to him. Hadn't coerced her to respond. To cling to him and moan with pleasure.

Never mind that he would never violate anyone, let alone his wife! He was a natural protector. He would give his life before he would harm her or anyone in his care.

Because, like it or not, she was in his care. His wife. His responsibility.

It didn't mean he couldn't be brutal or fierce. As the masquerade, he was required to deliver Yadili justice as ruthlessly and relentlessly as needed. He wouldn't be one of the most respected Yadili enforcers of his generation otherwise.

Still, he would concede the possibility she felt helpless because she was incarcerated. And while she was unwilling to accept him as her husband, she would see him as the enemy there to take advantage of her.

Therefore, he'd decided he wouldn't go down to the basement. He needed to deal with the seemingly constant battle between his anger at her and his need to protect her. Best thing was distance. Until she was ready to accept him as her husband.

"Dad, can I go down there and see her?" Abuchi's question cut through Maddox's thoughts.

"No!" he replied a little too vehemently, considering their previous light mood. "She's not an animal in a cage for your entertainment. It's not a zoo."

"Okay." His son reared back, looking shocked. He obviously wasn't expecting his father's response and glanced at his uncle before meeting Maddox's gaze. His Adam's apple bobbed as he swallowed. "I'm sorry, Dad. I didn't mean any disrespect."

Maddox sighed and shut the laptop as he stood. He walked over to his son and patted his shoulder. "I know."

Abuchi was a good lad. Boisterous, yes, but he was never disrespectful. Maddox was proud of the man he was becoming. He and his family had worked hard to raise his son as an Ejiofor. Maybe one day, he would continue the family legacy as a Yadili enforcer. But he was still young and had much to learn about life and relationships.

Maddox carried on walking towards the door. He needed to regain control of his life and relationship before he could school his son without hypocrisy.

"Where are you going?" Jax asked.

"I'm going to see my wife," he replied, walking into the corridor and stopping at the door leading down to the basement.

He turned the handle, opening it. The sound of a female voice reached him. Zoe's voice.

"So you said the other day that Maddox saved your life? Where was this?"

He was stunned into inaction at her question. His muscles became rigid, his posture stiffening as he listened.

He'd assigned a female crew member, Agatha, to watch over Zoe. He'd thought Zoe would ignore the woman or tolerate the guard's presence for her convenience. A security camera was installed in the basement, recording video and audio, but he'd switched it off since Agatha took over.

He hadn't known they'd been discussing him.

"It was years ago when there was a militant attack, an ethnic cleansing in Sabon Gari, where we lived," Agatha spoke softly. "Usually, when that happens, no military or law enforcement show up until it's over. But this time, soldiers came to our neighbourhood—a team of thirteen led by Maddox. They saved lives that day. I was fighting off some men who wanted to rape me. He intervened and killed them, but one of them managed to cut him with a machete. He was seriously wounded. He didn't have to step in to save me. To save us. In fact, he and his team disobeyed their superiors by being there. It's part of the reason he left military service. Joshua, Josiah, and Otito were all part of that team. They couldn't stand by and watch what was going on. They deserved medals of honour. Instead, they were threatened with punishment. If Maddox's father wasn't high up in the military, I believe Maddox would have been court-martialled. He had to resign his commission to avoid a court-martial."

As Agatha spoke, the memories came rushing back at Maddox, making his scalp prickle with unease. He didn't like reliving those times. But he bet it was worse for Agatha. She'd lost so much. Her family. Her home. She'd had to relocate afterwards. Thankfully, she'd found love and happiness with Otito, and they'd married.

"I didn't know." Zoe sounded choked up, pulling Maddox out of the haze of memories.

"Your husband is a good man," Agatha said quietly.

"I know that."

"So why are you trying to kill him?"

"I'm not. I…" Zoe trailed off as if unsure of how to reply. She couldn't very well admit that she'd been sent to kill her husband.

Maddox's anger returned, prompting him to move. He knocked on the wood to announce his presence and descended the stairs, his footsteps echoing in the silence that followed the knock. He stopped at the landing.

Agatha stood at the bottom of the steps and dipped her head. "Afternoon, boss."

She was a curvy woman with low-cut hair, wearing dark denim and black T.

"Afternoon, Agatha. Take a break," he ordered, allowing some of his annoyance to seep through.

"Yes, boss." She glanced at Zoe, who nodded at her from where she sat on the edge of the bed. Then she walked up the steps, past Maddox and shut the door as she left the basement.

He strode down the stairs slowly, watching his wife as she straightened.

She wore an embroidered, knee-length, short-sleeved grey tunic and her hair was wrapped in a loose bun. She'd bathed daily with the bucket in the wet room. Most significantly, there were no cuffs or chains around her ankles.

He'd instructed Agatha to remove the chain while she was in the basement. He hadn't been worried about Zoe trying to escape from the woman. Agatha was a fierce warrior, and it seemed she had figured it out.

"So you're still alive then," she grumbled, eyeing him as he approached.

"I am," he replied smoothly, with zero inflexion. He was ready to battle if required.

"So why haven't you been to see me for five goddamned days?" She stomped towards him.

He stood his ground. "So you can accuse me of taking advantage of you?"

Her eyes widened as she halted, but she was already in his personal space.

She really couldn't help herself. She was a creature of impulse. Of passion. She just didn't know how to channel it properly.

Realising she was too close to him, she took a step back. But he followed her, extending his hand, gripping her nape. He leaned in, lowering his voice. "Am I taking advantage now?"

Unexpectedly, she sucked in a deep breath, and her lashes fluttered shut. But she said nothing.

"Answer me," he ordered. "Am I taking advantage of you?"

"No!" she bit out, her eyes blazing with heat. That passion would be his undoing. "Where the hell have you been for five days?"

He released her, stepping away, needing to escape her alluring scent. Fighting not to succumb to kissing her again.

"Didn't Agatha tell you where I was?" he played for indifference.

"No! She just said you were unavailable. Unavailable. You don't lock me down here and become unavailable, dammit!"

If he wasn't so wound up, he would have chuckled at her outrage. In fact, it gave him hope. Perhaps she was thawing. Maybe she'd missed him.

"You could have asked for me if you wanted to see me," he said, tilting his head to watch her.

"I shouldn't have to ask … You're my husband." She glared at him.

"Am I?"

"Of course you are!"

Her acknowledgement set his heart racing. This was a leap from where they'd been five days ago. Perhaps the time apart had been good for her, even if it hadn't been great for him.

"Did you miss me?" he said in a low voice, his tone seductive. He couldn't help it. Just being near his wife set his veins on fire.

She stumbled back, lowering her gaze.

He followed her. She turned away, hands trembling.

He realised she was afraid, and her vulnerability called to his protective side. From his research, this was new to her. She'd never been in a loving relationship. She'd had lovers, for sure, but no one significant.

"There's no need to be afraid. You are fearless. You have no problems showing me when you're angry. So you shouldn't be afraid to tell me you need me."

"I don't need you," she bit out, avoiding his gaze.

"You don't? Okay." He nodded and stepped towards her bed, stooping to grab the chain. It rattled as he pulled it out.

"What are you doing?" She eyed him.

"I'm going to chain you back up. Sit on the bed." He'd tried to go gently with her, but it wasn't working. His brother was right. He couldn't leave her down here indefinitely. Something had to give. And he'd reached his tolerance limit.

"Why? No!" she stumbled backwards.

"To tell you the truth, I've had enough of your shit," he said coolly.

She blinked several times. "What?"

"You heard me. I've had enough. So, I'm going to put you back in chains, and you can stay down here for the remainder of our marriage. Afterwards, I'll ship you back to your father. Of course, it will mean your father doesn't get any dowry."

"You can't do that. You can't keep me locked here for three months."

"Oh, I can. Since you seem to be enjoying it so much."

"I'm not enjoying it. How can you say that?"

"Well, you're doing nothing to get out."

Her breath hitched, and she eyed the stairs.

"By the way, if you're considering running up those stairs, you should seriously ponder the consequences. My son is home."

"He is?"

"Yes, and I will catch you and belt your ass in front of him."

She tilted her chin up in defiance. "You wouldn't dare."

"I very well would. Considering you killed my baby and tried to kill me, all kid gloves have come off. I spanked you in front of my men. I will flog you in front of my son. Is that how you want to get introduced to him?"

"No." She swallowed. Sweat glistened on her forehead, and her gaze bounced around the room.

He'd trapped her, and he wouldn't release the pressure.

"I will make this easy for you and simplify your options. You have two choices. Be my queen or be my prisoner."

She swallowed again. "What happens if I choose to be your ... queen?"

"To be my queen, you must submit to me as my wife. You won't threaten me or members of my family. You'll come upstairs and meet my son. You'll be a part of my family. A part of me." Emotions swarmed him as he spoke.

"And … if I don't submit to you?" she sounded choked.

"Then I've already said it. You'll stay down here for the remainder of the marriage contract, and I won't come here again."

"You won't?" She rubbed the back of her neck, and her foot bounced. "Why?"

"You said it yourself. You don't need me to guard you. I employ enough security personnel to do the job."

"So I won't see you for the next ninety days?" She frowned.

"No." He feigned nonchalance, rattling the chain. "So make your choice."

She rocked in place, hands clutching her stomach. "But I don't know how to submit."

The tension left his shoulders for the first time since he came down the stairs today, and he relaxed a little. They were finally getting somewhere. "The most important question is, do you want to submit to me?"

"Yes," she murmured.

"Are you sure?" he persisted, needing her certainty.

"Yes, but I don't know how," she sounded frustrated.

He lowered the chain and straightened. "The first step to submission is admitting you want to do it. But the most important element is trust."

Her hysterical laughter echoed off the concrete walls. "Then we won't get anywhere because I don't trust anyone."

"I can see you don't trust me," he said calmly. "But surely you trust someone."

"My parents." She shrugged.

"That's a given. Who else?" he persisted. He had an inkling but wanted her to say it.

She twisted her lips in contemplation. "Noah. I trust Noah."

"That's your second, right?" His muscles tensed again.

"Yes. I've known him for nearly ten years," she said nonchalantly.

A ball of jealous acid corroded his insides. This was the same man who had rudely interrupted their wedding. Maddox had been so enraged he'd wanted to put a bullet through the man himself. Only his respect for Zoe's mother had kept his rage in check.

"Did you fuck him?" he asked coldly. It was the only reason the man had the gall to interfere at their nuptials.

She gasped, eyes widening. She opened her mouth and closed it several times as if unsure of how to answer. Finally, she said, "Yes, a long time ago."

He nodded, the tightening in his chest loosening a little. "I will forgive his offensive interference at our wedding. But he can't touch you again."

She eyed him and nodded. "Okay."

He puffed out a breath, letting go of his jealousy. He would accept her promise. Trust was a two-way street.

"Good. Now, do you think that I will ever harm you?"

Her chin tilted up. "Yes. You locked me up here."

He shook his head. "Yes, I locked you up, for good reason. But did I harm you?"

She frowned, pouting her lips. "No, you didn't."

"And if you didn't shoot at me on our wedding night, would I have locked you in here?"

"No. I don't think so."

"Exactly." He moved over to the bed and sat on the edge. Then, he opened his legs and pointed at the space between them. "Kneel here."

"Why?" she appeared puzzled.

"It doesn't matter why? I'm telling you to kneel. Submission requires taking a step or two of faith. Have some faith in me, Zoe. Trust that I won't harm you."

She eyed him for a few seconds, biting her bottom lip. Finally, she pushed off the wall and walked gingerly towards him as if there were hazards in her way. She lowered her body onto her knees in front of him.

"Is this how you want me?" she asked in a breathy voice.

"Yes. This is exactly how I want you." He smiled, unable to contain his excitement as his heart raced.

"You like me like this?" The puzzlement was back in her voice.

"Yes, I like you like this." He leaned forward, cupping her cheek. "I like to know that my wife is open and receptive to me. And as you submit to me, I promise to honour and cherish you. I will protect you with my life if necessary."

She gasped, shaking her head.

"You'll protect me with your life, even though I tried to kill you? Even when I know you're angry, I aborted our baby? I don't believe you." She sounded angry and tried to push off the floor.

"Hold on." He held her shoulders, keeping her down.

"Why should I? I know you're angry with me. How can you be angry and still protect me as you claim?" she retorted.

"Yes, I'm angry with you, Zoe. But for the next three months, you are mine. My wife," he gritted out. "And you better believe that I will defend what's mine.

To death. I will defend you against the world. So help me, Chukwuokike."

The tense muscles on her shoulders relaxed as she puffed out a breath. For the first time in what seemed like forever, she smiled, lighting up the space. "I believe you."

"Good." He released her shoulders.

She shuffled forward, and the next thing, her arms wrapped around his shoulders and her mouth ascended to his with eagerness, catching him off-guard. For a few seconds, he was too stunned to respond immediately as her warm, soft mouth devoured him.

She shoved him flat onto the bed, climbing on top of him and straddling his hips. "That is the sexiest thing anyone ever said to me."

"What?" He drew shallow breaths as arousal flowed in his veins. Her heat settled on his groin as she ground on his erection. His heart pounded.

"That you will defend me against the world." Her eyes sparkled, and her lips curved in the most glorious grin.

He clasped his hand around her nape and devoured her mouth, succumbing to the taste and feel of her as she ground on top of him. Things had escalated fast from their conversation, but he didn't care about the interlude as long as she was in his arms. She was his, after all. His dick was hard and throbbing against his zipper.

As if she could sense it, she reached down and tugged at his belt buckle.

An alarm bell went off in his mind, and he gripped her hands, pulling her away. Then he rolled over, dumping her on the bed and pushed off.

"What's the matter?" she asked, seeming confused.

"That's the other thing I forgot to mention," he said in a gruff tone. "We're not going to have sex."

"You can't be serious," she chuckled. "Why?"

"Because I can't risk you getting pregnant and aborting my child again." He couldn't go through another loss.

TWENTY

Zoe leaned back, recoiling from Maddox's words. Her heart pounded in her ears.

One minute, she'd been all over him, ready to tear his clothes off and make good on the sensual promise shimmering between them.

The next, he dumped her on the bed and scampered off, filling her with confusion.

But his announcement that they wouldn't be having sex was even worse because he made her feel as if she had a contagious disease.

She didn't even want to confront his reason. It made her stomach cramp, the muscles tightening and loosening.

She'd had an abortion. Yes. Would he wield it over her head forever like an axe? Did he think he was the only one who suffered? The baby wasn't just his. It had been her blood, too. Her body. She'd paid physically and emotionally for the decision.

The memories of sitting in the waiting room, praying she was making the right decision. Of leaving the medical centre afterwards, feeling empty and lost on the drive home. The trauma of her body decrying the loss of the foetus. The haemorrhaging and subsequent surgery. She'd paid for her actions. Was still paying. She didn't need the constant reminders.

Pain bloomed in the back of her mind, and nausea ripped through her.

She bolted off the bed and ran into the toilet, throwing up into the WC.

"Zoe?" Maddox's voice came from behind her. It sounded like the tap in the sink was running.

"Get out!" she screeched, not wanting him to see her like this. To see this quivering, puking person. This wasn't her. Tears pooled in her eyes, blocking her vision as she got off the cold concrete floor and swirled water in her mouth, spitting out.

"What's the matter? Let me help you," he sounded concerned, which only wound her up. He was the one bent on accusing her of wrongdoing. Of murdering their baby.

"I said get out! Can I not have some privacy?" she choked the words out.

He'd helped enough. His help put her in this position, feeling overwhelmed with emotions strangling the breath out of her. She wasn't weak, damn it! She'd allowed herself to succumb to him and had fallen into his trap.

"Okay." He sounded dejected. Scuffing footsteps announced his departure from the bathroom.

Her breath seized, her larynx constricting. She couldn't swallow and struggled to inhale. Why did the sound of his misery hurt so much?

She shouldn't care. Yet she slid down against the wall, pulled her knees up, bent over and tried to breathe as her vision blurred.

Warm, strong arms wrapped around her, lifting her from the floor and carrying her out.

"I thought you were leaving," she protested weakly.

"I'm sorry, but I can't leave you like this," his voice was gruff as he lowered his body onto the bed.

"Breathe," he commanded gently, cradling her on his lap.

She turned her face into his chest, taking a lungful of his scent in a deep inhalation. Surprisingly, the constriction in her chest eased, and she took another breath and another, the panic attack easing.

Why did she even have one? The last time she'd had an anxiety episode was as a child when she'd thought her parents would split because Baba's mistress got pregnant. So, what triggered this one?

Maddox and his constant berating about the termination.

Yet here he was, comforting her, chasing away her panic.

Why wasn't he fighting her? Shouting at her, throwing accusations. She could handle the ruthless enforcer. Even the vengeful husband.

Not this protective spouse, this caring *lover*.

Except he didn't want to make love. Scratch that, have sex.

"Is this what you want? Me being weak. Does it make you happy?"

He said nothing, his fingers stroking her nape gently.

She lifted her head and tried to kiss him, but he didn't respond, didn't let her tongue in, although he didn't push her away.

She repositioned herself, straddling him and reached for his buckle.

He grabbed her hands, restraining her.

"If you want to help me, fuck me. Now," she demanded.

"That's not going to happen. I want you to talk to me."

Anger surged through her, and she shoved his chest, standing. "I don't want to talk. I want to fuck."

She didn't want to rouse those overwhelming feelings again.

He studied her with an inscrutable expression. "Why is it so hard to admit you did something wrong?"

"Why am I the only one who has to make admissions of wrongdoing? You wronged me. I don't hear you admitting it."

"How did I wrong you?" His eyes narrowed as he stood.

"You got me pregnant," she bit out.

His mouth dropped open, and he stared at her with a gobsmacked expression.

Then his eyes narrowed, and he shook his head. "I'm not going to argue with you. Clean up so we can go upstairs."

Huffing, she walked into the bathroom, tidied up and packed her toiletries into the overnight bag Agatha brought down.

When she was ready, Maddox took the bag and led the way up the steps. In the main foyer, he led her up to the top floor.

"This is the master bedroom. Our bedroom," he said when he opened the door to a large bedroom.

The colours were in a range of blue. The walls were the sky-blue of a clear sunny day, and the bed linen was the cobalt blue of a starry night sky, matching the rug.

Tall drawers in dark wood complemented the space. It was masculine but tasteful and understated.

"There's a walk-in closet where you can hang your clothes. I made space for you." He opened one of two doors leading off the room. Then he pointed at the other. "This is the ensuite bathroom."

"Okay.' She glanced into the white, tiled space with ocean-blue borders.

"There are four bedrooms up here. Abuchi's room is up here. Jaxon's room is downstairs. He has a self-contained annexe," he carried on. "I can show you around the rest of the property."

"No. I want to shower and change before I meet Abuchi."

"Okay. I'll leave you to it."

The first thing she did after he left was to dig out her phone from her luggage. Thankfully, it still had life when she turned it on. There were many messages from Noah. So she sent him a note.

Hi, Noah. I've just seen your messages.

Thank Goodness. I was getting worried. Are you okay?

Yes, I am. I've just been busy.

She lied. She felt uncomfortable about telling him what happened since her wedding night. Noah didn't like Maddox and would escalate it. She didn't need to give him reasons to hate her husband.

Busy? You disappeared off the earth for five days! Couldn't you just respond to my messages?

Her spine stiffened. Who the hell did he think he was?

I don't have to explain myself to you. Have you forgotten who I am?

He didn't reply immediately. A few seconds later, the phone pinged.

I'm sorry, Shugaba. I was just worried about you.

She sighed. It was his job to worry about her safety.

I know. But remember, I'm newly wedded. There's such a thing as honeymoon, you know. Do you need a blow-by-blow account of what my husband and I have been doing?

She hated lying to her most trusted ally. But she had to tread lightly and figure out many things, including her position and future.

No! I don't need to know the details.

She chuckled. She could imagine him cringing at the idea of Maddox having sex with her. Well, her husband refused to touch her, so Noah had nothing to worry about.

So when can we meet to discuss the plan? He sent. They had agreed that he would stay in Lori Osa and be her backup when she executed her father's orders.

Not yet. I'll let you know when I'm free.

There was something else she wanted to do tonight.

***

Ninety minutes later, Zoe had showered and changed into a silk navy mini cocktail dress. She'd styled her hair with the electric straightener and applied makeup for the first time since her arrival in this house.

Purse in hand, she headed downstairs and into the living room, her designer stilettos tapping on the marble floor.

The male occupants gasped as she entered, their gazes filled with awe.

"You must be Abuchi," she said to the young man beside Jaxon.

"Yes. Good afternoon." He stood and dipped his head respectfully. He had his father's eyes and nose, but his skin tone was lighter. Probably took after his mother there.

Bile rose in her throat, and she swallowed it, pushing away the flash of envy. She'd promised her husband she wouldn't threaten any family member.

"Afternoon. How are you?" she replied, surprised at the warmth radiating in her chest. This was her husband's son. *Her* stepson. Her family.

"I'm fine. Thank you," he replied pleasantly.

"Maddox went out, but he'll be back shortly," Jaxon said.

"Yes, I know." Maddox had returned to the bedroom while she'd been in the shower. He'd knocked on the door and opened it slightly but hadn't come inside. Coward! He'd said he'd had to pop out but would be back quickly.

She didn't mind because she had plans of her own. She wasn't about to spend the first night after her incarceration sitting indoors.

"I'm going to pop out too," she continued. "I told a friend I'd meet them this evening."

She purposefully used a neutral gender term to confuse Jaxon.

"You're going out? Does Maddox know?" he asked, pushing off the sofa.

"No. But I can message him."

"It's probably best if you wait until he returns."

"I can't. I already told my friend I was on my way. Is this going to be a problem?" she challenged.

If Maddox restricted her movements, all his talk about respecting and cherishing her and treating her like a queen was out of the window. And their deal was dead in the water.

Jaxon seemed to know it, too, because he puffed out a breath. "No. There's no problem."

"Then, please arrange for a car and driver. Otherwise, I'll book an Uber," she said to appease him. She didn't mind them knowing her destination. Arufin was a public venue. Well, a privately-owned public arena.

"No. I'll get you a chauffeur." He pulled his phone out and raised it to his ear. "My sister-in-law needs to go out. Tell Agatha to bring the X6." When he lowered the phone, he said. "She'll be here shortly."

***

The drive out was uneventful. Agatha was her usual professional self, handling business as her chauffeur-slash-bodyguard. The supped-up SUV had blackout windows, and she was in a cocoon in the backseat. A security guard held the car door when the car stopped outside the Arufin's VIP entrance.

"Good evening, Ma'am," he said as she stepped into the warm night.

"Evening," she replied, walking past him.

Before she reached the building, a man jogged up to her. "Zoe, hold on!"

She glanced back. "Noah? What are you doing here?"

"I could ask you the same thing. I followed you from the Odili estate."

"You followed me? Why?"

"I've been monitoring the place since you didn't respond to my messages, hoping to see you. Then I saw you get into this car, and I followed it. What are you doing here?"

She couldn't fault his actions. It was what she would have done if she were in his shoes. What she would have ordered him to do.

She sighed. "I have an appointment."

He glanced around and lowered his voice. "This is Arufin. What kind of appointment do you have at a nightclub?"

"I can't explain right now. But since you're here, you can wait for me in the lobby." She might as well use his presence as a backup.

She entered the dark lobby and approached the receptionist behind the glass screen. "It's Zoe. Idehen is expecting me."

She didn't care if she was recognised this time. She was here as Maddox's wife and under his protection. So technically, her father couldn't punish her. Also, he'd been the one who sent her to Maddox, so anything she did to achieve the mission was permissible.

"Of course, Ma'am. He'll be down shortly," the receptionist said.

As if he knew she was in the building already since there were security cameras, the lift pinged, and the massive Black man stepped out of it. He reminded her of the two bears—Joshua and Josiah.

"It's good to see you, Zoe," the man said.

"Same here," she replied. "This is my security chief, Noah. He'll wait for me down here. Is that okay?"

"Of course," Idehen replied as Noah nodded at the man. He held the lift doors open, and she entered it.

When the doors closed and they headed up, she asked. "Is the file I requested ready?"

"Yes, I've set up a private booth for you to review it," he said.

"Okay." She swallowed, gulping breaths as her heart raced, her trepidation mixing with excitement.

She would see the definitive evidence of what Maddox did to her on the night they'd had anonymous sex. She would have proof if he tampered with the condom she'd given him. Evidence that he'd known who she was and had wanted to trap her with the pregnancy.

Or not.

Because the past few days had her questioning herself, her actions, her loyalties. Her husband wanted her trust, but she could never trust him until she figured out what happened the night they'd had sex.

Then perhaps they could move on.
For better or worse.
Till *Death* do them part.

TWENTY-ONE

Zoe almost stumbled out of the lift. She braced her hand against the wall, trying to shake off the dizzy spell.

"Are you okay?" Noah's voice cut through the haze as he rushed to her side.

"No, I'm not. My world is upside down," she wanted to yell.

"I'm okay," she lied instead. She was doing this a lot recently, telling untruths to the one person who knew her better than any other man. Better than her parents.

He stared at her, head tilted as if he didn't believe her. Case in point. He knew when she was lying.

"I need a drink. Let's go into the nightclub," she said to distract him.

The frown lines on his face deepened. "Your father forbids anyone from going in there."

She huffed, shaking her head as she walked past him towards the door leading to the club foyer. "I think you should worry less about Baba and more about Maddox. He will flip when he knows I'm here with you."

Maddox would find out. No doubt. Jaxon would tell him she'd left the house. Agatha would confirm her location.

Wrath was coming her way, and there would be hell to pay.

Because for the second time in about two months, she'd messed up. Big time.

And all since she met Maddox.

So yes, let him come. She would wait.

The bouncer at the club entrance ushered them in when she flashed her VIP pass.

As soon as the doors opened, she was enveloped in loud music and heaving bodies. The place was jam-packed, putting Noah in protective mode. He placed one arm around her while clearing a path with the other.

"Coming through," his loud voice boomed, making people move out of the way.

"The VIP section is this way." She pointed at the cordoned-off steps leading to the mezzanine. With another flash of the gold embossed black card, they were ushered into the VIP lounge.

Unlike some other VIP lounges, this was totally exclusive. Only those with the premium cards were allowed here, regardless of how much cash they flashed. Hence, there were only a handful of people in it tonight. The music wasn't as loud because of the thick, transparent Perspex wall separating them from the three-storey club. She could see the dancers covered in tassels dancing in cages suspended from the ceiling.

They gave the illusion of dangling, but bridges and braces secured the cages.

She found a corner sectional and plonked herself on it. Noah sat beside her. A waiter approached immediately, taking their orders—a rum and coke for her and a plain coke drink for him. He never drank alcohol whilst on duty.

Plus, she needed him alert because her husband was coming. And anything could happen.

When the waiter left, Noah leaned close, scrutinising her. "What's going on with you. You're not yourself."

"You can say that again," she muttered, leaning back into the sofa.

"Zoe, we're friends. Talk to me." He placed his hand on her arm.

"… *he can't touch you again.*"

She remembered Maddox's words from earlier today.

She was breaking his rule by allowing Noah near her. But this wasn't about sex. It was about concern. She could see it in her Second's face.

Still, she brushed off his hand. "You shouldn't touch me. Maddox won't like it."

She couldn't even believe she was saying this. But regret knotted her belly.

"What—" Before he could finish, the waiter arrived with their drinks and placed them on the low table.

She grabbed hers, taking a large gulp as the waiter left.

"Did he threaten you?" Noah's brow wrinkled.

His persistent questions began to annoy her. "Tell me, would you let Mary go to a nightclub with another man? A former lover?"

"Of course not." He jerked back, and his eyes narrowed. "But you're not Mary. You've never allowed any man to tell you what to do."

True. She shouldn't care what Maddox thought about her. Hadn't cared until five days ago when he'd made her question everything she'd believed. Made her question herself. He'd knocked her off-balance.

Hence, the reason she came to Arufin tonight. She needed to regain her equilibrium. So, she'd requested to view the video from their night together in the Black Room. She'd expected to see him tampering with the condom she'd given him to use. Or worse, obtaining proof he'd known her identity before she'd revealed it to him.

However, her expectations were shattered to smithereens.

She'd watched the video from beginning to end and even replayed certain sections. Maddox had used the condom she'd given him, and he hadn't seen her face. Hadn't known her identity.

Idehen had confirmed it.

Yet, for the past three months, she'd blamed him for trying to entrap her with the pregnancy. It was the reason she'd been enraged and hadn't told him in advance about her plans to terminate the pregnancy. It was why she'd stood before his father and her parents and rejected his marriage proposal.

Sure, her father had commanded her to reject him anyway. But she would have warned him in advance if she hadn't been so angry at him.

All for nothing.

Maddox hadn't held ulterior motives when he'd proposed to her. Her distrustful nature had made her think the worst of him.

Now, her suspicions had been debunked. What next? What motivation would spur her to complete her mission? How could she justify obeying her father's orders and killing her husband?

"Why do you care what he thinks?" Noah's words sliced through her reverie.

"Of course, I care what he thinks. He's my husband," she snapped, suddenly feeling possessive about Maddox. "Why is it wrong to care what he thinks?"

She gulped down the rest of her drink as the alcohol buzzed gently in her veins. Placing the glass on the table, she rested against the leather cushion, closing her eyes.

"Zoe," Noah said in a low voice. He leaned in, talking into her ear so no one else would overhear. Although the nearest clubber was three sections away. "Have you forgotten why you're with him? You're going to kill him in a few weeks once he sends the final payment to your father."

Yes, how could she forget? She was going to kill Maddox.

Her chest contracted in pain, and her limbs trembled.

"No, I haven't forgotten why I'm here. Maddox Ejiofor is a dead man walking," she bit out angrily, whirling in her seat, facing her Second. She shook off the uneasiness as adrenaline spiked through her. "I am the Ice Queen, after all. But for now. He is *my* husband. *Mine*. Do you hear me? And I will enjoy him however I see fit. I will use him. I will fuck him. I will parade around town like a married woman if I want to because, you know what?"

She glared at him, and he shook his head.

"Because it's the only time I'm ever going to be married. It's the only time I will be addressed as Mrs Anyone. So, I'm making the most of it. If you have a problem with it, you can go fuck yourself."

He reared back, looking offended, but she didn't care. She would not have him questioning her behaviour until she figured it out.

She reached for her drink, realised it was empty, and waved for the waiter.

"Look, I understand," he said finally.

"Good for you. And another thing." She rounded on him again. "Do you realise that if I don't play the role of a wife well? If Maddox isn't seduced by my charms, he won't pay the dowry? And this mission will be a failure."

He sighed. "I know."

"Good." She looked towards the counter impatiently.

But movement from the entrance caught her attention. Her husband had arrived. He strode towards her like an angry cloud obliterating the sun.

"Maddox is here," she said to Noah. "Make yourself scarce."

"He looks furious. I'm not going to leave you alone with him." He stood, moving to the edge of the sofa as if on guard.

"It's your funeral," she muttered, hoping the testosterone explosion wouldn't get bloody. She shifted to stand because she didn't want to sit while Maddox stood over her. A power move.

"Stay." Maddox pointed at the sofa as he reached her section.

She bristled, ignoring his order and straightening. "I'm not a dog."

"Sit the fuck down, Zoe!" Maddox demanded, invading her personal space.

"Don't talk to her like—" Noah took a step and was cut off when, in a flash, Maddox pointed a handgun between his eyeballs.

"I dare you. Finish that sentence," Maddox growled, fingers hovering around the trigger. He must have come in here with the gun in his hand because she didn't see him pull it out.

Noah's face puffed up in anger, but he said nothing, the two men in a glaring contest.

Zoe resisted rolling her eyes heavenwards. Usually, this ridiculous show of machismo disinterested her.

Still, watching Maddox display this level of primal possessiveness for her somehow made something melt inside her. She knew instantly that his promise about defending her against the world was genuine.

If she wanted to use him as a weapon against anyone, she could. An exhilarating discovery. Yet, she couldn't help wondering who would defend her husband from her. From her father. Because she was dangerous to him, and so was her father.

Right now, he looked impenetrable. Behind him were the two bears—Joshua and Josiah. Idehen was here, too, talking to the other guests and having them ushered out by security.

Her body temperature rose, and her skin tingled. What kind of influence did her husband wield? He could walk into a club VIP section and flash a weapon without interception by security?

She wasn't afraid. Maddox wouldn't harm her.

However, there was no guarantee for her Second. He was outnumbered and, honestly, outmatched. To save him, she had to defuse the situation.

She lowered her body onto the sofa. Hopefully, obeying Maddox's command would soothe him a little.

"Noah, apologise to my husband immediately," she ordered coolly.

He blinked several times, turning to look at her with a what-are-you-doing expression.

"You have no right to disrespect Maddox. He is my husband, and I've emphasized it to you several times. I am Mrs Maddox Ejiofor. So, apologise right away."

Noah flinched as if she'd hit him. And she might as well. She was using him as a scapegoat to salvage the situation. Moreover, she'd warned him, but he didn't listen.

Maddox couldn't be seen to lose face in front of his men or Noah. It was vital for him to be seen as vicious and fierce, ready to take down anyone who disrespected him.

It would keep him alive for longer.

Otherwise, if her father got a whiff of Maddox softening or being easily manipulated, he would send the boys after him. And not wait for Zoe to do it herself.

She needed to keep her husband alive. And if anyone was going to kill him, it would be her.

"I'm sorry, Mad—" Noah started.

"It's Mazị Ejiofor to you," Maddox interrupted.

Noah grimaced, shifting uneasily. "Mazị Ejiofor, I didn't mean any insolence."

"If you insult me again, you won't live to apologise. Now, get out!" her husband gritted out.

Noah glanced at her, nodded, and walked out with clipped footsteps.

She puffed out a sigh, but the relief didn't last long as Maddox holstered his weapon inside his jacket and swivelled to face her.

His eyes were dark, burrowing deep into her. It was like he was calculating what to do with her. How to punish her.

And as he stood there looking like he would make her pay for her misdemeanours in the most painful, most ecstatic ways possible, she made a realisation.

She wanted her husband.

Not just physically. Not just sexually.

She wanted him as her husband.

She needed him in all the ways she should need her husband.

Their night together, two months ago, had been the most exhilarating sexual experience she'd had. She'd been with other men but had never been able to relax until then. Until Maddox.

Despite everything she'd done to him and his fury, when he stared at her, he saw her. Not her status. Not her family. Not her father's empire. Just her.

He wanted her.

She wanted him. A scary notion, sending tremors through her. Not about the impending punishment. But for wanting her husband when she shouldn't.

Her heart was a drum beating loudly in her ears.

She tried to stand again. Maybe it was best if they left.

But he shook his head and approached the low table to sit beside her. He placed one arm around her shoulders and waved at the waiter with the other. When the lady came over, he ordered a bottle of water. The woman rushed off and returned with a dewy magnum, which she opened and poured some into the glass she had brought.

She hurried off again.

Maddox lifted the tumbler, directing it to Zoe.

She was reluctant to dilute the fizz of alcohol in her veins, hoping it would mask the pain coming her way. She swallowed before speaking. "I don't want it."

"Drink it," he ordered.

Sighing, she took the glass and drank some.

"All of it."

"Fine."

It was refreshing and quenched her dry mouth. But she didn't bother giving him the satisfaction. She gulped the rest down, and he placed the glass on the table.

His arm stayed around her shoulders, fingers gripping her skin. They stayed silent. He watched her while she watched the dancers through the Perspex. The two bears seemed to have left with Noah, and the VIP lounge was almost empty except for the service staff.

The loud music faded, and she was in a cocoon with him.

He took a deep breath, making her turn to glance at him.

"Why, Zoe? I finally give you the freedom of my home, and the first thing you do is to come and see your ex," his voice was low, calm.

Still, his anger remained apparent in the tightening of his jaw and the hardening of his lips.

Lips which kissed her five days ago, and she'd bitten him.

Lips she'd tried to kiss this afternoon, but he'd rejected her.

Lips she wanted to kiss tonight. Heaven help her.

"Do you just like to irritate me?" he continued. "You've been provoking me since you arrived."

"I can't help it. It's who I am," she replied, and it was the truth.

His eyes narrowed, and he tilted his head, studying her again.

"I've tried to be gentle with you. Tried to go easy on you. But it doesn't work. Is it that you want me to be stern and tough with you? Is that how you want me?" he asked quietly, making her strain to hear him.

She swallowed the lump in her throat because he hit the nail on the head. "Maddox, you must be tough."

A weak man couldn't endure her or her father. She wanted her husband to live. He needed to stay strong and relentless. Ruthless.

"With you?" he asked as if for confirmation.

"Yes, with me. With everything. If you want to survive this marriage. You must be tough with me," she said, trying not to choke on her words. Hoping he could read between the lines and know that one day, she could fire the bullet, which would end his life.

He nodded once before Idehen approached.

"Maddox, your suite is ready," the big man said, holding an electronic card. "The Purple Room is on the third level."

"Thank you, Idehen." Maddox shook hands with the man and took the key.

"Let us know if you need anything else." Idehen dipped his head at Zoe before walking away.

Maddox booked a suite at Arufin? Didn't he say they wouldn't have sex? Why would he book a suite?

He turned and extended his hand towards Zoe.

She reached for him, accepting his soundless invitation. Was the suite for them? She didn't want to ask him. Didn't want to jinx it. Trepidation and excitement rolled through her as he pulled her up.

Silently, they walked out of the VIP Lounge, through the busy club and back into the exclusive foyer before taking the lift to the third level. He didn't release her hand as he inserted the key into the door and pushed it open.

Soft jazz music reached her as the light flicked on. The walls were a glittery charcoal colour. The furniture uniquely handmade from black metal, and the soft furnishings covered in purple velvet, giving the place a luxurious, romantic atmosphere. Potted plants sat in the corners, while a bouquet of pink roses sat in a vase on the table.

He shut the door, locking it. Then he released her hand.

"Say something, Maddox. Why are we here?" she asked, his silence rattling her nerves.

He shrugged his jacket off, walked to the wardrobe, and hung it up. When he faced her, the black holster over his left shoulder and black shirt was visible.

"Go into the bathroom. Use it. Then strip everything off, Zoe. Everything, before you come out," he ordered quietly.

"Why?" Her body trembled a little because she could guess why.

"Because I'm going to punish you," he said calmly as if it was the most natural thing in the world.

She swallowed. "I didn't come here to fuck Noah."

She didn't want him to think of her as the cheating kind. She abhorred all forms of spousal cheating.

"I know," he said just as quietly as before.

"Then, why?"

"Because it's what you need."

A feeling of serenity settled onto her for the first time tonight, and she nodded. He understood. Maybe not everything, but enough to matter.

TWENTY-TWO

Zoe's stomach churned as she stripped off her clothes in the bathroom. She knew what was coming. She wanted what was coming, inexplicably. Yet, she couldn't stop her hands from shaking, making her take longer than usual to remove her clothing.

She half expected Maddox to stomp into the bathroom and drag her out because she was delaying the inevitable. However, he didn't. This was another compelling aspect of him. Despite his anger, he remained composed.

Sure, he'd pointed a weapon at Noah, but her Second had been out of order, interfering in a private matter between husband and wife without invitation. Hell, she would have shot him if his disrespect had been directed at her and he was a rival.

However, after Noah's departure and Maddox focused on Zoe, his poise was intact. He hadn't raised his voice since. Not even when he'd ordered her to go to the bathroom and strip.

A man who could control himself even when faced with provocative situations was rare in her circles.

Maddox had broken the myth of what she thought enforcers should be.

Norbert, her father's late enforcer, had been a vicious man who lost his temper and self-control at every irritation. It was the reason the boys feared him. No one wanted to be on the receiving end of his violent outburst.

A part of her had expected Maddox, wanted him to be as violent as Norbert, to justify her actions when she eventually killed him.

Instead, despite the many times she'd provoked Maddox, he'd shown restraint and patience. Sure, he'd locked her in the basement. But that had been for her safety as well as his.

If she'd married Norbert as her father had once planned, the man would not have tolerated her actions. He would have beaten her and probably attempted to force himself on her as per his rights as her husband. She would have had no qualms about killing him at the earliest opportunity.

However, now she was struggling to find reasons to follow through with her father's command to execute her husband.

Hence, the reason she was in this suite with Maddox tonight.

This was another test of his merit.

She needed to know that he was strong enough to handle her. Strong enough to deal with her father. Her family.

Because Heaven help her, she wanted her husband alive beyond their three-month marriage contract.

Naked, she sucked in a deep breath and walked to the bathroom door. She paused on the threshold as her heart slammed in her chest.

Maddox stood at the other end of the room, where there was clear space on the tiled flooring, away from the bed, table, chaise lounge and the deep shaggy rug. He was half-undressed—holster, shirt, shoes, and socks gone. Facing away from her, his back and arm muscles rippled.

She remembered tracing his skin with her fingers during their one-night stand. Remembered the scars. Now, she stared at them across his back. Long jagged contusions that could only have been made by weapons, a knife, maybe.

Agatha had mentioned Maddox was injured when he'd saved her. Was that when he'd received those injuries?

In reflex, Zoe's hands curled into fists, and she wanted to rip out the hearts of those who'd hurt Maddox. She'd never wanted to commit murder as much as at this moment, seeing her husband's old injuries for the first time.

He seemed unaware of her presence, fiddling with a metal T-bar with rubber grips suspended from the ceiling on a D-ring. Leather cuffs were attached to the ends. Was that for her? Would he restrain her?

Her limbs tingled, and her breath accelerated.

"Come here," he said, not looking at her, and his deep voice enveloped her.

She was startled out of her thoughts, realising he'd noticed her presence, although she was still at the bathroom entrance.

Obeying, she walked around to face him. Her usual compulsion to disregard orders seemingly vanished. The carpet was soft under her bare feet until she reached the cold, smooth, hard tiles.

Then she stopped in front of him, and the cool breeze from the air conditioner swirled around her body, making her nipples tighten.

His onyx gaze flickered with intense hunger, trailing heat over her body. Blood whooshed in her ears, and she couldn't look away from him either.

Their initial encounter had been under the cover of night and with no illumination. So this was the first time she saw him without clothes.

He was more than she expected.

Broad, muscular, rugged. Scarred.

Skin of walnut brown. Scent of bergamot and spice.

Added to the fierce slant of his full lips, the sharp cheekbones and the tight jawline.

He was gorgeous.

And he was hers. Her scarred, dangerous, gorgeous husband.

Her insides turned to jelly, and she wanted to reach out and touch him. Lean into his powerful chest.

But she waited because this was his show. And she didn't want to disappoint him. Didn't want to add to her regrets.

"Turn around," he ordered quietly.

She shuffled and gasped.

They stood in front of the full-length mirrors covering the wardrobe doors, providing a panoramic view of the suite. She could see everything he did to her from this angle.

And he could see everything. From the swell of her breasts and the taut nipples to the tiny strip of designer-waxed hair between her legs.

"Look up and grab the T-bar," he said.

She hesitated. He hadn't explicitly said what he would do to her as punishment. Aside from the T-bar, she couldn't see any immediate instruments of torture.

Unless leaving her holding the handles while naked was his preferred method. Still, she doubted it.

"Do I need to restrain you?" he asked in a stern voice.

"No." She swallowed, grateful for the option. "I don't want to be restrained."

"Then, do everything I tell you to do. Everything. Punishment time is not for questions or hesitations. If you can't trust that I won't harm you, then tell me to stop. I'll end it, we'll go home, and you'll be back in the basement in chains."

Shit. No. She didn't want that.

He was being strict. She'd requested for him to be uncompromising. So she couldn't fault him.

"Okay." She met his gaze in the mirror. Then she shuffled forward, stood on tiptoes and grabbed the bar handles.

Once she secured her palm around the rubber grip, she realised she couldn't return to normal standing. She would have to stay on tiptoes, which would strain her leg muscles. Her whole body. The only way to get comfortable would be to release the bars. Which would mean he would tie her up, or they would go home, and she'd be back in the basement.

The alternative would be the leather cuffs, which would restrain her, but she would have to give up control. She wouldn't be able to let go until he released her.

She met her husband's twinkling dark gaze in the mirror. An ingenious man, he'd set it up like this on purpose.

Her immediate options were to give up comfort or give up control.

Despite herself, she smiled, acknowledging his clever strategy. He'd figured her out, known she would choose no restraints and had adjusted the discomfort level to almost unbearable so she would have to give up control to get comfortable.

Perhaps there was hope for him. Maybe he could handle her, and he was precisely the man she needed.

She didn't know how long she would hold onto the bar, so better to have some comfort and room for manoeuvre. Her calf muscles were already protesting.

"Do you want to change your mind about the restraints?" he asked, still holding her gaze.

"Yes." She swallowed. "Please."

She had to trust that she was safe in his hands. He hadn't harmed her so far, even though he'd had plenty of opportunities to do so. Only her ingrained suspicions made her default to wanting to be in charge of everything.

Right now, he'd made it impossible.

He nodded and stepped close to her. His body heat caressed her back as he reached up and grabbed the first leather cuff. He secured it around her right wrist, the insides soft, cushiony, and yet, the strap firm. The cuff was linked to the bar by a chain. Then he did the same thing with her left wrist. "You can release the bar."

She lowered her hands, and her feet returned flat on the floor, yet her hands stayed above her head. In this position, she could move and remain attached to the bar.

Tension tightened her shoulders, and her jaw clenched.

"Are you comfortable?" he asked as if sensing her unease.

"No," she grumbled. "I don't like being restrained."

His flashed white teeth like a shark. "You're not supposed to like it. It's a punishment."

Still, surprisingly, he lowered his hands onto her shoulders, squeezing and massaging them.

"Oh," she sighed. Her lashes fluttered shut, and her muscles relaxed. His touch burned his skin, waking parts of her, sparking desire. This wasn't so bad for a punishment. The urge to lean into his chest sizzled in her veins. She wished for his arms around her, holding her tight. Wished for his kisses, his caresses. Floated in a daydream of the two of them intertwined.

The swish of leather against fabric woke her, and her eyes flew open. In the mirror, she watched him pull his belt out of the loops and fold it in half.

Her breath locked in her throat.

Shit. He was going to belt her like he'd threatened this afternoon.

***

Maddox sensed Zoe's presence as soon as she exited the bathroom.

At first, he'd thought she'd been unsure of what to do as she stood on the threshold. However, he'd felt the heat of her gaze on his back as he adjusted the T-bar.

She didn't argue or hesitate when he ordered her to come over. And as she stood in front of him, she'd appeared uncertain. It was strange to see one of the most fearless women he'd ever encountered this way.

She appeared subdued and had obeyed his order. Perhaps for the first time since her arrival in his house. Since she became his wife.

Adrenaline flowed through him. It was such a rush to finally have her submit in this way. In fact, it was surprising, considering how their wedding night had ended.

But today had brought a few surprises.

First, seeing her distress in the basement and her refusal to allow him to soothe her. Instead, she'd demanded sex and had been furious when he'd refused.

Then she'd left the house and had come out to Arufin. He'd popped out to run an errand, and Jaxon had called him to say that she'd gone. Then he'd called Agatha, who'd told him of their location.

Finding out she'd come to Arufin had set off alarm bells. Of course, Agatha had also informed him that Zoe had met Noah here. That had jacked up Maddox's anger.

It wasn't until he'd arrived here and met with Idehen, who'd informed him about her viewing the footage from their one-night encounter, that it had clicked.

Zoe had come here because she didn't trust him and wanted evidence from their night together to substantiate her suspicions. She was looking for reasons to escape their marriage.

So when he'd shown up in the VIP lounge, he'd been expecting a fight and had gone prepared, gun in hand. No way would he give up his wife before the agreed date. He would have shot her second-in-command if necessary.

However, Zoe had stunned him. By publicly acknowledging he was her husband and demanding an apology from Noah on his behalf. It was the blanket that smothered his rage. So when Noah apologised and left, he took Maddox's anger with him.

All he was left with now was a determination to correct his wife's misdemeanours and set them both on a new path, which would hopefully help them heal from the past.

Now that she was naked, standing in front of him, restrained by the cuffs, she was beautiful.

His imagination, based on their encounter in the dark, had not done her justice. She had the perfect balance of boobs and ass, the curves dipping in at the dainty waist before sloping out. This close, her hair was a dark brown rather than black as he'd originally thought. She wrapped it in a bun, giving him an unimpeded view of her back. Her skin was pristine, smooth, and dark, like roasted coffee.

He knew she'd never been this exposed to any other man. Never been this vulnerable with anyone else.

His dick hardened. His fingers itched with the urge to claim her, to make her his, to make her scream.

He grabbed the remote and increased the volume of the Bluetooth speakers playing jazz music. Then he pulled his leather belt from the hoop and folded it in half, holding onto the edge and buckle.

Her eyes widened in the mirror, her mouth popping open.

"Don't twist around. I don't want to mark your front," he said, moving to the side.

He wanted her tears. But he didn't want to damage her skin.

She smiled nervously and nodded, lowering her gaze as if not wanting to see what he was about to do.

He flicked his arm, connecting the leather strap to the flesh of her bum in the first lash, burning a line into her skin.

She gasped, and her body rocked forward, making the chain above her head rattle.

Their gazes met briefly in the mirror before she bowed her head, settling again.

The second lash lined up just above the first. This time, she cried out as if the air was pushed from her lungs.

When she settled down, he delivered the third and the fourth in quick succession, not giving her time to get out of position.

She jumped out of reach and glared at him. "How many am I getting?"

He didn't reply. Instead, he pointed at the spot. "Get back into position."

"But I told you I didn't come here to fuck Noah," she grumbled.

"This isn't about your ex. This is about you, Zoe. About your attitude since we got married. About you shooting at me. About you constantly provoking me. After tonight, your slate is wiped clean, and we start afresh. We will live together as husband and wife. You want that, right?"

"Yes!"

"Then get back into position. Now!" His fist tightened around the belt.

After a beat, she shuffled back into position. Her hands were clenched, and her shoulders tight. She squeezed her eyes shut as if it would block out what he was doing.

He settled in place and delivered another strike. This time harder than before, making her gasp. Making him glad he increased the volume of the music. He continued lashing her, again and again, her sounds mixing with the jazz in glorious symphony. Each line was laid carefully and neatly from the small of her back to the back of her knees with no intersections or crosses, ensuring the skin wasn't broken.

Zoe breathed hard, struggling to stay in position and failing but too vain to beg for mercy. His fearless Ice Queen.

At ten, he paused and stepped close to her, pressing his rock-hard crotch to her bum. "Are you wet, Zoe?"

She startled, her red-rimmed gaze darting around as she licked her lip. "What?"

"You heard me. If I put my fingers in your pussy, will I find you wet?"

"You're crazy."

"Am I?" He pinched her nipple with the hand holding the belt and slid the other down her belly. He rubbed his fingers between her folds and met slick flesh. "What's this?"

She avoided his gaze, craning her neck upwards, although she didn't move her bum away from his crotch.

Okay. There had to be a different way to reach her, to soften her, because the pain alone wasn't affecting her.

He fisted his hand in her hair, making her tilt back. Then he whispered in her ear. "Mimi, would you like Nnanna to make you come?"

Her breath hitched, and she tried to nod.

He flicked the belt on the back of her thigh. "Beg for my hand."

For the first time, tears welled in her eyes and dripped down her cheeks. "Please, I need Nnanna to make me cum."

He dropped the belt, wrapping his arms around her, one hand squeezing her boobs, pinching her nipples. The other slid into her pussy, rubbing her clit.

He watched her face in the mirror as she gasped and moaned and writhed against him.

"That's my Mimi. My queen. Come for me," he whispered, cajoling and tweaking her nipples and clit.

As if she'd been waiting for his command, she splintered, her body rocking against his arms, moaning hard first, and then she started sobbing as her orgasm ebbed.

He leaned up, releasing the cuffs and chain from the bar. She curled into him as he carried her cuffs and all to the chaise lounge, situated nearer than the bed. He settled on it with her on his lap and let her cry. And she allowed him to hold her for the first time since they married.

Finally, she submitted to him.

TWENTY-THREE

One minute, Zoe flew in ecstasy, floating on a cloud of blissful climax. The next, she was knocked out by a wave of overwhelming remorse. A lump sat in her throat, her eyes welled up with tears, and unable to stop it, she'd sobbed, burying her face in his chest as Maddox carried her to the settee.

When he changed tactics by adding pleasure to the punishment, it unlocked something tremendous inside her. It stripped away all the defensive layers around her heart and mind. It laid her bare. As bare as she'd been the night they made love months ago at Arufin. He'd done something to her no other lover had ever done. She'd relaxed in his company and allowed him to love her like no one else.

This afternoon, he'd tried to soothe her when she'd had a panic attack. However, she'd rejected his gesture because she feared appearing weak.

Yet, now she allowed him to hold her, to comfort her like never before. As he cradled her in the cocoon of his arms, she re-examined all the choices leading her to this moment.

Throughout her life, she'd been conditioned to withstand pain—emotional and physical—because there was so much of it around her. Although she couldn't claim to be immune to pain, she could detach her mind from it, a technique she'd learned over the years from living with her father.

Having to deal with knowing she wasn't good enough for her father because she'd been born female. Having to prove herself repeatedly with the goal post moving each time she achieved one.

She'd come from an environment where every life was disposable. Taking and losing lives was par for the course in the Himba clan. A rival's life. An enemy's life. Even someone who showed you the slightest disrespect. A bodyguard was there to take a bullet for the boss. A shugaba was there to serve the boss. If the boss ordered you to kill anyone, you wouldn't hesitate, even if it was someone you were entangled with. Because the boss was the law.

Hence, she'd been quick to threaten Maddox and fire her weapon at him. And why the decision to abort her baby to save her position in the Himba clan had been inevitable.

Yet, Maddox had shown her a different way of life. He was concerned about saving lives and protecting people—his family, team, and clan.

Even her.

"I will defend you against the world," he'd said earlier today, and she believed him.

Yet, she couldn't offer him the same reassurances, making her feel more wretched. She'd become entangled with her husband in a way she hadn't expected.

"I've got you," he whispered into her hair, rubbing her back gently. "I've got you, Zoe. Twenty-four-seven."

"Do you promise?" she choked out as her throat clogged. She almost didn't recognise her voice. Herself. Who was this soft woman who yearned for everything he was offering?

"I do. I'll always have your back. Trust me," he said quietly, confidently.

He wasn't boasting to win her over or being forceful.

He was making a solemn vow he would honour with his last breath.

And she was supposed to be the one to end his life.

Weighted with regret, she squeezed her eyes shut and clung onto his neck, head on his shoulders, his body keeping her warm in the otherwise cold room. "Why, Maddox, why? Can't you see that I can't make the same promise to you? I can't promise to have your back in return."

"That's okay."

"No, it's not."

"Listen to me, Zoe. You don't have to make any other promises except to be my wife and accept me as your husband."

She leaned back, blinking to see his face. "Is that really all you want from me?"

"For now, yes. Let me take care of you. You've spent so long being on guard, not letting anyone close enough to care for you. Let me be your guard. Let me watch your back for a change so you can experience how it feels. Perhaps by seeing me take care of you, you'll learn to reciprocate."

"You hope," she said because there was no guarantee she would care about him the way he expected. Then again, why was she filled with regret—belly knotted and struggling to take deep breaths—if she wasn't falling for him. She, who had never opened herself up to a lover before, was getting attached to the man she'd been ordered to kill by her father?

"I hope," he said, his lips curving into a grin. "I also hoped we could get away for a few days on a break."

"A break? You mean like a holiday."

"Yes, a mini holiday. A honeymoon."

"A honeymoon. Us?" she giggled. It sounded ridiculous.

"Yes, us." He tilted her chin up, grinning. "We are newlyweds, and this is still our honeymoon period."

"True." Warmth spread through her as he stared into her eyes as if she were his sole focus. "The past few months have been hectic, and I could use a break. But I have work and meetings with clients next week. I didn't plan on being wedded so soon."

She smiled at him, and he chuckled, the rich, rumbly sound melting her insides.

"That's fair enough. We'll take a few days to rejig our schedules. Then I'm taking you far away from here, where it's just the two of us."

"And we can finally consummate our wedding?" she asked, remembering what he'd said about no sex. "Are you serious about us not having sex?"

She could not understand why he'd made the decree. He was attracted to her. She saw his desire in his demeanour. In his heated gaze.

Yet, his features rumpled, and he moved her aside before standing. He scrubbed his hand over his head, looking agitated. "It's the one thing I can't get over, Zoe."

"Are you saying you don't feel desire for me?" The idea made her sick. Then again, he'd sported an erection when he'd pressed up against her earlier while he'd been punishing her.

"That's not what I'm saying. Far from it. I want to fuck you from here to next Sunday. But I can't deal with another loss, Zoe. I can't. You aborted my baby without telling me, and you could do it again. I'm struggling to shake off the dread."

Like being hit by a ton of bricks, his pain and grief suddenly made sense. She crumpled under the weight of remorse.

"Oh no." Her chin quivered, and she held her stomach, fighting nausea.

"Maddox, I'm sorry," she apologised to a man who wasn't Baba for the first time. "I didn't realise you would hurt like this. It wasn't my intention, believe me."

She swallowed the lump in her throat. "I've spent my life surrounded by men who have no qualms ordering women to abort pregnancies that I never considered you would be attached to or care about yours. Plus, I was angry at you for the wrong reasons, so I didn't tell you in advance. For that, I'm sorry. I really am. Please forgive me."

She bent over, staring at the floor, body shaking. Why did she feel awful for hurting him? She'd never cared before. Shouldn't care. Yet, she craved to hear the quiet rumble of his voice, reassuring her everything would be okay between them.

He didn't respond for several minutes.

The knot in her belly tightened. She kept her head down as silent tears ran down her face. She couldn't blame him for not forgiving her. She wasn't sure she would forgive him so readily if she'd been the offended party.

"Look at me," he said eventually.

She lifted her head, swiping her face with her palms.

"Why are you sorry? You weren't sorry when we got married. You weren't sorry this afternoon. What's changed?"

She swallowed and nodded, deciding to come clean about some things. "Since we married, your actions and words have differed from my expectations. You've made me question certain things about myself, leaving me conflicted. For example, when I found out I was pregnant, I couldn't believe it. I'd been with other men using the same brand and never gotten pregnant. Yet, with you, it didn't work. I thought you must have tampered with the condom I gave you to use that night."

"What?" He took a step back, eyebrows raised. "Why would you think that?"

"It was the only thing I could think to explain the pregnancy."

"Accidents happen, Zoe!"

"Not to me! Anyway, it's what I thought, and it made me angry at you. I knew I couldn't keep the baby anyway because it would scupper my father's succession plan. And Baba wouldn't let me have a baby outside wedlock. Then there was the marriage auction, which I hated."

His forehead furrowed. "You hated it? Why?"

The muscles on her neck stiffened in remembered annoyance. "Because all those suitors were there because of the business deal with Baba. I was just the sweetener. Valuable merchandise but still merchandise. I didn't want to marry any of them."

"And then I showed up and made a bad situation worse," Maddox said and started pacing. "You were already feeling shitty and angry at me. Then I showed up as one of those suitors you didn't want, trying to make a deal with your father, and you hated me even more."

"Yes?" She grimaced as he reprimanded himself.

"Shit," he swore, pacing some more. She hadn't seen him this agitated before. "Shit."

"What is it?" she asked, not understanding his sudden change.

He swivelled and strode to her. "Move over."

She shifted, and he sat on the settee beside her, taking her hand.

"What is it?" she asked, searching his face.

"I need to explain something. After our night together, I wanted to see you again and hoped you would contact me. So when I found out who you were, I called immediately, hoping to see you again. When you told me you were pregnant, I didn't even consider that you didn't want the child. Then, when you said you didn't want contact with me, there was no way I would let you raise my child without my input. I saw the marriage auction as an opportunity to convince you and your parents that we could work things out. So, I asked Chief Odili for permission since you'd already rejected Mason's proposal. I didn't consider for one second that you were being bullied into participating in the marriage auction." He shook his head. "I'm sorry for not seeing it earlier."

"You have no reason to be sorry," she countered, rushing to defend him as he couldn't have known her situation at home.

"I need to apologise because I didn't give you any grace. It's the reason Amaoge was angry at me when she said you were brave enough to do what you needed. You had to deal with the pressure from your parents. Pressure from the marriage auction. Pressure from me, the stranger you'd had a one-night stand with. Pressure with the pregnancy. Something had to give. And it was the pregnancy. I get it." He sounded choked.

Tears clogged her eyes that he could be so understanding.

"I finally get it," he continued. "And I'm sorry that I added to your stress. I showed up at your house with my family and put you on the spot when we were little more than strangers. I was arrogant to think you would accept my proposal. Please forgive me."

"How did I get this lucky?" she said huskily. She couldn't believe he was asking for forgiveness, considering how angry he'd been. "I forgive you as long as you forgive me."

She leaned into him, pressing her lips against his tentatively, not knowing if he would reject her again.

He cupped her face, taking her cheeks in his hands, wiping her tears with his thumbs before leaning in and kissing her, pulling her towards him.

"I forgive you," he said, breaking the kiss to look her in the eyes.

The constriction in her chest eased a little, and she confessed in a husky whisper, "I need you."

In response, he scooped her into his arms and carried her to the bed, laying her flat. Without breaking eye contact, he pushed his trousers down, stepping out. "That's all you ever have to do."

"What?" she croaked.

"Speak your need for me, and I'm yours."

Her heart picked up speed. It was what he'd meant this afternoon. All she had to do was confess her need for him, and he would deliver it. Just like he was about to break his own rules.

He leaned over her, hands braced on the mattress as he lined himself up with her sore. Then he pushed in, holding her gaze and not flinching. Stretching her, filling her up until he was all the way to the hilt.

So close that he couldn't possibly get any closer.

Her breath hitched, and her body heated.

It was so good to feel his weight on top of her and solidity inside her.

"Mimmiii," he growled in a guttural voice. "I missed you."

"I missed you too," she said huskily.

When he used her middle name, the name they'd first known each other intimately, she knew it was just the two of them. It was the husband and wife. The lovers. There was no enforcer here. No shugaba. Just two people who needed to share a private, sensual moment.

Two people who needed to love each other.

Her heart jolted, and her body overheated.

What was she thinking? Was this love? Would she even be able to recognise love if she felt it for him?

She'd just told him something she hadn't told anyone else, and she probably would never experience anything like this with anyone else.

But was it love?

She'd never felt so vulnerable, like she was fracturing, breaking apart.

Yet she wasn't afraid because somehow he would put all her pieces together.

He was making love to her.

The slow, deep thrust was not like their first time. This was different. Like he was taking time to savour every inch of her tight, warm depths.

There was a tautness in her chest. She leaned up, reaching for and kissing him sweetly like she'd never kissed anyone.

Her heart swelled with warmth. "Nnanna…"

"Yes, Mimi." He caressed her cheek and jaw, tracing the lips down to her throat and the delicate hollow of her collar. "I almost forgot how much I love your pussy."

His dirty talking was as devastating as his lovemaking, fueling her need, feeding her desire.

His hand curled around her shoulder to her nape, and he lifted her head, kissing her deeply as she wrapped her legs around his hips. He carried on with the slow, deep fucking, and she couldn't get enough of him.

Then he gripped her knees, bending them forward, spreading her wide. He glanced at where they were joined to see himself sliding in deeper.

The fever started tingling through her, sending her towards the edge of bliss.

"How do you feel? Is it good—"

"Yes! I'm coming."

The pressure built slowly with each thrust, his hips rolling, grazing her clit and adding to the sensations engulfing her.

"Good, Mimi. Look at me. Let me see you come," he growled, watching her face as she clawed his shoulders.

Then she was trembling, squeezing, and going soft all over, turning into liquid, crashing with a long, "Oh… Oh."

"Fuck." He grabbed her hips, his dick ramming into her pussy as his hips snapped against her until he was grunting his release into her.

He stayed over her, watching her, his dick still throbbing inside her as if he couldn't get enough of her.

The realisation dawned. They'd made love without a condom.

Where would they go from here?

TWENTY-FOUR

The following morning, Zoe opened her eyes, expecting to see dawn's grey light from the wet room window, illuminating the off-white basement ceiling. Instead, darkness surrounded her.

She blinked several times, glancing around. Slivers of grey light slipped through the edges of the blinds, obscuring the floor-to-ceiling glass taking up most of one wall. This wasn't the basement she'd slept in the past week. The fresh air blowing on her face from an overhead AC was another clue.

Yesterday's events flashed through her mind.

Maddox coming down to the basement for the first time in almost a week. Their argument. His ultimatum.

"Be my queen or be my prisoner … To be my queen, you must submit to me as my wife."

Then she'd admitted she didn't know how to submit. How to be a wife.

And he'd promised to defend her.

More than anything else he'd said or done, those words cracked the barrier around her heart. For the first time since their one-night stand, she'd been receptive to him. Had wanted a re-enactment of their night together.

Then he'd insisted they wouldn't have sex, which threw her into turmoil.

She'd wanted a way to reseal her heart. To stop the trickle of emotions before they turned into a wave she couldn't control.

And she'd thought visiting Arufin would provide the answer to her dilemma. But she'd discovered something totally different in the video replay from the Black Room.

"Your husband is a good man," Agatha told her yesterday.

That video had substantiated those words.

And he'd proven it when he'd eventually turned up at Arufin to claim his wife like she'd expected he would.

Sure, he'd punished her. The smack of the leather belt on her skin exacerbated the remorse inside her. However, she hadn't realised the pain could turn into something so blissful, so cathartic, until he'd touched her intimately. She'd exploded into the most intense orgasm ever, ripping her open and exposing all the concealed emotions.

She hadn't felt constrained by her life, the personality she was expected to always wear. Don Himba's daughter. A shugaba in the Himba clan. None of those things mattered last night.

She'd felt safe with Maddox. Safe enough to confess some of her secrets.

Instead of anger, he'd apologised and begged her forgiveness—the last thing she'd expected. He'd disarmed her, removed any hangups, and left her defenceless.

No, not defenceless. She was guarded by the best, physically and emotionally.

He'd promised to guard her with his life, and she believed he wouldn't abuse the access he had to her emotional well-being.

He'd been right. She'd never allowed anyone close until him.

Her limbs ached in the most gratifying way as she stretched, turning to stare at the man in bed with her.

Her husband.

For the first time since she signed the marriage contract, she didn't feel resentment or scepticism about the status.

Instead, warmth suffused her chest as she watched the sleeping figure tangled in the sheets beside her. He lay on his side, head on a pillow facing her, his arm curled over her waist, one leg thrust between hers.

Miji na. The Hausa phrase meaning 'my husband' whispered in her mind. *Mine.*

A covetousness she'd never felt made her heart swell and her rib cage tight.

Maddox was hers. Hers to claim. Hers to possess.

She was a selfish lover, domineering and controlling. Regardless of the brevity of her previous sexual affairs, she demanded total devotion from her lovers.

However, this feeling was more than just a jealous streak or a need to possess Maddox.

There was an unexpected and alien protectiveness. An urge to keep her husband safe.

In a short while, he was pulling strange, new reactions from her.

She was in uncharted territory and conflicted, her body becoming heavy.

What did this mean for her plans? Her mission? Her father's command.

Protecting her husband meant disobeying Baba. Something she'd never done before. Her father was her boss. Going against his order had never been an option before.

Was it now?

Her chest squeezed tight.

She couldn't consider hurting her husband or killing him.

Her hand clenched around the sheet as her jaw tightened. A headache loomed, and she closed her eyes, inhaling and exhaling to draw air deep into her lungs, hoping to stave the opposing emotions.

He murmured intelligibly, shifting closer, his musk filling her nostrils.

After the session at Arufin, they'd returned to his home—her home too for the next two months and three weeks—and continued the lovemaking. Their time in Arufin had been tame compared to what they'd done in this bedroom.

Her entire body heated in remembrance, her clit pulsing.

Their clothes trailed from the doorway, where they'd started tearing each other's garments off as soon as the bedroom door was shut. They'd been insatiable, thoroughly indulging in each other.

Sex with her husband was ah-may-zing! Passionate and mind-blowing. She'd come so many times, countless. He was a considerate lover, vigorous too. She could still feel him everywhere. Her pussy, her skin, her mouth. Her body ached delightfully.

For sure, her incredible husband knew how to satisfy her. How to make her yearn for him.

She squirmed as her pussy throbbed and intense craving twisted in her belly.

Momentarily, her breathing accelerated with her racing pulse as terror gripped her.

This euphoric, encompassing need for her husband had to be wrong. Surely, nothing this good could last. It certainly couldn't end well.

And it was screwing with her. Had the potential to ruin everything she'd worked for all her life.

Yet as she watched Maddox sleep, his vulnerability at this moment called to protective instincts she'd never felt.

He had no one else to defend him right now. He was powerless. Unguarded.

She was his last line of defence. His security.

Woe betide anyone who tried to hurt him. They would have to deal with her.

There would be consequences. But she wouldn't think about it now.

She had two months and three weeks with her husband. And she would enjoy every minute of their time together.

Her stomach growled. Yet she was reluctant to tear herself away from her man to search for food. She hadn't eaten much since lunch yesterday. Just a suya bought from an outdoor restaurant near Arufin, which they'd eaten on the drive home last night.

Each time she stared at Maddox, her heart took up a staccato rhythm. Puffs of air from his slightly open mouth fanned her forehead, his chest rising and falling in pattern, the scars and muscles rippling with his breathing.

She was tempted to pepper his scars with kisses, to wake him from slumber and arouse him into making love.

But she remembered their first night together. Remembered the video she'd watched. How he'd covered her up after she'd fallen asleep and had just held her when it was apparent he'd wanted more sex. Even when he'd had to leave, he'd instructed Idehen to ensure that she was undisturbed so she could sleep.

Her considerate husband had foregone his pleasure for her comfort.

It was about time she started doing things for him in appreciation.

Reciprocation. She was learning how to care for him from the way he cared for her.

Reluctantly, she detached her body from her husband's as gently as she could and slipped out of bed. Her feet hit the rug, and she padded across the room, grabbing the discarded clothes littering the place and smiling like an idiot.

How could seeing their trail of clothes leave her feeling giddy with joy?

Perhaps because she could picture them at each point in the trail of clothes. Tearing his shirt off at the door as he kissed her. Ripping her panties off before burying his face in her pussy. Using his tongue to bring her pleasure as he shoved his trousers down.

She walked into the bathroom and used it briefly before grabbing a fresh pair of knickers. Then, without rhyme or reason, she pulled on Maddox's shirt—the one he'd discarded last night. She had her luggage here, her clothes. Yet she preferred his used shirt. It was too big and almost knee-length. She had to roll up the sleeves to see her fingers and hand. Yet each deep inhale filled her nose with his spicey scent.

And that grim returned to her face. She loved how his smell surrounded her like a warm, soothing blanket. Marking her skin.

With another glance at Maddox, she grabbed her phone and tiptoed into the hallway and down the stairs, walking to the kitchen. It wasn't massive like the one in her father's house, but it was impressive and modern, fitted with gadgets found in contemporary kitchens.

Surprising, considering the only people who lived here were men until she'd arrived. He didn't have live-in staff, although a cleaner came twice weekly.

She wasn't a domestic goddess, although she knew how to cook. Her parents' home was equipped with servants catering to her needs. However, she'd lived away from while she'd been at university and Law School afterwards.

Anyway, her husband had been feeding her all week, even going out of his way to provide some of her favourite meals. He'd been exceeding generous while she'd been difficult for the past week.

Perhaps she could start by cooking his favourite breakfast meal. Shame she didn't know what it was. Hopefully, his sister would know.

She grabbed her phone and sent Amaoge a brief text. Then, she set the coffee machine to brew as she checked out the food store. The fridge had fresh food, while the freezer held stacks of labelled containers filled with already prepared frozen food.

Maddox had some of his meals prepared by a chef and then frozen. So he didn't have to cook from scratch at every meal or order takeaway. Clever and a handy alternative to having a private chef.

Her phone pinged, and she grabbed it. The notification was from Amaoge.

Maddox likes omelettes for breakfast. If you add fried plantain and yam, even better.

A second text came immediately.

You're making breakfast for Maddox? When you get a moment from your honeymoon, call me! I want to hear the full gist.

Zoe smiled as she sent a reply: *Thank you. Will call you soon.*

She could understand Amaoge's surprise. She was cooking breakfast for Maddox. For a man!

However, Maddox made this easy for her. He wasn't forcing any archaic gender roles on her, and she wasn't doing it because he expected it. She wanted to do something nice for him. Period.

She went about gathering and preparing the ingredients. She'd finished frying the plantain when Maddox strolled into the kitchen wearing a pair of low-slung khaki shorts.

"That smells yummy." He stood by the door, surveying the scene.

She became speechless as the gorgeous man walked toward her. His broad shoulders, toned chest, and ripped abs left her breathless. The scars on his body only added to his masculine beauty.

She blatantly gawked at him, and his gorgeous smile took her breath away.

"I'm making breakfast," she explained the aromas, snapping out of the sexual fog.

Locking his arms around her from behind, he pressed his body flush against hers. He pushed her hair away from her face and buried his nose in her neck, inhaling deeply.

"I'm not talking about the food on the cooker," he whispered, his voice heavy with lust as his erection brushed her bum. His fingers crept under the hem of the shirt, caressing her bare thigh.

"Oh," she muttered, pulse race accelerating. Her yearning returned.

"I love you in my shirt." He nipped her earlobe before kissing the exposed skin on her neck and shoulder. Intoxicated, she dropped the knife she'd used to slice the plantain and switched off the hob. She leaned her head against his chest, arching into him as his fingers roamed her hip. "Are you sore, Mimi?"

Whenever he used her middle name, it was full of affection, an endearment. She melted for him, shaking her head. "No. But I was making an omelette for you."

She whimpered as his fingers slipped past her undies, prodded her folds and drove inside her.

"Thank you. But I'm going to eat you first, then breakfast later," he growled as he thrust his hips against her. "I love that you want to cater for me. I love that you're always so wet for me."

He lifted her up, making her squeal as he placed her on the central island granite counter.

"What about your brother? Your son?" she asked. She hadn't seen them when they'd returned last night and hadn't minded being noisy in their bedroom. It didn't mean they weren't in this house. They could show up any minute.

"They're both out. Won't be back until tonight. Take the shirt off," he ordered, his eyes blazing with lust.

She didn't protest as she tugged the shirt off, letting it float to the marble floor. Holding his gaze with her sultry one, she tugged the knickers down and kicked them off her legs.

"You're so beautiful, Mimi." He couldn't keep his eyes off her, tracking her actions, surveying her naked body. A dark patch on his tented shorts indicated he was leaking precum.

"Lie back. Let me feast on you." His voice was thick with arousal, and her only response was obedience when he was so raw and passionate.

The granite was cold on her skin, but she didn't mind as his gaze heated her. She turned her head to the side, watching him.

He parted her thigh, exposing her private parts to his gaze. It was the first time he'd seen all of her in the daylight. He parted her labia with his thumbs, and his hot tongue laved her slit.

An unexpected whimper escaped her, and she arched her quivering body.

He seemed to take that as his cue and went to town, feasting on her pussy as he'd promised.

"Yes, that's it. Eat my pussy." she rasped, thrusting her hips into his face as he shoved his tongue deep into her before pulling out and swirling the tip around her clit.

"You like that? Then this is Nnanna's pussy. Remember that." he hummed against her sensitive flesh.

"Yes!" she cried out at his dirty possessive words. They did something to her. Echoed the way she felt about him. Lit a fire inside her so hot it would incinerate her. "Nnanna better remember it too. Because he can't eat any other pussy except this one."

"I promise to only eat this pussy from now on." He glanced up at her as his tongue laved her clit, meeting her gaze and holding it.

She wrapped her legs around his shoulder and watched as he ate her pussy as if it was nourishment for his body and soul. Soon, she was coming apart at the seam, flying off into nirvana aided by his skilful tongue and magical fingers, purring with satisfaction.

She didn't land before his thick dick was pushing inside her. She clamped her legs around his hips, clinging onto his shoulders as he fucked her hard on the island counter. It was as if last night's session didn't happen because he was re-energised, his hips pivoting, driving into her with a mixture of fast thrusts and slow grinds.

Through it all, they stared into each other's eyes, speaking silently. It was intimate in a way she'd never experienced. It was as if she was staring into his soul. And vice versa.

They had a connection beyond sex. Something exhilarating and yet scary. Something she didn't think she could let go.

The thought rattled her, and she blinked several times. As if he sensed her unease, he leaned in, grabbed her nape and kissed her fiercely. It was her undoing, and she climaxed again, clenching around his dick as he pumped his release into her.

Afterwards, he didn't withdraw, and they stayed locked together, his forehead pressed against hers. The affectionate way he held her didn't hide his turmoil.

"Something is bothering you," she said in a whisper.

He pressed his lips against hers briefly and lifted his head, meeting her gaze.

TWENTY-FIVE

Maddox reluctantly withdrew his dick from Zoe's pussy, fighting the fear creeping up his spine.

A fear that had developed when he'd awoken this morning to discover she wasn't in bed with him. He'd experienced momentary dread as he'd searched for her in the ensuite bathroom to no avail. He'd grabbed the first item of suitable clothing he could find before going downstairs. It wasn't until he'd smelled the aroma of the frying plantain that his panic had receded, replaced by relief.

Seeing his wife standing in his kitchen dressed only in his shirt was the sexiest thing he'd seen, sparking a longing he couldn't resist. Before he could rationalise his actions, he was promising that she would be his only lover henceforth and burying himself inside her for the umpteenth time in twelve hours.

He couldn't get enough of her, which was crazy.

Because wasn't this all supposed to end in less than three months?

She was still here to kill him. She still hadn't admitted it, nor had she withdrawn the threat.

So why was he losing his inhibitions and lowering his guard in her presence? He'd been so relaxed in her company that he'd slept through and hadn't noticed when she'd left the bedroom.

This was dangerous.

This woman could end his life.

But she could do even worse.

His gut twisted as he stepped away from the granite counter. Zoe tried to get down.

"Stay there for a minute." He hurried to the laundry room, needing to get away from her to clear his head. He opened a cupboard, grabbed a clean towel, ran some warm water in the sink, and returned to the kitchen.

Zoe still sat on the counter, but she watched his every moment.

His heart constricted, and warmth filled him because something in his wife had changed. He had to admit that. She seemed different to the one who arrived at his home one week ago.

The fact that she sat still when he'd ordered her to do so was proof. The Zoe of a week ago would never obey his order without question, especially when she knew something was wrong with him.

He returned to between her legs, gently parted her thighs and cleaned their mixed juices off her skin tenderly. His skin prickled under her silent gaze, and he hurried back to the adjacent laundry room and tossed the towel. When he returned, he picked up his discarded shirt from the floor and helped her put the shirt on.

"Maddox, talk to me," she said, grabbing his arm when he moved back.

"We'll talk. But let's eat first," he said, conscious that she must be hungry. Best to tackle the heavy subject on a full stomach. "I'll set the placemats while you finish the cooking."

She stared at him as if sensing his avoidance before climbing down the counter. "Okay."

Busying himself, he cleaned the central island and set a place for two. Then he poured the coffee into mugs while she made the omelette. It was unbelievable watching his Ice Queen cook. Yet, it soothed his troubled soul and provided hope there could be more to them than just great sex.

She served the meal in two plates, placing them on the counter.

He pulled out the stool and held it, waiting as she walked around. Then he placed his hands around her waist and lifted her onto it. Then he settled on the other stool beside her.

"This actually smells delicious," he said, cutting into the omelette before lifting his fork and placing a morsel into his mouth. The savoury, buttery flavour on his tongue was unexpected. "Wow. This is good."

She jerked away, side-eyeing him. "You say that as if you didn't think I could cook."

His cheek heated, and he grimaced. She was right. "Honestly, I didn't know what to expect. But I'm pleasantly surprised. Thank you for making this."

His gratitude seemed to mellow her out, and she nodded, returning to her meal. "Don't expect me to do this regularly. Me cooking is a once-in-a-blue-moon affair."

He chuckled. He had no problem with it. He led a hectic lifestyle and expected she did, too. There was rarely time to go grocery shopping, let alone prepare the food. "Noted. It's a good thing I have a chef who delivers our meals once a week. I'll give you the details so you can place your orders."

"Okay." She continued eating but didn't eat a lot.

"You don't like the food?" He'd almost finished the omelette and plantain.

"I do. But I'm not really a big eater." She pushed the plate aside, barely eating half of the portion she served.

He scrutinised her face, and she averted her gaze. She appeared uneasy.

"You lost your appetite," he said, feeling guilty because he thought he'd contributed to it.

She shrugged and tried to get off the stool. But he reached for her arm and lifted her hand to his lips, kissing the back of her hand. "I'm sorry for causing your unease."

"I just want you to talk to me. You made me open up to you yesterday. Now you're the one clamming up." She turned to face him.

He sighed, still holding onto her hand. "It's this thing between us. It seemed to have developed very fast over the past week. What I feel for you. I've never felt for any other woman."

"Really?" She shook her head in disbelief. "How can that be? You're saying you never felt this—" she waved her free hand between them "—for your ex-wife."

"No. It was different with her. There wasn't this intensity. This feeling of jeopardy. This overwhelming need to keep you by my side. Can you believe it? When I woke up this morning, I had a moment of panic."

"Panic? Why?" She frowned.

"I thought you'd gone. That I wouldn't see you again."

"You're afraid that I'll leave?"

"Isn't that ridiculous? Especially since this marriage is temporary, and you'll be gone in less than three months."

"Yeah." She said unenthusiastically as her forehead furrowed deeper. The expression she gave him was even more curious as if the thought of their marriage ending confused her too. Then she looked down at the table.

But he wondered if he should tell her the true reason he panicked. The reason he was worried about her leaving.

"And we haven't talked about the elephant in the room, Zoe."

"What is that?" she glanced at him.

"We're having unprotected sex. You haven't said anything about it."

"What is there to say?" she looked away, biting her lip.

He placed his hand under her chin, turning her head to face him again. "You could get pregnant."

"I can take the morning-after pill. I have up to seventy-two hours. It's been less than twelve."

That cut him like a knife, and the constriction in his chest returned. He released her hand, taking his plate and hers from the counter and walking over to the sink.

He didn't want her to see how disappointed he was that she hadn't changed her mind about not having his baby. But it was better this way than finding out after the fact like last time. Perhaps she wasn't the nurturing kind and wasn't ready.

But you are.

No, this wasn't about him.

"You should check online for a clinic or pharmacy that would have the pills," he said as he washed the dishes, needing something to do to keep busy, although he had a dishwasher.

Her breath hitched. "You really want me to take the pill?"

She sounded shocked.

He swivelled, his turmoil getting worse. "This is about you. As you reminded me the last time, it's your body. At least I know in advance this time."

"Why are you angry then?" she snapped.

He opened his mouth to dispute that he was angry but shut it. He wouldn't lie about this.

"What is the point of me getting pregnant when this marriage is only temporary? You set the marriage duration, remember? Yet you want to get angry at me because I don't want to get pregnant."

She was correct. He'd arranged the temporary marriage contract as a vendetta to punish her. However, his plan seemed to have backfired because he woke up this morning almost terrified of losing her.

"You're right." He stalked towards her and wrapped his fingers around her nape. "I'm angry because I want you for more than three months. I want you as my wife, permanently."

She gasped, staring up at him. "You do?"

"Yes. I can't bear the thought of you leaving. I want you as Mrs Maddox Ejiofor forever."

"Oh God." Her gaze darted around the room. "Is that even possible?"

"Anything is possible, Zoe. You've got to want it bad enough."

She licked her lips. "Don't you think this is happening too fast?"

Frustration made his grip tighten on her chin. "It doesn't matter how fast it is. Do you want me bad enough?"

She frowned, averting her gaze.

He knew why she was reluctant to answer—her mission to kill him.

"Fine. You don't want me as much as I want you," he bit out and released her chin. She still intended to kill him.

"No. It's not that." She grabbed his arms, preventing him from walking away. "I want you so much. But this is all new to me. And there is so much at stake. My life. My future. I told you being a wife was never part of the plan for my future."

"You don't think I can give Zoe Himba a good life as my wife?" He couldn't hide his cynicism. He just wished she would tell him the truth and admit the real reason she'd married him.

"That's not what I said. I just need some time, please," she pleaded, and his heart softened.

"You have less than three months, Zoe. Make it count," he said, his anger deflating.

"I will. You asked me to trust you. Now I'm asking you to trust me. I will find a way to make this work."

Her expression appeared determined, and for the first time, he believed she was having a change of mind about killing him.

TWENTY-SIX

"I miss working out with you," Zoe said two days later as she ran on the treadmill in the hotel gym, looking out onto the sunshine reflecting off the swimming pool outside. At only 07:30, it proved to be a glorious day.

She'd woken up to Maddox's text message this morning—*Be good for me, Mimi. Have a wonderful day*—and it made her feel like nothing could touch her. Her body tingled, and she bounced on air.

I'll try. Have a wonderful day too, she'd replied.

She'd never considered herself a good girl. But for her husband, she'd try.

Was this what being loved up felt like?

"Same here," Xandra replied with a smile, cutting into her reverie, her feet pounding on the next gadget.

Unlike Zoe in the running shorts and tank top, Xandra wore full-length sports leggings and a long-sleeve top. Although the space was airconditioned, it was still strange to see a person almost covered from head to toe without a hijab. But the outfit hid the burn scars trailing down Xandra's side and back, not out of modesty.

The woman didn't cover up like this previously. This was all because of Norbert's brutal idea of punishment. All because of Don Himba's order to punish Xandra for going to Arufin.

Regret wormed through Zoe's gut. She'd let her friend down because she hadn't done anything to prevent it until it was too late.

Spending the time with Maddox had made Zoe realise she'd been wrong in many aspects. She'd been so keen to curry favour with her father. To prove herself to him that she'd neglected to protect the only person she'd classed as a friend and sister.

Which brought her to the actual reason Xandra was in FCT.

Maddox had suggested they should go on a short holiday abroad, and she'd agreed the break would be great for them. However, she'd had some business she couldn't avoid this week. So they'd made arrangements for the trip next week.

So yesterday she arrived at the FCT for a business meeting. Although she'd protested the need for extra crew since she had a team already, Maddox had sent a skeleton crew comprising Agatha and Joshua.

When she'd arrived at this hotel in the afternoon, Xandra had been in the lobby, checking in. They'd planned to meet at the gym this morning because she'd been focused on catching up with Noah last night. However, Zoe suspected the other woman's presence was more than a coincidence.

"So why are you really here?" she asked.

The woman was an assassin, retired mostly since she got involved and set up home with Ebuka Njoku. However, she suspected the woman hadn't lost her killer instincts. And she could be here on an assignment…

"Maddox called me," Xandra replied.

Zoe's heart kicked in her chest, and she stumbled, quickly gripping the sides of the treadmill to steady herself.

"Are you okay?" the woman reduced the speed on her device, slowing her pace.

"No, I'm not." She put her device on warm-down, allowing her to walk. Then, she met the assassin's gaze. "Why did my husband call you?"

"He wants me to keep an eye on you."

What was Maddox playing at? So, with all his reassurances about trusting him, he didn't trust her. She'd thought they'd reached an understanding two days ago. What exactly did he think she'd come here to do?

"What? As in, spy on me?"

"No. As in, keep you safe."

"Keep me safe? He sent a team with me." Zoe indicated at Agatha who currently stood a few metres away at attention. Although she couldn't see him from this angle, Joshua was probably not far away. Noah and his team were out making arrangements for the meeting this afternoon.

"He said you declined to have a full entourage. And he thinks you will be more comfortable with me around."

"You mean *he* will be more comfortable having you around me." Zoe sniped, irritation coursing through her. She never liked other people controlling her life.

Of course, Xandra was now part of the Odili crew, so she no longer held any loyalty to the Himba clan. She was answerable to Maddox, not Zoe.

Xandra's treadmill stopped, and she stepped off, grabbed her reusable bottle, and took a sip. Zoe got off her when hers stopped, taking her phone and water bottle. She walked to the mats and started her stretches, trying to shake off her conflicted emotions.

Xandra joined her, speaking in a low voice. "Don't get wound up about this. Sure, the Odilis are paying me to be here. But I'm also here because our friendship is important, and I want to protect you however I can."

Her words pulled at Zoe's heartstrings, and she mellowed. "But I have Noah and his team to protect me. You didn't have to come all this way."

"I know that. But it can't hurt to have extra hands on deck. And if Maddox is anything like Ebuka, he's on a lifelong mission to protect you. He will go above and beyond."

"You think so?" Zoe couldn't help smiling at the thought of a protective Maddox.

Xandra grinned. "From what I know about these Odili men when they fall for their partners, they go hard. Look at Duke and Carla or Mason with Sophie—"

"Or you with Ebuka," Zoe added as something clicked inside her mind. She wanted the same type of relationship with her husband. The fierce and uncompromising love.

Mason challenged his godfather's authority because of Sophie.

Duke didn't hesitate to take on The Baron because of Carla.

Xandra faced down Norbert's wrath because of Ebuka.

Was Zoe willing to defy her father's order because of Maddox?

Blood drained from her head, making her dizzy. She lowered her body to the floor mat and wiped the sweat from her face. She didn't want to choose between her father and her husband. Nonetheless, she might not have a choice.

"What is it?" Xandra sat on the floor beside her.

"I just realised that I want what you just described with Maddox. I must be crazy." She pulled her knees up, wrapping her arms around them.

"There's nothing crazy about wanting to be loved by your husband."

"Oh, there is." *When you're supposed to kill said husband.* "A week ago, I was barely talking to him. I shot at him, and he locked me in the basement."

She pulled at her hair tied in a ponytail while her gaze bounced around the gym.

Xandra watched her with a concerned expression. "You tried to kill him? Why?"

She leaned close to her friend, lowering her voice. "After we got married, he tried to take my weapons. I pulled out the body-concealed handgun and fired at him." She barked a nervous laugh, shaking her head at the memory. "He dodged it, and it hit a framed painting instead. Joshua grabbed me and didn't let go until I was disarmed."

"Zoe, that was an extreme reaction. He's your husband. You could have hurt him." The censure in Xandra's tone pulled her up short.

Her cheeks smarted. "I know. But I had my reasons."

Although she trusted Xandra to an extent, she couldn't tell the woman about her mission to kill Maddox. Agatha was nearby. And she wasn't sure if they were listening to her conversations.

"Anyway, that isn't even the problem. I didn't want to marry Maddox. Remember when we last chatted? I mentioned he could have done it on purpose. It turns out he hadn't. I watched the video from Arufin, and

Maddox used the condom. He didn't do anything wrong."

"That's good. So you guys made up, and things are good now." Her friend sounded enthusiastic about her marriage.

How the tables had turned. Xandra had been the loner when they'd been younger, while Zoe had her affair with Noah. Now, Xan had a stable relationship while Zoe floundered in her marriage.

She sighed. "Yes, things are good now."

Her husband had unlocked the caring and protective person hidden inside her. He seemed happy to accommodate her idiosyncrasies.

"But things shouldn't be this good. The closer I get to my husband, the more I lower my guard. The more I feel for him. It can only lead to trouble. How can that be a good thing?"

Her chest squeezed tight, and her hand flailed in the air.

Her friend's eyes widened. "You care about him?"

"I do. Can you believe it? Me? Care about anyone outside my parents? It's never happened before." She leaned forward, gulping in the air to stop the oncoming panic. She's allowed Maddox to humanise himself by being friends with his sister and having unprotected sex with him. She didn't think about him as a rival anymore or someone to be conquered. "The other day, he told me he wanted me forever. I don't think our marriage would last the year, let alone ten or twenty. What am I going to do, Xan?"

"Why not talk to Maddox. If he wants you and you want him, surely you two can work things out."

"It's not that simple. There is my father to contend with."

Silence hung heavily in the air for a few seconds.

"Let's finish the stretches," Xandra said finally, scooting forward until they faced each other on the mat. "Whatever happens, I've got your back."

The reassurance made a lump form in Zoe's throat. She couldn't believe she still had the woman's deep friendship and loyalty after everything.

She raised her legs and arms in the boat yoga pose, and Xandra did the same, placing her feet against Zoe's and holding her hands. She felt the stretch across her core, hips, vertebral column and shoulders. The stretches relaxed Zoe. By the time they headed up the lift to shower, she wasn't as stressed out as earlier.

Xandra said, "I can't speak for you and Maddox. But I know what it feels like to be loved by a man who will do anything for me. Despite all the challenges we had, I won't change anything—"

"Even with what Norbert did to you?" Zoe shook her head in disbelief.

"Even with that. It made us stronger. Made the feelings more intense. We share an unbreakable bond because of what we went through. I know that if my life is ever threatened, Ebuka will move heaven and earth to protect me. And I feel the same way about him."

"That is amazing."

"From what I've heard and seen of Maddox, you can have the same thing. Frankly, you deserve a man like him. Plans can change. I'm the proof. If I'd killed Ebuka as planned, I don't even want to think about how miserable my life would be now. No matter what your intentions for Maddox were before you got married, if you feel different now, change the plans. Allow yourself to be a woman, to be *his* woman. Enjoy the moment, the feeling, and let it become what it will. You'll never know unless you allow it."

The lift pinged, and Zoe thanked her friend before getting off.

***

Two hours later, Zoe and Xandra were together in the backseat of an SUV en route to a scheduled appointment a thirty-minute drive from her hotel. Agatha and Joshua followed in a separate car. Noah had gone ahead with the rest of the security team to prepare for her arrival.

Her phone pinged, and she checked the updates from the private investigator she'd hired to monitor her husband.

Old habits died hard.

Naturally suspicious, she couldn't shake the feeling of dread and looming disaster. Regardless of Maddox's promises or how well they got along, she still needed the reassurance of knowing exactly where he was at all times. To know he was safe.

Moreover, he had his security team following her around. So he was doing the same thing to her. More or less.

She clicked to read the chain of messages and looked over the photos. There were shots of Maddox leaving the house and arriving at an airport.

Hmmm. Maddox hadn't told her he would be travelling. Where was he going? Was he keeping secrets from her?

Sure, he ran a security business. As the Odili clan enforcer, he travelled to the South East regularly. However, he should have mentioned his plans.

If he couldn't be honest with her. How did he expect her to reveal her secrets?

And how was she supposed to change her plans about killing him if she couldn't trust her husband?

She didn't want to hurt Maddox. Still, disobeying her father would put her in the firing line, along with everyone who supported her. Xandra, Noah, and their loved ones would both be at risk.

Then again, if she killed Maddox, his family would seek revenge. And all the people she loved would be at risk. She would be killed, and the whole thing would come full circle. It could become a never-ending cycle because any Himba survivor would seek revenge.

She closed her eyes, clenching her hand around the phone. Her chest burned with pain. The whole thing was messing with her head.

Maddox had scattered her mind and divided her loyalties. Now, she was questioning everything.

The car horn beeped, pulling her out of the depressive thoughts. They arrived in a rural location outside the guest house on the city's outskirts. Sometimes used as a BnB for those tourists and ramblers who came to explore the local natural attractions—Karshi Waterfall and the surrounding hills.

The driver pulled into the driveway, and Xandra went out first.

"Are we secure?" Zoe asked when Noah opened the back door.

"Yes, boss," Noah replied, and she stepped out.

The other vehicle with Agatha and Joshua stopped behind them.

"Boss, I'm not comfortable with the Odili crew being here," Noah whispered in her ear.

"Well, it's a good thing you're not the boss then," Zoe said, walking past him towards the entrance.

She wasn't about to argue with him. He'd clarified his opinion before they'd set out for their meeting, and she'd overruled him. She wasn't about to reject extra security while she had the feeling of impending doom like a constant alarm. Worst case scenario, they could dump this site if things didn't work out with Maddox. There were several alternative safe locations.

"Welcome, ma," the guy who ran the place greeted and ushered her into the bar lounge.

Xandra came in with her and stood behind the sofa facing the entrance. It was the best spot. Behind them was the wall.

Zoe had barely settled on the sofa when Simon Ali walked in with one of his goons. The other members of his crew would wait with Noah and her crew. It was all about balance and fairness.

Simon was a light-skinned, tall man with sharp eyes. He swaggered in with the arrogance of a man who knew he was good-looking and traded on it frequently. He was smartly dressed and middle-aged, yet there wasn't a speck of grey hair on his beard because he dyed it. For obvious reasons, the crew referred to him as Ali Baldy, a play on Ali Baba. Also, there were other Alis in the crews. It was a popular surname in the region.

"Zoe," he said, walking up to her sofa. "It's good to see you."

"Same here," she replied, keeping her tone cheerful although she did not get up. There was tension in the air, maybe projected by the stiff way he walked.

He was a shugaba loyal to her father, and they were on similar levels in the hierarchy, although she was also her father's adviser, which put her on a level above him. She didn't want to give him any liberties for him to abuse. He took them anyway sometimes.

"Would you like a drink," he asked, walking to the bar.

"No. I'll have a drink once we finish discussing business," she said.

"Okay," he returned to the sofas and settled on an adjacent one. "What business did you want to discuss?"

"You might be aware that I acquired business premises in the FCT, and I'm in the process of setting up offices there."

He frowned. "In the FCT? No one told me about this. Are you not newly married? Your husband lives in Lori Osa."

He sounded like his ego was bruised because she hadn't informed him before she started setting up shop in his territory. Technically, it was her father's territory, though.

"What does where my husband live have to do with this?"

"You can't live in Lori Osa and work in FCT."

"Who says I can't? I can do whatever I like. And anyway, the marriage ends in less than three months, so I'm not changing my plans for the business premises."

"If you say so." He shrugged, but he didn't look happy.

"This brings me to the other matter," she ignored his sour mood. "About the other matter we discussed previously. Have you managed to bring any of the other parties on board?"

She'd approached him months ago when she'd been looking at options to avoid the marriage auction about brokering a deal with the different crews operating in the central region and creating a network of associates similar to Odili franchises. She would work as their fixer if they paid Don Himba a percentage fee. She'd thought the volume and income would guarantee she could buy out any of the suitors at the auction and marry herself. That had been before Maddox showed up and demolished her plans.

Still, the plan was good if she could acquire the key stakeholders.

"Well, it's taking a long time to convince them," Simon sounded dismissive, which annoyed her.

"Why? Who is on the fence, and who said no," she insisted on getting more details.

"Taraba and Adamawa are definite nos."

She could understand those. Two suitors who'd eventually pulled out of the auction were from those states.

"And the maybes?"

"Plateau and Nasarawa." He met her gaze.

"You mean you're a maybe? How can you be a maybe? I thought you were a yes."

"Well, you haven't given me an incentive to back your plan."

"An incentive? What do you mean?" she tilted, watching him as he got off the sofa and walked over.

He sat down beside her, leaning close to her. "What you're asking me to do has not been sanctioned by your father. So this is your personal project."

"You knew all these things when I suggested the plan to you months ago. What is different now?"

"Things change. Situations change. I don't have to be the one to talk to the other shugabas or the crews across the region. If you really want this so badly, you can make it happen. Just open your legs, and you will speed it up. Fuck as many of them as possible."

Indignation and anger rush to the surface, boiling Zoe's blood. "Excuse me, Simon. What do you take me for?"

"I don't see what the problem is. Use your seductive charm. They will all fold and sign up."

His insinuation that Zoe's success was because of her seductive ability was a massive insult. She's worked damned hard to get where she was using a mix of strategy and sassiness.

She'd known Simon could be a prick, but she hadn't expected him to be this bold and in her face about it.

Still, the alarm bells were going off in her head, and she had to tread carefully to get to the root of the problem. She would deal with the insult at a later time.

"And if I don't fuck my way through the shugabas, are you saying you're going to throw away this opportunity?" she bit out.

"No need to get all wound up about it. I was just giving you options." He ran his knuckles down her cheek, and she fought the urge to shudder. "Is this because of your husband? Has he tamed you with his dick?"

"Why would you say that?" She pulled away from his grasp. "Maddox is my enemy. He will be dead in a matter of weeks."

She had to reiterate that because these people were loyal to her father. She couldn't let them see that she was straying from the path her father had chosen for her.

"Then you won't have a problem letting me fuck you as an incentive for me to back your plans." He shifted to the sofa's edge as if in preparation.

Pure rage flowed through Zoe because this had become utterly ridiculous and unbearable. Not only was the man insulting her, but he was trying to manipulate her, too. She would not tolerate it.

She stood. "The deal is off because I'm never going to fuck you, Simon."

Even if she wasn't married, she wouldn't touch him with a bargepole.

He straightened and grabbed her arm. "Don't be so quick to rush—"

Before he could finish, she withdrew her gun from the concealed thigh holster, jammed it against his groin and released the safety. "The quickest way to become dick-less is by touching a woman without invitation. Get your stinking hands off me."

"Don't!" Xandra had her weapon pointed at Simon's goon before the man could raise his gun. She was a skilled markswoman. And everyone around here knew her reputation. If the man flinched, he was dead.

Simon raised both hands, eyeing Zoe balefully. "Before you do anything irrational, I have a gift for you."

"Don't play games with me. You won't like what I'll do to you." She dug the weapon deeper, meeting only pliant flesh. If he'd sported an erection previously, it had long withered.

"It's not a game. Let me show you on my phone." He croaked and reached for his jacket pocket.

"Easy. No sudden movements unless you want to become a eunuch." She warned.

He pulled out his phone, fiddled with it and held it up for her to see.

Her heart dropped into her stomach at the sight of the woman on the screen.

Maddox's sister was bound and gagged in a chair.

This could not be happening!

TWENTY-SEVEN

"What the fuck is going on?" Zoe bit out as she glared at Simon's smirking face as if he knew something she didn't. She shoved her gun deeper into his groin, making him grimace. "Tell me why you have a photo of my sister-in-law tied up."

She said it in that manner to alert Noah, who was listening on an earpiece.

"Take it easy." Simon sounded uncomfortable. It would be when the barrel of the Beretta Nano was digging into his genitalia while her fingers were on the trigger. He knew she was trigger-happy. "Look, I'm only trying to help out."

"What the fuck are you on about?" she retorted, not letting up on the pressure.

"Don said your husband was delaying paying your dowry. He wants the cash sharp sharp. So I proposed a solution."

As soon as he said it, the penny dropped.

She'd suspected something was up. Imagined it even before she'd left the hotel. Guessed it as soon as Simon walked into this lounge. She'd worked with these people for so long, she knew the way they carried themselves when they were on a mission and had a target in their sight or claws.

But she hadn't expected this move. Hadn't expected them to go there. To hit her where it fucking hurt!

"You abducted Amaoge to demand a ransom from her family," she said in a calm voice, surprisingly keeping her composure when she wanted to squeeze the trigger and pump metal pellets into the man's flesh, blowing his dick to smithereens.

His sexual insults and innuendos were nothing compared to this. Those were aimed at her body. At her ego.

This was different. This time, he was threatening her heart. Threatening to wreck it.

And there was nothing she'd protected before more than her heart. Her heart had been in a cage, locked up tight, until she met Maddox and Amaoge.

Amaoge showed her a genuine, guileless friendship like she'd never known.

Maddox treated her with respect, honour, passion and devotion.

Now, she realised that Maddox and Amaoge owned her heart in different ways. They'd claimed her heart without her realisation. They were her heart, as her husband and sister-in-law.

Because they'd released her heart from its cage. Freed it to feel. To love. To protect. To cherish.

To love with compassion and selflessness.

To cherish the wonder and preciousness of life.

Yet, her heart thrummed hard in her chest and loud in her ears. She could barely hear Simon's response.

"Yes! Am I not a genius." He grinned. "Why wait three months to get the money from your husband when we can take his precious only sister and make him pay for her return right now."

The more he spoke, the more her anger flared. The man had no fucking clue what he'd triggered. How her mind was making calculations at a mile a minute. But she had to tread carefully. She needed information about Amaoge's well-being and location before she revealed the extent of her rage. The image was a still and was probably taken on his phone. So she wasn't sure what happened to Amaoge since then.

First things first.

"Does the Don know about this?" she asked, studying his expression.

"Of course, Don knows. I'm not an idiot. I will not do something like this without his sanction. In fact, he ordered it."

She believed him. He had a tell when he was lying—scratching his neck. But he didn't do it this time. Also, this was what Simon did for a living, extorting money out of people through abductions and ransoms. His crew operated in this area, and Don Himba always got his cut.

This meant her father had ordered this kidnapping to get his money. He must suspect Zoe of defying his order and decided not to wait for the end of her marriage.

Or this was part of his plan and another angle to extort money out of her husband.

Whatever the case, Zoe couldn't let it slide.

For one, they had bypassed her, which was another insult.

Emotions aside, the moment she married Maddox, he and his family became Zoe's remit. They fell under her possession. Her territory.

Hence, under her protection.

So Simon kidnapping Amaoge was akin to him breaking into Zoe's house and stealing her property.

"Simon, are you insane?" she barked.

"What?" He appeared bewildered.

"Do you truly know who that woman is?"

"No be your sister-in-law again." He laughed awkwardly.

"You said it. *My* sister-in-law. *My* property. As in na me own am," she spoke in Pidgin, a universal language amongst the Nigerian criminal underworld. It was the only language they truly understood. The only way to make him appreciate the gravity of the situation. Anything else was just phonetics and grammar. Big words.

He blinked several times as if suddenly realising his mistake. That she wasn't pleased. "Eh, I know. But the boss ordered it."

"You had no fucking right to take her without informing me first. No fucking rights. Where is she?" She capitalised on his seeming confusion and defensiveness. Otherwise, she didn't think he would give the information.

"She is close by," he said nonchalantly.

She glanced at his goon. "Call the person holding her to bring her here."

"No. There's no need—"

She didn't let him finish and pulled the trigger. The shot wasn't ear-deafeningly loud. More of a pop than a bang because of the proximity to flesh and bones. But anyone nearby would recognise it.

Simon's eyes went wide, and he looked down in shock at his bloody groin where his dick had been as blood splattered onto Zoe. He staggered backward, groaning, and collapsed on the sofa, clutching his non-existent dick.

"Bitch, you shot my dick." He stared at her as if he couldn't believe what she'd done.

"You didn't really think I would tolerate your earlier insult, or you stealing what belongs to me?"

"Fuck you!" He reached for the gun still holstered in his belt.

"Go to Hell." She raised hers and shot him in the head.

His eyes glazed over as he expired.

She swivelled towards the entrance. Footsteps indicated people were coming. Hopefully, Noah heard the conversation and gunshot and was prepared. The guards appeared from both teams—a mix of curious and shocked expressions when they saw Simon's bloody, lifeless body. They all had weapons on display.

Simon's goon stood still. The man hadn't reached for his weapon. Clever man. He wanted to live another day.

"Are you Simon's second-in-command?" she asked because she didn't recognise him. Simon's usual deputy had been killed since they'd last met face-to-face. So, she hadn't met the replacement.

He nodded, his expression blank.

"Tell your men to stand down unless they want to join Ali Baldy in Hell." She spat out.

"Weapons down. Now," he barked the order.

Five men shuffled, holstering their weapons. Noah had the same number of people. Zoe was glad she'd brought Agatha, Joshua and Xandra along to boost their numbers and give them the advantage.

She studied the man now in charge of Simon's crew. He had a scar above his left eye. He was dark-skinned and dressed in a dark suit with no tie. She could see the bulge of the shoulder-holstered weapon.

"What's your name?" she asked.

"Bruce Ali," he said with a deadpan expression, and he watched her with seemingly intelligent eyes.

She hid her smile. Alis were littered around the place, but she still had to check. "Are you related to Simon?"

If they were related, she would have to kill him, too, because of the danger of reprisals.

"No. I'm from Plateau. He's from Nasarawa."

"Good. You heard what I was saying to Simon. I need my sister-in-law brought here. Can you do that?" She held his gaze, weapons down but still in her hand.

He needed to know that she was ready to shoot everyone in their crew one by one until she found the person who would bring Amaoge to safety.

"Yes. I can send the message. But it needs to be from Simon's phone. Otherwise, they will suspect something is wrong and might kill her," he said.

That made sense. These kidnappers operated a tight ship to avoid detection.

"Do it," she ordered.

He moved to where Simon's body lay and grabbed his phone. He swiped Simon's thumb on his trousers to clean off the blood before swiping it on the screen, unlocking the phone. Then he typed on the screen.

"I want to see it before you send it," Zoe said, her suspicions rising. She couldn't take any chances with these people.

He showed her the screen message.

Change of plan. Bring the merchandise to the guest house.

"Fine. Send it," she said, and he tapped on the screen. "Give the phone to Noah."

Noah stepped forward and took the phone, but it started ringing.

TWENTY-EIGHT

"It's official. The Maximo brand is coming to this city. The contracts have been signed, and we'll be officially breaking ground on the site within months," Duke Odili announced, and the men seated in his living room cheered and raised their glasses.

This constituted a major achievement for the Odili clan since they started their expansion into the Southwest region and the megacity in particular.

They met in the Odili underboss's house for local Yadili meetings rather than in the office building they'd acquired on the Island overlooking the marina.

"This is fantastic," Mason said. As the clan legal expert and fixer, he'd flown in from the Opal City to oversee the contracts and stayed as a guest in Duke's house. He was Duke's partner in the Maximo Ventures brand they created ten years ago. "After all the problems when you first moved to Lori Osa, I didn't think we'd get to today so quickly."

"Indeed. Maddox and his crew are the ones who made sure we were secure to work in this city," Duke said before taking a sip of brandy.

"I didn't do it alone," Maddox said, grinning at the praise. "The lads worked hard and have been vigilant. I'm proud of them because we've had minimal casualties over the last year. Although we were fighting skirmishes at the start."

"Please pass on our gratitude to your crew," Duke said. "And as I promised when we moved to this city, everyone who's worked on this project is due for a bonus. I believe the funds have been made available for you to distribute as required."

"Yes, I got the notification from the bank," Maddox replied before his phone buzzed. He pulled it out of his pocket. The caller ID said it was from his brother Jaxon, who knew he was in this meeting with the other Fierce 4 members. There must be an urgent reason for the call.

Was it about Zoe? His heart slammed against his chest.

She travelled to the FCT yesterday for a business meeting today. He couldn't go with her because he had this Maximo thing to handle yesterday. But he'd sent Agatha and Joshua as her bodyguards and even called Xandra an extra.

Zoe had thought it was overkill that he'd sent an entourage with her. But he'd been concerned because she would be near her father, in his region of influence. Who knew what would happen.

He stood from the sofa. "Excuse me. I have to take this."

He strode into the foyer. The layout was similar to the one in his house.

"Jaxon," he said as soon as the call connected.

"We have an emergency. Something happened to Amaoge."

His stomach dropped, and chills covered his body. "What happened?"

"We had a distress signal from her personal alarm. I called her phone but got no response. I've called Emeka, and he hasn't seen her since he left for work. The baby is at daycare. Then Emeka called back just now. He received a ransom demand. Amaoge was abducted."

"Fuck!" Maddox swore loudly. "I'll be over in the minute."

He popped his head back into the living room door. "I have to go. My sister was abducted."

"What!"

Both men rose to their feet and walked towards him.

"Where?"

"What happened?"

"I don't have the full details, but there's been a ransom demand. Jaxon is investigating. I'm going to find out more."

"Okay. Let's head over there so we can figure out what's going on." Duke walked to the front door and opened it.

Bright sunshine glared down at them as they took the short walk across the front lawn and hedge to Maddox's house. As soon as he got inside, he called his brother-in-law, reiterating his brother's words. The ransom demand was for forty million naira, which was ridiculous, but no one argued about it because they would pay it if that was what it took to get Amaoge back safely.

However, abducting the daughter of a vice admiral and a respected member of the Yadili network was a slight no one was going to ignore.

So, while Jaxon coordinated the investigation, Maddox packed a bag. He was heading to the FCT because Jaxon had picked up the GPS on their sister's phone, and it was in the same region.

This reminded Maddox that his wife was also in the same area.

Alarm bells rang in his mind.

Hmmm. Was it just a coincidence that a day after his wife went to the FCT, his sister was abducted? Don Himba's business associates were involved in kidnappings for ransom. This was no ordinary coincidence. Don Himba was involved in this. By default, so was Zoe.

If something had happened to his wife, one of the team members he sent with her would inform him. His last update was that they were preparing to attend a meeting.

Still he sent a message to Joshua.

What's the update?

Maddox, Jaxon, Tito and Josiah headed to the airport in two cars driven by other crew members. Duke told them to use the private plane, saving them time from trying to catch a commercial flight.

Joshua sent back: *Still at the hotel but should be heading out soon.*

Ninety minutes later, they were in the FCT and were picked up by the navy special ops team Maddox used for his visit to Don Himba's house the last time.

His parents knew that Amaoge was missing, and his mother had picked up her grandchild from the daycare so Emeka could concentrate on dealing with the kidnappers on the phone.

Luckily, Jaxon had tracked the location where they were keeping Amaoge. Maddox and his crew headed straight there from the airport. It took about an hour to get to the house in the bush. With a mix of stealth and surprise, they took out the group of five men at the location.

Relief washed over Maddox when he saw his sister huddled in a corner of a room.

"Amaoge, are you okay?" he said.

"Maddox!" She looked up, her eyes welled up as she hugged him tightly. "I knew you'd come."

Jaxon walked in then, and she hugged him, too. "Thank you so much."

"What happened?" Jaxon asked.

"I was on my lunch break and just parked my car outside the mall when a man with a gun shoved me into a car. They took my phone but didn't know about the personal alarm with the location trackers."

"It's good because that's how we found you. The phone was only on briefly and was switched off."

Now that his sister was safe and unharmed, Maddox could concentrate on finding out who was behind this abduction. First, he messaged Joshua again: *Update?*

A reply pinged back: *At the meet location. Z and X are inside with Ali Baldy and his 2nd. Rest of the crew are outside.*

Maddox sent a reply. *Ping me the location.*

A second later, a message with the location pin appeared on his screen.

He returned to the room where they'd bound all the captured men.

The special ops guys were watching over them.

"Who is in charge here?" Maddox asked angrily.

No one said anything.

He pointed his gun at the bandit kneeling on the extreme left and shot him through the head, killing him on the spot. The rest gasped and shuffled in shock. Maddox didn't care. He wasn't about to take prisoners. He would kill them all, anyway.

"Let's try this again. Who is in charge?" he bit out again.

"He's not here." The man on the extreme right replied.

"What's his name and where can I find him?"

Someone coughed, but no one replied.

He lifted the gun and fired at the man next to the dead one.

"Ali Baldy is our boss," the man who'd spoken previously replied.

"And?" Maddox raised his weapon again. He knew the name by the bandit's reputation. This was his territory. But worse, Joshua confirmed that Zoe was meeting with the same guy. This was the proof that his wife was involved in his sister's abduction. Two days ago, they'd been living in what seemed like bliss. How could she do this? To Amaoge. Nausea rolled through him, and he fought the blanket of rage descending on him.

"I don't know where he is, but I can call him to come here," the bandit said.

"Okay. Mak, bring the phone." Maddox said.

Mak, or Makuochi, one of the special ops guys, stepped forward and withdrew the phone from the man's pocket because his hands were bound. He raised it to the man's phone for his biometric to unlock it. Then he handed it to Maddox.

It buzzed as Maddox grabbed it. He read the incoming message:

Change of plan. Bring the merchandise to the guest house.

Maddox's spine stiffened. He raised the phone for the bandit to see. "Is this from Ali Baldy?"

"Yes, na him." the man replied.

"And the merchandise is my sister?"

The man nodded.

Maddox's muscles tightened in anger, and he fired two shots, killing two more of the bandits, leaving only one.

"Right. Stand up. You will take us to the guest house," he ordered and headed for the exit.

TWENTY-NINE

"Shugaba … it's the Don on the line," Noah said as he stared at Simon's vibrating phone in his hand like it was a venomous snake.

A murmur passed through the gang gathered in the guest house bar lounge.

Shit. If Zoe needed conclusive proof that her father was involved in Amaoge's abduction, this was it. He was probably calling Simon to get an update on the ransom.

Simon was dead, and Amaoge was coming to the guest house. Zoe would make sure she returned to her family safely. There would be no ransom paid.

Not today. Not ever.

The concept sent a surge of adrenaline through her. There was only one thing to do.

"Give me the phone," she said without analysing her actions or the consequences.

She would do what was needed, To Hell with the consequences.

Noah handed her the phone.

"Silence," she ordered the group, swiping to answer the call, holding the gadget to her ear without saying a word.

"Simon, what's the update?" her father's deep voice rang clear in her ear. There was no mistaking it.

"Baba," she said in a husky voice and swallowed.

"Zoe? Where is Simon? Put him on the phone." His dismissive tone killed the last hope of her father caring about her.

He really didn't care and saw nothing wrong with his behaviour. It wouldn't have bothered her in the past. But she'd learned that a father should feel compassion for a child. Maddox had taught her this. He'd felt a love for a foetus that he hadn't seen. He'd felt loss and grief when she'd terminated the pregnancy.

She'd lived for thirty-five years, and suddenly, she realised that her father would not mourn her loss. He would miss the money and wealth she provided to him. But not her. She was disposable. Replaceable.

Finally, she saw her father for who he truly was—devious, manipulative, and traitorous. A violent narcissist who lacked empathy. A true psychopath.

Not to mention his other awful prejudices.

An unsettling ache descended in her chest, and she felt cold. She fought the disillusion, threatening to wrap its claws into her with determination and lowered the phone from her ear, clicking to switch to speakerphone. She would make everyone a witness.

"Simon is dead," she spoke loudly so everyone in the lounge would hear, and she increased the volume of the loudspeaker. No one made a sound as they all watched her.

"What?" her father's voice boomed. "What do you mean he's dead? I spoke to him about an hour ago."

"I killed him," she said calmly.

"You did what?" he sounded shocked.

"I said I killed him. First, I shot him in the balls because he insulted me. Then I shot him in the head because he stole from me."

"Insulted you? Stole from you? What are you talking about? You had no right to kill him."

"No rights?" Zoe snapped as her anger escalated. "You want to talk to me about rights? He had no right to encroach on my territory. To steal from me. Maddox and his family are under my remit. Mine, damn it. You had no right to sanction Amaoge's abduction without my permission."

"Your permission?" he bellowed. "How dare you, Zoe? I'm your father!"

"Then bloody well act like it for once in your life. No matter what I do, you don't appreciate it. All you do is undermine me. So much so that the men think it's open season and they can take potshots at me. I'm not even protected as your daughter. You are willing to sacrifice me. To sacrifice anyone for your gain. Enough is enough."

"Have you gone mad, Zoe? I'm Don Himba, for fuck's sake. Your boss."

"No. I'm not mad. Actually, for the first time in years, maybe all my life, I can see and think clearly. You are the boss only because I let you be the boss. If you want to stay as boss, you will keep your hands off my properties. And for your information, Maddox will not be paying any dowries to you. And he will remain untouched. He and his family are off limits."

"Oh, you have definitely lost your mind if you think you can threaten me."

"This is a promise, Baba. And before you rush off to order my punishment, remember that I know how you operate. If anything happens to any member of my crew or family, a certain retired admiral whose daughter you abducted will get full details of your operations. Don't forget I have the info on the offshore accounts and every asset you've acquired. You think you have financial troubles now? See how quickly your accounts get frozen if you dare threaten me."

Her father stayed silent for a few seconds. It seemed she'd hit a raw nerve. He didn't play with his money. So, threatening to cut off his finances would definitely give him pause.

"If the accounts get frozen, your mother will suffer it," he said in a subdued tone.

"Don't worry about my mother. I have made provisions for her welfare in the event of your demise," she said coldly, not hiding the threat. His demise could be his loss of wealth or his expiration. He could interpret it as he pleased.

"You will never inherit me!" he lashed out.

She barked out in humourless laughter. "I was never going to inherit you. That is the whole devious illusion you kept up for years. You made me think that if I worked hard and proved myself, you would consider me a worthy heir. But you never intended to make me your heir. I can see that now. But don't worry. I will build my own empire. And if I want it, I will take yours."

"Zoe—"

"Goodbye, Baba."

She pressed the button and ended the call., not wanting to continue the conversation as disappointment and hurt hardened her stomach. She dropped Simon's phone on the sofa.

Silence descended on the lounge. And for a few seconds, Zoe felt untethered as emotions rushed over her, threatening to overwhelm her. She felt like her world had collapsed. Everything she'd believed was essential vanished at the end of the phone call. She fought to maintain her composure, not to crumble in front of all the eyes that were focused on her.

For the first time since she got married, she missed her husband. She wished he was here right now. Hoped she could steal an embrace and he could comfort her. She'd never thought she needed comfort as an adult until now, when her world felt like it had ended.

Her mother was good at giving hugs. But it wasn't her parent she needed.

She needed Maddox. The way he held her in his arms and whispered softly in her ears while rubbing her back gently.

She wanted to call him and explain what happened. But she couldn't contact him until she'd seen Amaoge and verified her sister-in-law was well.

In the meantime, she had to deal with the group of people surrounding her. She'd quit her position as her father's deputy in their presence. They might think it meant they were not answerable to her any longer. She needed to set the record straight.

She coughed to clear her throat. "As you all heard. That was Don Himba on the phone, and I just resigned as one of his shugabas."

A murmur went through the group, but she continued.

"But that doesn't mean that I'm no longer your boss. It just means that from now on, I'm your only boss. In fact, I'm The Boss."

"Shugaba—" Noah started.

"Do not interrupt me again," she cut him off. "You just heard me say that I'm now the boss. From now on, you should refer to me as Boss. I'm not Don Himba's deputy anymore. Some of you might think you don't want to work for me, especially if it means going against the Don. But I can reassure you that if you pledge your allegiance to me, I will care for you like my family. You and yours will be protected. For one thing, I will never ask you to sacrifice your loved ones to prove your loyalty to me. That I can promise you."

"Yes!" some of them cheered.

"I will be strict, but I will be fair. There will be rules of engagement. First one, there will be no more kidnapping of women and children."

"But na how we dey make money," someone grumbled.

"I know. But hear me out. I know they are the easiest prey. But the trauma, especially for children, is not something I would accept. So if you drop that demographic, I will cut my fee as boss from twenty percent to ten."

"Wow." Their eyes bulged.

"You're serious," Bruce said.

"I am. There are other ways to earn money without terrorising the populace. But we'll get to those later. The other thing is that I will give you the choice to stay or leave now. If you walk out, you're not just leaving the premises. You're leaving the state. You cannot live or operate in this region. So I will give you a minute to make up your minds."

"Boss," Bruce said. "Who will be in charge of the crews?"

"If you choose to stay, Bruce, you'll be the shugaba in charge of what's left of Simon's old team. Noah will be the shugaba in charge of his team," she said, effectively promoting the two men on the spot.

"Sounds good to me," Bruce said, prostrating on the floor. "I'm happy to pledge my allegiance to you, Boss."

She hadn't expected the prostration, but she liked it. "It's good to have you on board, Bruce. You may rise."

She stepped forward and shook his hand firmly when he straightened.

Then she turned to Noah. "And you?"

"You always have my allegiance, Boss." Noah prostrated. He'd never done it before. But Bruce had set a precedence he couldn't deviate from in front of the crew. When he rose, She shook his hand to seal their agreement. Then he ordered the rest of the crew. "Leave now or prostrate in allegiance to the new boss!"

Surprisingly, no one left and all ended up flat on the floor except Joshua, Agatha and Xandra. They were Odili crew and couldn't pledge allegiance to Zoe.

"Rise. I promise you won't regret sticking with me," Zoe said, relieved for the base crew. Considering this wasn't how she'd planned the day, it wasn't too bad. "Noah, arrange for cleaners to get rid of Simon's body. Bruce, post a team outside to prepare for the people bringing Amaoge."

"Boss," they both replied and gave instructions to their teams.

Xandra came up to Zoe and spoke in a low voice. "Well done. You handled the situation very well, considering the circumstances. But I'm sorry about your father."

"Thank you, but I don't want to discuss it now." She needed to handle so many other things before she would analyse her conversation with her father.

Someone hurried in and announced, "Two cars are approaching, but I don't recognise them."

"That's Maddox," Joshua said.

Zoe's heart slammed in her chest. "He's here. You've been in contact?"

"Yes," he replied.

Shit. Of course, Joshua and his crew were here to spy on Maddox's behalf. She tamped down her irritation.

"Let them in. Welcome them nicely. Weapons down," she ordered. Her priority now was to protect her crew.

From what he knew about her husband, he would be on the warpath and would kill anyone who resisted.

She found an armchair in a different section away from Simon's body and settled down, still holding her blood-splattered gun. She should clean it. However, it would have to wait. Maddox needed to see this side of her—the uncompromising person who would do anything to protect her family.

Soon, her disarmed crew walked back into the lounge with raised hands while men in camouflaged uniforms pointed military-grade weapons at them. And leading them was her husband, looking murderous in his blood-stained clothes, a gun in his hands.

THIRTY

Zoe had never thought deadly intent attractive until she saw it in her husband's dark gaze as he entered the guest house bar. Twilight was approaching, the setting sun casting long shadows inside the dimly lit space.

Maddox looked like a dark avenger with his dark suit, bloody hands and weapons.

It didn't escape her notice because her appearance matched his.

They made a bloody pair. A perfect match.

As he strode towards her, winged creatures fluttered in her belly, and her pulse skyrocketed, devotion and desire sending euphoria through her.

He was the sexiest man alive, and he was hers.

"Where is Ali Baldy?" His deep voice held a stern tone, granite eyes drilling into her.

She reared back, coldness replacing the warmth she'd felt at his arrival.

Why was he being rude to her? Sure, he was angry about Amaoge's abduction. Still, it didn't warrant the attitude towards her. She was tired of being disrespected by men. First was Simon. Then, her father. She had no problems taking her husband down a peg, too.

She rode fluidly from the chair and sashayed into his personal space, her heels making her eyeball him. This close to him, the urge to lean forward gripped her, to kiss his stiff lips, making them go pliant for her. She ignored the urge and glared at him instead.

"I haven't seen you in two days, and *that* is the first thing you say to me? No, hello, wifey. No, how are you, Zoe?"

He raised his free hand and gripped her chin tight.

"I'm not in the mood for games," he growled.

His touch sent tingles down her skin, making her want to press her body against his. Damn, she'd missed him. Instead, she jammed her gun muzzle in his groin.

"I've shot one man in the balls today. I'll do it again if you don't show me some fucking respect, Maddox. Look around you. We're not in your basement anymore."

He scowled for a few seconds before glancing around.

Bruce and Noah stood behind Zoe with weapons ready, although not raised. Around the room, the rest of the crew, who hadn't been disarmed yet, were all alert, watching them, including Xandra, Agatha and Joshua.

He blinked, seemingly realising he was in her territory. Her turf. Sure, he could start a bloody battle right here. But his men and hers would be injured. His first instinct would be to protect his crew.

And she had to protect hers. She was on trial for her new team. Everything she did in public mattered and would be scrutinised for weaknesses. She couldn't be seen to be manipulated or disrespected, even by her husband. Otherwise, she wouldn't last long. They would either decamp or kill her if they felt she wasn't strong enough to lead them.

"Fine," he bit out, stepping back, capitulating. And her respect for him soared. It took a man confident about his stature in life to concede to a woman in his business.

"Good evening, wifey." His deep voice rumbled through her, making her heart skip a beat. She wanted to lean into him, but his next words stopped her. "Are you happy now?"

"No. But it will have to do," she sniped.

"Then tell me where I can find Ali fucking Baldy!"

"Over there." She pointed at the bank of sofas where a bedsheet covered the dead body.

He walked over and used the tip of his weapon to push the sheet, revealing Simon's head with the bullet hole, and the sheet slid to the floor, unveiling the extent of the man's fatal injuries.

"Grrr." Maddox didn't sound happy as he swivelled. "Who killed him?"

"I did." She said boldly, tilting her chin up.

"You did. Why?" His face crumpled in a frown.

"He disrespected me and stole from me," she said simply. There was no need to go into details. If he wanted those, they would have to talk privately.

But Maddox didn't seem interested. He shrugged in dismissal. "I want all the men who work for Ali Baldy."

"There is no one here who works for Ali Baldy." It wasn't a lie. No one here worked for Ali Baldy because Ali Baldy was dead.

"Don't fucking lie to me." He stomped towards her.

She stood her ground. "If you're looking for the men who kidnapped your sister, then you already found them at the hill lodge where you rescued Amaoge."

She figured he wouldn't waste time here looking for Ali Baldy if he hadn't already rescued his sister.

His eyes narrowed, confirming her theory. Her sister-in-law was probably outside the guest house with Jaxon and other bodyguards.

"Tell me what I need to know," he bit out angrily.

"I've told you already. You can see Ali Baldy is dead, and I'm sure you took care of the crew at the lodge. Take your sister home. The matter is over."

"No. It's not over until I say it is. They abducted Amaoge. Why are you protecting these people?"

"These people are my crew!"

His breath hitched, and he jerked back as if she'd slapped him.

Her heart clenched, and she wanted to reach out to him but couldn't. She had to protect the people who pledged allegiance to her.

"They are my crew," she said in a quieter tone. "And I'm their boss now, which makes them mine to protect. The boss has to protect the crew. That's what you taught me."

He paced a few times, bent over and growled. His rage must have turned into bloodlust because it looked like he really wanted to kill more people, and Zoe was standing in his way.

His red eyes hardened as he lifted his weapon and fired.

Bruce groaned, clasping his shoulder.

Xandra moved up beside Zoe, partially blocking her from Maddox's line of fire.

"No!" Zoe shouted, raising her hand to prevent anyone from shooting in retaliation. She didn't want to hurt her husband. He was in pain already, hence his current behaviour.

"Maddox, I understand that you're angry."

"You don't know how angry I am. You let them take Amaoge!"

"I didn't know Ali Baldy took her. And as soon as I found out, I made him pay. But I understand if you still need more heads to roll. I am responsible. So, if you want to retaliate, aim your weapon at me. No one else."

"No!"

Zoe glanced up at the soft voice, and warmth filled her heart as Amaoge walked further into the lounge. She looked intact, although her usually fabulous afro curls were askew.

"Amaoge, get back into the car. It's not safe here," Maddox ordered.

"Nowhere is safe in this country. That's the lesson I learned today." Amaoge ignored her brother and continued walking until she stood between Zoe and Maddox. "More to the point, if you're going to shoot Zoe, you might as well shoot me."

"And me too," Xandra said.

Agatha moved from where she stood beside Joshua and joined the other women shielding Zoe from Maddox. "Sorry, Boss. But I'm with them."

Maddox's muscles went rigid, and he fired his weapon up at the ceiling, showering the lounge with shards of glass and plaster as people ducked.

"I said you would sacrifice my sister to further your ambitions, and you've proven me right. The only thing you care about is power." He bared his teeth. "I can't do this anymore. The contract is done. Over."

He stalked out of the lounge, shaking his head.

Zoe felt like she'd been kicked in the gut. For a moment, she stood frozen, not knowing what to say or do as her mind went numb.

She didn't know when Amaoge turned around and faced her until her soft voice reached her. "Zoe, can I give you a hug?"

Unable to help herself, she nodded, although a part of her warned against hugging in public, especially in front of her crew.

Yet, as she was surrounded by Amaoge's warmth and softness, she held on tight for a few seconds and closed her eyes, relishing the comfort.

Earlier, she'd yearned for her husband's embrace after her devastating conversation with her father. Now, she was glad to have her sister-in-law's reassurance.

"Just give Maddox some space and time. I'll talk to him. He'll come around," Amaoge whispered to her.

"I doubt it." She swallowed the lump in her throat. "But thank you. And I'm glad you're okay."

"Yes, so am I." Amaoge leaned back, giving her a bittersweet smile. "I have to go now. I'll call you, okay?"

Zoe nodded as her throat locked up, and she didn't think she could use her voice.

Her sister-in-law waved at her as she left the lounge.

Zoe walked over to the armchair and lowered her body to avoid collapsing as her legs weakened and her heart broke.

She and Maddox were at an impasse. He was bound on revenge, and she wouldn't give up members of her crew. The situation was impossible.

The whole day had been impossible.

First, finding out about Amaoge's abduction.

Then, walking away from her father.

Finally, it seemed her marriage of two weeks was over.

Talk about a catastrophic day.

THIRTY-ONE

It was past midnight when Zoe walked into her hotel suite after Agatha did a quick visual check.

The sight of the empty room made her pause at the entrance. "Do you mind staying with me for a little while," she said.

"Of course," Xandra replied, stepping in after her.

"Sure," Agatha said, following them in and shutting the door.

Zoe walked to the nearest sofa in the lounge and lowered her body. She tugged her heels off, sighing with relief when her feet were free. She loved her stylish designer stilettos, which completed her power suits and never thought she would envy Xandra or Agatha, who wore sturdy leather trainers. But the day had been *long*.

"Sit down. Relax," she told the women. "Xan, please check if there's any rum in the minibar. Actually, call room service and order a bottle of rum and bottles of coke for the mixer. Get some food as well. Whatever is available at this hour."

She hadn't eaten because her stomach had been in knots earlier. Now, it rumbled with hunger pangs. She leaned back into the sofa and closed her eyes while Xandra ordered room service.

The day had been hectic, nonstop, since she left the hotel room about twelve hours earlier.

After Maddox left the guest house, Zoe hadn't even had time to fully take in what had happened because she'd been back in boss mode.

First, they had to sort out the removal of Simon's body. Then, she'd arranged for a care package to be sent to his widow. Bruce would go and see the woman and explain that her husband had been killed during an operation that had gone wrong.

Then Zoe had called in the medic who dealt with their emergencies in the region. The man had arrived and tended to Bruce's gun wound. It was lucky that no one else in the team had taken a bullet from Maddox, considering his rage.

Once Bruce was patched up, the man who ran the guest house, who was now part of Zoe's crew, brought out food and served everyone in the dining hall. Then Zoe and her new deputies sat in a meeting discussing strategies.

The short-term focus was survival. Survival meant protecting the team and securing their families—anyone who could be targeted as collateral damage if a war erupted between her crew and her father's crew or anyone else who wanted to target her. Some might need to relocate and go into safe houses unknown by other Himba crews. She tasked Noah with identifying any vulnerable relatives of the crew, including his family and ensuring they were moved to secure locations, at least temporarily. Although she had threatened her father if he targeted her crew, she knew her old man would not take her rebellion lightly.

The medium-term goal was finance. She'd calculated that she had enough funds to cover relocations for the crew for a few months. However, they would need a cash injection to boost their numbers and fund the long-term goals. She'd tasked Bruce and Noah to brainstorm ideas to improve their cash flow.

The long-term objective was growth and expansion. The best way to do it was through partnerships. She would revise her original idea to form a network of Himba associates across the central region. Except this time, she would be the boss, not her father. She would also collaborate with business partners outside the area, like Chief Odili. If her husband didn't block her deals.

This brought her back to thinking about Maddox and his anger. How she wished her father hadn't put her into the problematic situation in the first place. She hoped Maddox's rage would calm over time, and he would see she had no choice but to do what she'd done.

Just before she'd headed back to the hotel, she'd called her mother, who was in the USA. The time difference meant it was still day over there. They'd chatted briefly while Zoe explained the situation with her father. Her mother became furious after learning about Amaoge's kidnapping, but she seemed happy about how Zoe dealt with it.

"You must have your hands full. So concentrate on sorting out what you need to do. I will handle your father," her mother said ominously before they said their goodbyes.

Zoe hoped it meant that her mother could convince her father not to punish Zoe for her rebellion.

But to be honest, her father wasn't her biggest concern.

Her greatest source of anxiety was her husband.

Was Maddox serious about ending their marriage?

"Can I turn on the TV?" Agatha's question roused Zoe from her thoughts.

She opened her eyes and waved her hand at the large flatscreen mounted on the wall. "Sure."

Agatha pressed the black remote controller button, and the screen flickered.

"Agatha, does Maddox know you're still here with me?" Zoe asked. She was surprised that the bodyguard stayed after Maddox and the special operations team left the guest house.

"Yes, I guess so." Agatha sat on an adjacent sofa. "I haven't been reassigned to another job. So I'm with you until someone tells me otherwise."

"And your husband, Otito. Was he at the guest house this evening?"

"Yes, he was."

"And he didn't mind you staying?" Zoe frowned.

"Oh, he minded. He wanted me to go with them. But I told him I would stay with you until I get reassigned. He can't reassign me until Maddox tells him." Agatha shook her head and smiled.

"Well played." Zoe burst out laughing.

"Indeed." A grinning Xandra settled on the sofa beside Agatha.

"I want to thank both of you for standing up for me earlier. I will never forget what you did."

Xandra nodded. "You handled a difficult situation very well."

"I agree," Agatha said. "I admit I was annoyed when I heard that Amaoge was abducted. But when I got inside and saw that you'd already killed the Ali Baldy guy and then witnessed the messy phone call between you and your father, I had to step in when Maddox showed up."

"I'm sorry to say this. But your father is cold," Xandra said.

"Yes, he is." Zoe nodded. "I didn't fully grasp the extent of his coldness until yesterday, and then it hit me. Bam. How much he undermines me. Why? Just because I'm a woman. If I had a dick, he wouldn't treat me the way he does."

"I concluded a while ago that he hates women," Xandra said. "That's why he was so hard on me when I went to Arufin. No one else was beaten for going to a sex club. You can be sure the men do worse things, but none were ever punished."

Zoe tilted her head, thinking. "I never thought of it like that. But you're right. He does hate women. He lives with three women, but he hasn't treated any of us well. He cheated on my mother. I'm sure he's physically abusive to Brenda. And we all witnessed his attitude towards me. I don't think there's any woman he treats right."

Her father was indeed the worst.

Maddox's words returned to haunt her.

"…Have you considered that the most misogynistic and sexist person in your life is your father?"

He'd tried to warn her about her father's faults, but she hadn't wanted to listen. Had hoped that despite his faults her father cared about her.

Hurt, he only wanted to manipulate her.

She'd been exposed to an environment where people genuinely loved others. Amaoge, Maddox, and the rest of their family didn't hide affection and gave it generously, even to people who weren't their blood.

But there was no point stressing about her father. He was too set in his way. There would be no changing him.

She had to focus elsewhere. On her future. On her marriage. On Maddox.

How was she going to resolve their impasse?

A knock on the door roused her from her thoughts.

Agatha went to answer it.

"Room service," said one of the two security men posted outside.

Although she had Agatha and Xandra, Noah gave her a new dedicated security team. They had to double her security as the new boss because she was now a target.

The bellman walked in, pushing a trolley. He unloaded the covered dishes onto the small dining table with an unopened bottle of rum and soft drinks. Someone had gone to the trouble of preparing a meal for them this early morning.

Zoe walked to the safe, opened it and withdrew two cash bundles. She split one in two and walked to the bellman.

"This is for you—" she gave him the smaller bundle before placing the unopened one on the trolley. "—and this is for the kitchen staff. Make sure they get it. I will check."

"Yes, ma. I will give it to them. Thank you, ma." He bowed before exiting.

Zoe, Xandra and Agatha settled around the table. They opened the dishes—jollof rice served with fried plantain and beef stew.

Zoe opened up the bottle of rum and poured generous amounts into each glass, and they topped it up with the coke. They ate, drank, and talked about trivia, watching the African movie channel Agatha had switched on.

After eating, Zoe grabbed the almost empty bottle of rum and her glass and decanted onto the sofa. Xandra and Agatha cleared the table, and Agatha moved the tray into the corridor as Xan held the door. Then, they joined her on the couches.

On the telly, the woman who had previously argued with her husband was now on her knees, begging for his forgiveness in the movie.

The scene annoyed her because it was almost the same scene in all Nollywood movies. The wife was expected to go and beg her husband after an argument. Just so there would be peace.

Why was the onus on the wife to create a peaceful atmosphere?

Right now, she missed Maddox. But begging him wasn't even on her mind.

"Is that really the way the world sees us?" Zoe pointed at the screen. "Weepy and compliant. I'm sorry I have to ask. But is that how you apologise to your spouses. To Ebuka or to Tito?"

"Yeah, right," Xandra scoffed. "That would be the day. I think I've only been weepy once with Ebuka, and that was the day I realised I loved him. It was an overwhelming feeling. Something I'd never felt before."

"What about you, Agatha? Would you cry and beg Otito like that." She pointed at the screen again.

"No. I've never had to do that. But maybe if I did something terribly wrong and didn't want to lose him, I would grovel. But that day never reach," she joked in Pidgin.

Zoe smiled, but her words gave her pause. "Do you think I did something terrible yesterday by not handing over Simon's old crew to Maddox?"

"No! That's not what I meant. You did nothing wrong," Agatha said.

"You did exactly what you should have done. Maddox would have done the same thing if he were in your shoes. He wouldn't have given up his crew either," Xandra commented.

"I don't feel like I've done anything wrong, and I don't feel like grovelling either. But I could see he was hurt, and I didn't know how to soothe him. I hate that I don't know how to soothe his rage."

"I think you know. You just don't realise it," Agatha said. "When Maddox married you, he knew you would never be compliant. That there would always be a push-pull pull-push about your relationship. He's not foolish. He worked that out early on. I think it's the reason he brought you peace offerings."

"Peace offerings? Like what." Zoe frowned.

"Like, although you'd shot at him, and he locked you in the basement, he ordered me to go buy your favourite breakfast the next morning."

"Oh," Zoe remembered, and her cheeks heated.

"And even when he didn't go down to the basement for a few days, he instructed me to release you from the chains and give you some of your personal items down there."

"That's true. So you think I should offer him a peace offering."

"Yes. Offer him something he wants more than to punish Ali Baldy's old crew."

Zoe nodded as the realisation dawned. She knew exactly what to offer Maddox. At least, she hoped it would be enough of a peace offering to restore their marriage.

THIRTY-TWO

A phone vibrating on a hard surface woke Zoe, and she moaned for Maddox to pick up his phone. He was the one whose device rang at odd hours. She loved his dedication to his job. Yet the interruptions could be disruptive when trying to get some shut-eye.

"Ka nom-m, answer your phone." She reached for her husband and encountered cold, flat sheets.

Groggily, she lifted her lashes, blinking. The bed was empty beside her, and the room wasn't in their home in Lori Osa. Her memories returned. She was in the FCT hotel suite. Daylight cracked through the edges of the curtain, and the phone continued vibrating.

Who the hell was it?

She'd finally gone to sleep about five this morning after giving her deputies the morning off because of yesterday's wahala. So she wasn't expecting them to call her except in an emergency.

Her heart slammed in her chest, and she reached for the phone. The caller ID indicated it was her sister-in-law, and she answered it immediately.

"Amaoge, is everything okay?" her voice was croaky.

"Oh, Zoe. Yes, everything is fine. I'm sorry. Did I wake you?" the woman sounded regretful.

"I had a late night, but it's fine. What time is it?" She flopped onto the bed, closing her eyes in relief that it wasn't an emergency. Yesterday's disaster was enough for the week. For the year.

"It's just gone quarter past eleven in the morning. I'm calling because I forgot you had a viewing today. I got a notification from my calendar. I'm so sorry. After yesterday, I decided to take today off, but I forgot our appointment. I'll have one of my agents do the viewing with you."

"No need to do that if it's not convenient. I understand. I totally forgot myself."

She'd told Amaoge to help her find properties in the FCT since she was setting up an office. It made sense to buy a house, too, so she didn't have to pay for hotels. She'd planned to surprise Maddox once it was sorted so they could have the two homes and commute between them. It would be near his family and even nearer to Amaoge.

"No." Amaoge insisted. "I don't want you to miss out on the houses in the new estate behind mine. They are going fast. I would love to have you as my neighbour, please. So, I'll give you an extra hour to prepare, and you can come for the viewing. Is that okay?"

"Sure. That works. Thank you."

"I'll send you the address by text message. The agent will be waiting outside the property when you arrive. If you have any problems, just call me."

"Okay. Talk to you later."

Amaoge hung up, and Zoe returned the phone to the bedside table. She lay on the bed for a few minutes, dozing on and off. Remembering Maddox, she grabbed her phone to check for messages. Nothing new from him. He'd texted her yesterday before heading out to wish her a good day. Yet, today, nothing.

She puffed out a sigh.

She could call him but wasn't ready to talk because she needed to sort out her peace offering. Also, she wanted to speak to him in person.

When her mind seemed more alert, she rolled out of bed and padded into the bathroom, completing her morning cleansing routine. Once dressed, she entered the living room.

Agatha sat on the sofa, waiting for her.

"What's the plan for today?" the bodyguard stood.

"I have an appointment to view a house, and we need to head out shortly. I'll just grab a coffee." She walked to the kitchenette.

"Oh, Xandra went out to run some errands. We didn't think you'd want to go out until the evening."

"It's okay. You can come with me, and my regular chauffeur can drive."

"Okay. That works," Agatha said, walking to the door to talk to the men in the corridor. She returned as Zoe poured coffee from the machine. "It's all arranged."

Zoe smiled, loving the way the woman transitioned to leading the bodyguards. "Have you thought about the offer I made you last night?"

Agatha looked at her with curious eyes. "Were you serious? I thought it was one of those things people said when they were drunk."

"I wasn't drunk. Yes, the rum relaxed me, but I know everything I said last night."

"So you want me as your head of security?"

"Yes, I need a replacement now that Noah is a deputy, running his own operations. I need a dedicated head of security, and I think you would be great at it. You're capable and adaptable. No one else I know can do the job as well."

"There are people in Maddox's team who have been in the security services for longer than me."

"I don't know them, and I don't trust them. I trust you."

"That's kind of you. What about Xandra?

"Yes, I trust her. But as you heard last night, I offered her the enforcer job. I want you two in my inner circle with Noah and Bruce. I need the female perspective to balance out all that testosterone." Zoe smiled.

Agatha laughed. "I know what you mean. It's an exciting job offer, and I would love to work with you. But I have to talk to my husband first. Also, can I ask you to talk to Maddox and resolve your problems? I don't want you two to be on opposing sides because it will leave me with divided loyalties, which will not be fair to either of you. I told you he saved my life, so I owe him a lot."

Zoe could understand her reservation and stepped closer to reassure the woman. "I totally understand. And I promise you that my marital problems will be resolved. I will work things out with Maddox. I'm not going to walk away from my marriage."

"Good," Agatha said.

"Right. Let's go house hunting."

They left soon after that and headed to the estate.

Her phone pinged with a notification from her bank, and she checked it.

Payee: Zoe Mimidoo Himba
Amount: ₦70,000,000.00
Payer: Maddox Nnanna Ejiofor

Reference: DOWRY

Zoe's stomach dropped as she logged into her online banking and checked. Sure enough, Maddox had sent her seventy million naira. The severance pay to end their marriage.

What the Hell?

So he'd been serious. What was the matter with him?

Did he really think she cared about the goddamned money? Her father had been the one who insisted on a dowry. She supposed she should be happy he'd sent it to her instead of her father.

Still, it wasn't the point. She didn't want her marriage to end. And she sure wanted to tell Maddox directly.

"Aah," she clenched her fist, agitation roiling through her.

"Are you okay?" Agatha twisted in the front passenger seat to look at her.

"No. I need to talk to Maddox."

"Should we turn around and head to his parents' house?"

"No. I need to do the viewing first. Amaoge arranged it specially. I don't know when I can do it again after today."

She'd planned to head back to Lori Osa tomorrow. Another plan that seemed scuppered.

But she'd had enough of giving Maddox space. She was going to confront him sooner rather than later.

The car stopped at the main gate, where the security directed them to the show home. He said the agent was waiting. As they drove down the street, it appeared the construction was almost completed for the ten detached houses in the estate. Aside from the security personnel at the entrance, the place was deserted. It was a public holiday.

The car stopped outside the show home, a beautifully positioned house with a front green lawn and pavement, plants and hedges surrounding it. Of course, the plants were still young, but they would look wonderfully green and lush once matured.

The whole structure was designed to show what the other building would look like once finished. Excitement pulsed through Zoe as she stepped out. The house wasn't the largest, yet it appeared majestic as she walked towards it.

At the same time, someone got out of a car parked in the house's stone-paved driveway.

Mesmerised, Zoe caught sight of polished black shoes and long, sturdy legs in tailored trousers as he stepped out of the SUV. She didn't see his face immediately, just the tall, lean, muscular body wrapped in a suit designed to fit his body. His dark hair was cropped close to his scalp in a low fade. As he turned, the dark stubble indicated he hadn't tidied his beard in a day or so. But it only accented his chiselled face.

As recognition dawned on Zoe, her skin tingled with the thought of having his rough beard rubbing the sensitive skin on her inner thighs.

Her husband was here.

No wonder her body awakened. It acknowledged her lover before she saw his face, and her brain made the connection.

He lifted the pair of aviators shading his eyes from the sun as if he doubted their tinted view.

"Zoe? What are you doing here?" He took steps towards her, seemingly drawn to her by an invisible string.

"I came for a viewing," she said, stunned into standing still. "What are you doing here?"

"I'm supposed to show a house." He reared back, blinking rapidly. "Hang on. You're here for a viewing? You're Amaoge's client?"

"Yes. And you're the agent?" she asked tentatively, unsure what was happening.

"I told her to take it easy for a few days, and she roped me into acting as the agent for the viewing. I'm supposed to give you the portfolio and lock up once you're done. But she never told me you were the client."

"And she didn't tell me you were the agent."

They stared at each other silently for a few seconds, her ears ringing, her mind blank.

Then he turned. "I can't be here. I have to go."

He walked back towards his car, and she followed him, heart racing. "Why do you have to go? I've only just arrived. I haven't viewed the house."

Desperation clawed through her. Now that she'd seen him, she couldn't let him disappear again.

He leaned into the car through the open door and took something from the other seat. A small black velvet box slid across the glossy folder. Was that a jewellery box? Her heart jolted, and heat skittered over her skin.

"Fuck!" he muttered under his breath and slipped the box into his pocket quickly. Then, he held a branded marketing folder towards her. "Here's the information pack and the keys. You can lock up and hand the keys in at the gates when you're done."

"No. I don't want to do the viewing by myself." She stepped back, avoiding the pack he held out. Her mind went in different directions? She didn't want him to leave. Yet she couldn't shake the bile rising in her throat. Who did he buy jewellery for? Had he moved on already? No. Not happening.

"You've got Agatha with you, so you're not alone," he said, shoving the pack into her hand. "Tell your driver to move out of the way."

"No. I won't. What's the matter with you?" she shouted. She'd never been the clingy sort. Never been in a relationship she couldn't walk away from. Yet here she was with a tightness in her chest and manic energy making her want to shake some sense into her husband. She paced the distance between the side of the car and the hedge.

He ignored her and called out to Agatha, who stood outside her car. "Agatha, tell the driver to move out of the way."

Agatha met Zoe's gaze, and Zoe shook her head. Agatha didn't budge from the spot.

He rubbed his hand over his face, looking stressed. "Zoe, I don't need this right now."

She took a step towards him, hands trembling. "Just talk to me."

"I have nothing to say to you."

"You're my husband!"

"Not anymore," he said gravely.

She flinched, and her breath hitched. "You're serious about this. That's why you sent the seventy million."

"Yes. You can use it to buy your new home."

Nausea rolled through her, and a painful tightness clogged her throat. She struggled to breathe. "It was meant to be our home, Maddox. Our home. But you know what? You can go. There are plenty more men willing to take your place."

She turned away from him and pulled out her phone. Then she pressed the number she needed. It rang once before being answered.

"Hi Noah, I need you to come do a house viewing with me," she said.

"Are you okay?" he sounded confused because she was inviting him to do a house viewing.

She ignored his question. "It's a beautiful estate. You'll love it when you see it."

Maddox grabbed her arm, making her swivel. "What the hell do you think you're doing?"

She put the phone on mute and glared at him. "It's none of your business."

"The hell it isn't." His eyes raked over her body as if he was suddenly seeing her for the first time today.

She wore a strappy tight-fitting black dress which dipped low between her breasts, showcasing her braless boobs and toned stomach. It flared at the hips and reached the knees, making her legs appear endlessly long in the navy-print, peep-toe stilettos. The navy blazer gave her a modest appearance, and her makeup and hair were on point.

She knew she attracted attention in this attire. Her husband would have to be asexual or gay not to take notice.

"If you think I'm going to let your ex come here, you have another think coming," he continued.

"You don't have a choice. We're no longer married, remember? Let go of me." Zoe snapped, spitting fire at him with her eyes.

Agatha leaned away from the car as the driver came out. The two approached Zoe and Maddox cautiously, sensing the tension.

"To hell with that. If he comes here, I will kill him," Maddox bit out and pulled his weapon out of his pocket, pointing it at Agatha and the bodyguard. "The two of you, get back in the car."

Agatha hesitated, glancing at Zoe for direction. Maddox might be paying her, but Zoe was her primary concern. Her job. Zoe really needed the woman on her team.

"Agatha, both of you, go back into the vehicle," she said.

They obeyed instantly, getting into the front seats.

Maddox pocketed his weapon and stared at Zoe. "Why are you doing this? Why are you trying to aggravate me by inviting your ex here?"

She shoved his chest, extracting herself from his grasp and glowering at him. "You said our marriage was over. What does it matter if I invite my ex here to fuck? You don't want me anyway."

"Damn it, Zoe." He stepped forward, demolishing the distance between them. His heated gaze travelled over the swell of her breasts. The evidence of his arousal strained against his trousers. Nothing new there. She knew the effect she had on him. "You are not fucking your ex."

"You can't have it both ways, Maddox." She jabbed his chest, but he didn't budge. "We're either married, or we're not. Make up your mind because I still have Noah on the line."

He shoved her back against the SUV. "End that call now. If anyone is going to fuck you, it's going to be me."

THIRTY-THREE

As Maddox watched her with eyes blazing with heat, Zoe clicked the button to unmute the phone and raised it to her ear. "Noah, are you still there?"

"Sure," he replied, still sounding bemused. "What's going on?"

"Never mind. It's nothing to worry about. Maddox is here now, and everything is under control. Talk to you later," she replied breezily as if she hadn't just hooked her husband by using Noah as bait.

Well, no harm done. Noah was safe at home with his family. While Maddox looked ready to explode from the sexual energy oozing off him.

"I'm going to fuck you so hard, grind my dick into your hole, make you scream and plead for more until you're sore and addicted to my dick. To me," his gruff voice was loud enough for the bodyguards in the car to overhear the words.

Her husband had finally lost control of his emotions.

She'd done it. She'd pushed him, cranked his rage and desire to stratospheric.

She swallowed, sucking in air, her chest heaving, her nipples hardened and poking through her dress like bullet tips. Pushed against the SUV, her jacket lapels had fallen open, ensuring her bra-less nipples were displayed to her husband's smouldering gaze.

She'd never been one for public displays of affection. But right now, she didn't care that they were outside. Sure, they were shielded by plants and shrubs, and the area was deserted except for the two vehicles. However, Agatha sat in her car at the bottom of the driveway with her bodyguard, and the security men for the estate were about two hundred metres away.

"Send your security team home," he growled, thrusting his erection against her belly. "Unless you want them to hear everything I do to you. I doubt if the house is sound-proofed."

Her breath hitched as her pulse skyrocketed.

After three days without Maddox, a little dirty talk and she was about to spontaneously combust from desire. She was so ready, and so was he.

"Agatha!" Zoe called out, her gaze not wavering from Maddox.

"Boss?" the woman replied.

"Go back to the hotel. I'm in safe hands."

"Yes, boss."

Neither Zoe nor Maddox moved, restraining themselves until the engine started.

Her husband rubbed against her as the vehicle did a three-point turn and headed towards the gates they'd entered.

Then his lips smashed onto hers in a punishing kiss as her spine arched against the SUV and his hips, his body, pressed against her.

"Look at what you've turned me into," his words were gruff with anger and lust. "You're making me seem like a man who cannot keep to his words. A man who doesn't know his own mind. A man of low scruples and principles."

She'd already figured this out about him. He was a determined, decisive, principled man. He never reneged on a promise. Once his mind was made up, he stuck to his guns. So his about-turn on their marriage was out of character.

But she said nothing because she didn't want to sound triumphant. After all, she'd forced him into this situation. She would eventually explain her reasons. But she wanted him beyond the point of no return first.

She wanted to reclaim him and be claimed by him. If it meant he was a creature of primal instinct at this moment, then so be it.

"I want my husband back," she said between panting breaths. "Is that so wrong?"

His reply was to scoop her into his arms and carry her across the drive, under the portico and to the front door.

"What are you doing?" she yelped.

"What I should have done when we got married." He softly brushed his lips against hers as he inserted the key in the lock. "I will carry my bride over the threshold and fuck her in every room to make memories."

Her limbs felt light as happiness pulsed through her, melting her insides into mush. She'd never known she would feel ecstatic about a cliché, but here she was, ready to offer her heart and life to this man.

She beamed up the most euphoric smile. "But this isn't our house."

"Then we're buying it. Because after I fuck you in it, I'm damn well not going to let anyone else live in it." He pushed the door open and carried her across the threshold as promised.

Damn, the man's possessive streak matched hers. She was obsessed with him. There would be no going back for her.

They hadn't even viewed the place, but she didn't care. "I guess your sister made a sale."

"She sure did." He didn't take her far and lowered her onto the marble-covered foyer floor.

She glanced around, impressed by the ivory walls and spiral staircase. A narrow, polished teakwood table stood against a window beside the front door.

"Place your hands on the table and push your bum out," he ordered with a gravelly voice.

The same lust flowed through her veins like a life-sustaining force.

Surprisingly, her usual aversion to being ordered around didn't rear its ugly head. In any case, she wanted her husband in charge right now. She would give him this. He'd been patient enough. Despite all the wahala she'd caused him and his family, he was here with her now, a testament to his endurance.

She swivelled, facing the window, arching her back and lifting her hips. He shoved her dress up to her waist, exposing the barely-there thong, making her realise the air conditioner must be on as cold air breezed over her bare bum.

With a savage tug, he tore the lace, and it floated to the floor around her stilettoed feet. A feral rumble flowed from his lips as his hand descended on her bum in sharp swats.

"Ow." She yelped from shock. Her exposed flesh stung, yet her core clenched with need.

"That is for constantly giving me a hard time," he said before she felt a second sharp sting across her butt.

"But you don't mind me giving you a hard time," she retorted, moving one hand to cover her bum.

He grabbed her hand, shoving her body flat over the table before raining down more spanking in quick succession. "That's not the point. That I can live with it doesn't mean you should do it constantly."

He caressed her backside briefly, soothing the ache and followed it up with another volley. "And that's for moving your hand from the table."

She kept quiet, letting him have his moment. She realised the first time he did it that it was a stress relief for him more than anything. It didn't hurt or make her feel belittled. Instead, it sent heat to her core, almost like a vibrator.

The telltale sound of a zipper made her whimper, her core clenching with need.

Heat covered her back when he bent over her, blanketing her with his body. His warm breath tickled her eardrum. His teeth nipped her earlobe as clothing rustled, and then his skin flushed against hers. A delicious shiver skated over her body at the feel of him surrounding her on all sides. His erection pressed against her bum.

"I won't be gentle." He gripped her hips as he straightened.

"Don't be." She admitted. A messy ball of emotion clogged her throat because he was warning her, preparing her for what was coming and getting her permission.

He really was a principled man. Right from their first night together, he'd sought her consent before he'd done anything with her. She couldn't have asked for a better lover, a better husband.

He dipped two fingers inside her. Her greedy pussy gripped his digits tightly as he pumped in and out of her.

"Your pussy is dripping, begging for my dick."

She whimpered as delicious tremors marched over her entire body.

He wasn't lying. She would beg for his dick if he didn't fuck her soon.

The air shifted, and his wet tongue teased the lips of her pussy, running up and down her slit for a few seconds before withdrawing.

"No, don't stop," she grumbled.

"I would eat your pussy, but naughty Mimi gets punished."

He straightened, gripped her hips and tilted her bum. Then his dick nudged her slick entrance, and before she could fully prepare, he slammed into her in one long thrust.

"Maddox!" she screamed, pushing back against his groin as he rammed in and out of her. Her pussy clenched and relaxed with wanton need.

"Oh…oh." His stiff, hot length pounding into her was almost enough to send her over the edge.

"Mimi, you feel so good," he panted, gripping her hips tighter to control the angle of his thrusts. "Your hot pussy is squeezing me so tight."

"Nnanna … Oh," she moaned as he sped up, fucking her brutally and slamming her pelvis into the table. She would have bruises, but she didn't care. She only cared about chasing the orgasm building at a steady pace but not fast enough. Not nearly enough. "Nnanna … please."

"Tell me what you want?" he grunted, driving his dick so deep, she felt as if his sperm would fertilize her egg tonight.

"Make me come." She shoved against him, gasping as stars burst behind her retinas when he rutted into her like a savage creature, digging his fingers into her hips to control the motion.

"Nnanna will always take care of his Mimi." He moved his hand to her breast, squeezing and kneading before rolling and pinching the nipple like putty, making her squirm and tingle. A jumbled noise left her mouth as he worked her body like a finely tuned instrument.

He repeated the action with the other breast, leaving her aching and trembling for release. "Beg me again."

"Please," she urged as his hand skimmed down her belly to the sensitive skin between her legs, finding her clit swollen and throbbing.

"Yes," she cheered as he rubbed her in sync with the action of his rolling hips and thrusting dick. Her orgasm built and climbed, grew intense with the pressure he applied to her sensitive clit.

He clamped on her clit with his thumb and finger as he rammed his dick into her, burying himself so deep he hit her cervix. Powerful shudders ripped through his muscular body as he found his release, grunting while he deposited his seed inside her.

"Nnanna!" she screamed as a crescendo of bliss crashed over her. Wave after wave of orgasmic ecstasy lays siege to her body, leaving her whimpering and panting. She didn't move for a while, savouring the orgasm, floating in bliss. She'd never felt better or more sated.

THIRTY-FOUR

A few minutes later, a beeping phone interrupted the blissful silence and sent Zoe crashing back down to earth. Behind her, Maddox withdrew from her body, quietly, slowly, as if he was reluctant to be physically separated from her.

Thickness bloomed in her throat, and she missed his hardness and heat instantly. Her body ached, and her legs wobbled, but she wouldn't change anything.

She closed her eyes, lying still and listening to fabric rustling as he moved. Fabric swiped her intimately, tenderly, and she opened her eyes, watching him clean her with his handkerchief. Then he pulled her dress down, covering her bum.

For a man who'd just fucked her ruthlessly, his aftercare was ten out of ten. Same as the first night they'd met. Another ten-slash-ten for consistency.

A palm settled on the small of her back. "Are you okay to stand?"

The concern and awareness in his tone disarmed her. Despite his anger at her and what her father did to his sister, her husband still cared about her and felt protective towards her.

Unable to use her voice because of the lump in her throat, she nodded, pushing off the table slowly and swivelling.

She straightened, ready to apologise. Regardless of her conversation with Xandra and Agatha last night, at this moment, she realised she could grovel. He'd earned it, and honestly, she was desperate to hold onto this marriage. There was an ache in her chest that just wouldn't budge. A tremor in her limbs she couldn't squash.

Time stood still as they stared into each other's eyes. His, a gorgeous midnight hue, scrutinised her face just as she did his.

There were lines at the corners of his eyelids that hadn't been there weeks ago when he'd come to her house to ask for her hand in marriage.

Her chest tightened. Were they stress lines, and had she contributed to them?

She reached up and caressed the edge of his left eye, trying to smooth out the crease. "I wish I wasn't such a difficult person to live with.

He raised his hand and covered hers on his warm cheek. "I knew it wouldn't be easy when I married you. Anyway, If I wanted a simple life, I wouldn't do the job I do."

"True. But…" she paused and moved nearer to him so he would see the jumbled emotions chasing each other on her face and know that she was genuinely vulnerable to him. "There are things I need to tell you. So many secrets I held onto when we got married. I don't want to hide them from you anymore."

Her stomach churned, and her skin heated, her mouth drying out.

How would he receive her words? She'd managed to trick him into getting intimate. But he was not guaranteed to stay when she confessed her dark secrets.

He cocked his head to one side, his lips pursed. "Okay. Sit over here."

He took her hand and led her to the intricately hand-carved wooden armchair with a zebra-effect upholstered seat on the other side of the front door.

She settled in it, and he released her hand, moving away. He walked to the spiral stairs with the metal and wood balustrade. Black metal spindles with ornate flourishes travelled from the wooden handrail and embedded into the cream marble steps. The elaborate design on the balustrade matched the glittering chandelier above her head and the black metal wall sconces in the foyer and the wall leading upstairs.

The attention paid to the details was exquisite. She hadn't seen the rest of the place. Still, she was confident the same quality ran through the remainder of the house.

Amaoge and her husband had outdone themselves. Emeka owned the construction company, and Amaoge was the estate manager. It seemed the pair were a winning couple regarding residential architecture and interior design.

There was a landing on the penultimate to the last step, and he lowered his tight butt onto the marble, his long legs bent, his elbows at his knees, hands clasped.

"Why don't you sit on the bench?" She pointed at the other functional furniture in the foyer. The other fixtures were art pieces, dark-wood feminine sculptures strategically placed to catch the eye and invoke thought.

"That thing doesn't look like it will take my weight." He grinned, setting butterflies aflutter in her belly.

He was right. Although padded for seating, the bench appeared delicate because of the narrow, curved, spindly legs.

"We can sit in the dining area." She indicated the open-plan section a step lower and behind the foyer with a polished dark wood table surrounded by eight chairs with zebra-striped upholstery. Another chandelier dangled from the ceiling above it. Further down, a double door led to what she assumed was the back garden.

"Zoe," Maddox's deep voice held censure, grabbing her focus once more. She met his dark gaze. "Don't get distracted. We'll tour the house later. Right now, you have my attention. That's what you wanted, right?"

He understood her so well.

She swallowed, cheeks heating. "Yes."

She wanted him to stay so they could talk and solve their problems. But she was using the house as a distraction to hide from what she had to say to him. To hide her anxiety about how he would respond.

"Then, talk to me," he said in a soothing voice.

"Okay. I'm going to be eating humble pie and apologising often. So bear with me." She leaned forward, matching his pose, elbows on knees, hands clasped together.

"Now, this I have to hear." He chuckled, shaking his head. "The domineering Zoe Himba apologising without prompting. What triggered this change?"

"You triggered it. You've earned my apology. And for the record, this is Mrs Maddox Ejiofor speaking. Outside, I'm Zoe Himba when dealing with the business world. When I must be someone that I don't want to be with you. But right now—" She placed her palm over her chest "—I'm Mrs Maddox Ejiofor. Your wife. I hope you understand they are two different personas. Two different hats I have to wear."

"I understand." He nodded, his smile encouraging.

Her muscles weakened, and she suddenly felt giddy. "You don't know how relieved I am to hear you say it. I was worried you wouldn't understand after yesterday. But we'll get to last night's events later."

"I agree," he said simply. "Continue."

"First of all, I wasn't really going to fuck Noah. I would never cheat on you. I think marriage should be sacred between the people involved." She shifted in the chair, uneasy because she was baring her soul to him, revealing secrets he could hold against her. "I just used Noah as bait to keep you here so we could talk."

"You manipulated me," he said, eyes boring into her.

"Yes, I'm sorry." She shifted again, lowering her hands. "It's a method that has worked all my life, for me, for my family. A method we use to control people. Find something they value or a trigger point, capitalise on it to take advantage of them."

His forehead rumpled, and his eyes narrowed. "You do realise that while it might be suitable for exploiting your enemies or business rivals' weaknesses. It's a horrible and unacceptable approach for your family. For the people you love."

Her breath hitched at the implication of his words. He was correct.

She loved him.

It was the reason she became uncomfortable after they made love. The reason she itched to confess her darkest secrets to him.

He seemed to realise it, too. Hence, the raised eyebrows and questioning gaze. The stiff posture and air of readiness about him. The reason he gave her an audience.

He hoped she loved him.

She lowered her head, nodding. "I realise that now, after living with you for two weeks. I realise that my family is dysfunctional, and there are so many things I need to unlearn about how to treat people I care about."

She looked up and met his gaze. "And I care about you, Maddox. In a way, I've never cared for anyone before. It's like I've become someone I don't recognise. This person who feels despair at losing her husband. It's the reason I was frustrated earlier and manipulated you. It's the reason I fear losing you. Please promise me that whatever I reveal to you, you won't disappear again. That you won't end our marriage."

He sat up, shaking his head. "This is another form of manipulation by emotional blackmail. To accept whatever bombshell you're about to explode."

"No. No. I'm not asking you to accept it. You can get angry at me. Punish me if you wish. But don't walk away again. Please." She held her breath, her anxiety spiking.

He puffed out air and leaned forward again. "Okay. I promise I won't walk away or end our marriage. Why are you afraid?"

She exhaled the breath she was holding. "I'm going to get to it shortly, I promise. But I also wanted to mention my personality. My toxic trait. I know it is toxic, but it's also me. The day you came to my house and proposed, you told me you'd been married before and had a son. Instead of accepting the info you gave genuinely and innocently, my response was jealousy and anger. I hated that you were married before, hated that another woman bore you a child."

"What?" He pushed off the steps, body angled away. "Are you saying that you hate my son?"

"No! Far from it. He comes from you. He is family. My stepson. I feel as protective of him as I do of Amaoge. I would never harm him. I just wished he came from my womb, not another woman's." Unbidden, tears filled her eyes, and she wiped her palms across her cheeks.

He said nothing. What was there to say? She had the opportunity to bear his child and chose a different path.

"Anyway, I was trying to say I understand how you feel about Noah being my ex. I hated your ex-wife as soon as you told me about her. If I walk into a room and she's touching you, I'll shoot her."

If she walked into a room and the woman was there, Zoe would probably shoot her anyway.

"Hmmm," he murmured, nodding. "I understand, but I want you to promise not to hurt her. She is Abuchi's mother. If you care about Abuchi, you won't hurt his mother. Promise me."

She growled in frustration.

"Promise me, Zoe."

"Fine. I won't shoot her."

He eyed her but nodded. "What else did you want to tell me?"

She sighed. "After you came to my house and I rejected your marriage proposal, my father's marriage auction collapsed. All the suitors withdrew because they found out about my abortion."

"I know."

"You know? How?"

"When you humiliated my father and sister by rejecting my proposal the way you did, I had a plan for revenge, which included cutting off your father's sources of income. One of them was the marriage auction. I was going to use our family contact to ensure the auction failed. My eldest brother is married to a politician's daughter. Her father is connected to some of the families participating in the auction. A whisper in the right ear would have spread the rumour. However, someone else beat us to it."

"Who?" she was still too shocked by his revelation to fully process it.

"Your stepmother."

"Wait. My stepmother did what?" she sat up, staring at him like he had two heads.

"She's the source of the rumour that shut down the auction. My sister-in-law was at an event, and heard her talking about you. She's a well-known gossip in certain circles."

"Goodness! Now, it makes total sense. She's had it in for me. She's the one who made me confess the pregnancy to my parents, and then I had no choice but to abort it. And then she had the guts to blame me for the auction failing. When I set eyes on her again, she is dead."

"Zoe, forget about her. She is inconsequential."

"True. Anyway, when the auction failed, and several of Baba's business associates got attacked, he was looking for cash injections. That's when he commanded me to marry you so you would pay the dowry you'd offered with your original proposal."

"So you're saying you married me for the money I would pay your father."

"Yes, but that wasn't the only thing he ordered me to do." She stood and paced, needing to work off the agitation coursing through her. "This is big, Maddox. You're going to hate me."

"Tell me anyway. I'm not going to end our marriage. I promised you."

"I know. But I'm still scared."

"Fear is a healthy emotion. It's a survival mechanism. But you don't need to be afraid."

His words were encouraging, making her realise they were in this together. He wouldn't abandon her.

"When my father ordered me to marry you to get your money, he also ordered me to kill you," she finally admitted. "I married you, knowing I would kill you one day."

His expression remained unchanged.

"Say something," she said.

"The day you went to Arufin, you'd changed your mind about killing me, and you'd gone there to find the justification to kill me." His expression was unreadable.

"Yes." She frowned, confused about his reaction. "You don't sound angry."

"I'm not angry. I assume you don't want to kill me any longer."

"No. I wouldn't purposefully hurt my husband. I couldn't justify killing you when you'd done me no harm. It's why I got furious yesterday when Simon, Ali Baldy showed me Amaoge's photo and said he'd abducted her. He said my father had sanctioned the operation, and I lost it. I ordered him to bring Amaoge over, but he refused, and I shot him."

"In the balls," Maddox commented. "What was that about?"

"He insulted me by implying that I rose through the ranks and got results by sleeping with men. He even wanted me to have sex with him so he could champion one of my projects. Then he dared to touch me. I just shoved my gun into his groin and blew it away. Then, I shot him in the head to ensure he was dead. I'm sorry I stole your thunder because you wanted to kill him yourself."

"No. Don't apologise for that. He deserved to die when he did and the way he did. By your hands."

His understanding seemed a contrast to his reaction yesterday. Then again, yesterday had been intense. He had a day to cool off and reflect.

"Thank you. But I don't understand how you're so calm about finding out I wanted to kill you."

"Sit down, please." He waved at the chair.

She lowered her body back into the padded seat and stared across the foyer at him. He returned to the landing and sat down.

"I don't want any secrets between us any longer, and since you've shared yours, I have a confession to make," he said calmly.

Shit. What could he possibly have to confess? He'd always seemed straightforward to her. Had he been hiding things from her all along?

Her spine stiffened, and she braced herself for devastating news, wrapping her arms around her midriff. "What is it?"

"The day I came to your house to propose, I was hopeful for the best, but I had also planned for the worst. We suspected that your father didn't want to engage with the Odili family and might try to ambush us, so we came prepared. I brought some of my key team up, but we also had a backup team of Yadili men loyal to my father."

"Really? I don't remember seeing any military men with your entourage."

"Actually, every person in my entourage that day has been in the military. But I get what you're saying. The currently serving special ops naval officers were in mufti. They waited for our signal to intervene somewhere else. As soon as I left your house, I ordered surveillance on your family. But the surveillance team didn't get into position until the day after, and they couldn't get into your house to plant bugs. We bugged your half-brothers' phones, but they didn't yield much.

Then, to cap it off, you seemed to disappear for a week. The surveillance team couldn't track you. Then, one day, they followed Noah to Abuja. Lo and behold, you were there. That was the day you first had lunch with Amaoge."

"Oh." She said, still not sure where this was headed.

"Yes. We thought it was the best opportunity to plant a bug on you. So I ordered the surveillance team to clone your phone."

"My phone?" she dug into her pocket and pulled out the digital device. "What do you mean you cloned my phone. Are you saying this is not my phone?"

"No. That's your phone. It's just that we have another device that mimics and records everything you do on this phone—calls, messages, emails. Everything."

"What the hell?" She'd known he'd had her under surveillance since they got married. But this went back to…

"Does it listen to my offline conversations, too?"

"Yes, that's the beauty of it."

"Beauty?" She jumped off the chair. "You invaded my privacy!"

"You aborted my baby without telling me. You humiliated my family. I was bent on a vendetta. I was going to destroy your father's empire and leave you all with nothing." He slashed his hand through the air.

"Oh, my God!" She couldn't think straight. "Did Amaoge know my phone was cloned?"

"No. I distracted both of you with the phone call. I didn't want her involved with it."

"You didn't want her to be friends with me. She wouldn't have let you bug my phone."

He nodded. "She had a fondness for you right from the first day she met you, which I couldn't understand. I mean, you showed up at my house and married me intending to kill me."

"You knew that all along. Yet you allowed me into your home. Why would you?"

"Because I thought I could control you. I wanted to punish you. It's why I cleared the basement in preparation for your arrival. I didn't think I would fall in love with you."

Her mouth dropped open as she gasped. Her heart raced as she stood, walking towards him, her anger forgotten. "You're in love with me?"

He chuckled. "I think I've been in love with you since the first night at Arufin. The way you responded to me, your bossiness and backtalk. And the way you fell asleep in my arms afterwards. It showed you trusted me on an intrinsic level. It was like a drug in my veins. I wanted more of you. Then, six weeks later, I finally got your details and called you, and everything turned upside down."

THIRTY-FIVE

Zoe stayed silent for a few seconds, Maddox's words swirling in her mind. She stood straight, chin tilted. Her lungs expanded with pride even as warmth suffused her with joy.

Maddox loved her.

She allowed the words to sink in.

He was in love with her just as she was in love with him.

But…

A light quiver in her stomach triggered some doubt. So much had happened between them. She'd hurt him, and he'd sought revenge. Could they get past it and move on?

Could they have a happy life together?

Not if her father had anything to do with it.

Then there were his parents. Could they forgive her actions?

"What happens now? Where do we go from here?" she asked the questions bombarding her brain, swallowing more than usual. A tight pain spread across her chest.

He straightened and came closer, wrapping his hand around her shoulders. His eyebrows rose, and he offered a questioning gaze. "What do you want to do?"

"I want to be your wife beyond today, beyond the original three-month agreement." She bit the inside of her cheek. "But I know nothing about relationships, even less about marriage. My parents are not a good example. I don't want what they have. I guess that was my biggest reason for not wanting to get married in the first place."

He puffed out a heavy breath. "We won't do what they did. We are different people, and we want different things from them."

"Yes, I do." She raised her hand to his chest. "I want you. No, it's more than want. I need you to see me. To understand me. To commit to me like you've never committed to anyone before."

A slow grin spread on his face. "Oh, you don't ask for a lot, do you?"

"Maddox, I'm serious." She clutched his shirt tight, although a smile played on her lips. "I need to know that I'm your number one person."

His knuckle under her chin tilted her head up. "And am I your number one person?"

His voice was deep, making her belly quiver.

"Yes, without a doubt. There's no one above you," she made the vow solemnly.

"Unh." He groaned and closed his eyes. "That's the sexiest thing you've said to me."

Her heart fluttered in her chest. "Really?"

"Yes." He opened his eyes, grinning. "And for the record. You are my number one person. The day I offered you the option to be my queen, I was offering you the number one spot. All I wanted was for you to meet me halfway."

"Wow. Really?"

"Absolutely. I'm not claiming to be the best at relationships. I envy my parents the love and companionship they share. And after my first marriage ended, I felt like a failure as the first divorcee in my family."

"A failure. Never."

"It's true. I lost the confidence and inclination to sustain a long-term relationship. This is why I enjoyed the casual encounters at Arufin. The no-strings-attached meant I didn't have to invest myself again."

She frowned, cupping his hairy chin. "What actually happened between you and your ex?"

He stepped away as if he was uncomfortable. She followed him. He took her hand, and they walked down to the open-plan dining area. To the right was a spacious sitting room, split into two sections separated by a bookcase with potted plants and books.

He sat on one of the upholstered sofas and tugged her beside him.

"Many factors affected my first marriage. Firstly, I think Ifeoma and I married too young to fully understand the implications of marriage and commitment. We wanted everything there and then. She was bratty. I was impatient. To cap it off, I was mostly away, deployed on active duty while she was pregnant with Abuchi. It was at the height of the war against terror. So, I was sent to remote locations, and she couldn't reach me. Of course, she had my family and hers nearby. But I should have been there too. When I came home, she was distant and obnoxious. We would argue. In the end, I started avoiding home and stayed away longer, taking more assignments because I couldn't bear coming home and arguing with her. Then, one day, I came home, and she was gone. She returned to her parents, and when I showed up, she said she wanted to get out of the marriage. I didn't fight it. I let her go. She filed for divorce, and I didn't contest it. Abuchi lived with her until he became a teenager. He was at boarding school. During the holidays, he would stay with my parents. And then with me after I left military service."

Zoe held onto his hand as he spoke, his hurt and disappointment in his voice and posture.

"I don't think you are a failure," she said quietly. "If you were a failure, then so was I because I couldn't even sustain a relationship, let alone have a marriage. Hell, I couldn't even sustain a pregnancy."

"Don't say that." His grip on her hand tightened. "You were manipulated into giving up those things. In any case, it no longer matters because we're both starting afresh, right?"

"Right."

"So we can build the relationship we want. A relationship without manipulation. We will be open to one another. We will open our hearts and our minds to each other."

"Yes, I want to do it. You will have to be patient."

"I'm learning to be more patient. I promise to not bail out because you're being difficult." He grinned.

"And I promise to not let you go even if you bail." Her smile widened.

He chuckled. "I see you're not promising to not be difficult."

Her cheeks heated because he knew her too well. "Oh, I won't promise something I can't deliver. But I promise to stay and take the spankings when I get too difficult."

"I see. You're beginning to enjoy the spankings a little too much."

"Perhaps." She fluttered her lashes coyly.

He shook his head, still grinning. He pulled out the small black box from his pocket. "Since we're starting afresh, I would like to offer you this token of my devotion to you."

He opened the box, and the black diamond and platinum ring glimmered.

Her mouth dropped as she glanced up at his face. "You bought me a ring?"

How was that possible? He'd cancelled their marriage, hadn't he?

"Yes, this was my gift to you the day I came to propose, but I never got the chance to give it to you. I gave it to Amaoge to sell. But she obviously didn't and slid it into the folder where I found it this evening. That woman is sneaky."

"And I love her. And you." She leaned forward and kissed him deeply. Her body trembled as he slipped the ring onto her finger. "Oh, my goodness. You bought me a ring."

She couldn't contain her excitement as he chuckled. "Amaoge said the ring suits you."

"Absolutely. This is me. You know me too well."

"Then I think we'll do just fine. But I need to clarify something, and that's just because I don't like to have unanswered questions."

"Yes. What is it?"

"After I visited your parents' house to propose, where did you go for a week? Did you travel?"

"No." She shifted, feeling uneasy because this was a touchy subject for both. They'd talked about the reasons she'd had an abortion and some of their feeling about it. However, they hadn't discussed the physical implications of the procedure.

"After you left our house with your family, I fainted and became unconscious," she continued, her insides twisting into knots.

"What?" His eyebrows drew together, and he tilted his head, meeting her gaze. "You were unwell?"

"Yes, I was admitted to hospital that night and underwent surgery."

"Surgery?" He froze, his voice deepening. "That's serious."

"Yes, it was. I'd been in pain for a few days after the termination, and I put it down to a side effect of the procedure. But it turned out I was haemorrhaging due to complications. I was transferred to another hospital in the FCT for the surgery because they couldn't perform it in the first one. After I was discharged, I stayed in a hotel for two days. That's when I saw Amaoge in the shopping mall."

"Oh, no." He pulled her close, wrapping his arms around her. "I'm sorry. I didn't know."

She leaned in, pressing her head against his chest, circling her arms on his back. She savoured how he held her, the comfort and reassurance of his embrace.

He caressed her back gently and spoke tenderly. "Are you okay now? I mean physically. Will you need further operations?"

"No," she replied. "Doctor said I should be fine. I haven't had any other complications since."

She remembered her thoughts when she'd woken for the surgery, wondering if it wouldn't have been better to have a hysterectomy. But she was glad she still had her ovaries intact.

"We talked about the possibility of getting pregnant again. Are you still okay with it?"

He didn't reply immediately, and her heart sank. Her reluctance the last time had changed his mind. She couldn't blame him.

"I understand if you've changed your mind," she said.

He leaned back and met her gaze, his expression pained.

"That's not it," he said, shifting to face her properly. "I'm going to reveal something to you. Something private. Something that only sworn members of the Yadili know. I'm telling you because you're my wife. You must swear to keep the secret, Zoe."

Her body tensed as her pulse rate sped up. "I promise to keep your secret, Maddox."

He nodded, threading his fingers between hers. "As you know, Yadili is a secret organisation; we take oaths when we join. Once you join, there are different levels and subgroups. Different challenges and rituals are required, depending on the individual's goals. Everyone takes the oath at the sanctuary. However, because I took an enforcer oath, mine involved the Ofor challenge, where I had to prove that my hands were clean and I stand for equity and justice. As part of the ritual, blood was spilt to cleanse me of past misdeeds."

Her eyes went wide. "Whose blood?"

"Mine." He tilted to the side, pulled his shirt seam from the trousers and exposed the scar on his back. "That came from the masquerade during the Ofor challenge."

"Oh." She traced the welt with her fingertip.

"I told you before that my blood does not spill in vain. What that means is that anyone who spills my blood pays the price. Usually, these are enemies on the battlefield since I'm a warrior."

A cold sliver travelled down her spine. "What if it's not an enemy on the battlefield?"

"Then the consequences could be dire for them."

He held her hand as her heart raced.

"You think something is going to happen to me because I aborted your baby."

He nodded. "Not just you. The repercussions will impact both of us because you're my wife. I didn't think about it before because I was angry at you. But now that you mentioned your haemorrhage, I remembered that I also had a nosebleed and a searing headache that same day you told me about the abortion."

She wasn't superstitious, but dread filled her at his words. "What do you think is going to happen?"

"I don't know the exact consequences this time. However, when a loved one spills an enforcer's blood, it weakens them because blood cleansing needs to be performed again. But it's worse this time because you will be affected too. The haemorrhaging makes me think we might struggle to conceive and suffer miscarriages if we don't fix the problem."

THIRTY-SIX

"Oh no!" Zoe cried, pulling away from Maddox as she paced the spacious sitting room from one end to the other. "What have I done?"

She appeared distraught, wringing her hand, and her voice sounded broken. "How am I going to fix this?"

When she looked up, her glistening eyes tore at his heart.

She'd already apologised for not telling him about the abortion. But this was different. This time, she was hurting, and he didn't like it.

"And to top it off, I challenged my father yesterday and resigned as his deputy, setting up my independent operations. This is going to bring his wrath down on us. He will take it out on you. We already know he has no problem attacking your family. Now, I've practically posted a target on your back. He will think you convinced me to defy him."

"As if I have that level of influence over you." He stood and went to her, blocking her path. "Zoe, calm down."

"How can I be calm?" She reared at him, shaking her head. "What I did could ruin everything. What if my father orders a hit on you? What if I can't have your child? What if I aborted my only chance to have a child?"

He honestly didn't know the consequences of her actions. "I don't know the full implications. But I don't want you worrying about it until we learn more."

"But I'm worried. My father aside, I know how much you wanted the baby. I saw your face when I told you I'd had an abortion. You were heartbroken. What would it do to you, to us, if I don't conceive again."

He again pulled her into his arms to quell her agitation and stop her from pacing.

"Zoe, I love you," he whispered into her hair.

She sagged into his arms, gripping him tight.

He caressed her back tenderly. "I didn't marry you because I wanted more children. I married you because I want you."

"Oh, Maddox, I don't know how I got this lucky," she sounded croaky and leaned back to look up at him. She lifted her arms and wrapped her hand around his neck. Then she stood on tiptoes and pressed her lips to his. "I never knew that I could feel this way about anyone. I love you so much."

Her words made his soul sing with joy. He'd suspected she might be in love with him when she returned to Arufin to view the video from their first night together.

But he'd worried she might not be ready to let go of her father's influence until yesterday. Until Amaoge's abduction.

At first, he'd thought she was involved until he'd shown up at the guest house ready to raze the place to the ground.

Then he'd seen his wife, looking bloody and brutal like the kingpin she aimed to become. And even as he'd argued with her, he'd tumbled into her allure. He couldn't sustain his rage at what her father had done to Amaoge, especially after seeing the dead body of Ali Baldy, whom she'd killed.

Still, it annoyed him when she didn't hand over the rest of Ali Baldy's crew. It seemed she'd instigated a coup and had taken over the group, making herself a kingpin in waiting. What she'd always wanted.

Even more shocking, Amaoge, Xandra and Agatha, whom he'd paid to provide security, had supported her without question. She'd earned their trust more solidly than she'd received his.

But that was yesterday.

Joshua had informed him about Zoe's telephone conversation with her father, which had removed the last of his reservations.

Today, his sister had engineered this rendezvous, and Zoe was like a different person. There was no sign of the callous woman from months ago.

Instead, she was soft and fragrant and pliant in his arms. Having her like this was a dream come true. He didn't mind her being the kingpin with others as long as she stayed his wife like this.

He tilted his head, deepening the kiss, feeding off the passion she gave in abundance. His ice queen has thawed into a passionate goddess.

He broke the kiss to catch his breath. "It's time to check out the master bedroom."

Her eyes heated, making his dick harden. He ground his hips against her belly, making her feel his solidity, how she made him feel.

"I don't think we'll be seeing much of the room. But I'm ready to check it out."

He scooped her up and headed towards the stairs so they could explore their new home and each other.

***

While Zoe slept in the massive bed in the master bedroom of the house she'd come to view, Maddox called Tito to send a security team to their location.

Although he'd told Zoe to send her team home this afternoon, he wouldn't leave her without protection, a day after she'd quit as her father's shugaba and appointed herself as boss. A day after, Amaoge was abducted and rescued.

She was a lone wolf in a sea of sharks. Her new team was untested, and he doubted people who made a living through extortion would make great warriors.

Zoe was a queen who needed to conquer territory to claim a kingdom.

Maddox would conquer the kingdom for her and install her as empress.

After the call to his security team, he called Amaoge, and after thanking her for reuniting him with his wife, he told her that he and Zoe were buying the house. She laughed and said she thought as much. She would take this one off the market and prepare another property as a show home. Thankfully, they were the first to viewers, so no one else had traipsed through it since it was completed.

Phone in hand, he headed downstairs to the kitchen. Amaoge mentioned there were drinks and small chops in the fridge. She'd really gone all-out to reunite Maddox with his wife.

He found the takeaway boxes as she'd described and grabbed a glass of water. He finished drinking it when his phone pinged with the constant beeping he recognised as a security alert.

He decoded and read the message.
Intruder alert. Hostiles approaching your location.

THIRTY-SEVEN

Hostiles meant one thing. Trouble had arrived. Don Himba was about to rain on Maddox's parade.

Instinctively, he flicked off the light switch, turning the kitchen into darkness. He grabbed his phone from the counter and glanced outside. Dusk had descended, although he could see the back garden through the window and the reflection of the swimming pool. But he couldn't see anyone.

Still, it didn't mean the intruders weren't out there.

He pressed the button to dial the number, heading upstairs.

"Boss," Tito replied.

"What's the update?" he asked.

"A guard from the Ogeka Estate triggered an alarm. We were already heading to you, and I pulled up the livestream. Four intruders in a flatbed truck just entered the estate."

Maddox was glad he'd ordered his team to come over. They stayed in Amaoge's guest house, only a few minutes from here.

"Are you able to intercept?"

"Moving into position now."

"Good. Keep me updated."

The mobile phones will have to be their mode of communication since he didn't come out geared up for duty. Meanwhile, he needed his clothes.

Zoe stirred as he entered the room and switched off the light. He didn't want to give away their position by having the lamps on. Dusk light from the fading sun came through the window.

"What's going on?" Zoe asked, sitting up.

"Get dressed. We have a situation." He picked her clothes strewn over the settee at the foot of the bed and tossed them at her before pulling his on quickly.

"What situation?" she asked but started dressing.

He was glad she obeyed him, although she asked a valid question. This proved they were on the same page regarding their relationship. Out there, she was the kingpin. In here, he was the king.

"Intruders are heading for the house." He finished dressing and checked his weapon. He always examined and cleaned his gun every morning and after every use. A habit from his days in military service. He'd used it yesterday, so he'd cleaned it this morning. The Glock 17 handgun had seventeen rounds in the magazine, and he had another magazine in his jacket pocket. There was extra ammunition in the car. He doubted he would get out there before the firefight began. But he should have enough to stall the intruders.

Zoe put her clothes on silently. She followed his lead and checked her Beretta Nano. The magazine held six rounds, and there was one in the chamber.

He walked to the edge of the window and peeped out. The streetlights were not on. He glanced at his phone, expecting an update from his men. Nothing. Instead, there was the sound of a faint pop and crackle, like discharged firearms in the distance. Perhaps the use of a silencer close by.

"Something is wrong." He pulled his gun from the holster and unlocked the safety. "Stay here. Let me go check."

"Not happening." She snorted in brief laughter and held his gaze. Even in the shadows, he could see her icy determination. "I love you as my knight, but I'm not a damsel in distress. We're in this together. So, we do this together."

His protective instincts urged him to wrap her in Kevlar and keep her safe. But she was right. So, he didn't argue.

She looked ready to take on the world with her power suit, killer heels, and loaded gun. And she turned him on like nothing else.

He moved towards the door before he got too distracted by her allure.

"Hold on." She stepped in front of him, blocking the exit. "Regardless of what happens, I need you alive," she murmured, reaching up to cup his face.

"And so do I," he growled, the protectiveness and possessiveness swirling together as he grabbed her nape and slammed his mouth against hers in a brief, passionate kiss. "I need you in one piece and alive. So, if things get dicey, do what I say."

"Okay." She pressed tight, rubbing her belly against his crotch, making his dick swell and throb. Then, she traced her tongue over his lips. "And when this is over, I want you all to myself for at least a week, somewhere no one can interrupt our honeymoon."

There was a mix of flirtation and anxiety in her words that reflected his state of mind. Neither of them was in a hurry to get into the melee, hence the need to bask in the comfort of each other's arms.

Unease rippled through him, along with arousal heating his veins. Apprehension triggered by her earlier revelation about her haemorrhaging. He knew he didn't have his usual protection before going into battle. It was tainted because of the abortion. It was a crack in his armour, a defect his enemies could use to maim him or worse.

All because he'd married her and stayed married to her without fixing the problem. He hadn't known things would progress this quickly between them after a fortnight of living together. He'd assumed he had weeks, perhaps months, to repair the fracture.

Even worse, he hadn't prepared for her father hitting out as relentlessly as he was doing. First, Amaoge abduction for ransom only yesterday. Now, these intruders were here for them.

Regardless of his concerns, he had to stay upbeat and positive. He had to believe they would conquer the challenges, however persistent they became.

"Agreed," he said, grinning, matching her flirtation. "I promise to devote at least two weeks in the near future when my only duty will be servicing my queen."

She giggled, her eyes bright, her body posture relaxed, the anxiety vanishing.

Instinctively, he relaxed as well, and his grin widened with the realisation that they would be so in sync and mirrored each other's moods readily. She was his other half, indeed. His perfect match.

The Star-Arufin app had been accurate.

"I love the sound you make when you're happy." He brushed his lips against hers tenderly as warmth suffused him.

Outside, a battle was raging on. But between the two of them, their conflict was resolved.

"And soon, I want to hear the sound of those assholes meeting their makers."

"You are so bloodthirsty." He chuckled low. "After seeing what you did to Ali Baldy, I almost pity all your father's goons who are about to lose their balls."

"For attacking us in our new home, they deserve everything they get."

"True. Stay close. Watch my back." He walked to the door, weapon at the ready.

"Roger that," she said in a light tone and followed two steps behind, matching his steady, cautious motion.

They descended the spiral stairs without event, and he paused on the landing.

"Check the dining area. Keep your eyes on the back door," he said in a low voice, listening and sweeping the foyer with his gaze.

"Nothing here," she replied in a whisper and, after a minute, added, "Maybe it was a false alarm."

"Maybe." He didn't move. Just waited for the sign from his team. They were out there.

"Let's just get into the car and leave." The air shifted as she moved, hurrying down the last steps, making the hair rise on his nape in alarm.

"Stay back!" Reflexively, he reached out and grabbed her jacket, yanking her out of the way as a blast exploded in the street. He ducked, taking her down with him. "Keep low!"

She nodded, looking unfazed about the ongoing battle at the doorstep.

He scrambled across the foyer and sat on the floor before lifting his head to peer out the window. Sure enough, his men were out there, under attack. The continuous rat-tat-tat of heavy gunfire concerned him.

"Shit!" he swore aloud, sitting back down on the marble and pulling out his phone. He pressed the button to connect to Tito.

"What is it?" Zoe asked, following him across the foyer.

He held up his hand as his head of security answered the call. "What's the status?"

"We're under heavy fire but holding," Tito replied. "There are at least ten hostiles with assault rifles and a grenade launcher. Three down so far, leaving nine that we can see."

How did they go from four to ten? Maybe the others were hidden from the cameras when Tito reported earlier.

"Do we have any casualties?" he asked, heart racing.

"Yes, Mike was seriously injured with the blast."

"Shit." Mike had been with his team right from the start.

"Boss, we're not going to be able to hold them off at this rate without reinforcements."

They'd come to the FCT with a bare team because it had been a last-minute trip. The rest of the team couldn't be here at short notice. However, there was an alternative backup.

"Okay. I'll call Dad's Special Ops team." Then he thought of Zoe's suggestion. "Do you think you can hold them off for me to get my wife out of here?"

"Yes. But we'll need to disable the grenade launcher first."

"Do it, and let me know when it's safe." The call ended, and he turned to his wife. "We're going to get you out of here. Be ready to run for my car as soon as I give the word."

Her face furrowed in a frown. "It's bad, isn't it."

He sighed. "Yes. They have AK47s and grenade launchers, the preferred weapons for militants and terrorists across the earth."

Her frown deepened. "But Baba has no ties to …" she trailed off, eyes widening. "Shit … shit."

"What is it?"

"It must be Abdul Sani. He controls the militants in Medogri. His was the first proposal I rejected from Baba's marriage auction. The arrogant bastard didn't like it one bit. I'm sure he was happy to get revenge when Baba asked him for a favour."

"Abdul Sani?" Maddox's hands balled into fists. "Wasn't he working with Marlon Owo, Carla's brother, against Duke? He even attempted to abduct Carla before she married Duke."

"Yes, I heard about that. The man is a snake." Zoe nodded.

Maddox's spine stiffened. If that was the case, then Abdul Sani was also trying to get back at the Odili family for taking Carla away from him and punishing Zoe for rejecting him. He was attempting to kill two birds with one stone.

Maddox didn't like this one bit. "We need to get you out of here."

He stood, tugging Zoe up with him. "Get ready to move fast on my say-so."

A deafening blast exploded through the front door and careened Maddox forward. He kept his arms around Zoe, protecting her body as they crashed onto the hard flooring.

THIRTY-EIGHT

Zoe blinked several times, trying to get her bearings. It was difficult to see through the smoke surrounding her, and her ears rang as she lay on the cold floor. It took her a second to remember where she was.

In the house, she'd come to view with Maddox.

"Maddox!"

She glanced around the gloomy, smoky foyer, searching for him. He was here a second ago. He'd fallen on top of her and covered her with his body. Now, he was gone.

She blinked again, trying to remember. She must have blacked out from the explosion. How long had it been? Where was he?

Panicking, she tried to move, grappling to push off the floor. Her body ached, and her hands were slippery and sticky. She lifted them, staring at the dark stains. Blood? No!

"Maddox!" she yelled again, scrambling onto her knees.

Debris lay everywhere, and there was a gaping hole where the front door used to be.

"Zoe." The sound of her name was distorted, almost otherworldly, because of the ringing in her ears. Two dark figures appeared out of the gloom, surrounding her. One had a torch light focused on her.

Her heart raced as she searched for her gun. She'd had it in her hand when the front door exploded. She spotted it a few inches away. It must have dropped when she fell.

"Zoe, it's Jaxon." One of the dark figures leaned over her.

At first, she jerked back and blinked. Then she saw his face, recognition dawning and making her understand what he'd said.

"Are you okay?" he asked, looking her over. "Can you stand?"

"Yes." She pushed off the floor, and he held onto her arm when she stumbled.

"Are you injured anywhere?" He stared at the blood on her body.

"No. It's not my blood. Where is my husband? Where is Maddox?" Her voice rose as her panic returned. The blood must be from him.

Jax shook his head. "Let's get you out of here."

"No. I want to know where my husband is."

"I'm sorry, but he was taken. We couldn't stop them. We're two men down. Only me and Tito are left standing." He indicated the other man standing watch at the entrance.

"They took him! And you're still here. Why didn't you go after them?" She tried to pace but hobbled and stopped. Her knees and ankles hurt. The heel of her shoe was broken.

"We can't leave you here unprotected. We've really got to move—"

"Maddox is your brother! And you're concerned about me. He's the one you should protect. Don't you get it? This blood—" She lifted her hands "—is not mine. He's seriously injured. If his injuries don't kill him, those men will! … You know what? I'll go find him myself."

She reached for her gun, but Tito grabbed it before her.

She straightened, narrowed her eyes, and stretched out her hand. "Give me my weapon."

"No. Do you know what your husband will do to us if we let you walk out of here without protection?" He stepped out of reach. "You are Mrs Maddox Ejiofor, and I have a duty to protect you. Until he tells us otherwise."

"And if he's…" she trailed off, not wanting to contemplate that her husband was no longer part of this existence. An existence that would mean nothing without him.

"I know this is difficult," Tito said calmly. "But we have one positive note. They took him, which means they want him alive. He is more valuable to them alive. So that buys us a little time to prepare to rescue him. But we can't do that effectively if we're also worried about your safety. So, please. Come with us to the Ejiofor residence, where the war room is set up. You can contribute and make suggestions on how your husband is rescued."

His reassuring tone calmed her panic and anger. He made sense.

Except she'd always be an impulsive, reactive person. An attack on her always produced an immediate brutal response. She would act first and ask questions later.

But this was different. This had been a calculated attack, probably instigated by her father, but she had no proof. Since Maddox was taken, perhaps a ransom call was coming.

And if she was going to confront her father, she needed her team.

But that also led to another problem.

For now, she would go with Maddox's team.

"Let's go." She said, walking towards the hole where the door had been.

Tito led the way, weapon ready, past Maddox's SUV and down the street, where another car was packed. He opened the back door and held it for her to climb in and shut it.

Jaxon got into the driver's seat, started the car and drove away from the pavement.

"Is Tito not coming?" she asked, turning to stare at the man they left behind.

"No. He's waiting for the clean-up crew. We need to spin this as an armed robbery intercepted by the security team. Otherwise, Amaoge and Emeka will lose business. A good thing there were no witnesses, and it's a public holiday, so there were no workers. The security team are our employees."

"Of course." Zoe hadn't even thought about the other implications of the attack. Then she remembered. "You said you lost two men tonight. I'm sorry for your loss. Did I know them?"

"Thank you." Jaxon's throat bobbed as he swallowed. "We've never had this much casualty since we set up the security firm. Mike was part of the FCT crew and worked for us for years. I have to call his family and tell them the bad news."

"I'm so sorry. That's not going to be an easy call to make."

"It isn't. The worse will be if Josiah doesn't recover."

Zoe sat upright. "Josiah? He's hurt."

"Yes. Seriously. Joshua had to rush him to the hospital. He'll likely need surgery."

"Oh no." She bent over, stomach cramping with guilt and grief. She'd brought this trouble onto their doorsteps and made it much worse.

Josiah was in Maddox's close circle, and she'd grown fond of the fraternal twins she'd nicknamed the bears. His loss would be too close to home.

She covered her face with her hands.

How was she going to fix this?

***

The trip to Elder Ejiofors' house took about thirty minutes.

When Zoe glanced up from her wristwatch, Jaxon pulled into the modestly large compound surrounded by neatly trimmed hedges and uniformed military personnel. It seemed news of Maddox's abduction had reached them already because she didn't think they would have this number of people milling about usually.

When Jaxon parked the car in one of the spots, someone she didn't recognise opened the door for her.

"Good evening, ma," he said, stepping out of the way for her to climb out.

"Good evening," she replied as the warm night embraced her.

"Zoe," someone called out and hurried across the gravel driveway.

"Agatha," she called out in recognition, pleased to see the woman unharmed. "How did you get here."

"Tito called me earlier and told me to check you out of the hotel and bring your luggage here. I just arrived a few minutes ago." She pointed at the car Zoe had been using parked in one of the bays. Next to it was the driver who'd been with her earlier.

Zoe's blood boiled as soon as she saw the man, and her first reaction was to pull out her gun and shoot him. But she realised Jaxon held onto it.

Instead, she stomped across the driveway, the stones digging into her bare soles because she took her broken shoes off in the car. She didn't care, fired by adrenaline and fury.

He straightened, shifting his position as she approached. "Good evening, boss."

In response, she jabbed her fist into his face. His eyes widened in shock as his head hit the car, and he cried out. He slipped away and tried to run. But Agatha blocked his path.

He turned, nose bleeding, eyes wide, darting across the driveway, looking for escape. He knew exactly what had caused her ire.

"You swore allegiance to me, yet you betrayed me," she shouted.

"What?" Agatha kicked him from behind and sent him crashing onto the gravel.

"What's going on?" Jaxon asked as Agatha pulled the man up to a kneeling position.

"He told them where to find me and Maddox," Zoe snarled.

"How do you know it was him?" Jaxon asked.

"Well, think about it. No one else outside your family knew where I was. Not even other members of my team. Except Agatha and him. Agatha wouldn't betray Maddox. That leaves him. He's my father's mole."

"Lieutenant," Jaxon called.

One of the men standing around approached, "Sir."

"Interrogate him and find out what he knows about the attack and my brother's abduction," Jaxon ordered.

"Yes, sir." The man indicated for the other military officers to take Zoe's driver.

"Boss, abeg," the man cried as he was dragged up. "I no know where dem take am."

"But you thought it was a good idea to cross me. Even when you saw what I did to Ali Baldy," she bit out, not appeased.

"Na Don order me. E just say make I tell am everywhere you go. As soon as we reach hotel, I message am address wey I drop you. Nothing again. I don't know say dem go attack una. Abeg."

His words only fuelled her anger because his actions were intentional.

"And now, my husband is missing, and he's lost good men. All because you betrayed me." She turned to the military men taking him away. "I want him tortured. Make him bleed."

The lieutenant glanced at Jaxon, and he nodded. The military men dragged her pleading driver towards another building at the entrance.

"Agatha will take you inside and show you to Maddox's room so you can freshen up," Jax said.

"Freshen up?" Zoe tilted her chin up. "I thought you said there was a war room. We need to make plans to get my husband back."

"Yes, we do. But the rest of the team isn't here yet. My parents are out and on the way back home. Duke is flying in tonight. Amaoge is on the way over, too. So are a few other people. We cannot make decisions about Maddox in isolation. He matters to many people who want to contribute however they can."

Maddox had a vast, strong family looking out for him, and they were not all connected by blood. He had his immediate blood relatives, security colleagues, and the Odili clan. He was an essential part of a community that would miss him.

If he didn't come home, it would be her fault.

A lump lodged in her throat, and she couldn't speak. She swallowed as her chest ached.

Jaxon seemed to notice her distress, and his voice softened. "Go inside and freshen up. Get something to eat and some rest if you can. It's going to be a long night."

***

At midnight, Zoe sat in the war room. It had been five hours since the attack at the show home.

One of the living rooms had been converted into a makeshift war room. Desktops, computers and laptops were stationed on the dining table, and a large regional map tacked onto the wall.

She'd showered and changed clothes, grateful Agatha brought her bags from the hotel. She'd declined food because she couldn't stomach anything, and the thought of food made her queasy. She's been drinking black tea with honey, though.

She'd called Noah and updated him about the situation and the mole. She'd instructed him to investigate and find out who the other moles might be in her team. Also, she'd ordered him to capture Vershima and Dooshima and keep them in a safe house until she got back to him. She would use them as bargaining chips if necessary. If her father was going to threaten her loved ones, she would do the same to him.

Maddox's parents had returned while she'd been in the shower. His father was in the sitting room, talking in low voices with Duke, who'd arrived about half an hour ago with his best friend.

She still hadn't met his mother, who'd gone into a meeting after her return.

At the table, Mason sat next to Jaxon, who was typing on the keyboard. He'd mentioned he'd tried to track Maddox's phone, but it was currently switched off. He could get the last known location if it was turned on again.

Xandra sat beside her on the sofa. She'd also arrived while Zoe had been in the shower. Amaoge was here too, but she'd gone to put the toddler to bed.

Agatha had gone out to help Tito and the guys investigating and cleaning up the home invasion. Law enforcement showed up, but there wasn't much they could do. The story was that armed robbers had been intercepted, resulting in a gun battle with the security crew. They seemed to buy it. Emeka was handling the PR as the owner of the estate.

Joshua was still in the hospital with Josiah, who was undergoing surgery. Mike's body had been taken to the morgue.

Jaxon suddenly straightened. "Maddox's phone is back online."

Everybody shifted, turning towards him.

"Can you track it?" Mason asked.

"If it stays on long enough, yes," Jax replied.

At the same time, Zoe's phone started buzzing, and she lifted it from the coffee table. "It's from Maddox's phone."

Her heart jerked in her chest.

"It's probably the ransom call. Remember what we discussed," Jax said.

She nodded and pressed the button to connect. "Maddox?"

"Is this Zoe Himba?" the distorted voice said on the other end.

"I'm Zoe Ejiofor, Maddox's wife. Who is this?" she said slowly, calmly.

"That doesn't matter," the person snapped. "What matters is that I have your husband?"

"I'd like to talk to Maddox."

"No. If you want to see your husband again, you will pay one hundred million naira."

Zoe's heart jumped. That was more than the demand for Amaoge.

"Where am I supposed to get that amount from?"

"You're not serious about getting your husband back. I guess you don't love him."

"Of course, I love him. I'll get the money. I just need time. But I need proof that he's alive. Can I talk to him?"

"No!" The call cut off.

"Aargh." She growled, jumping off the sofa.

If that was Abdul Sani, she would kill him if they ever crossed paths again.

"Did you get anything?" she asked Jax, who was typing furiously.

"Yes." He looked up. "They are currently six hours away and heading north-west towards Medogri."

"We can intercept them," Duke said. "We'll fly out to Medogri and be there in two hours. We can lie in wait for their arrival."

"But won't someone tip off Abdul Sani about a private jet arriving in the early morning?" Mason asked.

"Not if it's a military aircraft delivery supplies to our troops fighting the war on terror in the state," the admiral said.

"Great idea," Mason said.

"I'm going to make a few phone calls." Mr Ejiofor Snr left the living room, followed by Duke.

"Don't you think it's odd that they're taking Maddox to Medogri. My father is in Lokogi, which is in a different direction. And if they want a cash delivery for the ransom, surely it will be somewhere local."

Nobody replied as she glanced around the room from Jaxon to Mason to Xandra.

Suddenly, her legs trembled and gave way, making her slump onto the sofa with dizziness.

"They're going to kill him even if we pay the ransom, aren't they?" her voice held tremors and sounded shrill.

"We're going to stop them before they do," Mason said, walking over to her sofa and settling beside her. Tonight was the first time she'd seen him since she declined his proposal during the marriage auction. He looked well, and it seemed his marriage to Sophie was going great. "Maddox will come home to you. You have to believe it."

"Of course, he's coming home," she said with determination. "I'm going to be there with you guys to bring him home."

"No, you're not."

A sharp female voice came from behind Zoe, and she swivelled.

An elegant older woman with low-cut silver and black hair, dressed in a flowing white lace gown, looking like Onyeka Onwenu, walked into the living room.

Maddox's mother.

She wore no expensive jewellery. Instead, a simple coral bracelet adorned her wrist and around her neck was a pendant dangling on a black fabric.

"Ezenwanyi, good evening." Mason stood and bowed like the woman was royalty. He hadn't greeted Maddox's father with the same reverence.

Zoe followed his lead out of courtesy since she'd never met the woman. So, she curtsied. "Good evening."

Xandra did the same thing, too.

"Good evening, my children. Excuse us. I want to talk to Jaxon in private." She walked over to where her son sat, still typing.

"Hi, mum," he said, barely looking up as Zoe followed Xandra and Mason into the corridor, shutting the door.

Mason continued walking, and Zoe went with him.

"What's with all the bowing? You treated Maddox's mother like she was royalty," she said.

"That's because she is," Mason said in a low voice, pulling her into the kitchen. "You know Chief Odili is our godfather. Ezenwanyi Ejiofor is the female equivalent."

"Female equivalent? You mean there are female Yadili."

"Of course, there are female Yadili, and they have their godmothers. The women of Umudike, wives and daughters, pledge through Ezenwanyi. She is a powerful nurturer and a fierce protector."

Zoe nodded. It made sense. "But if Chief is the Umudike godfather, shouldn't the godmother be his wife?"

"It doesn't exactly work like that," he replied. "But as you know, Chief's wife is late. So technically, it should go to my mother because of my father's position in the Yadili hierarchy before he passed. But if you meet my mother, you'll know she's neither a nurturer nor a protector. The women didn't want her as their leader. She tried to take over after Chief's wife died, but Maddox's mother overthrew her."

"My mother-in-law sounds fearless."

"She is. Don't mess with her."

"No wonder she birthed warriors."

"A lioness will birth lions."

Zoe smiled. She liked Maddox's mother. Then she frowned.

"But she doesn't want me to go to Medogri. I need to be there. I can't bear not knowing what's happening with my husband."

Mason walked to the fridge and pulled out a bottle of water. "My advice to you is to do what she says. If she doesn't want you to go with us, she must have a good reason."

THIRTY-NINE

Mason's advice stayed on Zoe's mind. However, after ten minutes of watching the activities as the men changed into Kevlar-reinforced clothing and packed their battle gear, Zoe got restless again.

It was like all the activities were happening around her without her. She wasn't used to being sidelined or even taking a back seat.

Even worse, she'd never cared for anyone like she cared about Maddox, and she felt helpless, almost useless. Surely, there was something she could do to help and bring him home.

She left the men in the war room and searched for Maddox's mother. She hadn't seen the woman since their initial meeting. When Zoe returned from the kitchen, she'd left the war room.

Xandra told her the women were in the second reception room, so she knocked on the door.

"Come in," someone she didn't recognise spoke.

She turned the handle and pushed the door in.

The living room was elegantly decorated with soft furnishings and flowers. It was clear that this was Mrs Ejiofor's space compared to the war room, which had a more masculine tone.

Yet there was no mistaking the authority of the woman seated on an upholstered armchair at the far end of the room flanked by sofas on either side, forming an aisle in the middle. Despite the feminine tone of the space, it looked like a throne room with Maddox's mother at the helm.

Seated on the sofas on either side of the older woman were Amaoge and a woman Zoe didn't recognise. Her sister-in-law smiled, but the other woman didn't look pleased at her presence. She hadn't seen much of Amaoge tonight. What were they discussing?

"Mrs Ejiofor," she curtsied again. "Can I talk to you, please?"

"Come back later. We're in a meeting," the woman she didn't recognise replied. She was older than Zoe and Amaoge, probably in her forties rather than her thirties. The woman didn't like her by her tone.

"She is his wife. She should be in this meeting too," Amaoge said.

Zoe flinched. They were discussing Maddox. Why hadn't they invited her?

"Maddox ended their marriage and paid her severance. They're no longer married," the other woman said.

That answered Zoe's question about why she hadn't been included. They thought Maddox ended their marriage, which he'd done. But…

"We made up. Maddox is my husband. We're still married," Zoe said, lifting her hand to show off the diamond ring he'd given her yesterday.

"That's what you say. For all we know, you set him up to be abducted and killed," the woman interjected.

Zoe's breath hitched, and she clutched her stomach.

"Ifeoma, stop," Mrs Ejiofor warned.

Huh? Ifeoma? The woman was Maddox's ex? What was she doing here?

Zoe reached up reflexively to grab her gun and realised she didn't have it. Damn it. She would have shot the woman on the spot.

Then she remembered her promise to her husband to not hurt Abuchi's mother. She sucked in a deep breath. But her irritation remained.

"Is that what you think I did? That I set Maddox up to be abducted?" Zoe snapped.

"What else are we supposed to think? You haven't given us reason to think otherwise," Ifeoma said.

"How does this even concern you. Who the hell are you?" Zoe rounded on the woman getting thoroughly pissed off at her attitude.

Ifeoma stood, hands on her hips. "I'm Maddox's first wife."

"His ex-wife, you mean."

"The mother of his first and only son."

"And that's the only reason I haven't shot you already."

Amaoge burst out laughing.

Ifeoma rounded on her. "You think it's funny that she is threatening to kill me?"

"Ifeoma, take a chill pill," Amaoge said, still giggling. "You're always so serious."

"This is a serious matter. Maddox's life is at stake," Ifeoma said.

"I know that. But I'm trying to point out that if you stop for a second, you'll realise that you and Zoe have commonality. You both care about Maddox. You are both alike."

"I'm nothing like her." Ifeoma groused. "I would never kill my baby like she did."

"So, you didn't have an abortion." Zoe stepped up to her and got in her face. "But you gave up on Maddox. You gave up on your marriage. You have no right to stand as judge and jury over me."

"She is not the one who will judge your case," Mrs Ejiofor said. "I am."

"What?" Zoe jerked, turning to the older woman. "You're judging my case."

The other women returned to their chairs.

"Yes," Maddox's mother said. "We are gathered here because of Maddox. This also means we must consider what to do about you."

"About me?"

"Yes, whether you would become part of our family?"

Zoe frowned. "I thought being Maddox's wife makes me part of your family?"

"Not necessarily. There are two aspects to our family. There is the Ejiofor relatives, which you are automatically invited into as an Ejiofor wife. Then, there is the Yadili sisterhood, which requires a special invitation. They are similar and yet different."

That was why they hadn't invited her to the meeting about Maddox. They were trying to decide if to invite her into the sisterhood.

"What do I have to do to get the special invite?" she asked.

"You will have to submit yourself to my judgement," her mother-in-law said.

Zoe's spine tingled. She hated losing anything, and a part of her thought that the woman would find her guilty regardless. Zoe had so many crimes against her. The abortion. Humiliating her family. Shooting her son. Amaoge's abduction. Maddox's abduction. The destruction of the new estate Amaoge's husband built. The men who had died at the attack. And the list went on. Zoe had no chance.

"This is not the right time for this while my husband is out there," Zoe said.

"Who—" Ifeoma started but stopped when Ezenwanyi raised her hand.

"Do you think there's something more important for you to do now?" Ezenwanyi asked in a calm voice.

"Yes. Going with the men to Medogri to bring my husband home," she replied.

"Are you a warrior?" the older woman asked.

"No."

"Have you ever been on a rescue mission? Ever saved anyone's life before?"

"No."

"So, what makes you qualified to take up limited space on a military aircraft that should go to a soldier trained on search and rescue missions?" the woman's gaze pierced her as she spoke in a stern tone.

Zoe's cheeks heated, and she shifted from one foot to the other in unease.

The woman was correct. She had no reason to be on the mission except to be there when her husband was rescued.

"I'm his wife, and I can handle myself with a weapon," she said, knowing it was a weak argument.

"If that's the case, then I should also be on the aircraft as his mother. Or do you think you can handle a weapon better than me?" The woman eyed her.

"No." The woman lived in a house with military men. Zoe was confident she could handle firearms. But she still couldn't let it go.

"But Ezenwanyi, I feel useless just staying here while Maddox is god-knows-where."

The woman sighed. "I understand your predicament. Trust me, I do. You've spent most of your life trying to prove that you're as good as the men or even better. Constantly trying to prove yourself worthy means you've lost some attributes that make you unique and strengthen you."

Zoe swallowed because the woman was speaking the truth.

"You're a natural-born leader," Ezenwanyi continued. "But your trust has been eroded so much that you don't trust anyone. So tasks you should delegate, you do them yourself. That's why you want to be on that aircraft with the men. First, you want to prove that you're as good as the men, which is ridiculous because you don't have to prove anything. Those men are at your service. Sending them to battle doesn't mean you're weak. Secondly, you don't trust them to bring your husband home safely without your presence. Which is also ridiculous because those men are warriors. They've seen things and done things you cannot contemplate."

Zoe lowered her head because the woman was looking into her soul and exposing all her secrets.

"You're right. I'm sorry. I just want Maddox to come home safe." A lump clogged her throat. Then she lifted her head. "I will submit to your judgment."

"Good, because we need to get it out of the way so we can focus our energy on bringing back the warriors safely," Ezenwanyi said and leaned into the seat. "Like every case, there is a prosecution and defence. Ifeoma is acting as your prosecutor, and Amaoge is your defence. I've listened to both sides. But I will allow them to round off their arguments before I make my final judgement. Ifeoma, do you have anything else to add quickly?"

"Ezenwanyi, my final point is based on the statutes of our organisation," Ifeoma said, still sitting. "A woman who cannot nurture her child cannot be welcomed in our midst. This is the foundation on which we are formed, birthing and nurturing the future Yadili generations. How can we then accept a woman who murdered her baby? It will weaken all of us and destroy our purpose ... I rest my case."

"Thank you," Ezenwanyi said and turned to Amaoge. "Do you have anything to add?"

"Yes, Mum," Amaoge said. "I beg you to give Zoe a chance. She was coerced into aborting her baby and didn't understand the full implications concerning Maddox or our family. Moreover, there is nothing that says she cannot nurture children even if she didn't birth them. Other women in the Yadili have adopted children before. From what I see, I know she cares about Abuchi. She loves Maddox. Let her pay a fine and purify herself so we can accept her into our fold. This will strengthen her bond with Maddox and repair the fracture. It will strengthen Maddox. That's what we all want."

"Is that what you want, Zoe? Do you want to make Maddox whole again?" Ezenwanyi asked as she reached into a drawer on the side table and pulled out what looked like a necklace similar to the one she wore. She rose from the armchair.

"Yes, please." Zoe's body trembled as the woman approached her. It was a weird sensation she couldn't explain. She had to force herself to stay upright.

"Even if it means severing your father's hold on you?"

"My father doesn't have any hold on me. I don't work for him any longer."

"Oh, child." The woman shook her head. "Your father has you in bondage, and you don't even know it."

Zoe staggered. "What?"

"You are tied to your father. You are his siphon. He drains power from you and uses you to drain power from others. He is using you to drain my son. That's why you had the abortion. That's why you married Maddox. Your father set it up."

"No. You're wrong." Zoe wasn't superstitious, and this was the exact reason. The woman was crazy. "My father didn't even know it was Maddox's baby until he turned up at the marriage proposal meeting."

"Then you really don't know your father. Or the lengths he would go to grow his power and wealth."

FORTY

Asudden tightness crushed Zoe's chest, and her vision blurred. Realisation dawned with Ezenwanyi's words. Like repairing blurry vision, she saw the depth of her father's betrayal with clarity.

And it hurt more than any other experience.

All her life, she'd done whatever she could to please her father. To support his business interests and expand his empire. Even when it meant hurting other people. She'd gone above and beyond to prove she could run his operations and preserve his legacy.

And with each new challenge he'd thrown at her, she'd conquered it, thinking it was just his way of preparing her to take over the helm.

However, she'd begun to rebel at his edicts over the past few months since he announced his intention to set up the marriage auction and use her as the bargaining chip in his trade negotiations.

After she got together with Maddox, she realised her father was undermining her.

Yet, everything she'd assumed and known was smashed by Ezenwanyi's words.

Because despite everything else, Zoe knew her father would go to any lengths to grow his wealth. After all, he'd put his own daughter on the auction block.

Was it so far-fetched to imagine he would use her in other, more devious ways, even if she didn't believe in those things?

She looked down at her hands, shaking her head.

"You doubt my words, child?" Ezenwanyi asked sternly, pulling Zoe from her thoughts.

She lifted her head and met her mother-in-law's piercing gaze. Her eyes were as sharp as a hawk, the eyes of her son. Maddox's eyes.

Pain returned at the back of her throat. Her husband was still in danger.

"You don't have faith," the woman continued.

"I believe in what I can see and feel," Zoe replied. "I know my husband is in danger, and I believe you have his best interests at heart. I know that my father wants to kill my husband, and I believe that he is using me to weaken Maddox. My father is manipulative and uses people to achieve his goals. However, you make it sound like my father's sole purpose for me is to be his tool to success. This means he started using me a long time ago. Wouldn't my mother have known this? She would have told me."

"And what would you have done if your mother had told you this five years ago, ten years ago?" Mrs Ejiofor asked.

"I don't know," Zoe conceded.

"You would have doubted her. You might have assumed she was trying to discourage you from your ambitions. It would have created a rift between you and your mother. Perhaps your father would have killed her."

Zoe's breath hitched. "No!"

"Look. I'm not saying I know the exact extent of what your mother knows about your father's deviousness. But consider this. Your mother came to us for help with you."

"What?" Shock rippled through Zoe.

"She came here and asked me to help free you from your father's tyranny."

"When?"

"When your father ordered you to marry Maddox. She saw it as a great opportunity for you to break free."

"But my father ordered me to kill Maddox."

"She hoped you wouldn't go through with it. She hoped you would fall in love with my son."

"Wow." Zoe covered her face with her hands as she remembered the day she'd married Maddox and her mother's peculiar behaviour. Now, it all made sense. Her mother had been in on the plan for Maddox to marry Zoe on the spot. "She planned it, but she didn't tell me."

"She suspected you would not have gone through with it if you'd known beforehand."

"True. Maddox ambushed me and left me reeling that night." A smile curled Zoe's lips as she recalled it all. "And you're right. You were all right. I fell in love with your son despite everything. And I will do anything to have my husband home again safely. Tell me what I must do, please."

Ezenwanyi nodded. "Knowing you are willing to go the extra mile is good. However, Ifeoma is right. We cannot let you into our fold without penance and purification. You will have to pay for your crimes and be spiritually cleansed before you can become a full Yadili sister. This will require travelling to Umudike."

"Oh." Zoe frowned. "Isn't that going to take time?"

"Yes. But right now, getting Maddox home is more urgent. This means we need a temporary solution, a workaround." Mrs Ejiofor lifted the pendant on the end of the fabric necklace. "We need to block out your father's eye on you."

She tapped Zoe on the forehead with the pendant.

Instantly, Zoe lost control of her limbs. Her knees crumbled, and she collapsed onto the cold floor. She must have blacked out for a few seconds. When she blinked her eyes open, Amaoge and Ifeoma were on her sides, helping her sit on her heels.

Ezenwanyi stood in front of her, holding the pendant and swinging it in a circular motion around Zoe's head.

"Aside from the abortion, have you intentionally hurt anyone since you married my son? Confess any actions that might weaken your protection." The woman asked, still swinging the pendant.

"I shot at Maddox on our wedding night," she said, cheeks heating up.

"That doesn't count because I'm sure Maddox made you pay for your actions." Ifeoma rolled her eyes as if she knew precisely what Maddox did to her for shooting at him. She supposed she could guess, considering she'd been once married to the man. Had Maddox chained her up, too, for misbehaving?

Amaoge smiled and shook her head. "Try again."

Zoe sifted through all the things that had happened. None of the bad things that had happened had been her intention except, "I shot and killed the man who abducted Amaoge."

"He deserved what he got, and he will continue to pay for his crimes in the afterlife," Ezenwanyi said.

"Ise!" the two women beside Zoe chorused.

"As your hands are clean, may no wicked intentions befall you."

"Ise!"

"May the tongue that speaks of you only speak good."

"Ise!"

"May you be protected from evil eyes."

"Ise!"

Ezenwanyi bent over her, lowering the necklace until it settled around Zoe's neck, the pendant resting on her collar. "You will wear this necklace for the foreseeable future. It is for your protection. Do not remove it even when you're in the shower or asleep. Do not remove it even when you're making love to your husband."

"Oh. Why?"

"Because I told you this is a temporary solution. Until you pay your penance and get cleansed, which will give you a permanent break from your father's hold when you officially join the sisterhood. This necklace is a temporary solution because it taps into my powers. In other words, you are borrowing from me to break the connection with your father rather than using your powers. If you remove it, the connection will get reestablished with your father."

"Are you saying I will have powers when I join the sisterhood?"

"Yes, you're a powerful woman. You just don't know it because your father is stealing your power. The sisterhood will allow you to regain your powers and show you how to defeat him if he tries to enslave you again."

"Thank you. But how does this help Maddox?"

"Now that the connection with your father is broken, we can use you as a point of contact to refuel Maddox. Three of us can channel vitality and lifeforce through you to him. Once he regains some of his drained power, he can fight his captors, and with the rescue team on the way to him, there is a greater chance he will live to see the daylight and come home."

Zoe heart raced. "Yes. Let's do it."

"Rise," Ezenwanyi commanded.

Amaoge and Ifeoma held her arms and supported her as she regained the use of her limbs and stood slowly.

"Go to your room and get changed into loose, comfortable clothing. Remove any jewellery except the necklace I just gave you, and bring an item that reminds you of Maddox. Something that, if he sees, will also remind him of you. When you're ready, Amaoge will bring you to the sanctuary."

FORTY-ONE

Maddox floated in and out of consciousness. He'd been barely conscious when he'd been dragged out of the destroyed heap that was the foyer of the new house he'd been checking out with his wife when an explosion ripped through the front door.

He'd been conscious enough to place his body between the blast and Zoe, protecting her as they'd been thrown across the foyer by the explosion.

He'd known he'd been injured and had tried to wake an unconscious Zoe. Then, men in bandanas and balaclavas entered the house through the gaping hole in the wall.

The men had hit him and searched him, taking his weapons and smartphone. He'd been barely conscious at that point. His body losing blood fast. He must have hit his head when he'd fallen because the blood was getting into his eyes, blurring his vision while he'd slipped in and out of consciousness.

He'd been immobile and unable to react quickly enough as they'd dragged him outside. The men had been firing shots, but Maddox's men hadn't retaliated when they'd seen him come out of the building. They probably didn't want to cause more harm.

He slipped into darkness, where shadows loomed like giant trees moving in and out of focus. Disjointed voices spoke to him, but he couldn't make out their words. Pain filled his body, immobilising him.

The smell of smoked weed floated around him, as well as laughter.

Voices called his name, but he couldn't make it out.

Then a soft voice spoke, "Nnanna, wake up."

Recognition made him blink, and he found himself lying on the bed at home. Still, something felt wrong, but he couldn't put a finger on it.

Zoe stood by the doorway, dressed in yoga pants and a loose t-shirt. Not exactly how he expected her to dress when she used the endearment.

"Come here," he ordered huskily, wanting her to climb into bed with him.

"No. You come here," she replied, smiling coquettishly.

"Get into bed. I'm tired." His body felt cold and exhausted. Any other day, he would get up and chase after her. Now, he felt drained and closed his eyes.

"Maddox, wake up," she said in a firm tone, the playfulness gone.

He opened his eyes, and she was pointing her gun at him. Something was definitely off.

"Zoe, what are you doing?" he frowned.

"I need you to get up now," she ordered.

"I am the masquerade. You dare to point a gun at me?" he blinked.

"I'm not afraid of the masquerade."

"You should be. I will punish you hard for pointing a weapon at me."

"Good. But you have to get up first."

She lifted the gun and aimed at him.

He'd known she would do this one day. But he'd prepared for her, hadn't he?

"Don—"

The words died in his throat as she fired.

He tried to move but couldn't. The bullet hit him in the chest. But instead of pain, a blast of energy surged through him.

He jolted awake, and his eyes flickered open. He wasn't at home in bed. That was a dream. He was injured, lying in the back of a lorry, a *gwongworo*. Around him were sacks of onions and *aki awusa*.

He lifted his head. Beyond the sacks were men sitting on the bed of the truck. They were smoking weed and cigarettes, swigging drinks straight from the bottles.

Maddox checked himself. The way congealed blood stuck to the back of his head and neck, he must have sustained a head injury when there was an explosion at the house. But he'd stopped bleeding, so that was good.

The men must think he was dying or dead. Otherwise, they should have bound his hand, at least. Instead, they'd tossed him on the floor with the smelly sacks of onions.

The truck kept moving, rolling over potholes and tarred roads in their journey. From the position of the stars in the cloudless sky, he assumed they were headed north. There were no street lamps. And he didn't think they'd passed another car yet. So they were probably between towns.

Maddox stayed still, waiting to see if anyone would check on him. He counted from one Mississippi to one-twenty Mississippi, and no one approached him. They probably didn't care if he was alive or dead.

He could fight the two men who were awake. But it could wake the sleeping ones. In his weakened state, his chances were not good.

A few minutes later, a couple of cars went by. It must be approaching dawn since more cars were on the road.

Maddox knelt and crept behind a pile of sacks, biding his time. He would wait for the right opportunity. He advanced towards one of the men sleeping on the sacks nearest to him. His AK47 and sheathed dagger were beside him.

Whoosh. Whoosh. Whoosh.

Maddox recognised the sound of the approaching helicopter in the distance. The watchmen shouted and pointed at the sky, giving him his opportunity, and he sprang into action. He ignored the assault rifle and chose stealth with the dagger. He pulled it from the sheath and slit the man's throat where he lay. Then he crept along using the darkness and sacks as cover. The second man woke and grunted as the knife slit his throat.

An explosion took out the front cabin and sent the truck bed twenty feet into the air, taking men and onions with it.

FORTY-TWO

Maddox was on the upward trajectory from the explosion, clinging onto the wooden slats on the side gate of the lorry, when he spotted the special ops paratrooper hanging on the end of the descending line, a shadow against the skyline.

His brain registered the implication just as he collided with the paratrooper who snatched him out of the air.

"Lieutenant Ejiofor," the man wearing night vision goggles said, lifting the sling in his hand. "Put on the harness and hold tight."

Maddox barely made out the words because his ears were ringing from the blast. But he understood what was required, accepting the paratrooper was here on a search and rescue for him. Also, the man had addressed him with his military designation.

Maddox clicked on the harness under his arm as the paratrooper held his waist and then secured himself to the other man using the metal clips. They'd trained for this in his military days, but he'd never had to do it in active battle until today.

"He's secure. Go, go!" the paratrooper spoke into his headset.

Maddox glanced up at the helicopter hovering above the road as the winch pulled them. It was a stealth helicopter with a unique blade designed to reduce noise used in combat to scope out and destroy enemy targets, not search and rescue.

Someone had to pull a lot of strings to secure this. Probably his father.

He exhaled in relief, grateful that they'd gone to so much trouble for him.

The gunner in the cockpit was having a whale of a time with the automatic cannon as they pulverised anyone who'd survived the initial impact from the rocket. All Maddox could see as they flew away was the *gwongworo* fireball.

Ten minutes later, they were dropped off at a military airfield before the helicopter returned to its base.

Maddox was glad to have his feet back on the ground as he detached the harness.

"It's good to see you alive and well, Lieutenant," the paratrooper shook his hand.

'Thank you for your help, Officer Belu," he read the man's name on the badge. "But you know I'm no longer in the teams."

"I know that. But you're still one of us and a very well-respected and legendary member of the special ops teams. It is an honour to be part of this mission." The man stepped back and saluted.

Maddox returned the salute. "At ease, Officer."

Men approached them across the field, and he recognised Tito and Joshua amongst the special ops team members. A medic attended to and dressed his injuries.

They didn't hang about after that and boarded the aircraft to fly to the FCT. He was debriefed on the plane during the flight. The intelligence provided meant the tactical team reached the airbase in Yobe, where the helicopter had been dispatched to intercept the bandits. They'd been able to track their movements using the GPS on Maddox digital watch, which one of the men on the truck had stolen. The special ops team engaged in a firefight with the bandits and captured a prisoner. Hopefully, he would provide information that could be used to track the rest of the gang.

Josiah was out of surgery, and it looked like he would make a full recovery.

When they landed, the drive to his parents' house seemed interminable but was only twenty minutes. The sun was rising as the car pulled into the driveway.

A group awaited him outside as he exited the vehicle. His brothers-in-arm and blood. Duke, Mason, Jaxon.

"Welcome home."

"It's good to have you back."

"We were worried about you."

They clapped his back and hugged him, their relief palpable.

"Maddox," a female voice called out.

Was that Zoe? His heart skipped a beat. He swivelled as Amaoge barrelled around the side of the house and collided with him in a tight hug. "I'm so glad to see you."

"I'm glad to see you too," he replied, looking her over. She wasn't his wife, but he was still pleased she was here. "Have you been here all night?"

"Of course. You know Mum needed the prayer warriors on site." A huge smile lit up her face as she held onto him. She was tactile, and she expressed affection through touch.

"Of course." He grinned, holding her hand because the contact was healing, and he didn't feel so exhausted.

Prayer warriors was a phrase used by his mother to describe the group she assembled whenever an emergency required mystical intervention. These were usually the female members of the family, especially the ones inducted into the Yadili who possessed arcane powers no one else could match. They were a powerful force that had shielded him and other family members in the past. He had no doubt they contributed to his survival this time.

He lifted his head and saw his ex-wife behind Amaoge. He released his sister's hand. "Ifeoma."

"Maddox." She stepped forward and embraced him briefly. "I'm glad you're home."

"Thank you for coming," he said, leaning back to look her over.

She wore an outfit similar to Amaoge's—sports leggings, a t-shirt, and trainers. Her hair was natural in a low cut. She was integral to his mother's inner circle and prayer warrior, so he knew she would be here. But she didn't have to show up for him because they were no longer married. So he was always grateful for her help.

After the initial resentment fuelled by the divorce, they maintained a cordial relationship because of their son. Over the years, they'd been able to reestablish their friendship. They were no longer lovers or spouses, but they were friends.

"Don't mention it. Not like I can disobey Ezenwanyi." She smiled, stepping back.

"True." He grinned, rubbing a hand over his chin. "Did you speak to Abuchi?"

"No. I didn't want to worry him. He'd only just returned to the academy."

He nodded. It made sense.

The others headed indoors, and he turned towards the front door, eager to get inside. His wife must be in there. Tito mentioned he'd brought Zoe here. She was probably sleeping. It was only dawn.

"Are you coming inside?" he asked Ifeoma, who seemed to be going in a different direction.

"No. My job here is done. By the way, I finally met your wife. She really has a thing about shooting people, doesn't she?" she said in a severe tone.

He narrowed his eyes. "What did she do?"

She looked unharmed, but it didn't mean that Zoe didn't shoot her. Then again, Zoe had promised she wouldn't harm his ex-wife.

"She threatened to shoot me." Ifeoma chuckled, shaking her head.

"That sounds like her," Maddox said warily. "You're not angry."

"No." His ex-wife shrugged. "I kinda understand where she's coming from. And she genuinely cares about you, so I can forgive her this time."

Maddox nodded, but he didn't miss the veiled warning. "Has she been accepted into the sisterhood?"

Ifeoma was his mother's enforcer and responsible for keeping the female members of the Ejiofor clan in line. She would have the power to punish Zoe if she was inducted into the Yadili.

"Ezenwanyi put her on probation," she said. "She will have to travel to Umudike, pay the penance and undergo the purification ritual before she can be fully inducted."

"That's good." Definitely a step in the right direction. It meant his wife had been accepted by the members of his family. She just needed to be welcomed by the wider Yadili sisterhood. He really needed to see her.

"Yes, I thought you would say that. I have to go." She grinned and winked before walking towards her car parked under the port. Her house was in the same estate as his sister's. He'd bought the house for her because it was also his son's home.

"Maybe one of the security men should drive you," he stepped up to the car as she got in, his protective instincts kicking in.

"Don't worry about me. I can take care of myself." She started the engine. "I think you should worry more about her. You're going to have your hands full." She pointed out of the window.

He swivelled as his nerve endings prickled.

Zoe stood at the corner of the house, arms crossed over around her midriff.

His heart leapt, and he stepped back as Ifeoma reversed the vehicle. She drove out of the compound as he strode towards his wife. She dressed similarly to his sister and ex-wife and must have been at the sanctuary with the other women.

She walked towards him with the same urgency zipping through him. They collided in the middle of the driveway. He cupped her nape as she stood on tiptoes and wrapped her arms around his shoulders. They didn't need words. The relief and joy were palpable as they kissed passionately, clinging onto each other as if they weren't outside his parents' house.

FORTY-THREE

Three months later, Zoe was in Maddox's hometown of Umudike. Instead of the two-week honeymoon she'd wished for, they'd had to overhaul their plans following the recent attacks on the Ejiofor family, with Amaoge's and Maddox's abductions.

Zoe had cancelled all personal leave time for members of her crew. Noah and Bruce were doing a great job as shugabas. They'd locked down the teams to ensure security and had conducted a mole hunt. They'd discovered three people working as spies for her father, excluding her former driver. Making four in total.

They had all been punished, and she'd allowed them all to walk away afterwards, only because they hadn't been directly involved in Maddox's or Amaoge's abductions.

She'd shown mercy only because Maddox and his family had taught her to be gracious. She'd come into their lives as her father's assassin, sent to murder

Maddox. They'd known of her intentions in advance. Yet they'd been tactful and lenient. Sure, Maddox had punished her, but locking her in the basement had been more inconvenient and uncomfortable than harmful.

Certainly not near the torture her former driver was undergoing in a military holding cell. She didn't care if he stayed imprisoned for life. He only remained alive because Maddox came home in one piece.

Meanwhile, she'd accelerated her plans to set up business premises in the FCT. She'd always planned to move offices to align with her plans to work as a fixer to the Himba business associates across the central region. But the transition would have been in weeks and months rather than days.

That had been before Ali Baldy doublecrossed her and took Amaoge. Before, she'd executed him and quit as one of her father's shugabas.

Now, she was her own boss, a member of the Ejiofor family through marriage and allied with the Odili clan. And it seemed her relocation to the FCT was serendipitous because she now had relatives in the area. She would live near Maddox's parents and Amaoge.

There was one significant change. She was married to Maddox. Not just for three months. But for life.

And for the first time, she didn't feel like a performing monkey, continually trying to prove that she was good enough to be who she was.

She was confident of her place in Maddox's life. Her position in his heart.

He loved her the way she was. Sure, he didn't want her shooting people unnecessarily. But she'd grown and learned to value life, especially those around her. Those she loved.

Because she loved. Loved Maddox. Loved Amaoge. Loved the new family she'd acquired—Abuchi and her in-laws.

She even loved her new team. Xandra had accepted the offer to be her enforcer, and Agatha became her new security chief. Both were being coached by the best in the business—Maddox, of course.

Zoe was unlearning all the toxic things she knew about leadership and was willing to put herself under the tutelage of the best leader she'd had the fortune to encounter. Ezenwanyi Ejiofor.

Like Mason had mentioned, her mother-in-law was a powerful nurturer and a fierce protector. Zoe had witnessed her esoteric brilliance in action the day Maddox was attacked and taken by men sent by her father.

She couldn't even explain the full extent of the woman's authority. Had been more than awed when she'd been in the sanctuary with the three women—Ezenwanyi, Amaoge and Ifeoma—meditating and channelling their reinforced protective and healing energy to the injured and captured Maddox. She hadn't believed in the positive influence of prayer until that day.

Until she'd lapsed into a trance and had seen what she believed was a vision of Maddox lying injured and dying on the back of a truck surrounded by his captors. For the first time, she'd feared losing someone dear to her. But Ezenwanyi had helped her turn her desperation into determination to bring her husband home alive.

It had worked. Maddox had come home.

He'd had a bandage around his head. But he'd walked without support from the car that brought him home. She'd stood aside and watched him exchange pleasantries with his family and friends who'd been there to welcome him home. They were entitled to him, to his attention, because they'd been a part of his life a lot longer than she'd been.

She'd even watched as he'd hugged his ex-wife. Her toxic instinct urged her to match across the front yard and yank them apart. Still, she'd tamped it down. She trusted Maddox. Couldn't believe she reached that state of mind. But she trusted her husband.

In any case, they didn't linger in each other's embrace. It had been a brief hug between friends rather than a prolonged welcome between lovers. Despite Ifeoma's initial behaviour when she'd met Zoe, once they'd entered the sanctuary, it became apparent the woman was there to help bring Maddox home. She had no interest in Zoe's husband except as her son's father and ex.

As soon as Ifeoma headed home, Maddox finally turned towards Zoe. His eyes sparkled with joy as he jogged across the gravelled driveway towards her. Her heart raced as she rushed into the arms he wrapped around her.

She'd never been so relieved, so overjoyed to see anyone. Their kiss had said it all. She'd poured everything into it, not caring about the audience of security personnel or other members of the family lingering outside.

Then he'd lifted his head, pressing his forehead against her and said, "Thank you."

"Why are you thanking me?" she asked breathlessly, still clinging onto him, wanting to savour his presence, scent, and feel.

"I saw you in a dream. You shot me." He chuckled low.

"I did?" She leaned away to see his face, confused about why he would find it funny.

"I was unconscious, and you were trying to wake me up. But I was dreaming that I was in bed asleep, and you were trying to wake me up for sex." He grinned, eyes sparkling. "I kinda knew it was a dream, but I wasn't sure it was really you in the dream. Until I saw you were waving a gun at me, and you shot me. Then suddenly I woke up at the back of the lorry. You roused me and ensured I had the strength to fight in time for the rescue team."

"Wow." Was all she could mutter.

She'd taken the weapon into the sanctuary because Ezenwanyi had told her to bring something Maddox would recognise as hers. She'd waved the gun at him too many times, so it was a significant item for them.

But she hadn't known how it would be helpful to Maddox until he'd explained his dream.

Zoe had developed the utmost reverence for Ezenwanyi. Since then, she'd come to appreciate the aspects of being a woman she'd ignored. Being a woman didn't make her lesser or even weaker than a man.

Ezenwanyi carried herself with the poise of an empress. No one would dare tell her she was minor compared to a man. Zoe hoped to attain that respect one day.

As for her father, his downfall had been spectacular. The Ejiofor family didn't let up. All his business associates were targeted and arrested. His accounts were frozen, and his arrest had been imminent. He'd seen the writing on the wall and went into exile abroad before he could be arrested. To top it off, his boy, the state governor, was impeached and ousted by the Supreme Court. So, Don Himba lost his stranglehold on the region.

Zoe had no regrets about it. She'd warned him about the consequences of harming a member of the Ejiofor family, and he hadn't listened. Her mother was back in Lokogi while Brenda was in exile with Don Himba and her half-brothers.

So today, she sat in the sanctuary in Umudike with other women, members and aspirants. The building wasn't what she'd expected. It looked like any other place of worship, with rows of chairs and an altar. The only difference was the chalk-like markings on the wall. Ancient symbols she couldn't decipher. The women were dressed in uniform like they were attending the annual August meeting. Only the new pledgers dressed differently.

Other people pledging included Carla, Duke's wife; Sophie, Mason's wife; Agatha and Xandra because they belonged in Zoe's crew.

The initiation ceremony involved a swearing-in and a baptism. Each person brought something from their past that they wanted to let go. Zoe took a photo of her father and a necklace he'd gifted her on her sixteenth birthday. At the back of the building, they made a giant bonfire from all the items the pledgers had discarded. The blaze signified breaking the hold of the past on their lives and a cleansing.

Afterwards, they bathed in the stream at the bottom of the footpath near the sanctuary, which completed the purification and signified a fresh start.

Then, they returned to the sanctuary where refreshments had been laid out. Ezenwanyi introduced her to some older ladies, including Mason's mother.

"So, you rejected my son as your husband," Mrs Maduka asked, looking her over with cold eyes. The woman obviously wasn't happy Zoe had married Maddox.

But Zoe wouldn't kowtow to the woman. "Mrs Maduka, I love Maddox."

"Yet you aborted his baby," the woman said in a snide tone.

Zoe gasped. Did everyone know about the abortion?

"Mabel, stop it," Ezenwanyi warned. "That is not to be mentioned in the sanctuary or anywhere else again."

"Ezenwanyi, you know I'm only irritated because you got such a wonderful girl as a daughter-in-law, and I got that ..." Mrs Maduka said with saccharine sweetness and trailed off, but she was obviously talking down about Sophie.

She could see why Mason's mother had been overthrown as leader of the Umudike Yadili sisterhood. The woman was cold.

Annoyance seeped through Zoe because the woman's attitude reminded her of being compared to her siblings because they were male and she wasn't. She hated the feeling of not measuring up in her father's esteem. She could imagine how Sophie would feel overhearing this conversation and being viewed as an inferior option.

She just snapped. "I don't see what your problem is, Mrs Maduka. Mason is obviously in love with Sophie, and as everyone can see, she is pregnant with your grandchild, which is better than I did to Maddox. So why can't you be happy that they're happy together."

Silence filled the sanctuary as conversations died and all eyes focused on Zoe.

Mrs Maduka gasped and glared. "Excuse me?"

"You heard me," Zoe retorted, hands braced on her hips. "Now, do you still want me as your daughter-in-law?"

Mason's mother glared at her speechlessly for a few seconds before turning to Maddox's mother. "Ezenwanyi, caution your daughter-in-law. Are you going to let her talk like that?"

"Mabel, you know the sanctuary is a safe space for every member. What happens here stays here. Nevertheless, you opened the can of worms. You can't blame anyone else if you don't like what you get from it." Ezenwanyi shrugged and turned to Zoe. "Zoe, go and mingle with the others."

"Thank you, Ezenwanyi, Elders." She curtsied before swivelling and walking off. She was glad to leave the elders now scrutinising her with hard eyes. She was sure they were glad she wasn't married to their sons.

Amaoge approached and hugged her. "Gurl, I'm in awe."

"Don't encourage her," Ifeoma said, although she was smiling.

"I'm just living vicariously through her. All of us are." Amaoge tugged Zoe deeper into the hall towards the food counter.

"And that's because no one wants to make an enemy of Mrs Maduka. Zoe already has her hands full. She doesn't need to add to her problems."

"True," Zoe said, watching Amaoge pill food onto her plate. She wished she had the appetite to eat all the delicious aromatic food. "But is the woman always like that?"

"Trust me. No one is good enough for her sons, especially Rocha," Ifeoma said.

It was interesting to see Maddox's ex being so relaxed and gossiping with the other women, unlike her stern attitude when Zoe first met her.

"Anyone except Sahara," Amaoge said.

"Who is that?" Zoe asked. She'd heard the name earlier.

"Sahara is Chief Odili's daughter."

"Oh, yes. I saw her earlier. Is she not already married?"

Zoe's curiosity spiked. The Yadili sisterhood only accepted daughters who were married or pregnant. But it was open to Yadili wives, women whose husbands were already sworn members.

"No. But Mrs Maduka obviously wants her as a daughter-in-law."

"Are you ladies talking about me?" someone said in a sing-song voice.

"Only good things," Amaoge said with a smile as she hugged the new arrivals, including Carla, Sophie and Sahara. "Have you all met Zoe?"

"No, we haven't met, and we're supposed to be neighbours," Carla said, coming forward.

"We have to remedy that. We must do something when we get back to Lori Osa. It's nice to meet you ." Zoe hugged Duke's wife.

"Same here. Finally. Yes, let's organise something." The woman giggled before stepping back.

"I'm glad to meet you too," Sophie said, wrapping her arms around Zoe. "And thank you for what you did with my mother-in-law."

"Oh. No need to thank me. From what I hear. The woman deserved it." She stared at the gentle slope of the woman's belly. "How are you and baby doing?"

Sophie's smile widened. "We're doing great. I've never been so excited about anything else. Mason is over the moon."

Warmth filled Zoe at her joy. If a brothel madame could find happiness in marriage and parenting, then, indeed, Zoe could do the same as a mafia boss.

"You are going to make great parents. You have your family around to support you, right?" Zoe could imagine that Mason's mother would be of little help.

"Not my birth family. But we have Ma Bagu." She indicated an older woman sitting in another group and waving at them with a smile. "She is like Mason's adoptive mother, and she fusses over me like mad. She is going to spoil this child."

Sophie placed her hand over her bump, beaming.

"I'm so glad for you." Zoe turned to hear the conversation between Amaoge and Sahara. It seemed the two knew each other well.

"So when is the date?" Amaoge asked.

"Date for what?" Sahara looked confused as she sipped from a glass.

"The wedding date."

"I haven't set a date yet."

"So, it's true. You're marrying Rocha." Amaoge gasped in shock as if she couldn't believe it.

"Rocha?" Sahara spat out the drink in her mouth and coughed.

"Oh no." Carla thumped her back, easing the coughing bout.

Sahara wiped herself with a napkin and grimaced. "Why do you think I'm getting married to Rocha?"

"Because Madam over there—" Amaoge tilted her head several times comically to indicate the altar where the elders sat "—has been talking about it in the sanctuary for yonks. How his firstborn son would marry Chief Odili's daughter."

"She has?" Sahara reared back.

"Yessoo. Then again, she would tell anyone who cares to listen that her Rocha should have been the Odili underboss, not Duke."

"Haba? How come I've never heard any of it before?"

"Because what happens in the sanctuary stays in the sanctuary. There are secrets shared here that we don't speak anywhere else."

"In order words, this is where to come if I want the latest gossip."

"Exactly. This is the main reason I come to these meetings. I get my information live and direct."

The women burst into laughter, drawing attention.

"Uh oh. The elders are staring at us."

But instead of quieting, they giggled some more.

Zoe felt at ease in a group gathering for the first time in a while, surrounded by all these women she now called friends or family. It was a great feeling.

"So, if you're not getting married to Rocha, then how come you came to pledge?" Ifeoma asked.

Sahara fidgeted, glanced around and lowered her voice. "You must swear to keep a secret."

"A secret?" Amaoge asked.

"Yes, a secret. Swear it," Sahara insisted.

"I swear," the women in the group mumbled.

"I'm pregnant," Sahara confessed.

Gasps and gaping mouths followed.

"And it's not Rocha's?" Ifeoma asked in a whisper.

"No."

"Do we know him? Is he Yadili?"

"No."

"Wahala dey."

"I know. He is so wrong for me. My father is going to flip when he finds out."

"Oh, Sahara." Amaoge hugged her first. "We're here for you."

The other women took turns hugging Sahara.

Zoe knew that whatever happened, the sisterhood would be there to support one of their own.

Thank you for reading the Tough Alliance. If you enjoyed this story, please rate it on the site of purchase and leave a brief review if you can.

Zoe, Maddox and the rest of the Odili clan will return soon in the next Yadili Series book.

To keep up to date on my upcoming book releases, sign up for my newsletter:
https://www.kirutaye.com/contact

For a full list of books in the Kiru Taye Universe visit: https://www.kirutaye.com/books

YADILI SERIES

Prince of Hearts
Killer of Kings
Bad Santa
Rough Diamond
Tough Alliance
Honour in Love and the Lawless anthology